Worthy of
Riches

BONNIE LEON

BROADMAN
&HOLMAN
PUBLISHERS

Nashville, Tennessee

0-8054-2154-8

Published by Broadman & Holman Publishers,
Nashville, Tennessee

Dewey Decimal Classification: 813
Subject Heading: Fiction—Alaska
Library of Congress Card Catalog Number: 2001037997

Library of Congress Cataloging-in-Publication Data
Leon, Bonnie.
    Worthy of riches / Bonnie Leon.
        p.   cm. — (The Matanuska series ; bk. 2)
    ISBN 0-8054-2154-8 (pb.)
    1. Alaska—fiction. 2. Women pioneers—fiction. I. Title.
PS3562.E533 W67   2002
813'.54—dc21

                                                        2001037997
                                                        CIP

2 3 4 5 6 7 8 9 10   06 05 04 03

Worthy of
Riches

Dedication

To my brother Bruce, who knows and loves Alaska.
Thank you for sharing your many adventures.
This story would not be the same without them.

Chapter 1

Jean added split birch to the firebox, then filled two cups with tea and placed them on the table. Then she took pen, ink, and paper from a kitchen cabinet and sat across from her daughter. "Thank goodness Susie's asleep. Now we can plan for the wedding."

Laurel stirred sugar into her tea and rested her face in her hand. "One more month and I'll be Mrs. Adam Dunnavant." She sipped her tea. "It's hard to believe that when I first met Adam I detested him. All I could see was an arrogant meddler." She grinned. "I must say, he was a handsome meddler though. Those blue eyes caught my attention right off, and the way his hair curls onto his forehead reminds me of a sweet boy."

Laurel slowly shook her head. "I was so wrong about him."

Jean brushed auburn hair off her neck. "I have to admit, in the beginning I didn't think too highly of Adam either. He seemed awfully bold and brash with his camera and pencil, intruding into everyone's business. Even if he *was* a reporter, it didn't seem right." Jean smiled, her amber eyes sparkling. "I'm glad I was wrong."

"Sometimes I wonder what would have happened if King Edward hadn't abdicated his throne for Mrs. Simpson," Laurel said. "Adam might still be in London."

Dipping a pen in ink, Jean said, "We need to get this list taken care of. We still have a lot to do before the wedding."

Laurel leaned on the table. "Jessie said she'd take care of the flowers. You know how much she loves plants and living things. I'm sure she'll do a beautiful job."

Jean wrote down Jessie's name. "It's too early for wildflowers."

"She knows a woman who grows flowers indoors." Laurel took another sip of her tea, then looked at the golden liquid. "Jessie's the one who got me drinking tea—all those hours at her place recording her husband's notes." A sad expression crossed Laurel's face. "After I'm married, I won't be able to work with her much. I'll miss it. I have to admit, working on a book about Alaska made me feel kind of important."

"You're not going to give it up altogether, are you?"

"No. Jessie said we'll keep working but at a slower pace."

"Good. I'm glad you're going to finish. Folks on the outside ought to know more about Alaska and its history."

"I still have so many notes to go through and record. I'm beginning to think we'll never finish." Laurel set her cup on the table. "It's sad her husband died. I wonder if she's lonely, especially since she never had any children." Laurel looked squarely at her mother. "Maybe we ought to find someone for her."

Jean held up her hands. "Oh, no. I'm not getting involved in matchmaking. Seems to me Jessie's more than happy just as she is, and she ought to know her own mind by now. She's lived alone for a good number of years. I don't think she'd appreciate our meddling."

Jean redipped the pen. "All right now, enough of this. Back to the wedding. Since it's at 11:00, people are going to get hungry. I think we ought to make some sandwiches and maybe have some salads. Norma Prosser said she'd bake and decorate the cake. She's a wonder in the kitchen."

"Good."

Jean wrote down Norma's name and beside it, *cake.* "The reverend said April 10 will be just fine. He asked if we could all be at the church the night before for the rehearsal."

Emptying her cup, Laurel said, "It seems strange to practice a wedding. I'll feel silly."

"We won't go through the ceremony. The reverend will just make sure we all know where to stand and how it's all going to take place." Jean set the pen in its holder. "Since Celeste is going to be your maid of honor, will her father be there?"

"Ray Townsend at a Hasper wedding? I think he'd rather die."

"Just thought I ought to ask since he's your best friend's father."

Laurel folded her arms over her chest and leaned back in her chair. "He detests me, and he hates Daddy even more. I think just the sight of an outsider gets him riled. Now he's threatening to turn in any colonist who bypasses the co-op."

"I'm still praying for him. Maybe he'll have a change of heart."

"He'll never change, and I'm sure he won't be at the wedding. I wouldn't want him there anyway."

"It would certainly raise a stir." Jean grinned. "Oh well, what Ray Townsend does or doesn't do is between him and God. It has nothing to do with us." She looked back at her list. "Oh, Celeste told me she'd talked to you about the bridal shower?"

"She said she wanted to have one and that we could use the community building." Laurel frowned. "I don't know how I feel about it. After what happened with Robert, it doesn't seem right. I mean, we had a shower when I was going to marry him; it doesn't seem right to have another one."

Jean reached across and patted Laurel's hand. "Everyone understands about you and Robert. They were surprised when you called off the wedding, but it's better to do that than to marry a man you don't love."

"I know, but I feel strange having another shower. It's only been a few months. I'm embarrassed."

"It'll be fine. Celeste is your best friend. She'll feel badly if she can't do this for you, and I actually believe she'll have more fun this time, considering how she feels about Robert."

Laurel smiled. "I'm glad they're going around together. She fell for him the first time she saw him." She took a deep breath. "All right. We'll have a shower."

"Did she tell you when she wanted to do it?"

"A week before the wedding, Friday, April 3."

"All right then." Jean wrote down *shower* and the date alongside Celeste's name. "We can serve coffee at the wedding, but I think we ought to have punch too. Grandma Hasper's punch recipe has always been a favorite."

"Can we get the lemons?"

"That shouldn't be a problem, but I'll check." Leaning back, Jean ran her hands through her hair. "There's so much to think about—so many details." She studied her daughter. Laurel was a taller, younger replica of herself, with long auburn hair and hazel eyes.

Laurel smiled. "The house is nearly finished. Adam's done a wonderful job. He's a good carpenter. I guess that's one good thing that came out of his growing up in that dreadful orphanage." She shuddered. "Every time I think of that horrible Mr. Hirsch and how he treated the boys, I want to cry."

"You can be proud of Adam, especially considering all he's been through."

"I can hardly wait to move into the house and make it ours. It's sad that so many colonists left, but at least the empty farmland is still available. Adam and I can be thankful for that. We'll have a fine farm one day."

Uneasiness settled over Jean. She wasn't at all sure that Adam should give up his career as a reporter. It had meant everything to him. "Are you sure farming's what you ought to do? Adam's a writer."

"It's new for him, but he's excited to try. I'm sure he can do it. He can do anything he sets his mind to do."

"Farming's a far cry from living in Chicago and writing for an important newspaper like the *Tribune*."

"He wants to farm, and he'll do it. Just look at the house he's built for us. And he's already making plans for sowing barley and wheat. We have a good piece of land. There's no reason why we can't make it."

Jean put on her kindest expression. "I know what it's like to be young and full of dreams. It wasn't so long ago that I was in your place. I haven't forgotten. But sometimes dreams don't turn out the way we plan. I just wish you two would step back a bit and pray about this."

"You don't want us to get married?"

"Of course I want you to get married. I think you are meant for each other. It's just that I wonder if Adam will be happy as a farmer. Maybe he ought to do something else. The depression has eased some with President Roosevelt's new ideas."

"He's already decided, Mama." Laurel's voice had taken on a sharp tone.

Jean reached out and covered her daughter's hand. "I just want you two to be as happy as your father and I have been. What if Adam wants to go back to Chicago? Or take up traveling again? What will you do?"

"He won't. He promised. In fact, we're planning on getting a tractor so we can grow more. The government is still helping out farmers by giving loans like they did for you and Daddy."

"Yes, well, our debt is still rising. I'm not so sure the tractor was a good idea." She looked squarely at her daughter. "Laurel, what if living here makes Adam miserable? Can you ignore that?"

Laurel didn't answer right away. "I don't know what we would do. If it happens, we'll work through it together." She scooted her chair away from the table, straightened her legs, and crossed them at the ankle. "Tell me about your wedding. Was it beautiful?"

"It was a wonderful day. We didn't have much money, and the only flowers were in my bouquet. They were just wildflowers, daisies mostly. My dress was simple and made of cotton, but I remember how your father's eyes lit up when he saw me."

Jean paused. "He was so handsome. I wondered how such a man could love me." Jean smiled softly. "He's still handsome."

"You were younger than me when you got married."

"We didn't want to wait to begin our lives together." She chuckled. "Twelve months after our wedding, you were born, and life got busy."

"Adam and I want children—as many as God gives."

"I thank God for every one of mine." Jean's eyes misted. "I just wish Justin . . ." She wiped her eyes with the back of her hand. "Sometimes it's still hard to believe he's gone."

"I think we all feel that way. I'll never stop missing him. He was a sweet boy."

"He was. I never knew a child who loved to read as much as he did." Jean leaned her arms on the table. "In spite of the sorrows, your father and I have a wonderful life. I can't imagine living without him."

"I feel the same about Adam, and I know we'll have a good marriage." Laurel carried her empty cup to the sink. "Laurel Dunnavant." Turning to look at her mother, she said, "I like the sound of that, don't you?"

"It's perfect," Jean said with a wink. More seriously she added, "I know you two will be happy."

"Help! Someone help!" Luke's cries carried in from outside. A moment later the back door flew open and he ran into the kitchen.

"What's wrong?" Jean asked. "Where's Brian? Where's your father?"

Luke struggled to catch his breath. "Dad's hurt."

"What happened? Where is he?"

"The tractor. It tipped and . . ."

"Laurel, stay with Susie," Jean called and raced out the door. Luke followed. Glancing at him, she asked, "Where's Brian?"

"He stayed with Dad."

She headed for the far field where Luke and Will had been working. Her heart pummeled her chest. "How bad is it?" she gasped.

"I don't know for sure. He's alive. I checked him, then ran for the house."

"He was alive when you left?"

"Yes, but he looked bad. He was unconscious."

Lord, keep him here with me. Please God, let him be all right, Jean prayed as she ran, her feet sinking into muddy earth. The freshly turned loam threatened to trip her as clumps clung to her shoes. The tractor lay on its side. She couldn't see Will. Although it had been a warm spring, she'd warned him not to start plowing so early.

Jean approached the machine, and then she saw him. Will sat with his back resting against a wheel. Brian stood beside him, his hand on his father's shoulder. Relief flooded the boy's face when he saw his mother.

"Will," Jean cried, dropping to her knees beside her husband. "Are you all right?"

He managed a nod.

She did a quick inspection. He looked pale. Blood dribbled from a gash on his head. Gently, she touched the wound where a lump had already formed. "Thank God you're alive," she said, fighting tears. She ripped off a section of her apron and pressed it to the injury. "Luke, keep pressure on that for me."

Luke laid his hand over the makeshift bandage and his father winced. "Take it easy," Will said, managing a smile. He looked at Brian and added, "It probably looks worse than it is. You know how head wounds can be. They bleed like a stuck pig."

"What do you mean?" Brian asked, his voice higher than usual. "Are you all right?"

"Yes, Brian, he's fine," Jean answered, then asked, "Where else are you hurting?"

"My hip's screamin' at me, but I don't think it's much. This is the biggest problem." Closing his eyes and gritting his teeth, he barely lifted a broken, twisted hand. Two fingers were splayed at odd angles; another was badly bent. Bone showed through a knuckle, and his palm was already bruised and swollen so badly that it resembled a bloated dumpling.

Jean sucked in her breath. "Dear Lord." For a moment she stared at the mangled appendage, then said resolutely, "We best wrap that up." She tore off another section of apron, tied it around his neck, and gently lifted his arm so it rested in the sling.

Will squeezed his eyes closed and sucked air through his teeth.

"I'm sorry, but we've got to hold it steady until we can get you to the doctor," Jean said. She ripped another piece of apron and wrapped it around his trunk and over the injured arm, bracing the limb so he couldn't move it. "Can you stand?"

Will nodded but cringed at the movement. "My head's pounding, but I think I can make it." His face bathed in sweat, he leaned against Luke as Jean and the young man helped him to his feet. For several moments he stood between the two, swaying.

"Dad, lean on me," Luke said, moving his shoulder beneath his father's good arm.

Will rested against his son. "The world's spinning. Give me a minute."

Brian stood close to his father. "You can rest your hand on me if you want."

Will managed to nod but didn't answer. His pale skin blanched more, and fresh beads of sweat merged with those already on his face. He compressed his lips.

The gash started to bleed more heavily, so Jean reached up and pressed down on the cloth. "Can you make it back to the house?"

"I'll try," Will said, his voice weak.

"We can bring the truck out here," Luke said.

"No. You'll end up stuck. I can do it."

Taking small, slow steps, they headed for the house. Jean didn't like Will's color. He'd gone gray and was shaking. He needed the doctor soon.

Laurel met them at the driveway.

Her eyes swimming in tears, Susie followed, dragging a dilapidated blanket in the dirt. "Daddy, are you all right?"

"He's gonna' be fine," Jean said. She looked at Laurel. "We've got to get him to the clinic. His hand is broken, and the gash on his head is going to need stitching. You stay with the little ones. Luke will drive us."

They guided Will toward the pickup and helped him in. Jean slid onto the seat beside him. With Will leaning against her, they headed for town.

"Darndest thing," Will said. "I didn't see that hole. I pulled out a stump last week and just plain forgot about it."

"What happened?" Jean asked.

"My right back tire dropped into the hole, and over I went. I tried to jump clear."

"Praise the Lord you're alive. It could have been worse."

Shivering, Will lay under a wool blanket on an examination table. His feet were elevated, and an IV with fluids dripped into his arm. Jean caressed his forehead and cheek. His skin felt cool and clammy. "I'm sure the doctor will be here any minute," she said, glancing at Will's misshapen hand.

A nurse stepped into the room and placed a thermometer in Will's mouth. "The doctor's treating another emergency, but he'll be here soon and have you fixed up in no time." She felt Will's face, took his pulse, then checked the reading on the thermometer. After shaking it down and replacing it in a container of alcohol, she headed for the door. "I'm sure it will only be a few more minutes," she said and stepped out.

Jean stood beside Will, keeping a hand on his shoulder. "How are you feeling?"

"Not so good, but I don't think I'll be dying anytime soon."

The door opened, and Dr. Donovan walked in. His graying hair needed the attention of a barber, but he was clean-shaven. Pushing his hair out of his eyes, he peered over small square glasses. "Afternoon,

Jean. Will." He crossed to the table. "So, you were out playing on that new tractor of yours, huh? Looks like the tractor won."

"I'll say," Will tried to move his leg and winced.

"That leg hurting you?"

"It's my hip."

The doctor pulled down the blanket and placed a stethoscope on Will's chest. He listened, then examined the head wound. "This'll need stitches but should heal fine. You'll probably have a doozie of a headache," he added with a grin. He ran his hands over Will's shoulders. "Any pain here?"

"Nope."

He felt Will's arms, then gently released the hand from its bindings. Turning it carefully, he studied the swollen, bloodied appendage. "We've got some real work to do here." He continued to probe. Will gritted his teeth and groaned as the doctor manipulated the fingers. "This'll need more than setting. It'll take surgery. You have a compound fracture in that one finger. We'll have to take it off."

Jean felt as if the floor had dropped out from under her. She gripped the table to steady herself.

"You mean amputate?" Will asked. The doctor nodded. "Why?"

"Danger of infection. You could lose your whole hand, or even your life. I don't want to take that risk."

"All right. Do what you have to do."

Gently placing the hand on Will's stomach, the doctor rolled him onto his side and palpated the hip joint. "Nothing feels broken here. More than likely it's just bruised with some muscle strain." He examined Will's legs and feet, and finding no further injuries, he said, "My nurse will stitch that head wound, then I'll see you in surgery."

"Doc . . . is it going to be all right? My hand, I mean. Will I be able to use it?"

"It's in bad shape, Will. I'll do my best." He turned as if to go, then stopped. "I've seen worse." He placed an arm around Jean's shoulders and guided her out of the room.

Out in the hall, Jean fought tears. "Do you have to amputate?"

"It's too risky. The bone is open to the air, and the chance of an infection is high."

"Is he going to be all right?"

Dr. Donovan massaged his chin. "I wish I could tell you he's going to be good as new, but I just don't know. That hand's a mess." He folded his arms over his chest. "My best guess is he'll get back function, but I can't promise the hand will be like it was. He'll learn to live with one less finger." He smiled. "He'll have to lay off for a while. I expect he'll hate that. I know how he loves his work."

"I'm not sure how we're going to pay you, doctor. Money's tight."

"Now's not the time to be worrying about that. We'll work out something." He rested a hand on Jean's back. "Well, I've got an appointment in surgery. I better get to it."

Chapter 2

"Anything I can get you from town?" Will asked, carefully cradling his injured hand against his body.

Brian dumped an armload of kindling into a wood bin. "Can I go?"

"Not today," Jean said, setting a coffeepot on the stove. "I need your help here." She looked at Will. "I can't think of anything I need. Are you sure you're feeling up to going?"

"Yeah. I'm all right." He glanced into the front room. "Where's that Luke? He knew we were leaving first thing."

"I haven't seen him."

"He's probably out in the barn." Will kissed Jean, wincing when his injured hand touched her arm. He looked at the swathe of dressings. "I never would have believed I'd say this, but I'll be happy to get a cast on this thing."

"Try to be patient. The doctor just wants to make sure there's no infection. And it's looking good; well, as good as it can look." Jean grinned.

"I'd sure like to get back to work."

Jean kissed Will's cheek. "I'm just thankful all you lost was a finger. It could have been worse."

"True." Will offered his wife a sidewise grin. "I'm not sure my hand knows how to function with only three fingers and a thumb, but I'll be glad to start using it again."

Jean felt a flicker of apprehension. Will had been acting as if his hand would be good as new, except for the missing finger. "Remember, Dr. Donovan said your hand could be stiff and might not work the way it did."

"I know, but he also said he did a pretty good job of fixing it. And he thinks it'll be functional." He shook his head. "I hate that word *func-tional*—sounds like I'm talking about a piece of farm equipment."

Jean smiled. "In a way it is. Where would we be without your two hands?"

He held out the bound appendage. The end of two fingers twitched and he grimaced. "I can't even move my fingers."

"Will! Don't! You know you're not supposed to do anything yet."

"I know. But I need to get back to work. As much as I appreciate Adam's help, he's got a lot to learn." He chuckled. "I don't think he's cut out for farming."

Luke walked into the room. "Can I drive you into town later? I was planning on going over to Alex's. He's actually going to test me on some of the native tracking techniques he's been teaching me. I'm getting pretty good."

"It'll have to wait. We need to get some shoes for the wedding, and we might have to order them."

"I don't see why I need new shoes."

Jean eyed his tattered boots. "You can't very well wear those."

"They clean up all right."

"Luke, you're going to be the best man. You can't stand up in . . ." Jean searched for the right words. "Well, those awful things." She studied her seventeen-year-old son. He'd shot up recently and now stood a good inch taller than his father. He hadn't yet filled out. It would be a while before his body adjusted to his six-foot-two-inch frame.

"I want some shoes," Brian said.

Two-year-old Susie held out a foot. "Me too."

"Brian, the ones you have are good enough," Jean said. "We just bought them a couple of months ago."

Brian frowned. "Yeah, but they're not new, and I want black ones like Adam's."

"They'll do," Will said. "Help your mama." He looked at Jean. "We ought to be back before lunch." Giving Luke a playful shove toward the door, Will followed him out.

Jean cleared away the breakfast dishes and stacked them in the sink. A cow's bawling came from the barn. "These will have to wait," she said with a sigh. "The milking needs to be done."

Laurel untied her apron, grabbed a coat off a hook on the back porch, and pushed her feet into rubber boots. Brian ran to get his coat and pulled it on.

Jean lifted Susie out of her high chair and carried her into the living room. "I'm thankful she's still content to stay in her playpen," she said, settling the little girl in the wooden enclosure. Handing her a doll with blue eyes that closed when she was laid down, she said, "You stay put and play with your baby. We'll be back in a few minutes."

Susie took the doll by the hair, chattered at it, then cradled it in her arms. "Baby."

"Brian, keep an eye on your sister for me."

Brian walked into the front room. "I want to help with the milking," he whined. "You said I could. You told me eight was big enough." He threw back his shoulders and pulled his four-foot-one-inch frame up as tall as he could.

Susie was happily playing with her doll. "All right. I s'pose she'll be fine for a few minutes."

"We can leave the door open," Brian said. "That way, if she cries, we can hear her."

"I suppose. And with the weather so warm, it'll be good to air out the house." Jean kissed Susie's golden curls, then returned to the kitchen. She filled a bucket with warm water, dropped a washcloth in it, then followed Laurel and Brian to the back porch. Each grabbed a clean, empty pail and headed for the barn. Jean left the door open.

Swinging his pail up and over his head then back down in a wide circle, Brian skipped ahead. A hen and brood of chicks pecked at the ground outside the barn door where oats had been spilled. Dropping his bucket, he headed for the chicks; they scattered. The hen bristled, making a low burring sound in her throat. Ignoring her warning, Brian grabbed for a chick. Golden feathers ruffling and wings flapping, the hen bustled toward him. Snatching up the chick, he easily stepped out of her way. Still complaining, the hen gathered the rest of her brood and led them away.

Brian held the chirping creature, careful not to crush it. "Mama, is this a rooster or a hen?" he asked, studying the golden ball of fluff.

"Don't know yet. We'll have to wait and see."

"I hope it's a hen. Otherwise, it'll end up in the pot. And it's awful cute." The chick's protests grew louder. The hen responded by squawking and fluffing her feathers.

"Put it back with its mother," Laurel said.

Brian set it on the ground. Flapping stubby, down-covered wings, it scampered to its mother and siblings.

"Brian, would you get the goat into its stanchion?" Jean asked.

Picking up his pail, Brian protested, "I thought I got to do the cows."

"I'm not sure you're ready for that just yet. You could get stepped on or worse."

"I'm big enough, and I'll be careful."

Jean knew it was time for Brian to take on more of the chores, but he seemed so young. With a sigh, she relented. "All right, but make sure you keep an eye on those two. Sometimes they're playful or get in a hurry for their grain and you're ..." She was about to remind him of his size but thought better of it and said, "You just watch out for them."

Brian disappeared through the doorway, the interior gloom swallowing him.

Jean and Laurel followed. After the bright outdoor sunlight, the inside of the barn seemed dark, but they knew the way and didn't slow their steps. The barn smelled of hay, oats, and manure. Jean pitched hay into the cribs while Laurel measured out small amounts of grain for each animal.

Brian appeared, towing the Guernsey. She balked, and he tugged on the lead. "Come on, get up there." The cow didn't move. "Penny," Brian said sternly, "come on." He pulled harder. Finally she plodded forward and allowed Brian to guide her to the crib where she immediately licked up her portion of grain, then buried her nose in the hay.

"She was testing you," Laurel said.

Brian patted the Guernsey's side. "I showed her who was boss."

"That you did." Laurel headed for the Jersey's stall. "I'll milk Molly."

Jean hooked a lead on the nanny goat and led it to a small stanchion. She set a stool beside it and sat down, then washed the goat's udder. Keeping an eye on Brian, she started milking. He sat, then while reaching for the udder, he tipped his stool, bringing his hand down on the bucket. Jean smiled, remembering how frustrated he'd been when she'd first taught him how to milk. After several failures he'd finally managed to get the knack of it.

Bucket and stool back in place, Brian pressed his forehead against the Guernsey's soft hair and grabbed two teats. "Brian, are you forgetting something?" Jean asked.

He looked at her with a puzzled expression. "What?"

She lifted the washcloth from the bucket.

"Oh," he said, retrieving the wet rag and cleaning the cow's udder. Again he sat, rested his head against the Guernsey's belly, and searched for her teats. His small arms barely reached, but he managed to grab hold of two and squeezed. At first the milk dribbled out, but finally narrow jets of white squirted and spattered into the bucket with a soft ring.

The animals munched, and the three Haspers settled into the rhythm of milking. Soon rich, frothy milk filled their pails. "Looks like they've been getting a good share of the early spring grasses," Jean said.

The Guernsey blew air from her nostrils, flicked her tail, and let out an anxious bawl. She stamped the floor with her hind foot. Brian leaned back. "Hey! Hold still!" The cow paid no heed and stomped again, this time plunking her foot inside the bucket and knocking it over. "Rats!" Brian shouted. "Now look what you've done!"

The Jersey also seemed nervous. She swished her tail and moved her weight from foot to foot. "What is it, Molly?" Laurel asked, patting the cow's side and removing the bucket.

Jean stopped milking and listened. Setting her bucket out of harm's way, she walked to the Guernsey and ran her hand over the cow's neck. "You out of sorts today, Penny?" The cow blew air from her nostrils, her skin shuddering as she looked at the barn wall, the whites showing around her brown eyes.

Molly's gaze followed the Guernsey's. "Mama, what's wrong with them?" Laurel asked.

Jean heard snuffling along the barn wall. "Shh." She walked toward the sound. Scratching joined the snuffling. Jean stepped back. "Something's out there," she whispered. Peering through a space between boards, her stomach dropped and the hair prickled on her arms.

A cinnamon-colored grizzly dug at the ground along the barn wall. It was trying to dig underneath! He stopped and sniffed the air, then returned to digging. He wanted in! Fear spiked through Jean. They had heard a few reports of mauled livestock. She wondered if this was the offender.

The animal stopped digging and lumbered toward the front of the barn. "Get up in the loft!" Jean whispered fiercely and ran for the door. "Now!" Brian and Laurel obeyed, their faces questions. She reached the double doors just as the bear rounded the corner of the barn. Thankful they hadn't opened both doors, she grabbed the open one and swung it closed, quickly dropping a wooden bar in place to secure it.

"What is it, Mama? What's wrong?" Laurel asked.

Jean didn't answer but walked quietly to the bottom of the ladder. Looking up at her children, she whispered. "It's a bear. Be still." Brian started down the ladder. "Get back up there."

His face blanched. "Can it get in?"

"No, but I don't want to take any chances."

The grizzly set to work, digging dirt out from under the door. After a few minutes he moved away, circling the barn and scratching at the ground and walls. With a snarl, his feet slammed against the south wall. He pushed, making the boards creak.

"He's going to get in!" Brian cried.

Every nerve on end, Jean watched the barn wall. The animal stopped battering at it and found his way back to the doors. Then he put his nose through the place where the two met and pushed. The doors moved and groaned. Jean stepped onto the first rung of the ladder.

The doors held, and the bear stopped its assault.

Jean looked up at her children and forced a smile. "Praise the Lord; Daddy does good work."

"Mama, what are we going to do?" Brian asked, his voice quaking.

"We'll be real quiet and wait until he leaves."

The cows continued to stomp their feet, swish their tails, and let out an occasional worried bawl. The goats seemed to have more sense and stood quietly. Jean walked to the cows and stroked their necks, talking softly. "It's all right, ladies. He can't get in. Shush now."

For several seconds the bear made no sound. *Maybe he's gone,* she thought, holding her breath and listening. Then she heard something that sent terror pulsing through her. Susie was crying! "Oh, dear Lord!" Jean pressed a hand to her mouth. "Susie!"

She tried to remember if the door had been left open or if it was closed. She ran to the double doors and peered out. The bear lumbered toward the house, his cinnamon coat glistening in the sunlight and his huge paws padding the earth. Jean's eyes traveled to the door. It was open! The bear was already at the back of the house. He stopped and sniffed the ground. Stepping onto the porch, he swung his huge head back and forth, smelling the air.

Jean felt as if she were drowning in horror. *Lord, protect my baby!*

"Mama," Laurel said from behind her.

Jean jumped.

"What's happening?"

"The bear's on the back porch, and the door's open."

There was no time to think. Jean wrenched open the barn door, throwing it wide. "Hey! Bear! Over here!" she yelled, running out and waving her arms. The animal swung around and looked at her. Mouth slightly agape, he stared at Jean, stepped off the porch, and ran toward her.

She stepped back inside, slammed the door shut, and bolted it. Near tears, she backed away. The grizzly rammed the barrier. The doors held. *Father, what should I do? What can I do?* She searched the barn, hoping to find something to use against the bear. The only weapon was a pitchfork, and it would be worthless against this beast. "I wish I had the rifle."

"Mama, what are we going to do?" Laurel asked.

In a rage, the bear snarled and pushed against the door. A board popped and splintered.

"Someone's got to get to the house and close that door!" Jean almost screamed. "I shouldn't have left it open."

"I'll do it," Laurel said immediately. "I can run faster than either of you."

"You can't outrun a bear. And it's too far."

Laurel paced and thought. "What if you distract him? I can sneak out one of the stall doors and run for the house."

Jean nodded. "That might work. But I'll go. I don't want you taking such a risk."

"No. It has to be me." Laurel stared at her mother. "Susie needs the one who can run the fastest." She sat down and pulled off her boots. "I'm ready," she said as she stood up.

Jean knew Laurel was right, but the idea of her daughter putting herself in the path of that animal was nearly unbearable. "All right."

The bear's attack on the barn doors ended. There was no sound except for Susie's cries. Jean peered out. The bear was headed back to the house. "We've got to do it now!"

"I'm going," Laurel said and ran to the back of the barn.

"I'll get his attention," Jean called. She glanced at Brian who was peering down from the loft. "You stay put. I don't want to have to worry about you. Not a peep now. You hear me? No matter what happens, you stay right there and be still."

His face white, Brian nodded.

Her stomach in knots, her heart thumping, Jean lifted the wooden bar and opened the door. "Laurel, are you ready?"

"Yes."

"I'm going out now." Jean stepped into the yard. The brute stood on the porch with his head inside the back door. "All right, bear! I'm here! I'm the one you want!"

He looked at her but didn't move. He seemed undecided about what to do.

"Come on, bear! Come and get me! There's nothin' in that house you need." Jean picked up a handful of pebbles and started throwing them at the intruder.

The grizzly took a step toward her, then stood on his hind legs. Small black eyes glared at her. She couldn't remember being so frightened. Susie let out a loud wail, and the bear looked back toward the house. Jean took another step away from the barn. "Come on, bear. Come on. I'm here."

Jean glanced at the corner where Laurel stood waiting. *She can't make it without the bear seeing her! He'll be on her before she gets halfway there!* Jean scanned the yard. *I'll have to draw him away from the house.*

The chicken house was only a dozen yards away, but it didn't have a door. It would be of no help. A pump house stood several yards beyond. Jean doubted she could make it there before the bear got her. *I have to try. If I don't . . .* She couldn't complete the thought. It was too horrible. If she could make it part of the way before the bear came after her, she might have a chance.

Father, give me courage. Help me run faster than I've ever run. And . . . if I die, take care of my family. Jean edged toward the pump house.

The bear followed her with his eyes but made no move.

Jean took another step, and another. She recalled hearing somewhere that the natives sometimes talked kindly to bears, and it seemed to calm them. Figuring she had nothing to lose, she said, "All right, bear, that's a good boy. Now, stay put for just a while." She tried to sound serene. "Everything's just fine." Her voice trembled. "No one's going to hurt you. Just let us get our little girl."

Mouth open, eyes trained on Jean, the bear bounced on straight front legs in a show of intimidation. Froth dripped from his muzzle. Jean had managed to make it nearly halfway. She kept moving, slowly, steadily. There was no turning back. It was now a longer run to the barn than to the pump house. The bear continued to watch her.

What if he doesn't follow me? Jean wondered. *Susie and Laurel could be killed.* She changed her tone and talked louder. "Come on, bear." She kept moving. "Come and get me. I'm right here."

Then she remembered something Alex had told her, "Never run from a bear. If you do, he'll chase you." *I need to run,* she decided. Once she started, she knew not to look back. Even one glance could slow her down enough to make the difference between safety and death.

Father, give me the speed of a deer, she prayed. "Come on! Get me," she yelled, then sprinted for the refuge. Her feet pounding the earth, she gulped air. At first all she heard was her own breathing and the blood surging through her head. Then she heard panting and heavy footfalls close behind. She fought the urge to look back.

Pumping her arms, lifting her legs, and stretching out each stride, she ran as hard as she'd ever run. She could smell the animal and hear his huffing! It was close! *Only a few more yards!* she told herself. *You can make it!* She lunged for the pump house, slammed her hands against the door, and leaped inside. Shaking, she pushed the door closed, latched it, then pressed her weight against it. Terror consumed her. She glanced around the small dark room. It wouldn't hold up against an attack.

The bear threw himself against the door, biting and clawing at the wood. The door bounced beneath Jean's hands. She closed her eyes and pressed against it, then stared at the splintering door. It wouldn't hold.

The bear broke off his attack and prowled around the tiny sanctuary, occasionally digging along the base of the building or scratching at the walls. Low, throaty growls served as a warning of his intentions. With a roar he assaulted the door again, laying it open. Strips of wood were shorn away. Terror strangling her, Jean stared at the fractured door and at the teeth ripping at it.

Gunshots reverberated, and Laurel yelled, "Get! Get out of here!" More shots were fired, and the assault stopped. "Go on! Leave us be!" Laurel called.

It turned quiet.

"Mama, it's all right. He's gone. Come on out."

Taking a deep, shuddering breath, Jean let the shredded door fall open. She stepped into the sunshine and glanced about, searching for the animal. Her legs shook, and she felt like she might faint. Jean sat with her back resting against the pump house.

Laurel kneeled in front of her and pulled her into her arms. "Oh, Mama. I thought you were going to die."

Tears of relief spilled down Jean's face. "So did I," she managed to say.

"Why did you do that?"

"It was the only way. If I'd stayed where I was, you couldn't have gotten past him." She glanced at nearby fields. "Where did he go?"

"He hightailed it into the woods over there." Laurel pointed at a grove of birch and alder at the edge of the pasture.

"Susie's all right?"

"Yes. Just angry. She had her leg caught between the bars of the playpen." Laurel smiled and said in a light tone, "Well, maybe Jessie will put this in her book."

Still shaking, Jean pushed herself to her feet. Her eyes searched the woods. She thought she caught a glimpse of glimmering cinnamon, but then it was gone.

Chapter 3

LAUREL STOOD IN FRONT OF AN OAK-FRAMED MIRROR AND STUDIED HER reflection. Her hazel eyes sparkled, and her mouth turned up in a persistent smile. "This is it. Your wedding day." Her heart quickened, and her stomach did a small flip. In less than an hour, she'd be Mrs. Adam Dunnavant. "Laurel Dunnavant," she said. She touched the lace on the princess neckline of her dress, then hooked a pearl button at the wrist.

A soft knock sounded at the door. "Laurel, may I come in?" her mother asked.

"Yes."

Jean stepped into the room, her eyes settling on her daughter. "You're beautiful." Her voice caught, and she retrieved a handkerchief tucked inside a cuff and dabbed at her eyes. "I'm sorry. I've been weepy all day."

Laurel rested a hand on her abdomen. "My stomach is full of butterflies. I think having the wedding in the morning is making it worse. My stomach always takes a while to wake up. I wish the train weren't leaving so early."

Jean smiled and replaced her handkerchief. "Every bride gets anxious." Reaching into a pocket, she pulled out a small box. "I have something for you." She opened it and lifted a delicate necklace with a single pearl. "This belonged to your grandmother. I wore it on my wedding day. I thought you ought to have it."

"Oh, Mama, it's beautiful."

"It will be perfect with your dress. Turn around, and I'll fasten it for you." Jean secured the necklace.

Fingering the teardrop pearl, Laurel gazed at it in the mirror. "It looks elegant." She met her mother's eyes in the mirror. "Thank you."

Again Jean teared up and brought out the handkerchief. "I don't know how I'll get through the wedding."

Laurel kissed her mother and hugged her. "I love you."

"I love you," Jean said, the words sticking in her throat. She straightened. "Well, it's nearly time to leave. You ready?"

Laurel blew out a breath. "Yes."

Organ music filled the sanctuary, and Adam's grasp was firm and sure as he and Laurel walked down the aisle as husband and wife. When they exited the doors, he stopped and faced his bride. "We did it! I love you, Mrs. Dunnavant!" He pulled her into his arms and kissed her eagerly.

Slightly embarrassed, Laurel returned his kiss.

"All right, that's enough of that," Celeste teased.

Feeling giddy, Laurel stepped out of Adam's embrace.

"What a beautiful ceremony," Celeste said, pulling her friend into a bear hug. "I'm so happy for you! Maybe it will be Robert and me next," she whispered.

"What about your father?"

"He's already fit to be tied because I'm seeing Robert, but he'll have to get used to it." A momentary flash of sadness touched her eyes, and then Celeste turned on a bright smile and gave Adam a hug. "You'd better take good care of my best friend."

"I will. I promise."

Robert stepped up to Adam. "Congratulations. I wish you both well."

"Thank you," Adam said, shaking Robert's hand.

Robert turned to Laurel. "I'm happy for you. You and Adam were meant to be together." He gave Laurel a brotherly hug.

Remembering the relationship she and Robert had once shared, Laurel felt a twinge of sadness—not because she hadn't married Robert, but because she knew how much she'd hurt him. "Thank you, Robert," she said.

Celeste linked arms with the lanky man. "I'm ready for a party. How about you?"

"Sounds good," Robert said with a grin. "But I think you have to stay with the rest of the wedding party and greet the guests first."

"Oh. Right." Celeste took her place beside Laurel.

The next two people to leave the church were Miram and Ed. Miram headed straight for Laurel. "You're the most beautiful bride I've ever seen!" she said in her high-pitched voice as she hugged Laurel. "I hope I look half as pretty on my wedding day." She batted her eyelashes and glanced up at Ed.

Laurel whispered, "You'll be beautiful, and Ed will be proud of you."

Miram blushed. "You think so?"

Laurel nodded. "Yes, I do."

Smiling, Miram crinkled her cheek to push up her glasses, then catching herself, she rearranged them with her hand and moved on to congratulate Adam.

Guests moved through the receiving line, and by the time the last one headed for the reception at the community building, Laurel felt as if she'd been hugged and kissed by most of Palmer.

At the reception there were toasts and speeches, followed by dancing and cake-cutting. Finally Laurel threw her bouquet to a cluster of single women anxious to capture the prize. Lunging past the others, Celeste managed to catch it and held up the bouquet in triumph.

Will and Jean stood at the bottom of the steps, their arms intertwined as they watched Laurel and Adam hurry for the train depot. Jean dabbed at tears and waved when Laurel turned and smiled her good-bye.

Laurel snuggled close to Adam and gazed out the window as the train headed north. "I'm glad you thought of Mt. McKinley. It's a perfect place for a honeymoon." She leaned her cheek against his arm, enjoying the feel of his worsted jacket.

"It's just a camp, not fancy."

"I don't mind. I'm used to tents, remember? We lived in one our first summer here." She hugged his arm. "Any place with you will be perfect."

Adam kissed the top of her head. "It's hard to believe you're my wife. I keep thinking I'm going to wake up and this will be a dream."

"This is no dream," Laurel said and nestled against her husband.

A few hours later the train chugged into the station at the entrance to Mt. McKinley Park. An open-air bus waited to take them and a handful of other passengers to the camp. A tall slender woman with short brown hair, wearing tan slacks and a lightweight jacket stood beside the bus. She was plain, but her eyes held a spark of humor and energy, making her look almost pretty.

"Welcome to Mt. McKinley Park," she said. "I'm Janet Holcomb. I'll be driving you to the camp." She grinned. "You can all be thankful for the warm spring weather. First thing, we need to get your luggage on the bus."

Adam grabbed two suitcases. "Where do you want them?"

"In the back. There's plenty of room." She picked up two other bags and stowed them beside the ones Adam had already loaded. Another man added more, and Adam hefted the last one on top of the pile.

"Where's the mountain?" a short, chunky woman asked. "I was told we would see it."

"It's there," Janet pointed toward Mt. McKinley. "But the clouds are hiding it. Sorry. It happens a lot. We get socked in here pretty regularly. The park has lots of beautiful and interesting sites, though. I think you'll enjoy yourselves even if the mountain doesn't come out of hiding." She opened the bus door. "Everyone on board." The people climbed in and found places to sit, while Janet slid onto the driver's seat and started the engine.

"How far to the camp?" a man smoking a pipe asked.

"It'll take about an hour to get there. Supper ought to be waiting for us." Janet shifted into first and pulled onto a dirt road. "It'll be a bit bumpy, but it won't be boring. There's lots to see."

Gravel crunched beneath the tires, and a cold breeze blew over the passengers. Taking in the surroundings, Laurel bundled deeper into her coat, her excitement growing. Stately looking mountains hemmed in broad valleys carpeted with low-growing grasses and broad patches of snow. Ponds left by melting snow dotted the landscape, and narrow rivulets wound their way through ravines. A few hardy flowers grew close to the earth, splashing the fields with bursts of color.

Birdsong echoed from all around. Sparrows, warblers, and finches flittered from low-growing bushes. Some balanced on frail willow limbs, while others were planted on the sturdy branches of stark spruce. Except for the lusty comical chortle of a willow ptarmigan, their mix of songs reminded Laurel of an orchestra.

"Oh, look!" the short woman said, pointing at a small herd of shaggy caribou sprinting across the road and leaping down an embankment on their right. "Why do they look so awful?"

"They're still shedding their winter coats," Janet said. "They'll soon look like themselves. In the meantime, they look pretty moth-eaten."

"Why does the herd only have males? Where are the females?" the woman asked.

Janet chuckled. "The herd has both males and females. All caribou have horns, even the cows, but the bulls have larger racks. The cows will be calving soon."

Laurel watched the animals trail their way into a small valley. "Aren't they something! I love it here!"

"I'm glad," Adam said, tightening his arm around her shoulders.

"There's a bear!" a man called, then asked in a tense voice, "How come this bus don't have windows?"

Janet slowed the vehicle and glanced at the brute on the bank above them.

"You don't have to stop," the man said.

"Don't worry. He's more interested in a meal than he is in us," Janet explained.

The bear stopped digging and looked at the bus. A few moments later he returned to digging.

"What's he doing?" Laurel asked.

"Probably after a ground squirrel, one of the bears' favorite foods." Janet moved on, expertly shifting through the gears.

The bus headed down a steep incline, splashed through a clear-running stream, ground its way up the opposite bank, and pulled into a camp made up of one log cabin and several tents. Stopping in front of the cabin, Janet said, "Here we are."

Adam looked at the tents and four outhouses. "It's kind of primitive." He raised an eyebrow.

"It's fine. I love it," Laurel said with a smile. Then she saw a monstrous mountain gleaming in the sunlight like a brilliant jewel.

Deep snows slashed by dark gashes of granite glowed pink and gold in the sunlight. This mountain towered above all the nearby mountains and hills. It had to be Mt. McKinley. She'd never been so close.

Hands on hips, Janet stared at the peak. "Well, how about that? It decided to show off for you after all." In a more businesslike tone, she said, "You'll need to register. Sign in at the main building. You'll get your tent assignments and a camp schedule. You have lots of activities to choose from. We've got horseback riding, hiking, mountain climbing, fishing, and sight-seeing, plus games. And after supper we'll have some good old-fashioned singing around the campfire."

The idea of horseback riding interested Laurel most. It had been a long while since she'd ridden. She placed her hand on Adam's arm. "Have you ever ridden a horse?"

"No."

"Would you like to?"

"I'm game."

"After we get our room, can we go for a short ride? It would be a nice way to see some of the park."

"Sure. If that's what you want." Adam sounded disappointed, but he gave Laurel a gentle squeeze. "We'll do whatever you want." He glanced at the log house and row of tents. "First we need to find our room."

After getting their room assignment, Adam and Laurel walked hand in hand between the row of tents. Adam glanced at a piece of paper he'd been given. "Number 8," he said, stopping in front of the one with a number eight painted on it. He set down his suitcase and stepped up to the door. Pulling open the flap, he peeked inside. "Not bad." He caught Laurel in an embrace and kissed her. "Do you think we might postpone that ride? Just for a little while?"

"Maybe," Laurel said, quaking inwardly. She was innocent and not quite sure what to expect. Should she be frightened?

He lifted her in his arms.

Laughing, Laurel dropped her suitcase with a loud thump. "What are you doing?"

"You're my bride, aren't you?"

"Yes."

"Well, I'm carrying my bride over the threshold. Isn't that how it's supposed to be done?" Circling her arms around his neck, Laurel leaned against Adam as he carried her into their temporary home.

The room was simple but comfortable. It contained two cots, each with a brightly colored quilt, a chest of drawers, a small table with two chairs, and a woodstove radiating heat. "How is this, Mrs. Dunnavant?" Adam asked.

"Fine. Just fine."

Adam looked at the beds. "I guess they'll have to do." Still holding Laurel, he crossed the room and sat on one.

Laurel remained in his arms. She'd wondered how she would feel at this moment. Now that it was here, she was aware of a deep longing for and devotion to her husband. This is how it was meant to be, man and woman together. A covenant created and blessed by God.

Looking into Adam's warm, blue eyes, she felt as if she were swimming in his love. She kissed him gently, slowly. Searching his face, she said, "I love you, Adam Dunnavant."

"I love you." Adam's voice trembled slightly. He held her tighter. "It scares me to think I almost lost you."

"I'm not lost," Laurel said smiling. "I've been found."

"I'll be a good husband. I'll never hurt you."

"You will. And I'll hurt you too. But after the hurts, we'll forgive and love." Laurel kissed him again and again. "Maybe we can ride horses tomorrow. Would that be all right with you?"

Adam answered with a hungry kiss.

Chapter 4

ADAM WALKED INTO THE KITCHEN AND SET A PAIL OF MILK ON THE COUNTER. "I don't know if I'll ever get the hang of milking. Seems the harder I try, the less milk comes out. Your father can milk four cows in the time it takes me to do one."

Laurel kissed him. "You worry too much. It takes time to learn. You'll figure it out." She set a plate of toast and eggs, along with a pitcher of milk, on the table. "Hope you're hungry. The hens have been busy."

"I'm starved." Adam sat at the table. "I figure I'll finish most of the plowing today. Might even get some of the vegetables in the ground."

Laurel filled a glass with milk and set it in front of Adam. "Great, but eat first." She pushed the platter of food toward him.

Adam slid three eggs onto his plate and took two pieces of buttered toast. "So, what do you think?"

"About what?" Laurel asked as she filled another glass with milk and sat across from Adam.

"Planting."

"We need to think about frost. It's still early." She took a bite of toast. "We can plant peas. The rutabagas and carrots are hardy, but we should wait another week or two before we put the cabbage and cauliflower starts in the ground."

"I doubt we'll have any more freezes. Why don't we go ahead and plant them?"

Wearing an understanding smile, Laurel slowly shook her head no. "We could lose all of them if we get a freeze. We can't take the chance."

"What about potatoes?"

"They should be all right."

Adam ate in silence, then asked, "Has that bear been back to your parents' place?"

"I talked to Mama day before yesterday, and she said she hasn't seen it. Hopefully he won't visit again."

"I haven't heard of any recent kills. Maybe the bear that was doing the damage has moved on. I hope so. It wouldn't take much to wipe out the few animals we have."

Laurel returned the milk to the icebox. "Maybe you can start planting after lunch."

Adam didn't respond. He stared at his plate. "I'll need you to show me how. I've never actually done it before." He drained the last of his milk.

"I was planning to help. It'll be fun doing it together."

"I'm beginning to think I wasn't cut out to be a farmer. I like being outdoors, and I like the physical labor, but I'm ignorant. I can't make a move without asking for help. You and your father have to show me the simplest things. I feel like a fool. I'm supposed to be helping your father, but I feel more like a nuisance."

Laurel walked up behind Adam and draped her arms around his neck, resting her hands on his chest. "Why do you think you should know farming? You've never done it before." Laurel moved to the chair beside him. "When you started working for the paper, did you begin as a reporter?"

"No."

"So why would this be different?" She leaned against his arm. "Adam, I've lived on a farm since the day I was born. It's all I've ever known. Of course I know more than you."

Adam took Laurel's hand and rested it against his cheek, then kissed it. "I know. It's just that for a long time I've been good at what I do."

"I know this is hard for you. I'm sorry." Laurel brushed back a strand of hair that had found its way onto Adam's forehead.

"I've got to go over to your folks' house this afternoon. Your dad needs help with the tractor." He gave her a wry grin. "I'm not all that much help. I can't seem to make straight rows."

Laurel patted his arm. "I just wish you didn't have to do so much. You've got work to do here. What about Luke? Can't he help?"

"He's swamped."

She sighed. "It doesn't seem right—you having to work both places."

"It's not for long. The doctor said your dad ought to get his cast off soon. I don't really mind. I just wish I were better at this."

"Why don't I take care of the planting?"

"No. I want us to do it together, and I want to start this morning. I can finish the last of the plowing tomorrow." He scooted his chair away from the table and carried his empty coffee mug to the sink. "I'll get the seed and tools and meet you outside." He gave Laurel a lingering kiss. "Maybe we can have a picnic this afternoon before I go to help your dad?"

"Hmm. Sounds nice. I'll make sandwiches."

"I don't know if we'll have time to eat them," he said with a grin.

Exhausted and dirty, Adam came in from working long after supper time. He washed up, then sat at the table.

"I missed you at lunch."

"I know. I'm sorry." He downed a glass of water. "I had more to do than I thought. Dinner smells good."

"It's not much. Just rabbit stew and biscuits." Laurel set a bowl of stew and two biscuits in front of him.

"Looks good," Adam said, dipping a spoon into the mix of meat and vegetables. He said little while he ate.

"Is something wrong, Adam? You look worried."

"No. I'm fine," Adam said, but he wasn't. He missed working for the *Tribune*—the busyness, the excitement of chasing down a story and then writing it. And as much as he hated to admit it, he missed the recognition that came with the job.

"No, you're not all right. I can see it in your face. Adam Dunnavant, you can't fool me." Laurel folded her arms over her chest.

Adam set his spoon in his bowl. "All right. I didn't want to say anything. I know everything will work out. I just need a little time."

"What is it?"

Adam took a slow breath. "You know I love it here, and I love being married to you. But . . . well, I miss writing. I feel like part of me is missing." Standing, he shoved his hands into his pockets. "I'm no good at farming. I don't know anything about it. And even if I did, all our hard work could be lost in a day."

"I thought we already talked about this."

Adam gazed at Laurel. "We did. And I know it's going to take time, but . . . I'm afraid. What if I do it wrong and the crop is no good? What if the weather turns bad?"

Laurel circled her arms around her husband's waist. "We have to trust God. He hasn't taken his eyes off us. We aren't alone."

Adam hugged her. "I'm trying, but it's not so easy. I can't even make a straight row with the tractor."

"You're getting better. Your furrows are mostly straight these days." Laurel grinned.

"It's not funny."

"I know. I'm sorry." She gave Adam a quick hug. "And I'm sorry you miss your writing."

"What will I do if I can't adjust? Sometimes I'm not sure how I'll live without writing."

Laurel was silent for a long moment, and Adam wished he hadn't said anything. Talking about how he felt wouldn't change anything. He'd chosen this life; now he needed to make the best of it.

Softly Laurel said, "I suppose you could try living without it, but if it's part of who you are . . ." She stepped back and averted her eyes. "I was afraid this would happen."

"I'm sorry I said anything. Everything will work out just like you said. I'm too impatient, that's all. I'll get used to it." He kissed the tip of her nose. "I will."

"Have you thought about putting out a paper of your own right here in Palmer?"

"We already have one, the *Matanuska Valley Pioneer*."

"Well, you could have another one, a better one."

"This town is too small for two papers."

"Could you do any other kind of writing?"

"I've been doing some journaling, but it's not the same." Adam pushed away the last of his stew. "I've thought about writing a novel."

"A novel? Do you know how?"

"Yeah. I guess."

"What would it be about?"

"I don't know exactly. I haven't gotten that far."

"I think it's a wonderful idea. It could be about a very handsome man who leaves the city to live in the Alaskan wilderness where he meets the woman of his dreams."

"Hmm, sounds like a good story. How does it end?"

"It has a happy ending, of course. The hero becomes a real Alaskan pioneer, and he and his wife live happily ever after with their five children."

"Sounds nice." Adam yawned. "I'm beat." He kissed Laurel gently. "I'm going to bed. I'm supposed to go fishing with Luke in the morning."

"Oh, Adam. You're already so tired."

He shrugged. "I told him I had to work, but he wouldn't take no for an answer, so we're going early—four o'clock."

"I'll set the alarm, and I'll make a basket of food for you and set it on the back porch."

"Thanks." Adam headed up the stairs.

The night passed too quickly. Still exhausted, Adam rolled over and shut off the clanging alarm. Longing for a couple more hours of sleep, he lay on his back, staring at the ceiling while he waited for his mind to wake up. Glancing out the window, he could see sunlight-touched clouds and wondered if he'd ever adjust to the long summer days. Yawning, he stretched, rolled onto his side, and dropped his legs over the edge of the bed.

"Are you going now?"

"Uh-huh. I didn't mean to wake you."

"Do you want breakfast? I can make you some." Laurel pushed back the blanket.

"No. Go back to sleep. I'll grab something."

"How about coffee?"

"Is there some left from last night?"

"Uh-huh," Laurel said groggily.

"I'll warm it up."

Laurel pulled the blanket up under her chin. "Don't forget the basket."

"I won't." Adam crossed the cold floor and grabbed his pants off the back of a chair. He pulled them on, then put on a work shirt. Taking a pair of socks from his drawer, he sat on the edge of the bed and dragged them over his feet, then stepped into boots, quickly lacing them.

He stared at Laurel. She was beautiful, even this early in the morning. Auburn hair spilled over her pillow and onto her shoulders. Long lashes caressed her cheeks, and a half smile touched her lips. He bent and kissed her cheek, then brushed the hair off her forehead and pressed his lips against her cool skin, longing to stay with her.

She smiled and murmured, "I love you."

"I'll be back soon," Adam said, straightening and pulling on his jacket. He glanced out the window. "Looks cold. I'll be expecting a pot of coffee when I get home," he teased and headed for the stairs.

He stopped in the kitchen just long enough to add wood to the embers in the stove, then grabbed the basket and walked out into a chilly morning. The grasses and spindly willows growing alongside the porch glistened with dew. After getting his rod and reel from the barn, Adam set them in the back of his pickup and headed for the Haspers'.

A disheveled, sleepy-eyed Luke met him at the door. "You ready?" Adam asked.

"Yeah," Luke said, sounding uncertain. He dropped onto the bench beside the door and pulled on boots and laced them. He glanced at Adam, scrubbed his face with his hands, then stood and lifted his jacket off its hook and shrugged into it. He yawned broadly. Stepping outside, he gazed at the gray sky. "Perfect weather for fishing. No rain, no sun." Pulling the door closed, he followed Adam to the truck.

"I'm counting on bringing home a salmon," Adam said, sliding in behind the steering wheel. He started the engine, shifted into first, and headed for the river.

"It's early in the season for kings, but I've heard they've been pulling a few salmon out." Luke smiled, staring at the road as it disappeared beneath the front of the truck. "I've been fishing this spot since we moved here. We ought to catch something."

"I got up too early to show up at home empty-handed."

"No guarantees," Luke said.

The two rode in silence the rest of the way. Adam longed for bed. He couldn't shake his weariness and preferred to be snuggling with his beautiful wife.

"Slow down. This is it," Luke said, pointing to a wide place on the side of the road. "There's a trail that leads down to the fishing hole."

The two grabbed their gear and headed for the river. Damp foliage wet their pant legs. Even if it wasn't good for fishing, Adam would have preferred sunshine. His feet skidded on wet grass, and he fell hard on his backside. He quickly found his feet. "There isn't a better trail?"

"Nope. That's why this is a good spot. Most folks don't use this hole." Luke moved on, undeterred by the steep, slippery track.

Adam hurried after him.

Finally they broke through the brush and stood above the river. In a foaming swirl, it tumbled over rocks. "The fishing hole is down here," Luke called over the roar of the water. He clambered over downed trees and through heavy brush, finally stopping at a place where the rapids emptied into a broad pool.

Adam sat on a boulder to catch his breath. "I'd better get me a fish," he said with a grin. "This is a lot of work."

"This is the first place Alex brought me when we moved here. And you will catch fish. It's a good spot." Luke set up his rod and reel. "I'll see if I can hook into one of those early kings."

"I'll try for a trout, and we'll see who comes up with a fish first."

Luke grinned. "All right. Sounds good to me."

"You get a hook into one, and I'll change gear and bait," Adam said, casting out his line. He watched the bait bob across shallow rapids and settle in the pool, then he leaned against a fallen spruce. It felt good to be still.

The forest was alive with the calls of birds searching for mates. Squirrels, grateful for spring, chirped and darted across the ground, then up tree trunks and out onto sturdy limbs. Leaves rustled, and a sharp crack sounded in the woods above them. Their tranquility momentarily interrupted, both men turned to look. Neither spoke, waiting to see what might emerge. More crackling resonated from the forest, then moved upriver. Something was making its way through the underbrush.

When it was quiet again, they settled back to fishing. "What do you think that was?" Adam asked.

"Hard to say. Could be most anything."

Adam pulled in his line, cast it, watched it bob over the froth, then find the pool and settle. As he reeled in and recast, he caught movement in the water. The long, sleek body of a river otter broke the surface, a fish in its mouth. Its fur slicked back, the animal shuffled up the bank and settled down to enjoy its prize.

"Hey," Adam whispered to Luke. "Look."

"Well, how about that. At least we know there are fish here. I haven't even had a nibble."

"Me neither," Adam whispered, keeping his eyes on the otter. Just as he spoke, he felt a tug on his line. "I've got one," he called, yanking on the pole. Unhappy with the intrusion, the otter picked up its meal and disappeared into the bushes.

Adam's pole bent, and his line zinged as the fish ran. "Feels like a big one!" He pulled hard, cranking the reel, then leveling the pole and hauling on it, reeling again as he dragged it upward. The fish broke the water's surface, wriggled in midair, then splashed back into the river.

"A grayling! And a big one!" Luke called.

Adam kept working the fish, pulling it closer to the bank. "This one's got a lot of fight in him." The fish splashed out of the water, battling to free itself.

"Be patient," Luke said. "He'll tire, and you'll get him. Keep playing him. He'll come to you."

Adrenaline pulsed through Adam as he worked the fish, gradually pulling it closer and closer. He imagined Laurel's pleasure when he returned with the prize.

Adam teased the trout into the shallows, and Luke clambered into the water with a net. "Get him over here by me," he hollered, holding the net just above the water. The fish flashed past him, and in one quick motion, Luke scooped it out. Cradling it in the net, he said, "It's a big one. Real fine fish."

Adam joined Luke and disentangled the fish from the netting. Hefting the large-bodied trout, he asked, "How much you think? Five pounds?"

"At least. More than enough for a good meal."

Adam removed the hook, knocked the fish in the head with a club, then kneeled in the shallows to gut and rinse it. He held it up and admired it. It wasn't flashy, but it was beautiful to him. He felt good—better than he had in days.

I need to stop worrying about what I've lost and be thankful for what I've gained. I have a good life here—a beautiful wife, spectacular country-side, great fishing and hunting, and most of all, good people. The life I left in Chicago doesn't exist for me anymore. This is what matters.

Suddenly he realized he was living a life some people dreamed about. A quiet voice said, *Maybe you should tell people what it's like to live in this place. After all, you're a writer.*

The voice was clear. It hadn't been his imagination, had it? He couldn't get it out of his mind. Outsiders might be interested to hear about life in the Alaskan wilderness.

He cast his line again, excitement catching hold of him as he imagined all the stories he could tell.

Chapter 5

Jean spread butter on the bread, then added sliced ham and cheese and topped each sandwich with another slice of bread. Sighing, she gazed out the kitchen window. Heavy clouds veiled the mountains. She'd hoped for sunshine for the Colony Day Picnic. It felt like winter. *We'll just have to wear our coats,* she told herself, slicing the sandwiches and deciding that nothing would ruin the day.

Will came up behind Jean and caught her around the waist. "So, what goodies do we get today? Any cake?"

"Yes. Chocolate. Your favorite." Jean nuzzled against him and rested the back of her head against his chest. "I wish it was warmer."

"We could stay home," he whispered in her ear.

Setting the knife on the countertop, Jean turned and gazed up into her husband's blue eyes. Her heart turned over. He could still send her pulse racing. "Sounds tempting."

Will kissed her. "We could send the children with the Lundeens."

Jean laid her cheek against Will's wool shirt. "We can't. Susie and Brian would have a fit. You know how much they love these picnics." She chuckled. "Brian told me he's going to win the sack race this year for sure. He's been practicing. The last couple of days he's been hopping back and forth between the garden and the barn. Said that way he'll be all practiced up and ready to win."

"We certainly can't miss that," Will said with a grin.

Brian bounced into the kitchen. "I'm ready to go! My hair's combed, my teeth are brushed, and I've even got on clean underwear." He grinned.

Blonde-headed Susie followed her older brother. "Ready," she said, holding a wad of green yarn in her hands, which stretched out behind her.

"Oh, Susie," Jean said, wiping her hands on her apron. "Where did you get that?" She took the yarn and started rewinding.

"She got it off your dresser," Brian tattled. "I saw her do it. She pushed the chair up to the bureau and climbed up."

"You saw her?"

"Uh-huh."

"Why didn't you stop her?"

Brian frowned and shrugged.

Will raised an eyebrow and smiled. "No harm done." Using his good arm, he picked up Brian. "I heard you've been practicing for the sack race."

Brian nodded. "Yep. I'm gonna win!"

"I'll be watching." Will set the boy on the floor. "You and Susie feed the chickens, and then we'll head out." He bent and kissed Susie's blonde curls. "I'll pack the blankets and fishing gear while your mama finishes making our lunches. We ought to be ready just about the time you two finish."

"All right." Brian started for the door.

"Don't forget your sister," Will said.

With a look of annoyance, Brian held out his hand. "Come on."

"Brian, get your coat. It's cold." Jean grabbed Susie's off its hook by the door and helped her put it on.

"I want to go to the picnic," Susie said.

"We will. Just as soon as the chickens are fed." She patted the little girl on the fanny. Susie took Brian's hand and allowed him to lead her out the door.

"S'pose I ought to get to it." Will stopped at the door. "Where'd Luke get off to so early?"

"You know him. He set out for Alex's first thing. They planned on doing some fishing. We'll see them at the lake."

"I don't doubt that. I've never known either one of them to pass up a meal."

"I don't recall your letting many pass you by."

Will stepped back into the kitchen and crossed to Jean. Pulling her into his arms, he gazed into her eyes. "That's only because you're such a fine cook." He kissed her. Looking at her adoringly, he added, "I believe you're more beautiful today than the day I married you."

"Oh, go on. I know better," Jean said, smiling and tucking back a loose strand of hair. "Now, scoot. I've got work to do."

With a wink he headed outside.

When they reached the lake, Will pulled the pickup to the side of road. The picnic area was already crowded. Children waded in the shallows, but many simply stood shivering, their lips tinged blue. Adults, bundled in coats, watched, and some crowded around a bonfire; others roasted frankfurters skewered on sticks.

Glancing at the youngsters in the water, Jean pulled her coat closer. "That lake's got to be freezing. How can those children stand it?" She looked at her own two. "No swimming for you. It's too cold, and I don't need you sick."

Brian's expectant expression crumpled into a pout. "It's not cold," he protested.

"It is." Jean glanced at Will who looked as if he might dispute her ruling. "Will?"

"We'll have to see. Maybe it'll warm up later."

Sulking, Brian headed toward a group of his friends.

"Looks like a lot of homesteaders are here. Do you think there'll be trouble?" Jean asked.

"No reason why there should be." Will lifted the picnic basket from the truck. "Folks have been getting along pretty good, for the most part."

"A lot of the homesteaders are still mad about us living in the valley, especially that Mr. Townsend. Nothing would make him happier than to see all the colonists leave." She nodded toward the big man. "He's here." Wearing a buckskin coat and well-worn jeans, Ray Townsend stood warming himself at a bonfire, along with several other homesteaders.

"No matter what Ray Townsend may think, he's not bigger than God," Will said. "We don't need to worry about him or the others; God will see to us and the rest of the folks in this valley."

"Yes, but he didn't make us puppets. Every person has a mind of his own; whether to hate or to love is up to us."

"True, but I believe folks will find a way to get along." Will's eyes roamed over the people gathered. "Anyway, looks like most are stickin' to their own friends." He handed the basket to Jean, then lifted Susie out of the pickup and set her on the ground.

The little girl spotted her sister. "Laurel," she called and ran for her, arms outstretched.

Jean draped two blankets over her arm and headed for Laurel. "She sure misses you."

"I miss her," Laurel said, gathering Susie up in her arms.

Will grabbed his pole. Gazing at the dark ceiling of clouds, he said, "Looks like rain." A mosquito landed on his arm and drilled. He slapped it. Another settled on his other arm, and one buzzed his head. "Maybe if we stay close to the fire the mosquitoes will stay away."

"I doubt it. They're determined." Jean walked back to the truck and took netted hats out of the back. She handed one to Will. "Seems the children are oblivious to the pests," she said, planting a hat on her head and pulling the netting over her face. Will swatted another bloodsucker. Jean raised an eyebrow. "You might have less trouble if you put on your hat and coat."

"I don't like wearing them," he said, putting on his hat, then grabbing his coat out of the truck and shrugging into it.

Laurel scratched a welt on her cheek. "We saved a place down by the lake." With Susie still in her arms, she moved toward their picnic spot.

Watching Laurel with Susie, Will said, "The kids have grown so fast. Susie's not much of a baby any more. Before we know it, she'll be grown and married too. And then it'll be just the two of us."

Jean leaned against her husband. "We've got a while yet. Brian's only eight, and Susie's not even three."

Taking Jean's hand, Will followed Laurel. Adam walked up from the lake and met them.

Jean gave him a quick hug. "I've been meaning to come by. I've just had so much to do, what with Will still trying to catch up after being off work so long."

"How's that hand?" Adam asked.

Will reached out his arm, straightened his fingers, and then bent them, the stub of a finger moving along with the rest. He repeated the movement a couple of times. "Feels pretty good. Nearly good as new, minus a finger. It takes a little getting used to. And my fingers are still kind of stiff. The hand is weak, but the doc says it won't take long to get back the strength." He flexed the hand again, then let his arm fall to his side. "I'd say I've got a lot to be grateful for. And it sure feels good to be working again."

"Yeah, I'll bet. I didn't know farming was so much work," Adam said, patting Will's back. "I've got my hands full at our place."

"Thank you for all the help. I'm real sorry I had to take you away from your chores."

"I was glad to do it."

"If you need any help or have any questions, just holler."

"I will, and probably sooner than you think." Adam leaned against a tree. "Did you hear about the calves killed at the Prosser place?"

Jean had started to sit but stopped. "The Prossers? No. What happened?"

"Looks like that same grizzly. Killed three calves and mauled his bull so badly they had to put him down. From the looks of it, though, the bull got the bear pretty good. His horns were bloodied."

Jean's face had gone pale. "Everyone's all right?"

"Yeah." Adam shook his head. "But now we've got an injured grizzly roaming about. Hope he stays away from our place."

"Sounds like a bad bear," Will said.

"Townsend's putting together a hunting party. He said it shouldn't be too hard to track him."

"I'd like to go along. 'Specially since it was probably the same animal that made a call at our place."

"You can't be sure, Will. It might be a different bear," Jean said. "Let Ray Townsend take care of it."

Will settled serious eyes on Jean. "God placed me as guardian over my family and my farm, and that includes taking care of marauding bears. It doesn't seem right to let someone else take care of my responsibilities." He pulled off his hat. "Besides, I've never tracked a bear. It would be a real Alaskan adventure and would give me a chance to use some of what Alex has taught me about hunting and tracking." He scanned the crowd. "Where did Ray go? I saw him a minute ago."

"He's over there," Adam said, pointing at a small band of men standing close to the largest fire.

"I think I'll talk to him."

"Will, no. Please." Jean rested a hand on her husband's arm. "Your hand's not even completely healed."

"It's good enough." He watched Mr. Townsend. "It's not up to Ray Townsend to watch out for my family."

Jean's eyes moved to Susie, who was sprinting toward the lake. "Oh, that little scamp. She's heading straight for the water."

"I'll get her, Mama," Laurel said and ran after her sister.

"I'll be back in a few minutes," Will said.

"You mind if I come along?" Adam asked.

"No. Come right ahead." Will kissed Jean and headed toward Ray.

When Will and Adam approached Ray, he was glaring at his daughter and Robert Lundeen as they walked along the lakeshore. He ignored the newcomers. Three of the men with Ray nodded. The fourth, a stocky man with dark hair and a friendly smile, said, "Howdy, Will. How you been keepin'?"

"I'm doin' all right. How about you, Frank?"

"Good. Been thinkin' about doin' some minin' this summer."

"Thought you had a good trapping season."

"I did, but the pelts won't see me through the year. Prices are down."

Ray cut in. "So, Hasper, what is it you want?"

Will faced the big man. He wasn't small himself, but beside Ray Townsend he felt puny. Ray's shoulders and chest were broad; he stood a good two inches taller than Will and outweighed him by twenty or thirty pounds. A tangle of curls had fallen onto his forehead. Glaring at Will, he swiped them back. Pulling himself up to his full height, Will met the man's angry eyes. "Heard you were putting together a hunting party for that bear."

"Yeah. So?"

"Well, he made a visit to my place awhile back. Tore apart my pump house and scared my family good. I figure I owe him something. I'd like to go along."

"You?" Ray sneered and shook his head in disbelief. "We don't need farmers along to botch things up." He looked at his buddies and snickered.

Will wasn't about to be put off so easily. He took a step toward Ray. "I mean to go. That animal threatened my family; he could have killed our livestock. I have a right to hunt him."

"Hunt him then. Just not with us." Ray grinned. "You'd be smart to stay put and watch out for your family."

Smelling a fight, onlookers encircled the men. Robert, with Celeste on his arm, joined Will.

Ray glared at the young man, then turned and picked up a piece of wood and chucked it into the fire. Refocusing on Will, he said, "You're a farmer, not a hunter or tracker. You try to hunt that bear, and he'll end up hunting you. Leave this to people who know what they're doing."

"I'm not as ignorant as you think. I know some about tracking."

"Why not let him go?" Frank asked. "He's a good man. We could use him."

Ray glowered at Frank, then turned a hate-filled glare on Will. "You're not needed, and you won't be coming with us."

Anger and resentment burned through Will. He fought to control his rage. He said nothing for a long moment, then took a steadying breath and said, "Have it your way. I'll pray for you and the rest of the men."

Will's compliance made Ray angrier, and Ray turned his ire on Robert. "I told you to stay away from my daughter," he growled. Glancing at Celeste, he said, "She can do better."

Robert looked squarely at Ray. "Maybe she's made up her own mind about us. Seems to me a twenty-year-old woman ought to be able to choose who she spends time with."

"She does what I say!" Ray bellowed, his face turning crimson. "And she ain't wasting time on no outsider!"

Celeste stepped between the two. "Daddy! Stop it! I told you how I feel. You have no say in this."

The red hue in Ray's face deepened. "You don't talk to me that way, girl! And you'll do as I say!"

Celeste's blue eyes blazed. "I won't. I'm a grown woman, and I'll make my own decisions."

Knitting his heavy brows, Ray compressed his lips, then said stonily, "Then it's time you found somewhere else to live." He turned and walked away.

Celeste stared after her father, her chin quivering. Robert placed an arm around her shoulders. "I'm sorry," he said.

"You don't have anything to be sorry about." Celeste wiped at tears and sniffed. "It's him." Her eyes refilled. "I don't know him anymore. I . . . I don't know what's happened to him."

"We should have stayed away from him," Robert said.

"No. He has to face up to this—you and me. I'm not going to hide from him. And he's not going to control my life anymore." With a shuddering sigh, she added, "I'll need help getting my stuff moved." Fresh tears emerged. "I don't know where to go."

"You can stay with us," Adam said. "We have plenty of room."

"Are you sure? I hate to impose."

"Are you kidding? Laurel will love having you."

"All right. If you're sure?"

"I'm sure."

"I'll help you move," Robert offered.

"No. You better stay clear of my place. I'll get someone else." She turned to go, then stopped. "I'm sorry, Robert." Without another word, Celeste walked to the road.

Robert watched her until she disappeared. "How can her father be like that?"

"I'm done trying to figure him out," Will said. "You have my sympathy. If you and Celeste stay together, you'll have a rough road."

"She's a special girl. I guess I'll have to put up with her father."

"Good luck," Will said with a grin and patted Robert on the back.

"I'm going to need it," Robert said glumly.

When Will returned to his family, Jean immediately asked, "Are you going along?"

"Where are you going?" Luke asked, walking up to his parents with Alex beside him.

Will looked at his son. "You have any luck?"

"Nope. Too early."

Alex grinned, his bright smile lighting up his face. "Next time, maybe."

When it was quiet, Jean asked again, "Are you going with them?"

"Nope. Seems they've got enough help."

She rested a hand on her chest. "Thank goodness. I don't want you traipsing off after a crazed bear, especially with your hand still weak. You need to keep close to home for a while, and you have lots of work to do anyway." She sat on the blanket. "It looked like Celeste and her father had words. What happened?"

"Ray doesn't want her seeing Robert. She took a stand, and he kicked her out of the house."

"Oh, no. That poor girl. What's wrong with that man?"

"I don't know. If he's not careful, he'll lose his daughter for good." Will gave Jean a small smile. "Let's talk about something else."

"All right. But where will she stay?"

"With us," Adam said. He looked at Laurel. "I told her you wouldn't mind."

"Of course I don't. I'm glad you asked her."

Jean looked at Will. "You hungry?"

"Always," Will said, sitting beside his wife.

Jean opened the picnic basket and took out a sandwich. "You want potato salad?"

"You have to ask? You make the best I've tasted."

"I made some too," Laurel said, taking out a bowl of salad. "It's Mama's recipe, but I doubt it will taste as good as hers. It's my first try." She looked at the road where her friend had disappeared a few moments earlier. "I hope Celeste's all right. Maybe I should go and help her."

"No. It would only cause more trouble," Will said. "Her father doesn't like you anymore than he likes the rest of us."

"I know. I just feel so sorry for her."

Jean scooped out a spoonful of salad and dropped it onto a plate. "We need to start praying in earnest for them every day. God has a way of working these things out."

"He has his work cut out for him with this mess," Robert said.

"I can't argue with you, but we've seen him do some amazing things." Jean scratched a welt from a mosquito bite. "I remember the day I stepped off the train and got my first look at the valley—and the mosquitoes." She looked up at the gray sky. "It's hard to believe it's been two years since we arrived."

"What a spring that was," Adam said. "All the rain and floods."

Laurel linked arms with Adam. "I'll never forget. Rain and more rain. What I remember most when the train pulled in was a town of tents sitting in the mud." She laughed. "I nearly fainted."

"Will, did you think you'd made a mistake?" Adam asked.

"No. I knew this was the place for us."

Jean took his hand and squeezed. "He made the right decision, but I knew it was going to be harder than we'd expected, and it was."

Brian ran into the midst of his family. "Is it time to eat?"

"You bet." Will took a bite of salad. "Your sister and mother both brought food."

"Oh, boy!" Brian dropped to his knees and took a sandwich his mother offered him. He bit into it. Through a mouthful, he asked, "Can I have some cake?"

"Absolutely," Jean said, "but first eat your lunch." She spooned salad onto his plate.

Will took a bite of Laurel's potato salad. His eyes opened slightly as he chewed. "This is good—almost as good as your mama's." He winked at Jean.

Susie grabbed for her father's plate. "No. You wait. Mama will get you some."

"Here, Susie," Jean said, handing the little girl a spoon and a small plate with salad and a sandwich.

Susie sat with the dish between her legs and sloppily spooned potatoes into her mouth.

Shouting broke out along the tree line. Two boys were fighting.

"What is it?" Jean asked, standing. "Who are those boys?"

"One of them's Jonathan Reis. Abe and Jessica's son. I don't know who the other one is. Haven't seen him before," Will said.

"Oh, that's mean old David Hirsch," Brian said. "He's the meanest boy in school. He doesn't like anyone, 'specially outsiders. He says we should've never come here."

Abe Reis and another man separated the boys. Abe leaned over his son. "What is this? You know fighting is wrong. What happened?"

"He called me a Kraut!" David yelled.

"That true?" Mr. Hirsch asked. "You calling my boy names?"

"No. I didn't say nothin'!" Jonathan shouted.

"Tell me what happened, Jonathan." Abe waited for him to answer.

Jonathan prodded the ground with his toe. "I called him a Kraut, but he told me . . . he called me . . ." he hesitated. "I can't say what he said."

Abe looked at the other boy. "Did you call him a bad name?"

David didn't answer.

"So, maybe he did," Mr. Hirsch said. "Boys will be boys. You know how it is. And you can't exactly blame him for being upset about you people—coming in here and changing everything." He squared his jaw.

"We just want to farm and raise our families. If you'd just leave us to our business, we'd get along fine," Abe said. "We've done nothing wrong."

"You don't say," Mr. Hirsch jeered. He grabbed his son's hand. "Let's get out of here." He gathered up his family and left. Several other homesteaders joined them.

A sick feeling replaced Will's pleasure over the celebration. All he wanted now was to go home. The hatred had been handed down to the children. What would it take to bring change to the valley?

Whatever it takes, Father, do it. I don't want my children living in a place filled with hatred.

Chapter 6

WILL GRIPPED THE STEERING WHEEL AND STARED AT THE ROAD. JEAN SCOOTED closer. "You're awfully quiet."

Will glanced at her, giving her a quick smile. "I'm all right. Just thinking." They bounced through a pothole, and he tightened his hold on the steering wheel, using his good hand.

"What are you thinking about?"

Will didn't answer.

"Clashes between the boys and their fathers have been going on for generations," Jean said. "Boys fight, and so do their fathers."

"Hey! Look!" Brian shouted from the back of the pickup. He pointed at a goose and her goslings. Susie stood and peered around the cab. Even Luke tried to get a good look.

Will slowed, then stopped while the goose and her little ones waddled across the road. "It's more than the boys fighting. It's Ray Townsend and his friends."

Jean rested her hand on Will's leg. "They are who they are. You can't change them."

"I know, but sometimes it's hard to accept. I've prayed; I've been patient and considerate with them; I've been a good neighbor and still . . ."

"Some men are more stubborn than others. Don't give up. They may still come around. And if they don't, there's nothing we can do. All of this is in God's hands. They're in God's hands."

"I know you're right; it's just hard to accept. And I hate to see the hatred being passed down to the children." He looked at Jean. "We can't let that happen to us."

"We won't," Jean said with assurance.

Brian jumped up and down, bouncing the bed of the truck.

Jean leaned out the window. "Brian! Sit down! Otherwise I'll make you come sit up front with us." Susie leaned out over the back. "Luke, could you keep a closer eye on her, please?" Luke grabbed Susie and planted her on her bottom just behind the cab. Brian kneeled and craned his neck to see over the sideboards so he could watch the goose and her family.

Jean gazed at the geese as they headed down the bank. "Baby animals are everywhere—new calves, foals, piglets, and chicks. I even saw a bear and two cubs the other day." Jean leaned against Will. "I remember the days when we were having little ones."

Raising an eyebrow, he looked down at her. "You want another?"

"No!" She laughed, then shrugged. "I miss the babies, the way they sound and smell."

Will chuckled. "Maybe it's time you were a grandmother. Do you think we'll have long to wait?"

"Don't rush things. Adam and Laurel have only been married a few weeks."

"I'd be real happy to be a grandpa," Will said with a grin.

"I'm too young to be a grandmother."

"No you're not, you old lady." Will's eyes crinkled in merriment.

Jean cuddled closer. "I'd love it. But it's not up to me." She patted Will's leg. "We have to leave this in God's hands, just like Ray Townsend."

Will sighed. "I'll do my best."

The truck crossed the wooden bridge just before their drive, its tires thudding hollowly. A cow and calf grazed alongside the road. Will stopped. "What are they doing out? Brian," he said with indignation. "He must have left the gate open." His eyes roamed over the pasture and the corral. Part of the corral was down, and other animals were roaming. "Something's wrong." He pulled into the driveway.

Fences were down, hay had been scattered, and a feeding trough had been shredded. A bloodied calf with its neck twisted and eyes staring lay alongside the trough. Part of its back leg was missing. "Oh, Lord! What's happened?" Jean cried.

Will stopped the truck close to the back door of the house. "You and the children get inside," he said, grabbing his rifle from behind the seat and climbing out of the cab. He scanned the yard. Their Jersey lay on her side, already stiff. Jean stared.

"I said, get in the house!"

Jean picked up Susie and grabbed Brian's hand. Both children gaped at the dead cow. "Come on. Inside." Jean pulled them into the house, then returned to the porch.

Luke ran inside, got his rifle, and joined his father. Together they searched the area close to the house and barn. Whatever had done the damage had gone. Will approached the Jersey. Her face was lacerated, and her stomach was torn open. Broad bear tracks led away from the carcass.

"Looks like a big bear," Luke said. "Wonder if it's the one that visited a while back."

"Probably." Will followed the tracks. They led west into the forest. Stopping and staring into the woods, he said, "No use trying to follow him today." He turned back toward the house. "I'll be going with Ray Townsend tomorrow," he stated and headed for the barn. "I hope that bear didn't get at our sow." Entering the darkness, he didn't hear the grunting or snuffling he'd expected.

It was clear the bear had been here too. Tools were scattered, grain bags were shredded, and he saw blood. He approached the stall that housed his pregnant sow. She lay in a pool of blood. Sickened and angry, Will turned away. She'd only been a day or so away from dropping a litter. This was a huge loss. He searched the rest of the barn and found a dead goat and a handful of naked, bloody hens, lying among their feathers. He didn't know how they would make up such losses. Shaking his head, he hurried to the house.

"Will, was it a bear?" Jean asked.

"Yep. A big one."

Brian and Susie huddled against their mother. "Will he come back?" Brian asked.

"No, I don't think so," Will said, unable to keep the discouragement out of his voice.

Tears slipping down her cheeks, Jean hugged him.

With a heavy sigh, he said, "Things happen. We'll get through this."
He looked at Luke. "I'll need you to help me bury the animals."

"Dad, how come it killed so many and didn't eat them?"

"Can't say. Sometimes a bear's just plain mean or mad."

The gruesome work of burial completed, Will took off his blood-stained clothing. Jean had a bath ready. Opting for a swim in the creek, Luke grabbed a bar of soap and was on his way.

Stepping into the bath, Will said, "We lost almost all of them." Shaking his head, he continued, "I don't know what we're going to do."

"Pray and work harder," Jean said matter-of-factly, handing him a bar of soap. "I'll make some coffee," she said and headed downstairs. By the time Will was clean and dressed, the aroma of apples and cinnamon filled the house. Jean had been baking.

"Sure smells good in here," Will said, combing wet hair back with his fingers. "But I don't think even your cake is going to help this time." He sat at the table. Resting his face in his hands, he managed a smile. "I'd love some cake."

Susie sat on the floor playing with Tinkertoys. Brian sat across from his father. "What you gonna' do?" His eyes filled with tears. "You gonna get that bear? He killed Molly and her calf. And Penny's calf too."

Will scooted back from the table. "You too big to sit on my lap?"

Brian shook his head no, rounded the table, and climbed onto his father's lap. He rested his head against the clean wool shirt. For a long while no one spoke. Finally Brian asked, "How come that grizzly's so mean? I think someone ought to shoot it."

"Well, someone will. I hope it's me."

Jean set a cup of coffee in front of Will. "I thought you said Ray . . ."

"He is. And I'm going with him. I'll make sure that bear never comes around here again."

Gripping her apron, Jean sat across from Will. "I don't think you should go. Let Ray Townsend take care of it."

"I thought you understood. I have to go."

"I do understand, but you can't go alone."

"I'm not. I'll go with Ray."

"I thought he said you couldn't. You'll just stir up trouble. Ray Townsend will get the bear."

Saying nothing, Will clenched and unclenched his jaw. Finally he said, "That bear destroyed most of our livestock, tore down fences, and destroyed feed. And he scared my family. I'm going to be part of that hunting party. I'm not talking about it any more. I've made up my mind." He slid Brian off his lap and walked out the door.

"Is Daddy mad?" Susie asked, her blue eyes wide.

"Yes, but not at us. He's mad at that bear." Jean picked up her daughter and cradled her against her chest. A sense of loss and fear enveloped her as she watched Will walk toward the barn. She knew that what she felt had nothing to do with the damage. It was something more, something terrifying. *You're being silly,* she told herself. *Seeing those dead animals just got you spooked. Those men know what they're doing. They've killed bears before.*

The following morning Will rose early, but Jean managed to beat him downstairs and was cooking bacon and eggs when he walked into the kitchen. "Smells good," he said. "You didn't have to get up and do this."

"Yes, I did."

Will kissed Jean, then sat at the table. "Good thing the gelding was in the far pasture. I'd hate to have lost him. He's a good packhorse."

"What time are Ray Townsend and the others leaving?" Jean asked, turning an egg and resettling it in bacon grease.

"Six o'clock. I'd better be on my way."

"Not before you have something to eat." She slid eggs and bacon onto a plate alongside two biscuits. Setting the plate on the table in front of her husband, she said, "You'll need a good breakfast if you're going to be traipsing through the countryside. I packed some food for you to take along. It's on the back porch."

"Thanks." Will reached across the table and kissed Jean, then sat back down and started on his breakfast. "Hopefully, we'll catch up to him today and I'll be home tonight. But if I don't show up, don't worry. From what I've heard, these trips sometimes take several days. Bears can cover a lot of miles, and some are smart enough to outwit trackers. But from what I've heard, Ray Townsend's one of the best. We'll find that grizzly and kill him. I'm sure of it." He bit into a biscuit, then took a bite of egg.

Luke came down the stairs and stood at the foot of the table. "I'm goin' with you."

"No, you're not, son. I need you here. Your mother needs you."

"Dad, I have a right to go. I'm not a boy anymore."

"I know you're not a boy." Will set his fork on the plate. "That's why I need you to stay here. That bear could circle back, and I don't want your mother here without a man."

Luke stared at the floor. "I'll stay if you say I have to, but I want to go."

"You're young, Luke. You'll have other chances. This time you stay. Besides, it'll be a fight just to get that bunch to let *me* go along." Will shoved the last of his biscuit into his mouth, took a gulp of coffee, and stood. "I'd better git', or they'll leave without me."

Jean held Will for a long moment. Stepping back, she looked into his eyes. "Please be careful. I need you to come home."

He smiled down at her. "I'll be back." Kissing her tenderly, he added, "Don't keep supper for me," then headed for the door.

Brian bounced into the room. "Daddy! Wait!" He ran to his father and hugged him.

Will tousled his unruly hair, then kneeled in front of his son. "I won't be gone long, hopefully not more than a day or two. I need you to do just as your mama says."

Brian nodded. "You gonna get that bear?"

"You bet." He kissed the boy's forehead, then straightened. "I'll see you all in a few days."

Jean followed Will onto the porch. "I wish you wouldn't go."

"I have to."

The knot had rooted in her stomach, and Jean pressed her hand against her abdomen. She'd had a dream and needed to tell him. "Wait. I had a dream last night. You were in a dark place, and then you broke out and were running across a field. The grass was high, all the way to your shoulders. I could barely see you. You kept moving away from me, and I kept calling to you, but you just kept running."

Jean stopped, remembering the emotions of the dream. She'd awakened, feeling lost and frightened. "The dream felt bad," she said. "You finally turned around, and I could see your face, but it didn't look like you. And . . . and your coat was soaked in blood." She grabbed Will's hands. "I'm scared. Will, I know something bad is going to happen. Please don't go." She pressed his hand to her cheek. "Please."

Will wrapped his arms around her and pulled her close. "Nothing's going to happen. It was just a dream." He kissed her forehead and smiled at her. "The bloody coat was about yesterday. My coat got bloodied pretty good. Remember?" He rubbed her upper arms. "You don't need to worry. I'll be with a whole group of men." He held her at arm's length. "I'll be back before you know it. And that bear will be nothing more than a bad memory."

Tears escaped Jean's eyes.

Wiping them away, Will kissed her cheeks. "Try not to worry. God will be with me."

Chapter 7

WHEN WILL ARRIVED IN TOWN, RAY TOWNSEND AND THREE OTHER MEN, Frank Reed, Joe Stanfield, and Mike Gilman, had already gathered. Will knew Frank well, but the other two he knew little about except that they mistrusted outsiders nearly as much as Ray.

Leading a large white horse, Townsend strode up to him. "What do you think you're doing?"

"Going with you."

"You're not." His horse blew air through his nose and jerked up on the halter. Ray yanked down hard.

"Yesterday I lost most of my livestock to that bear. He headed off into the woods from my place. I think we ought to start there. He's heading west."

Ray grinned. "He may be heading west now, but there's no telling where he'll end up. And as soon as he knows we're after him, he'll pick up the pace and take us on a jaunt you'll not soon forget." He raised an eyebrow. "You sure you want to go? I ain't baby-sitting you."

"You won't have any need to baby-sit me."

"Suit yourself then."

Leading a bay, Frank walked up to Will. "Glad to see you. Sorry about your animals. Family all right?"

"They're fine."

Ray cut in. "We're not holding back for you. You'll keep up or get left behind." He spat tobacco juice at Will's feet. "We'll start at the Hasper place." Climbing aboard his stallion, he headed out of town.

Ray sat his heavy-bodied stallion comfortably, his huge Siberian Husky padding along beside. Straining to pick up the pace, Ray's mount chewed on his bit, tossed his head, and pranced. Will was grateful for his steady Morgan. The gelding had little flash but was strong and dependable.

"Hope the rain holds off," Frank said, glancing at the gray ceiling.

"It'll be miserable if the clouds open up." Will sidestepped a puddle. "How long you think it'll take to track down the bear? My wife won't stop worrying until I get home."

"Depends on which way he's headed, how fast he's moving, and whether he's feeding or not. And some bears are trickier than others." Frank gave Will a sidelong glance. "You ever hunted bear?"

"Black bear. We used dogs to hunt them." Will's horse snatched a mouthful of grass, jerking on the reins. He eyed the pack. "I should have brought less so I could ride."

"Yeah, your feet will be hollerin'. You should have saddled him." He eyed Ray and the others who were quickly leaving them behind. "I'm not much for horses. I'd rather be driving a team of dogs." He glanced about at a farmhouse. "I'm more of a winter person. I like the cold, the yapping dogs, and the crunch of snow under my sled." He slapped his neck, then looked at his palm. Wiping off whatever he'd smashed on his pant leg, he added with a wry grin, "And I don't like bugs."

Frank nodded at Ray. "Now, he's a real mountain man. He loves this kind of thing—traipsin' out into the wilderness. No matter how dangerous, he can't wait to see what's out there waitin' for him." Frank spat tobacco juice. "Ray's done just about everything there is to do out here. Once he even tussled with a wolverine with just a knife." Frank grinned. "The wolverine got the worst of it, but Ray was laid up for a while."

"I'm not surprised." Will nodded at the husky. "What about the dog?"

"Ray says dogs are good to have around when you're huntin' bear, that is, if it's a good dog. And Jed is. Ray always takes him. Jed don't miss nothin'." Frank hitched up his pants with his free hand. "Ray's had that dog since it was a pup, more than eight years now. Don't know what he'll do when ole' Jed's gone."

Will nodded. He'd never thought of Ray as a person who cared much about anything, especially dogs. Maybe there was more to the man than met the eye. He didn't suppose Ray Townsend was much different from most folks. People wore all kinds of masks, depending on what they wanted others to know. He studied the big man and wondered how it would be if Ray were the one taking orders instead of giving them. Will doubted it had ever happened.

"So, you got a dog?" Frank asked.

"No, but we've been thinking maybe we ought to get one—especially after the bear. Heard bears don't like dogs."

"They don't, not usually. Course, if you've got a real ornery grizzly, it don't make no difference." Frank pushed his tobacco deeper into his cheek, then dug into his coat pocket and pulled out a leather pouch. Holding it out to Will, he asked, "You chew?"

"No. Never took up the habit."

Fishing out a pinch, he added to what he already had in his mouth, then returned the pouch to his pocket. "Just as well. Ruins your teeth. I started when I was barely in britches. My granddaddy chewed, my daddy chewed, and I chew." He grinned, and removing his hat, brushed back his short, damp hair. "Sweatin' already."

Passing through tranquil farmland, the men fell quiet. Finally Will asked, "You hunt bears much?"

"A few. It's not something I like to do. It's just plain hard work and dangerous. I like the pelts; they make good rugs. And the meat's good." Frank looked at Will and said earnestly, "This is serious business— huntin' grizzly. You do as you're told, and don't take nothin' for granted. A mean bear like this would just as soon tear you apart as look at you."

"You think he's going to give us trouble?"

"He sure will if he can, but we'll give him more." Frank grinned. "Ray knows what he's doing. Even though you two got bad blood between you, you listen to him and do as he says. That way you won't get hurt."

"I'll remember that," Will said, knowing he'd do exactly as he was told.

"I'd say this bear's smart. He's managed to get in and out of a lot of farms without gettin' shot. I'll be glad when he's a rug hangin' on someone's wall."

Ray stopped on the bridge just before Will's driveway. The men crowded together in the middle of the road. "This your place, Hasper?"

"Yep."

"Pretty nice," he said derisively. "Course, what would you expect—with all the help you've had." Before Will could reply, Ray asked, "Which way?" His horse danced under a tight rein.

Will's anger flared, but he forced it back. Fighting with this man would serve no good purpose. *Father, help me be a light. Don't let my anger smother whatever you're doing here.* He pointed toward the north field where Luke was working on the fence. "His tracks led off that way, then disappeared into the woods."

Ray kicked his heels into his horse's sides. Breaking into a lope, he led the men around the fence line. Thrusting a shovel into the sod, Luke watched the approaching riders. "Hi, Dad," he said when his father was within hearing distance.

"Morning, son." Some of the others responded. Ray simply asked, "So, he ran off through here?"

"Sure did," Luke answered. "He headed straight off that-a-way into the timber. I followed his trail this morning, but I never saw him. Sure would like to though. I'll plug him if I get a chance."

His face grim, Ray said flatly, "Don't be so certain. No one wants to just meet up with a bear like that. You hunt him, then you kill him." He climbed off his horse, kneeled beside a set of prints, and placed a hand in the center of one. Ray Townsend's hands were large, but the bear's prints dwarfed them. "He's a big one, all right." He glanced over his shoulder at his friends. "'Course, we knew that." He followed the bear's prints a short ways, stopping occasionally to examine the tracks and measure the paces between them.

"What's he doing?" Will asked Frank.

"I'd say he's figurin' the bear's gait and studying his prints. That way he'll be able to track him, and we won't end up following the wrong animal. Ray's good. He knows what he's doing. He's done more trackin' and huntin' than anyone I know. He's had his run-ins, though. Nearly got himself killed a few years back."

"Oh, yeah?"

Luke walked up to his father. His voice quiet, he said, "I can be ready in five minutes."

Frank overheard. "This ain't no place for youngsters. You'll be wise to keep to home."

Luke glared at the man. "I'm no youngster."

Will smiled. "We already talked about this. Your mama needs you and your brother and sister too. I've got to have someone here to look after things—someone I can trust."

Luke looked like he was about to argue, then said, "All right. I'll stay."

Ray walked back to his horse and mounted. "We need to make up some time. That bear's got a good head start on us." Baleful eyes rested on Will. "We'll be riding."

Without waiting, Ray headed toward the forest, leaving Frank and Will to repack the gear. Frank looked at Will. "Maybe you ought to get your saddle."

Will climbed aboard and glanced at the barn on the other end of the property. "It'll take too long. I've ridden bareback plenty of times." Will nodded at Luke. "I'll be home soon as I can. Tell your mama I love her." He kicked his horse, and he and Frank chased after the rest of the hunting party.

When they caught up, Ray was spouting orders. "Remember, this is a big brownie, and we know he's not afraid of people. He's dangerous. Stay alert." He picked up the pace, heading deeper into the forest.

Climbing out of the valley, the men left farmland behind. The terrain turned steep and was heavily forested. Trees and brush pressed in, and Will had a sense of being swallowed by the green wilderness. The grizzly was following a well-used bear trail. Unable to see beyond the edge of the brush, the men were constantly on alert. They could come face-to-face with the bear at any moment.

Seemingly unperturbed, Ray pushed on, occasionally stopping to climb off his mount to examine the tracks or bushes. Birds serenaded the men as they passed. Their music calmed Will's edginess.

After following the trail for several miles, the bear had cut into the woods. Ray didn't miss it. He stopped, climbed off his horse, and studied the prints. "Yep, it's him," he said, returning to the saddle. Will wished he'd saddled his horse. His backside and legs were aching. Without the saddle, he had to work harder to maintain his seat.

The men moved off the path, and the trees closed in around them. Will was jumpy. The muscles in his neck and shoulders were tight. Did the bear know he was being followed? Would he break out of the brush in a surprise attack?

The other men didn't speak to Will, their loyalty to Ray clear. Frank, on the other hand, seemed to enjoy talking with Will about his life and his plans for the future. Still, Will rode alone most of the time. He knew he wasn't wanted or needed and began to question the wisdom of going along. These men knew what they were doing and could easily hunt down a bear without him.

Why had he insisted on joining them? It wasn't like him to shove his way into anything. As he considered the situation, he still felt a driving need to be part of the chase. *Why?* he wondered. Did it have something to do with God's will, or was it simply his own stubbornness and pride that had brought him here? Either way, it made little difference. It was too late to change his mind. He was committed. He'd simply have to make the most of it and hopefully serve God in the midst of the adventure. Maybe he'd find a way to break down some of the barriers between himself and Ray Townsend.

The bear led them up steep hills and into hidden valleys, along narrow trails clinging to rock faces, and across shallow streams cutting through canyon floors.

All the while, Ray Townsend never missed an opportunity to belittle Will, throwing hateful looks and words at the outsider whenever possible. Refusing to retaliate, Will kept his mind on God's goodness. Relishing the world around him, he breathed in the scent of spruce and pine and enjoyed the birds and squirrels creating or repairing homes among the boughs.

At one point, the men made their way around a marshy area, stopping for a moment to watch a moose grazing among lilies and bog beans. Ray spat tobacco juice, and the heavy animal startled, then charged away, disappearing into the forest.

Hours passed, but the bear stayed well ahead of them. Will could feel his horse tiring, and his own body ached. Longing for rest, he gratefully climbed off his Morgan at a broad stream when Ray called for a breather.

"We'll water the horses and rest a while," he said. Throwing a disdainful glance at Will, he knelt along the bank, dipped his hands into icy water, and scooped it into his mouth.

Everyone drank, including the horses. Ray and the others sat on a grassy knoll and dug into their packs for food. Will sat alongside the stream, studying a beaver lodge on the far side while he worked his way through a cheese sandwich. He'd hoped to catch a glimpse of one of the hard-working animals, but the beavers stayed in hiding. His only entertainment was a duck and ducklings navigating the reeds along the bank. The mother occasionally dipped her face into the water, leaving a feathered tail bobbing.

The men talked about hunting and fishing and an upcoming fur sale. Suddenly, their voices quieted. Ray, Joe, and Mike glanced at Will more than once. An occasional snicker carried over the ground between them and Will. Frank ate in silence.

Knowing Townsend couldn't be trusted, Will knew he'd better stay alert. He didn't know what to expect from the homesteader, but it couldn't be good.

Will was still troubled about why he had come and wondered if he ought to return to his family. He didn't belong. He was a farmer. However, even as he considered leaving, he knew he would stay. He wasn't about to quit, not with Ray Townsend and the others hoping he would leave.

Leaning back on his hands, Will gazed at gray clouds and an occasional patch of blue. The sky looked less threatening than it had that morning. Sunshine would feel good. His mind wandered to Jean. She was probably working in the vegetable garden, her auburn hair shimmering under sunlight and sweat glistening on her face and bodice. He smiled. She was a fine woman. A loud laugh brought Will back to the present.

Mike, wearing a smirk, glanced his way. Will wondered who was more dangerous, these men he was with or the bear. He suddenly had a strong urge to head for home, and he almost rose to leave. But something stopped him. He had to see this through.

Ray sauntered toward Will, then knelt beside him, keeping his gaze on the water. "So, how you like tracking so far?"

"I like it fine. Seen some beautiful countryside."

He continued to stare at the stream. "You do, huh? Well, I wouldn't count on it staying so pleasant. You never know what might be ahead."

He settled his gray eyes on Will. They looked cold and dispassionate. His lips curved up in a smirk. "Stay alert. That bear could be almost any-where." As if to make his point, his eyes moved to the forest and across the creek. "He's a slick one."

Yeah, Will thought, *about as slick as you.*

"He knows we're after him." Ray stood, then strode across the clear-ing and mounted his horse.

The rest of the day, Ray continued to make derogatory remarks about farmers and colonists as often as possible, always speaking loudly enough so Will could hear. *If you're waiting for a counterattack from me,* Will thought, *you'll have a long wait.* He understood that Ray was trying to provoke him. Determined not to impede God's plan, he rode and prayed.

After an especially cruel attack, Frank joined Will. Bouncing along on his stubby mount, he asked, "You gonna' let him get away with that? Stand up for yourself, man."

Will measured his answer carefully before speaking. Frank was a good man but loyal to Ray Townsend. "What good would it do? I figure I'll just keep quiet and stay along for the ride. Maybe I'll be needed."

"After what he said, you're still worried about being needed?" He shook his head. "I never would have guessed you'd put up with that kind of malarkey." He sounded disappointed.

Will leveled a calm look at Frank. "You want me to argue with the man? Why?"

Frank didn't answer right away. "I just figured a real man would fight back."

"To be honest I'd like to, but like I said . . ."

"I know, won't do no good." Frank shrugged. "I s'pose you're right. Just never thought someone like you would put up with it. If it were someone else, I'd say he was chicken." He sized up Will. "You're not afraid."

Will smiled. "I came out here to get a bear. Did Ray have something else in mind?"

Frank was silent a moment, then said, "You know, he ain't such a bad fella'. He's been a good friend to me, and he's the best tracker and hunter I know."

"I believe you," Will said evenly. "You think there's anything that would pry his hatred for me and the other colonists out of him?"

Frank leaned forward and resettled himself in the saddle. "I s'pect he'll change if and when he's ready. He's a proud man, sometimes too proud." He grinned and kicked his mount. "Your not fightin' back is makin' him madder than that old grizzly."

"I thought he looked a little tight," Will said with a wry smile.

"You be careful. You get him real mad and—well, just be careful." He pulled his hat down in front, then moved ahead and joined the others.

That night they set up camp in a small clearing. Jean had packed enough food for the lot of them, so Will offered to cook a hot meal. Since no one else seemed inclined to do any cooking, and Will had venison, vegetables, and Jean's flaky biscuits, his offer wasn't challenged. During the meal the men seemed more amiable, and Will hoped he'd made a chink in their armor.

His hunger satisfied, he sat facing the fire and discreetly studied each man. They had all come to Alaska looking for a new and better life. They were more like him than they wanted to admit. His eyes rested on Ray Townsend, who stood in the shadows smoking a cigarette and staring into the forest. His long, curly hair nearly hid his face. *What does he want from life? And why is he so angry?* Will wondered.

Will knew very little about the man's background. He'd heard that at one time Ray had been considered generous and kindly, but that had been before his wife died. Will tried to imagine how he'd feel if something happened to Jean. A mantle of grief fell over him. Life would be empty. A rush of sympathy and compassion for Ray touched Will.

Lord, what will it take to reach him? Show me if I can help. The morning would come all too soon, so he said good night and climbed beneath his blankets and quickly fell asleep.

The next day was much the same as the first—long hours astride with Ray Townsend taking jabs at Will. The other men were different, however. They were friendlier; some even occasionally rode alongside the outsider and talked with him about their families and previous hunting excursions. Mike, who had seemed most distant, even asked

Will about his farm and his life in Wisconsin. Will smiled inwardly, knowing God was at work.

There was a drawback to the friendly conversation, however. It seemed to intensify Ray's ire. His temper flared, and now Will wasn't its only target. Ray hurried the pace, as if wanting to put an end to the trip.

Ray stopped and stared up at a spruce while his horse fidgeted. "Take a look at that." He nodded at deep slashes high in the tree. "That's him. He's letting us know this is his territory." Ray kicked his horse in the flanks and moved on. "We're getting closer." He glanced over his shoulder. Eyes alight, he said, "Watch your back there, farmer. Never know when he might sneak up on ya."

"I'll do that," Will said evenly.

The men saw many signs of the bear that day, but no bear. When they camped, it was understood that Will would cook. The men wolfed down the meal, and another chink came down. Ray kept to himself. When Will put out his bedroll that night, Ray was still up, sitting by the fire and staring at the flames. His hand rested on Jed's head, who now seemed to be his only companion.

Exhausted, Will fell asleep almost immediately. He woke to Jed's deep growl. Remaining motionless, he barely breathed. He scanned the encampment. As he stared into the darkness, his eyes caught the outline of a hulking shape. His flesh prickled. Something was there!

Jed's growl intensified; then barking ferociously, he hurled himself at the shadow. Everyone in camp was awake now. Will grabbed his rifle and backed away from a blur of gray and white dog and the snapping roar of a large animal. Heavy footfalls moved away from camp with Jed pursuing. The sound of splintering limbs and cracking underbrush carried from the surrounding woods. Jed's yapping and snarling continued as he lay into the interloper.

The camp resonated with shouting and cursing as men grabbed guns and stumbled out of their bedding. Someone tossed wood on the fire. It flared to life, but whatever had invaded the camp was gone. Jed's barking attested to that, moving further and further into the forest.

"Jed! Jed!" Ray called. "Come on, boy!" He waited, but the dog didn't return.

"Was that him?" one of the men asked. "Was that the devil?"

Ray grabbed the unlit end of a burning branch, and holding it up, headed toward the woods. Peering into the darkness beyond the light of his makeshift torch, he hollered, "Jed. Get back here! Jed!" Barking, the dog continued his pursuit. Then they heard a yelp and another yelp. Suddenly the forest turned quiet. "Jed!" The cracking of underbrush carried through the night air as the bear retreated.

Ray stood for a long time, torch above his head. Finally he returned to the campfire. "It was him. He doubled back on us. He's a devil, all right. We're lucky to be alive." He tossed his torch into the flames. "Fool dog." He sat on a log. "I'll keep watch," he said, his voice sad.

Will slept fitfully, his dreams filled with images of a dead calf, a bloodied sow, and Jean standing in the doorway of their house. Her face was etched with worry, and tears wet her cheeks. Will wanted to tell her that everything would be all right, but in his gut he wasn't sure. He was afraid. The bear was hiding, waiting for him. He knew it. He had to stay alert and watchful, but all he could see was blackness! He could hear footfalls!

Will startled awake and for a moment lay perfectly still, trying to drag himself away from the nightmare. The sky was alight, but the men were sleeping, all except Ray. He stood at the edge of the clearing with a scruffy-looking Jed sitting beside him. The bear hadn't gotten the best of him, although it was clear he'd tangled with the monster.

Will sat up and scrubbed his face with his hands. His eyes rested on Ray, who stared out into the forest, his expression resolute. Will knew he was thinking about the grizzly and that he was more determined than ever to get him.

The hunting party was up and moving early and on the bear's trail. Jed limped but managed to keep up. They were closing in. The tracks were fresh. Only now, the animal had circled around the men and they had become the prey.

"It's time to turn the tables on him," Ray said. "Time to get that devil." He climbed off his horse and tied him to a tree. Everyone else dismounted. "I want you to divide into twos," he said. "We'll round him up."

"You think we ought to go into that thick underbrush?" Joe asked, his face white.

"We've no choice. We can't wait for him. He's not going to show himself, and after what happened last night, we can't wait." He pointed south. "There's a ridge that runs along there. Frank and I will head west and circle around. You two, Mike and Jim, you come around the other way. We'll get this bear in a pickle and flush him out." Without even looking at Will, he headed into the woods.

Will was left on his own. He hesitated, not knowing which way to go. He felt anxiety well up, then told himself, *I know a thing or two about hunting.* He headed into heavy foliage, following Ray's path. The musty smell of earth and vegetation assailed him. He couldn't see well, but still he moved on, stopping frequently to listen. The buzz of insects, chirping birds, and squawking of squirrels were the only sounds he could hear.

Keeping his rifle at his hip, the safety off, and his finger on the trigger, he pushed through the brush, hoping the bear would be between him and Ray Townsend. He knew the bear was close. He could sense it. More than once he thought he heard the grunt or pant of an animal. Although he couldn't see, he continued, driven by a sense of urgency. He had to get that bear.

Chapter 8

EVERY NERVE BRISTLING, WILL MOVED THROUGH HEAVY BRUSH. HE COULDN'T shake the sense that he was being tracked. He stopped and listened. Nothing stirred. Even the raucous cries of cranky jays had ceased. Will smelled the air but detected only the scent of evergreen and earth.

He pushed on, his feet catching in a tangle of ferns, dead leaves, and cranberry bushes as he moved through aspens and willows wrangling with spruce for ground. Skirting a large devil's club, he nearly plunged down a steep embankment. Regaining his balance, he studied a ravine veiled by the heavy greenery. His eyes took in the upper ridge, searching for man or beast. He saw neither.

Suddenly the crackle of underbrush fractured the air. Off to his right, something crashed through the foliage. Rocks and dirt spilled down the gorge wall, followed by a tumbling body. Cries of pain and cursing accompanied the man. It was Ray Townsend. He didn't stop until he reached the bottom, then lay still, looking like a pile of limbs, boots, and clothing.

Forgetting about the grizzly for the moment, Will started down. Ray lay too still, too quiet. Keeping his body parallel to the hill, Will moved as quickly as he could, planting his feet in loose dirt and rocks and using vines and branches for handholds.

By the time he reached the bottom, he was out of breath and his thighs ached, but he sprinted to Ray. He felt for a heartbeat. It was strong and steady. Will carefully disentangled the man's limbs and rolled him to his back. Ray moaned. Brushing away dirt and leaves, Will quickly scanned his body. He didn't see any obvious injuries. "Ray? You all right?"

The big man opened his eyes and blinked, then spit dirt. "I think so." He pushed up on one arm and bent his leg. "Ahh," he hollered, grabbing his knee. "I think it's broke."

"Let me take a look." Will pulled out his hunting knife and cut open the pant leg. The knee was already swollen, and the leg above and below had begun to turn dark blue. He resheathed his knife. "You might be right. It doesn't look good." He leaned back slightly. "Can you stand?"

Grimacing, Ray pushed himself into a sitting position, then tried to rise. Letting out a cry, he crumpled back to the ground. Beads of sweat dotting his face, he closed his eyes. "I can't walk."

Will studied the landscape. Steep walls reached up on two sides, and a narrow gorge stretched ahead and behind. "Getting you out of here isn't going to be easy."

The sounds of splintering underbrush came from the ridge, and rocks and dirt skittered down the bank. Both men's eyes went to the crest and moved along the rim. Ray whispered, "I'd like to know where that bear is."

A surge of alarm swept through Will. He'd forgotten about the grizzly. "It's probably one of the men." He cupped his hands around his mouth and yelled, "Hey, anyone up there?" He received no reply. A branch cracked and bushes moved. "Who's up there?" No answer. Fear moved in. "We better get you out of here. I'll have to haul you up."

"And how do you propose to do that? It's a steep climb, and I ain't no sack of potatoes."

"Where's Frank? You started off together."

"He headed toward the other ridge." Ray searched the ground around him, then scanned the slope where he'd fallen. "You seen my rifle?"

Will made a quick search but didn't find the gun. "No telling where it is," he said. "We'll just have to go without it."

"I paid good money for it, and I'm not leaving without it." He made another visual search.

Concealing his frustration, Will looked again. When he didn't find it, he said as calmly as he could, "It could have ended up in a lot of places, and we don't have time to look. We've got to get you out of here. You need a doctor."

"Just hightail it. Find someone to help."

"Good idea, except you don't have a rifle, and I'm not about to leave without mine."

"You have a point." Again Ray scanned the hillside. "So, how do we get out?"

"Looks like it might be easier going along there." Will pointed toward a slope with a gentler grade. He handed his rifle to Ray. "I'll have to carry you. You can hang on to the gun." He thought for a moment. "This is going to take teamwork, and it's gonna' hurt—"

"Pain ain't new to me. Just tell me what you want me to do," Ray snapped.

Will silently prayed for patience. With half a smile, he said, "Like you said, you're not a small man. I need you to push yourself up with your good leg so I can get my shoulder under your gut."

"You're literally going to carry me?" Ray asked incredulously.

Will grinned. "You have another idea?"

Ray didn't answer.

"You'd be surprised what farming can do for a man's strength," Will said, grabbing hold of Ray's arm. "Come on, let's get to it. I don't much like the idea of becoming bear fodder."

To a tirade of cussing and groans, Will slung Ray over his shoulders. Bent beneath the weight, he started up the embankment. "Feels like you ought to lay off those extra flapjacks and syrup."

"Maybe you should keep your mouth shut and walk."

Tempted to dump his load, Will kept moving. "Just hang on to my gun and keep quiet." Will thought he heard a chuckle from Ray.

A low snarl accompanied by the sound of splintering twigs and cracking brush resonated from above. "He's up there," Ray said. "Just waitin' for us."

Will stopped. "Maybe it's something else."

"It's not." Ray swung the rifle around. "He could come out of there at any moment, and I can't shoot from this position. You better set me down."

Bending at the knees, Will lowered Ray to the ground. He took the gun and pulled on the lever. It was jammed. He tried again. "It's stuck."

"Should have known," Ray growled. "Give me that thing." Will handed him the gun. "You farmers don't know the first thing about what really matters. Don't you know you gotta keep your rifle in good shape? You gotta be able to count on it." He struggled to release the bolt. "Looks like the workings are rusted."

"It's old. It belonged to my father."

"Why didn't you get another one?"

"I have a newer one at home, but I left it for Luke. That gun's been fine for years."

Hands trembling, Ray worked on the rifle. He pulled the trigger. Nothing happened. Shaking his head, he said, "We're dead." More snapping of twigs and brush rose from the ridge. He followed the sounds with his eyes. "He's checking us out. Wants to make sure we're easy pickings." He glowered at Will. "Which we are."

Will's pulse climbed. He grabbed the gun, pulled on the lever again, then the trigger, then lever. It was still jammed. Finally he handed it to Ray. "S'pose you could use it as a club." He searched for a heavy branch. When he found one, he picked it up and swung it several times. "This will have to do."

"You think that's going to stop a grizzly?" Ray asked derisively. "You're more of a fool than I thought."

"David brought down Goliath with a sling and a rock."

Ray scowled.

Rocks tumbled down from straight above them, then the sounds of stirring brush and cracking limbs moved along the ridge. Will's pulse raced, and his stomach felt tight. He knew they were in trouble. "Father, we need your help. Do what needs to be done."

"If I were you, I'd be on my way," Ray said nonchalantly. "Leave me. At least that way one of us has a chance."

Will ignored him. "Let's keep moving. Sounds like whatever's making that racket is heading away. Maybe he'll leave us be." Still gripping the heavy branch, Will hoisted Ray onto his shoulders. Ray held the useless gun. One agonizing step at a time, they made their way up the slope, keeping their eyes trained on the place where the rocks and debris had come from.

The forest was silent, as if holding its breath.

His face and body saturated with sweat and every muscle screaming under the strain, Will scrambled over the top and gently lowered Ray to the ground at the foot of a spruce. "Do you think you could climb if you had to?"

Searching the forest, Ray said, "If I could have, I would have, and you wouldn't have had to carry me up that hill." His eyes continued to move over the brush. His voice low, he added, "He's close. I can feel him."

Will stood with his back to Ray and faced the brush. A moment later the big cinnamon-colored bear broke through a clump of willows and charged. Will swung the club at the animal and hollered. "Hah! Get out of here! Go on bear!"

The animal veered off, then stopped and studied the two men, his nose twitching. He stood on hind legs, then with a huff, dropped to all fours.

Will's heart beat hard and fast. This was a big animal, probably close to eight hundred pounds. His eyes rested on its huge paws and five-inch claws, then traveled to the animal's vicious-looking teeth. The branch would be no defense. He could climb a tree, maybe save himself. He looked at Ray and knew he couldn't do it. How could he abandon any man, even one as vile as Ray Townsend?

"You want to go, so go. Save yourself," Ray said. "There's not much time, and I'm not worth dying for."

"I'm not leaving you." Will raised the club and waved it at the animal. "Hah! Go on! Get out of here!"

Swinging its head from side to side, the bear paced back and forth and moved closer. "Go on! Get!" Will took a few steps toward the grizzly.

The animal didn't back away, and his small dark eyes watched Will. With a snarl, he charged. Will and Ray both shouted, raising their feeble weapons. Unbelievably, the bear veered off again. Will began to hope they had a chance. Maybe the brute was more bark than bite. He glared at the animal, hoping he looked intimidating. "What do you think he's going to do?"

"He's gonna come at us again." Ray held a knife in his hand. He looked at it and smirked. "Probably won't do much good, but I'll be hanged if I'm going to just *let* him make a carcass out of me."

"Where are Mike and Joe? They can't be far off."

"Hard to tell. There's a lot of ways they could have headed." He shrugged. "Holler for them."

Will cupped his hands around his mouth. "Frank! Mike! Joe! Where are you?" He listened, keeping an eye on the bear pacing a few yards away.

"Here!" came a call. "I'm coming!"

"That sounded like Frank," Will said. "He'll be here." *Hurry!*

His coat glistening, the bear snapped his jaws, then swiped the air with a heavy paw. He circled the two men.

"Hurry, Frank!" Will shouted. He remembered Jean's dream. Had it been a vision? *I'm sorry, Jean,* he thought, envisioning her amber eyes and warm smile. *Lord if this goes bad, please watch over my family.*

Without warning, the bear ran at the two. Will raised his club. In a matter of seconds the bear was on him. He managed to hit the grizzly across the face before the animal tore into him. With a roar, he knocked the branch away like a twig.

Blood ran into Will's eyes, but he felt no pain. He backed away. The bear kept coming at him. It took a swipe at his arm, and hot pain shot through his shoulder and across his chest. The arm hung useless.

"Hit the ground! Play dead!" Ray yelled.

Will did as he was told. Using his good arm, he pulled the injured limb in close to his body, then draped the arm over his head. He lay still, barely breathing. His pulse hammered through his body. Blood stained the ground. The bear batted him a few times, then sniffed him. Will remained motionless.

All of a sudden, a stabbing pain knifed him in the side. The grizzly bit into him, lifted him, and shook. "Ahhh," Will screamed. Then the bear let loose, and Will hit the ground. He hugged the earth, feeling it was his only refuge. Then he remembered his true refuge was in the Father, and his terror lifted.

Will's thoughts turned to his family. They needed him. He had to fight; he had to try. The animal sniffed at his prey and took hold of the bad arm. In one swift move, Will rolled onto his back and swung his good arm at the bear's face, bringing his fist down on the animal's snout. At the same time, a boom echoed. The bear released Will, and he lay on the ground panting, his cheek resting against the cool earth. The animal ran. Another blast resounded, and the bear fell. Will closed his eyes. The bear was finally dead.

The next thing Will heard was Frank's voice. "Will?" He felt himself being rolled over. "God almighty."

Ray crawled to Will and lifted him, cradling him as he would a child. "Why did you do it?" His eyes were confused and guilt-ridden. "Why?"

"Do what?" Will asked with a wheeze.

"You could have saved yourself."

"You would . . . have . . . done the same." Will struggled for breath. Pain burned through his middle.

"No." Ray shook his head. "I wouldn't have. I wouldn't have." Tears washed into his eyes.

Will could feel the life leaving him. He glanced down at himself. His clothing was blood-soaked. He was dying.

"We'll get you out of here," Frank said. "You'll be all right."

Will gave the man a smile. "Thanks for getting here."

"I came as fast as I could. I'm sorry it wasn't sooner."

Will's eyes found Ray's. "Look after my family."

"Don't even talk that way. You're going to be fine. I've seen men torn up worse than this who made it. You got to hang on." Ray glanced at the blood oozing from Will's stomach. "Just hang on," he repeated more quietly.

"It's all right. I know where I'm going. I'm not afraid."

"You're not dying. You can't. We've got differences to mend. We're not done with our business, yet." His voice softened, and he added, "Please live."

"It's not your fault . . . I stayed . . . because I wanted to."

"I can't figure out why. I'm not worth it. We were enemies."

"I never hated you." Will closed his eyes and groaned. It was getting harder to breathe. He looked at Ray. "God . . . has a life . . . for you to live. Live it."

"He has one for you too."

"Yep—but not here." He grimaced and swallowed. His strength was leaving him. "Jean. She's going to need help. And . . . Luke . . ."

"Don't give up. We'll get you to the doc."

Will's strength was gone and so was the pain. His body went limp.
"No!" Ray almost shouted. "You can't die!"

"Tell Jean I love her. Tell her I'm sorry."

Will stopped breathing. Stunned, Ray didn't move but stared at the man who had been his enemy. "I never meant for anything like this to happen. I just wanted you out of the valley. I just wanted . . ." Truth spilled over him. This man wasn't his enemy. He had never been his enemy. He hadn't deserved Will's mercy. His bitterness and hatred were swept away, and shame engulfed him.

Ray saw his own ugliness and was sickened. He gazed at the dead grizzly and realized he'd been more a beast than the bear had been. The bear had acted out of instinct; he had no understanding of right and wrong. *I knew what I was doing. I'm the one who should be dead.*

Ray turned his gaze to the man in his arms and wished he'd known him as a friend. "I'm sorry. I'm so sorry." He let loose of Will and buried his face in blood-stained hands.

Gentle arms lifted him. "Come on, we need to get you to the doc," Frank said. "We'll take you up on the litter."

"What about him?"

"We'll get him out too."

"And his family? Who's going to tell them?"

Frank didn't answer right away, then said, "I will. I'll tell them."

"I didn't mean for this to happen. I didn't mean for it to happen."

"It's not your fault. We never know what lies ahead of us when we're out here. That's the way it is. Nothing to be done about it. It's over."

Chapter 9

CELESTE HUNKERED DOWN IN THE SEAT AND SNUFFLED INTO A HANDKERCHIEF while Frank helped Ray into the pickup.

"I'm gonna need a hand here," Frank said.

"Oh." Celeste gently cradled her father's casted leg and settled it on the seat. Leaving her hand on the heavy cast, she glanced at her father but said nothing before sitting back.

Frank set a pair of crutches in the pickup bed, then hurried around and climbed in. Pushing in the clutch, he turned the key and the engine fired. Glancing at Ray, he shifted into first. "You don't have to do this, you know."

"Yes I do," Ray said, his voice weary.

Celeste dabbed at her eyes. "Thank you for driving us, Frank. I just don't think I could manage."

"Glad to help." Frank eased the pickup forward, pulled onto the road, and headed toward the Haspers. His brow furrowed, he gripped the steering wheel. "I don't know what you can say, Ray. Nothing'll fix what's happened."

Biting her lip, Celeste grasped her father's hand.

"I have to be the one. I have to tell them . . ." His voice broke, and he tried again. "I have to tell them how sorry I am." He could already envision the agony on Jean's face when she heard. *Oh, Lord,* he nearly groaned out loud. Pressing his hands against his face, he wished it were a nightmare and he'd wake up. This was his fault.

He ran his hands through his hair and stared at distant hills. It had happened up there. The heavy forests framed by snow-covered mountains looked peaceful, but they lied. Death had been waiting.

Ray turned his gaze to the road disappearing beneath the front of the pickup. His head throbbed and his stomach churned. His aching leg reminded him of the hideous scene. He tried to shut it out, but it persisted. He'd never erase Will Hasper's death from his mind.

What would he say to Jean Hasper? How could he tell her that her husband was dead? Sweat beaded up on Ray's face, and he thought he might be sick. He gripped the door handle. Will Hasper's death was his fault. How could he tell her that?

God, forgive me. I'm sorry. If only I had understood, maybe none of this would have happened. The truck bumped through a puddle, and Ray winced, letting out a moan.

"Daddy, you're hurting. You need to send someone else. You should be in bed with that leg up."

"I'm fine."

"She's right. You ought to be at home. I'll tell them." Frank slowed. "I can turn this truck around right now."

"No."

"Daddy, please. Listen to Frank." Celeste's eyes refilled, and she choked back a sob. "This isn't your responsibility." With that, Celeste started weeping again. "I can't believe he's dead. I just can't believe it."

"Frank, stop the truck," Ray said.

Frank pulled to the side of the road and turned off the engine.

"Give us a minute." Ray opened the door and gingerly eased himself out. Standing on his good leg, he grabbed the crutches out of the back.

Celeste followed. "What do you want? You shouldn't be doing that. Get back in the truck."

"No. I need the air." Ray hitched his way to a log and sat down. "Sit," he said, patting the rough bark beside him.

Celeste did as she was told. Her hands pressed between her knees, she stared at the ground.

Ray circled an arm around her shoulders. "This is bad. Real bad. I don't know how we're going to get through it, but we will . . . somehow." He squeezed her gently. "I wish I could make it all go away, but I can't."

Celeste leaned against his arm. "I know. I just can't believe he's dead. He was a wonderful man. You would have liked him."

"I know that now." Ray's eyes filled, and he wiped at them.

"Every time I think about Mrs. Hasper and Laurel and Luke, Brian, and Susie . . ." She started to cry again. "I remember how it was when Mom died."

"She was the best." Ray let out a shaky breath. "I let you down and everyone else. Ever since she died . . . well, I've been plain mad. I took out my hurt on the people around me. I'm sorry."

"Daddy . . ."

"No. Let me say this. I don't understand it all just yet, but I'm beginning to make some sense of it." He rubbed his hand on his thigh. "When your mother died, I wanted to die. There was a big hole where she used to be. And her death was my fault."

"You . . ."

He raised a hand. "Let me finish. Your mother didn't want to come to Alaska. It was me. It was *my* dream, and she loved me, so she came."

"Mom was happy. We all were."

"I know, but I could have made sure she was in a safe place when your baby brother was born. Instead, we were out here—in the middle of nowhere. If we'd been near a doctor or a hospital, it could have been different." He swallowed hard and blinked back tears. "I hated God for letting it happen, then I hated myself, and eventually I hated everyone." He looked at Celeste tenderly. "Except you, of course." He took a shuddering breath. "I don't know why things happen the way they do. I wish I'd turned to God instead of hanging on to the bitterness." He shook his head. "Now this. Will Hasper's dead, and it's my fault."

"It's not your fault."

"It is."

"You act as if you're the one who killed him. It was the bear."

"Oh, the bear killed him all right, but if I'd treated him decently, he might not have felt like he had to come along. And when he did, I should have made sure he had a partner to hunt with. The rest of us went off and left him."

"Mr. Hasper would have gone along no matter what." Fresh tears filled her eyes. "And if he'd stayed home, you'd be dead."

"That would be more fitting. He was a better man."

Celeste took her father's face in her hands and made him look at her. "No. He was just a man—good yes, but not better."

"I did some things you don't know about. I wish you wouldn't have to know, but . . . pretty soon everyone will."

"What things?"

"I'm not ready to talk about them just yet." He took Celeste's hands in his. "I'm sorry, honey. I'm sorry to bring shame on you."

"I could never be ashamed of you."

Ray managed a small smile and pulled his daughter into his arms. "You are so much like your mother. She was always quick to forgive. I should have been more like her." He pushed himself to his feet and leaned on his crutches. With a heavy sigh, he said, "Well, I've got something to do, and I'd better get to it."

Jean heard a truck pull up to the house. *He's home,* she thought and quickly set a rising loaf of bread in the oven warmer and walked to the door. Will had been gone longer than he'd expected. "It's about time," she said, opening the back door and stepping out on the porch.

But it wasn't Will. It was Frank Reed, Ray Townsend, and Celeste. Jean immediately knew that something was wrong. She pressed a hand against her stomach and stared at the truck as she went down the steps. Mr. Townsend slid out, then Celeste. Ray Townsend had a cast on his leg. Father and daughter both looked desolate. Celeste's eyes and nose were red as if she'd been crying. Afraid, Jean stood still and waited.

His face ashen, Ray hobbled on crutches toward her. Celeste stayed at his side, careful not to look at Jean.

Lord, what is this?

When Ray was about a yard away, he stopped. Leaning on the crutches, he stared at the ground, then looked at Jean.

Jean braced herself.

"Mrs. Hasper . . . I . . . I've always been a direct man, but I don't know just how to say what I have to say."

"It's Will, isn't it? He's hurt." She bunched up her apron and pressed it against her abdomen.

His gray eyes meeting hers, he said, "It's worse." He glanced at Luke, who stood in the doorway. Brian and Susie walked down the steps and stood beside their mother. Ray glanced at the children, then continued, "We were tracking that bear and split up into pairs. Figuring we'd have a better chance of cornering him, I sent my partner up on another ridge." He paused a long moment. "Will was following me." He leaned hard on the crutches. "I fell down a ravine and broke my leg." He glanced at his bad leg. "Will was helping me when . . . when the bear came at us. We only had one rifle, and it was jammed." His voice quavered, and he swallowed. "Well, ma'am, the bear got him."

The world tipped, and Jean thought she might fall. She managed to ask, "Is he alive?"

"No, ma'am. I'm real sorry—real sorry."

Anguish swept over Jean. The strength went out of her legs, and she started to fall. "No," she whispered.

Celeste ran to her and held her, then carefully lowered Jean to the bottom step of the porch. She was crying. "I'm so sorry, Mrs. Hasper."

"What happened?" Luke demanded, storming down the steps. "It's your fault, isn't it? Tell me!"

"Please, Luke, no," Jean said. "Not now."

Luke glared at Ray Townsend, then stumbled back onto the porch. He stopped at the door, pressed his forehead against the frame, and wept.

Brian stepped up to Ray. "You're lying. He's not dead! He promised me he'd be all right!" When Ray didn't answer, Brian turned and walked to his mother. "Daddy's all right, isn't he?"

Jean scooped the little boy into her arms. After a few moments she held him away from her, and looking into his frightened eyes, she said softly, "Daddy's gone to heaven."

His eyes filling with tears and his chin quivering, Brian shook his head no.

Susie joined her brother. "Daddy?" She started to cry, and Luke picked her up.

"Here, give her to me," Jean said and took the little girl. She set Susie on her free leg and held her two youngest close.

His eyes hard and jaw set, Luke jumped off the porch and stormed toward Ray Townsend. "How did it happen?"

"Daddy was hurt . . ." Celeste started.

Ray lay a hand on his daughter's arm to quiet her. "I fell down an embankment and broke my leg. Your father came to help me. I lost my rifle in the fall, and your father's was jammed. When the bear came at us, we were helpless. Your father could have saved himself, but he wouldn't leave me. I told him to go." Ray's gaze wandered to Luke's feet, then he looked into the young man's eyes. "It's my fault. When we split up, I let him go off on his own. Everyone spread out; we should have stayed close. That way, if someone needed help . . ." He stopped and shuffled his crutches. "I was in charge." He looked at Jean huddled on the porch with her children. "I'm sorry. Real sorry."

"Sorry isn't good enough!" Luke exploded, lunging at the man and hitting him.

Ray stumbled backward.

"This is your fault! And you're going to pay!" He hit Ray again, clutching his collar. "You'll pay!"

Celeste grabbed Luke. "Stop it! He didn't mean for anything to happen!"

Frank hustled out of the truck and stepped between the two. Gripping Luke's arms, he pushed him back firmly. "Settle down. This ain't gonna' help."

Luke fought to get past him, but Frank kept a tight hold on the young man. Finally he stopped struggling. For a long while he glared at Ray, then the fight went out of him, and he dropped his arms. He started to weep, and with a lurching run, headed toward the fields.

Leaning heavily on his crutches, Ray watched him. "I didn't mean for anything like this to happen."

Her voice hard, Jean said, "You better go." Turning tormented eyes on Celeste, she asked, "Can you send Adam and Laurel over?"

"Yes. Right away." She hugged Jean, then broke down again.

Jean held Celeste away from her, then without another word, picked up Susie, grasped Brian's hand, and walked into the house.

With Susie in her arms, and supported by Laurel on one side and Luke on the other, Jean made her way to the gravesite. She stared at the plain wooden casket. How could his lifeless body lay in that box? How could he be dead?

This is a nightmare. I'll wake up soon. She glanced around at family and friends. The minister stood at the head of the casket, his Bible in hand. Birds sang, the sun felt hot, and mosquitoes assaulted bare skin. This was real. Will was gone.

An unbearable ache squeezed her chest and throat; tears burned her eyes. *How will I live without him?*

Laurel tightened her arm around her mother. "It'll be all right, Mama," she whispered.

"No. It can never be all right."

A murmur moved through the mourners, and Jean looked up to see Ray Townsend and Celeste join the gathering.

"What's he doing here?" Luke asked.

"I don't know. I don't want trouble, so keep still. And I don't believe your father would mind him being here. He died for that man."

Luke didn't say any more, but he continued to glare at the intruder.

The minister met Jean and the children. Taking her hand, he said, "You have my deepest sympathy, Mrs. Hasper. Will was a good man, one of the finest I've known. We'll all miss him."

Jean only nodded, not trusting herself to speak.

The minister returned to stand at the head of the casket. He scanned the people, and finally his eyes stopped on Jean and her children. "Our Lord is a God of comfort. He will not forsake you in your time of grief. Lean on him and he will sustain you."

He opened his Bible to a place he had marked. "Isaiah 41:10 says, 'Fear thou not; for I am with thee: be not dismayed; for I am thy God: I will strengthen thee; yea, I will help thee; yea, I will uphold thee with the right hand of my righteousness.'" He lifted his eyes. "Grieving is a human emotion, and it is right and good for us to come together to mourn the loss of someone we love. Mrs. Hasper, I want you to know that we are all here to help you through your sorrow. You're not alone. Above all, remember it is God who upholds us all."

Heads nodded, and compassionate eyes sought out Jean and the children.

"On behalf of the Hasper family, I want to thank you all for coming." He paused. "We know the length of our lives is limited, that a day will come when each of us must face death. For some, life will be short, but all who belong to the Lord have an eternity in paradise waiting." He glanced at his open Bible. "Three days ago Will Hasper faced his day of death and began his eternity. He would want us to rejoice."

The minister scanned the faces and smiled. "Will would be pleased to see so many of his friends and neighbors here. He loved you all."

Many cried openly while others fought their tears. The reverend read several passages, finishing with Psalm 23. His own eyes moist, he went on. "We've lost a good man, but Will Hasper will dwell in the house of the Lord forever. He's waiting for us." He looked at Jean. "And those he's left can be assured that sorrow is only for a time. Joy will return."

He bowed his head and finished with a closing prayer. Then the choir broke out into a chorus of "Rock of Ages." People joined in. Jean tried, but grief choked off the words.

When the singing stopped, the minister looked out over the people. "Before we close, would anyone like to say something?"

Surprisingly, Miram spoke up almost immediately. "I remember when we were on the boat." She sniffled. "I thought we were sinking. Mr. Hasper was real kind to me, and he went right down to check to see what was wrong." She blew her nose softly, then continued, "He's always been that way—kind and helpful. I'll never forget him."

Drew Prosser was the next to speak. "I've only known Will since we met on the train two years ago, but I realized right off he was a good man, someone who could be counted on. He's been a friend to me and my family. I'm grateful I had the chance to know him."

Struggling to keep his tears in check and holding Laurel's hand, Adam faced the people. "When I first started out with all of you, I was pretty obnoxious." A flicker of a smile touched his lips. "Even so, Will Hasper treated me fairly and accepted me just as I was." He wiped his nose with a handkerchief. "He was the only father I ever knew. I grew up in an orphanage, but he was my dad. I've never known a finer man." He choked back a sob, and Laurel hugged him, crying softly.

Several others spoke up, and then it was quiet. The minister said, "Let's pray."

"Wait a minute. I have something to say." Ray Townsend stepped forward. "I know some of you don't think I belong here, and you're probably right, but I wanted to say good-bye to one of the finest men I've ever known." He cleared his throat. "And I need to say something to all of you." He gazed at the casket.

"You all know that Will Hasper saved my life, but he did something I don't think most of you know. He showed me Christ, and he saved me from an eternity without God." Tears washed into the big man's eyes. "He didn't have to stay with me. He could have left me and saved himself. Instead, he stood beside me and faced that bear with nothing but a club. I've never known anyone who gave his life for someone else, and especially not for an enemy." He glanced at the minister. "I've been in church a lot of years, and I heard about Jesus Christ and about how he died for mankind, but I never really understood it. To me Jesus was just a symbol of goodness, someone from history."

He searched the faces of his neighbors. "After all this happened, I closed myself off with my Bible, and I began to read . . . I'm ashamed to say for the first time in my life. Now I know Jesus is real. He lived in Will Hasper. Will gave his life for mine, and now I understand." Again tears filled his eyes and he wiped them away, struggling to go on.

"I'm the worst sinner in this valley, but Will stayed by my side. I'm the last one to deserve compassion. After everything I did, he should have hated me. But not Will Hasper. All he could see was another human being who needed help. So he stayed. And he died.

"I've been praying and searching for the truth. Will died in my place. Jesus Christ died in my place." He looked at Jean. "I understand now. I've accepted God's love and forgiveness; I'm not the same man I was three days ago. I'll understand if you don't forgive me. It's all right."

Jean only stared at Ray. What could she say? It was too soon to know what she felt. Right now, all she wished was that Ray Townsend were dead and Will were alive.

Ray turned back to the crowd. "This might not be the time or place, but I've got something else to say. I've been thinking on it, and I've got to tell you. Here it is." He took a deep breath. "I've done some terrible things, things I'm not proud of." He glanced at Celeste. "I'm sorry, honey. I have no excuse."

Clasping his hands behind his back, he continued. "Ever since Ellie passed away I've been angry—at myself and at God. For a long while I took it out on anyone who irritated me, and when the colonists came, I focused on them. They were an easy target, and I took out my bitterness on them. I figured if life was bad enough they'd leave, so I made trouble for them in lots of ways."

His eyes settled on Robert Lundeen and his mother. "I hired those men who beat you up. Celeste was fond of you, and I didn't like that." He glanced at his daughter who wore a horrified expression. Tears streamed down her cheeks. "I knew how you felt about him, and I wanted him gone." He turned back to Robert. "And . . . I hired the man who started the fire at your house." A crooked smile touched his lips. "You had more resolve than I figured. You stayed and rebuilt. Somehow I'll pay off the debt you owe to the government. I'm real sorry."

"Daddy, please don't say any more."

"I love you, honey. I'm so sorry." Ray awkwardly pulled Celeste into his arms and held her tight. Then smoothing her hair, he stepped back and continued, "I was the one who made sure no homesteaders bought your produce. And I stirred up trouble wherever I could and spread tales that weren't true. I'm ashamed. And I'm sorry, really sorry. I wish I could take it all back, but I can't."

He scuffed the ground with the heel of his boot, then looked at the crowd. "I don't expect forgiveness. I know that's asking too much. But I am asking you to forgive each other—stop hating. Will Hasper wanted this valley to be united, and now that I'm seeing with new eyes, I believe it's a better place because of the colonists. They aren't outsiders. We're all just folks trying to make our way here. Please don't do what I did and keep on hating. It'll only bring sorrow."

Ray's gaze settled on the sheriff. "I suppose I'll be going with you."

The sheriff looked at the crowd. "Anyone pressing charges?" No one responded. He looked at Ray. "Well, I guess that settles it."

"I wish they'd lock him up and throw away the key," Luke said with venom in his voice.

Jean felt a pang of fear go through her. Would the cycle of bitterness begin again? And could she forgive?

Chapter 10

WHILE HER FAMILY ATE BREAKFAST, JEAN MADE PEANUT BUTTER SANDWICHES and set them in a clean lard bucket used as a lunch pail, then added apples and cookies. Handing it to Brian, she said, "This is for you and Susie."

Brian took the pail without interest. He wasn't interested in anything since his father's death. Brian's sorrow stabbed at Jean. He was such a sad little boy. Kneeling in front of him, she rested her hands on his shoulders. "Things will get better soon. Then you won't miss your daddy so much."

Brian's eyes filled with tears, and his chin quivered. "I don't think that's true. I want him to come back."

Fighting her own tears, Jean pulled him into her arms. "I'm so sorry. I miss him too."

"Why did God take him to heaven? He already had Justin."

How did she answer a question she'd asked herself? Death was unfair and unkind. She held Brian away from her and looked squarely into his eyes. "I think that maybe God loved them so much he wanted them to be with him. Heaven is a beautiful place. I'm sure Justin and Daddy are very happy. And they're together."

"Will he come for me too?"

"No. He knows how much I need you."

Brian thought a moment. "Do you think Justin was lonely and needed Daddy?"

"No. I don't think Justin was lonely. In heaven no one is sad. But I do know Daddy missed Justin."

"I want to be with them."

"Me too," Susie said, climbing down from her chair.

Luke kept eating and didn't say anything.

"Can I go to heaven?" Brian asked.

"One day, but for now I need you to stay with me and your brother and sister."

"What if we all went?" Brian looked at Susie and Luke.

"Yeah," Susie said.

Jean smiled. "That would be nice. But we'd all have to die. And I don't think God wants that. He has plans for us here."

"What kind of plans?" Susie asked.

"I don't know for sure, but he'll show us if we keep loving him and talk to him."

"The preacher said we're supposed to love each other," Brian said.

"That's true. We are."

Brian managed a small smile. "I love you and Susie and Luke and Laurel and Adam and . . ."

"You're full of love." Jean hugged him. "And I love you. And you," she told Susie, touching the tip of her nose. Jean straightened. "Well now, we need to get moving. We have work to do." She hefted Susie into her arms. "Oh, you're getting heavy."

His face a scowl, Luke pushed away from the table and set his empty coffee cup in the sink. "I better get to the cabbages. They need weeding." He headed for the door.

"I'll take these two over to the Jenkins's and then I'll be back."

Luke nodded and stepped outside.

"You ready, Brian?" Jean asked.

"No. I want to help. Why can't I stay?"

"I need to know you're safe and out of trouble, and I can't do that when I'm working."

"Daddy used to let me help."

"I know, but today I need you to stay with Mrs. Jenkins and help her watch Susie." She steered Brian out the door.

"I can help. I'm big. I won't get into any trouble." He folded his arms over his chest and stuck out his lower lip. "Daddy would have let me help."

Jean sighed. "He probably would have, but he's not here. And just for today I need you to be a good boy and stay with the Jenkinses." Jean didn't feel up to battling. Will had been buried only five days earlier, and she was too weary and depressed to argue. "Please, Brian, just do as I say."

Staring at his feet, hands shoved in his pockets, Brian walked down the steps and ahead of his mother and Susie as they headed toward the Jenkins's place. Jean wished there were some way to lift his pain, but there wasn't. Only time would bring healing.

The months and years stretched ahead, empty and frightening. There was so much work to be done and no one to share the burden with. Jean still needed to be a parent, but she also had the responsibility of the farm. Alone it was more than she could handle. No matter how much she worked to construct a plan, she'd found no way to hang on to their home. There was just too much work. *Lord, if we have to move, where will we go?*

Brian kicked a stone, sending it off the road and into the weeds.

Jean searched her mind for something to cheer him. "Did you know the Jenkinses have new puppies?"

Brian stopped. "They do? What kind? When were they born?"

"I don't know what kind. A mix, I guess. They were born a few weeks ago. I'm sure John and Michael will show them to you."

Brian hurried his steps.

Adele Jenkins and her two boys met Jean and the children on the front porch. Eyes full of compassion, Adele smiled, brushing wispy blonde hair off her face. "Hello there. How are you?"

Before Jean could respond, Brian asked, "Can I see the puppies?"

Seven-year-old John asked, "Would it be all right, Ma?"

"Yeah. Can we?" five-year-old Michael asked, swinging from the porch railing.

"Certainly. You know where they are."

"Come on," John said, jumping off the porch. "They're in the barn."

Brian and Michael raced after John with Susie lagging behind.

"Those four are really something," Adele said, watching them until they disappeared inside the barn. She turned soft green eyes on Jean. "So, how are you, really?"

"How do you think?" Jean could feel raw emotions rising. "I'm managing."

"We're here if you need anything."

"Thank you. I sure appreciate your watching Brian and Susie for me."

"I'm happy to do it. They're a real joy to have around."

"If they get to be a bother, you let me know."

"I'm sure they'll be fine. Tom and I are hoping for more children, so we figure this will be good practice for us."

A pang of sorrow went through Jean. There would be no more children for her and Will. "Well, I better get back." She stepped off the porch. "I'll come by to get them this afternoon."

"Tom said he'd be stopping over at your place later. He'll bring the kids with him, and if there's anything you need done, he'll do it."

"All right." Jean turned and headed for home. She could hear the sounds of laughter coming from the barn, and another twinge of regret hit her. She hated leaving her children. Glancing back, she spotted Susie walking toward Adele with one puppy in her arms and another galloping around her feet. Jean hurried on, choking back tears.

When she approached the house, Jean stopped to watch Luke. He didn't notice her, his full attention on his work. He'd made it clear that he was determined to do as good a job as his father, and that meant vegetables free of pests and weeds.

Jean leaned on the fence, her eyes wandering to the tractor parked in the field. Will had been so proud and excited when he'd brought it home. Anxious to try it out, he'd started working immediately. Fresh tears seeped into her eyes. "You can't cry your life away," she told herself in frustration, wiping the tears away and heading for the barn.

Inside it was dark and cool. Jean was hit by the memory of the grizzly prowling around outside while she and the children hid. Fear and revulsion washed over her Jean. "If only I'd had a rifle. I would have killed him then, and Will would still be alive."

Fluttering noises came from above, and Jean gazed into the rafters. Daylight flickered through, and birds flitted in and out to care for their babies in hidden nests. Instead of enjoying the sight, all Jean could think of was that the roof needed repair. Her eyes roamed to the stack of hay. It was low. They'd have to replenish it soon. Would they have enough grain this year?

Snuffling came from outside the barn wall. Adrenaline shot through Jean, and she pressed her hand to her chest. *He's back! No. He's dead.* She moved toward the barn door and peeked out. Nothing. Fearfully, she edged her way around the barn.

Jean heard stomping and crackling. Something was there! Pressing close to the wall, she crept to the corner of the building, then took a quick look around the edge. A moose stood alongside the barn munching grass. Letting out her breath, she nearly laughed, then almost cried. Would she ever feel safe again?

She returned to the barn, picked up a seeder, and filled its canvas bag with oats. Slipping the halter over her head, she slung the broadcaster across her chest and headed for the field, careful to give the moose ample space. It was time to go to work. She needed to do anything but think.

Walking up and down the field, Jean turned the crank and watched seed shoot out and away from her. At first the job was easy, but after a while the sun grew hot and her legs and feet ached. She headed back to refill the broadcaster for the third time and wondered about the honesty of the company that had advertised it. They'd said it could seed six acres in one hour. She couldn't imagine how that could be true. *I suppose a man can carry more seed and make fewer trips to refill,* she thought, stopping at a cistern just outside the barn door. Taking a ladle from a hook on the wall, she dipped it into cool water and drank.

When Jean returned to the field, she watched Luke. He was still working steadily. *Maybe it will help use up some of his anger. Lord, give him peace. He could probably use a drink,* she decided and returned to the house.

She filled a quart jar with water from the faucet and headed to the front plot. "You thirsty?" Jean called when she was a few rows away.

Luke straightened, and using the edge of his shirt, wiped sweat from his face. "Yeah. Thanks."

"Figured you could use a drink," she said, handing him the jar.

"I could." He chugged down the cool liquid. "I should have brought some with me." He took another drink.

"You look like you've had too much sun. Maybe you should rest."

"Nah. I'm fine." He looked down the row. "It's looking pretty good, huh?"

Jean looked out over the field. "As good as your father would have done."

Luke's expression turned dark, and he drained the last of the water, then handed the jar to his mother. "I better get back to work."

Feeling miserable, Jean trudged back to the field she'd been seeding. Exhausted, she thought about all the chores she still had to do. She had supper to make, clothes to launder, and mending to do. Turning the crank on the broadcaster, she watched seed scatter and wondered how she would do it all.

With the oats and barley seeded, Jean headed for the house. Overheated and worn out, she imagined sitting on the porch and drinking cool lemonade. She had no lemons. Water would have to do. Shielding her eyes from the sun, Jean studied Luke. He'd been at it all day. It was time for him to quit.

"How about taking a break?" she called. "I think you've done enough for the day. I'll get us something to drink, then make supper."

"All right. I'll just finish the row, then I'll be up."

Half an hour later, looking tired and hot, his clothes caked in dirt, Luke walked toward the house. He sat on the front step and wiped sweat from his face. For a few minutes he said nothing, then looked at his mother. "I'm starved."

"I should have made us some lunch," Jean said. "I just didn't think about it."

"Figure I can make up for lunch at supper." He grinned.

Jean was happy to see him smile. "I'll get you some water."

"I'll get it." Luke headed into the house, returning a minute later with a quart jar of water. He sat and took a long drink. "Whew," he said, wiping his mouth. "I was thirsty."

Jean looked out at the fields and rocked in the chair. Fatigue seeped into her, and she rested her head on the back of the chair and closed her eyes. Memories of afternoons spent in this very rocker back in Wisconsin before the draught sifted through her mind. They had been good days.

"I figure after supper I'll work a few more hours," Luke said. "That's a good thing about this time of year—lots of daylight."

Jean looked at the young man. He was carrying a heavy load for a seventeen-year-old. "Maybe you ought to go fishing with Alex."

Luke gazed at the path leading to the creek. "Wouldn't be a bad idea. We could use the fish."

Tom's, Brian's, and Susie's voices carried from the road. They were singing, "She'll Be Comin' 'Round the Mountain." Jean rocked forward and pushed out of the chair, then stood at the top of the steps. A short-haired, black puppy danced around their feet.

"Look, Mom," Brian called. "We got a puppy!"

Wearing a sheepish grin, Tom said, "Hope you don't mind. Brian and Susie wanted one so badly. I told them to pick one out, but that you'd have to OK it. Adele and I figure it'd be a good idea for you to have a dog around the place."

Jean didn't want to be responsible for anything else, especially not a dog. She wanted to say no, but how could she—Brian was smiling.

He lifted the wiggling pup into his arms. "Can we keep him, Mom? Please?"

"All right," Jean said with a chuckle. "He is cute."

"He ought to be a good-sized dog," Tom explained. "And if he's anything like his father, he'll be a good watch dog."

Jean nodded slowly. "What should we call him?"

"I thought Spot would be a good name," Brian said as the puppy licked his face. "See, he has a spot on his chest." He turned the pup to show off a splotch of white. The squirming bundle of fur wiggled free and bounded toward Susie. Jumping on her, he toppled the three-year-old. Susie giggled and squealed as he washed her face, his tail beating the air.

"Spot?" Luke asked. "That's dumb."

"No, it's not. I like it," Brian argued.

"Well, Spot it is," Jean said, settling the argument. She looked at Tom. "Anything I can get you?" she asked.

"Nope. But I thought I'd take care of the milking and feeding for you while I'm here. Brian told me he'd help."

"Thank you. I do appreciate that." A sharp gust of wind blew across the open fields, raising the hair on Jean's arms. "I hope we're not in for a storm. I'd hate to see my new seeds end up at your place." Clouds looking like mounds of cotton gauze billowed above the mountains.

"Looks like we might be getting a little weather," Tom said. "I'll see to the livestock." He headed for the barn with Brian and the puppy tagging along behind. Susie started after them.

"Susie, you stay here. You can help me make supper." Jean waited for her youngest to climb the steps, then asked, "Luke, you want more to drink?"

"No, thanks," he said, keeping his eyes on Tom. "Feels strange having someone else do Dad's chores."

"I know." Another wind gust swept through the porch, and Jean rubbed her arms, studying the fields. Dust blew up and swirled into a cloud. "Oh, no," she said, leaning on the railing. She stared as more dirt, along with seed, lifted into the air. "I can't believe it. It's just blowing away—all my work, all that seed." She wanted to cry. "If it keeps up, I'll have to replant."

"Maybe it's just a few gusts," Luke said. "And if it's not, I'll take care of replanting."

They waited and watched, but the wind continued and carried away precious seeds. Jean sank into her chair. Shaking her head, she finally said, "I'm not sure we can make it. We don't have enough money, and there's too much work for the two of us."

"I can do it. And I'll get another job."

Jean looked at her son with a mix of pride and sorrow. "I know you mean well, but you can't do it all. And with the co-op doing such a poor job of selling our produce . . ."

"I've been thinking on that," Luke said, a note of excitement in his voice. "I've decided we ought to bypass the co-op and go straight to the buyers. We can do our own selling."

"But we signed a contract, agreeing to sell only through the co-op. I don't know . . ."

"The only farmers making it are the ones sidestepping the co-op. Dad and I talked about it."

"And what did your father want to do?"

Luke didn't answer right away. "He hadn't decided yet. But remember last year. We had a good crop, but most of it didn't sell. Instead, it rotted in the boxes."

"But last year the homesteaders weren't buying. This year will be different."

"There aren't enough of them. It won't make that much difference. We've got to sell directly to the towns—Anchorage, Seward, Cordova. I can do it."

"I don't know, Luke. How will you do all that and work the farm?"

"I won't have to do much traveling 'til the end of summer. Robert did a lot of selling last year. We could go together."

Jean nodded, considering the possibilities. "If we're caught, we could lose the farm."

"The government won't do anything. And like I said, I could get a job."

"How can you hold down a job and take care of everything around here?"

Susie had wandered off the porch and picked a buttercup. She carried it to her mother. "This is a pretty flower," she said, holding out the blossom.

Jean nodded. "Yes. Pretty." She looked at Luke. "And have you forgotten the agreement we made? No outside jobs. The government could take back the farm."

"Agreement!" Luke spat. "I'm sick of hearing about how we need to uphold our end of the bargain while the government does whatever it wants. The government promised us plenty of buyers, lots of work, and a good life. And what did we get? Nothing. What happened to the government's promises to us?"

"The government has helped a lot, Luke."

He strode across the porch. "They got us here, but they didn't tell us we'd have to make it on almost no money after we moved in. How are we supposed to pay back what we owe when we can't even make enough to live on? The government controls everything. Have you read the papers lately? They're saying this project is a flop, a disaster. And they're comparing it to Russian collectives." He squared his jaw. "I agree."

"Those reports are distorted, and you know it," Jean said as calmly as she could. She walked across the porch and leaned on the railing. Gazing at their fields, she asked, "Have you forgotten how rich the soil is or about the money the government has paid us for clearing our land? And what about the livestock they gave us? And don't forget about our community—a new school, a modern hospital, a fine church. We have so much."

"That might be true, but the government still controls us. We have no freedom to choose what's best for us."

"You know how newspaper reporters can be. They love to get things stirred up. You can't let what they say push you into doing something you'll regret. We just need to work hard and trust God. He'll see us through."

"You just said you don't think we can make it."

"I know I said that, but . . . I was wrong. I'm not thinking straight these days. God will see us through this." Susie leaned against her mother's leg, and Jean rested a hand on her blonde curls. "We can't give up." Her eyes teared. "I remember how hard it was for your father to leave Wisconsin—how we prayed and prayed, wanting to do the right thing. It wasn't easy. Your father left everything he'd worked for and the life he'd always known just for this chance. We have to keep the farm."

"That's what I'm trying to do," Luke said, his voice almost shrill. Without another word, he headed for the barn.

Chapter 11

LAUREL MOVED THE PERCOLATING COFFEE TO THE BACK OF THE STOVE AND slid the cast-iron frying pan over high heat. Dropping a spoonful of bacon grease into the skillet, she watched it liquefy and glide across the pan. The smell of aged bacon assaulted her senses, and her stomach roiled. She'd been queasy all morning, and it wasn't the first time.

Placing a hand on her abdomen, she wondered if she might be pregnant and decided if she were, she didn't mind being sick. She considered what Adam's reaction might be when he found out, and she smiled. He would be thrilled. Adam loved the idea of being a father.

Thoughts of her own father melted away her delight. *Why did he have to die?* she asked, still unable to comprehend why God hadn't protected him. Ray should have been the one to die. Laurel felt a twinge of guilt. If he had, then Celeste would be the one grieving. Why did anyone have to die? It didn't make sense.

She cracked two eggs and dropped them into the hot oil. Yellow yolks stared up at her, and Laurel's stomach churned. *Toast for me,* she decided. Sawing off three slices of bread, she placed them on an oven rack.

If I'm pregnant, maybe Adam will be happy again, she thought. Since Will's death, Adam couldn't seem to break away from his grief. He'd been quiet and kept more to himself. "All my life I wanted and needed a father," he'd said, "and when I finally find him, he's taken away."

Again Laurel rested her hand on her abdomen. It was all so confusing—one life ending, another beginning.

"Morning," Adam said, walking into the kitchen. He kissed Laurel. "You look like you're far away. You all right?"

"I was just thinking."

"About what?"

"Oh, Daddy and how confusing the cycle of life and death is." She opened the oven and turned the toast. "You look almost happy this morning."

"I'm better," he said with a sigh and leaned on the table. "It feels awful to me; I can't imagine how hard it must be for you."

Laurel offered him a smile. "It's hard—for all of us. Sometimes I still can't believe he's gone. I worry about Mama. She has a haunted look about her." She turned to Adam. "Don't ever leave me. OK?"

"I'll try to stick around, but I can only do so much."

Laurel slid the eggs for Adam onto a plate and set them on the warming shelf. "Maybe we'll die together."

"What about our children?"

Laurel hadn't thought about that. "We don't have any yet."

"We will one day."

Laurel forced a smile. "They'll just have to be grown up, that's all. And we'll be very old." Taking the toast out of the oven, she buttered it and put two slices on Adam's plate. She set the meal on the table in front of him, then taking one piece of toast for herself, she sat across from him.

"Is that all you're eating?"

"I'm not very hungry." She took a small bite. "You want coffee?"

"Sure."

She filled a cup, then returned to her place at the table.

Adam studied her. "This the fourth day in a row you haven't felt well. Are you all right?"

"I'm fine. Probably just a touch of something."

"Maybe you should see the doctor."

"If I'm not better in the next couple of days, I'll go." She'd already planned on seeing the doctor but didn't want to say anything about her suspicions just yet.

"I'd better go on over to your mother's this afternoon and give her a hand," Adam said, scrubbing his face with his hands, then yawning. "There's more to farming than I realized. The work never ends."

"It's always been like that and always will be. I've never known any-thing different."

"I have. And it's looking awfully good from here." Adam shook his head slowly. "I can barely keep up with the work here, let alone your mother's. I wish I could do more for her, but there's only so much of me to go around."

Laurel leaned over the table and laid her hand on Adam's. "I know this is hard on you—just learning how to farm and taking care of two places." She squeezed his hand. "Maybe you should stay home today. Mama has lots of help. Tom Jenkins, Drew Prosser, and Robert have been giving her a hand. And I can go over today." She smiled. "That way you can catch up on some of the chores around here."

"I thought you were going to Jessie's today. At the rate you two are working, you'll never finish."

"It can wait a little longer. Anyway, I'm not sure I want to finish. I love spending time with Jessie and going over her husband's notes."

Adam took a bite of toast and chewed thoughtfully. "Well, the weeds are about to take over, so I'll work around here today." He sipped his coffee. "And maybe I could find a little time to write."

"What are you writing?"

"I've mostly been thinking, but I'd like to write a piece about your father, what happened between him and Ray Townsend, and how he died. He was an extraordinary man."

"That sounds wonderful."

"I want to tell about how it's touched people's lives here in the valley. You know, the change in Ray Townsend and how people have started to trust one another and be real neighbors."

"What about Mr. Townsend? Have you asked him how he feels about it?"

"Yeah. He said he didn't mind. I think it's a good story, one people ought to hear." He leaned on the table and looked earnestly at Laurel. "I feel like I've got to write it—let people know what kind of man your father was and what kind of God we have."

"What will you do with it?"

"I figured I'd send it to the editors at the *Trib*, maybe as a personal interest story. They might be interested." He speared a bite of egg.

"That's a wonderful idea."

Adam dipped his toast in egg yolk and took a bite.

Watching Adam eat nauseated Laurel, so she looked away. She set her half-eaten toast on the plate. The sight of food and the smells in the kitchen were becoming too much. She thought she might be sick.

"Are you all right? You don't look good."

Laurel stood, bracing herself against the table. "I need some air, that's all." Shakily, she walked to the door.

Adam got to the door before her and opened it. Holding onto her arm, he guided her outside. "I want you to see the doctor today."

Laurel nodded and sat on the front step. After a few minutes in the fresh air, she felt a little better, the sweet smell of flowers and the clean aroma of summer grass reviving her.

"It's chilly out here." Adam disappeared inside, returning a moment later with her jacket. He draped it over her shoulders. "You feeling better?" he asked, sitting beside her.

Laurel nodded and rested her head against his upper arm. She smiled up at him. "You're so good to me."

For several minutes they sat quietly, taking in the Alaskan scenery. Reluctantly Adam said, "Well, I've got work waiting for me. Will you be all right?"

"Uh-huh. I'm fine."

"You sure?"

"Yes. Go on."

He stood. "I'm off to work then." With a sigh, he added, "Another day of farming." He headed for the barn.

Laurel watched him, her pride swelling. He'd done so well and worked so hard. Having grown up in the city, adjusting to farming life hadn't been easy. In the beginning he plowed crooked rows, and after much practice, had finally settled for rows that were almost straight. Laurel had shown him how to plant seed and starts. He learned quickly, but each vegetable had a different planting schedule and different instructions, so it took him a while to sort them all out.

Working with the animals had proven to be a greater challenge. Harnessing the horses was one of the more intimidating and frustrating chores. They often refused to cooperate. If they were in the pasture, they'd do all they could to avoid capture, and once harnessed, fought the yoke. It sometimes took Adam the better part of the morning to get them in harness. His greatest frustration was knowing that his own ineptness set the horses against him. He'd persevered, however, and finally managed to do a respectable job of harnessing and driving the Belgians.

Adam had so much to learn. He had never milked a cow before marrying Laurel. When he was first learning, more milk ended up on the barn floor than in the pail. Laurel nearly giggled out loud remembering the first time he'd killed a chicken. The headless rooster had taken flight and headed straight at an astounded Adam, splattering him with blood. He'd sworn never to eat chicken again. He did, of course, and actually became competent at killing and butchering the birds.

With a sigh, Laurel got up. *Some day he'll be a fine farmer.* Sadness touched her. Her father had talked about all he'd wanted to teach Adam and how they would work together.

Adam sat at the kitchen table, typewriter in front of him, while Laurel kneaded bread dough. Occasionally her eyes wandered to her husband. Deep in thought, his fingers eagerly struck the keys. Laurel shaped the dough into two loaves and placed them in bread pans to rise. She started working on sweet dough for cinnamon rolls, Adam's favorite confection. "How would cinnamon rolls be for breakfast tomorrow?" she asked.

Adam didn't look up.

"I'm making cinnamon rolls," she said.

"Good." Adam still didn't look up.

Laurel kept working, a smile touching her lips. Adam was so wrapped up in his work that he hadn't heard what she'd said. It was good to see him doing what he loved. His face was flushed, and his eyes were bright. *He's happy,* she thought, realizing the light had gone out of him even before her father's death. She'd known Adam wasn't a farmer, but she had hoped he'd learn to love it. Now she realized the enormity of the sacrifice he'd made for her. Writing was part of who he was; it had been his life.

Guilt crept over Laurel. Adam had given up writing for her, and she'd encouraged him to do so. She hadn't really considered what God had wanted for him. Maybe they should have moved to Chicago; then Adam could have continued to write for the paper. *I want him to be happy, but how can he be without writing? Maybe we ought to move.*

What about Mama? She needs me. Laurel knew she couldn't leave yet; it was too soon. And she had the baby to think about. The doctor had said it was due around Christmas. They'd have to stay at least until after it was born.

Laurel studied Adam. He was completely absorbed. She'd planned on telling him about the baby right after supper, but he'd gone straight to work on his story. Once he knew, what would he say about leaving or staying? Maybe she ought to keep it to herself until he could make a decision.

She set the rolls on the warming shelf beside the bread. "Would you like more coffee?"

"No thanks." Adam pulled a sheet of paper out of the typewriter. "You want to hear what I've written so far?"

Laurel sat at the table. "Absolutely." While Adam read, she rested her face in her hands and listened. It was a wonderful piece. He started with the bear's perspective, which was thrilling and frightening, then went on to tell how the colonists came to the valley and how hate had grown between them and the homesteaders. He used the prowling bear as an illustration of the enemy prowling through the valley, seeking to destroy. He talked about Will Hasper and Ray Townsend—how the conflict had grown between them and how the two ended up hunting the bear together. The piece ended with Will's death and how his example of love and sacrifice finally brought peace to Ray Townsend and to the valley.

By the time Adam finished reading, Laurel was crying. "It's beautiful," she said, moving around the table and sitting in his lap. She hugged him around the neck and wept. "Daddy would have loved it."

Adam held her closely. "I hope the paper likes it. I want people to read it, not just because I wrote it, but because they need to hear."

Laurel kissed Adam. "I know the editor will like it, and people *will* read it."

Adam mailed the story to the *Trib* the following morning. The waiting began. He went about his work, but the question of the story's fate stayed with him. He liked what he'd written, and now that his appetite had been whetted, he wanted to do more. Running the farm was important and even fulfilling in many ways, but it didn't satisfy his need and drive to write. He'd already decided that if the paper liked the story he'd propose a series of stories. He might even write a book.

Two weeks later a special delivery letter arrived. Laurel ran to the cabbage field, waving it in the air. "Adam, this came for you. It's from the *Tribune.*"

Adam brought his hoe down, burying it in the dirt. Then he looked at Laurel and the letter in her hand. "From the *Trib*?"

"Yep. I thought you'd want to read it right away." She handed him the letter.

He pulled off his gloves, shoved them into a back pocket, and tucked his hoe under one arm. "I hope it's good news," he said, ripping open the envelope and removing a letter. Silently he read.

"Well, what does it say?"

Adam kept reading, a smile emerging. Finally, with a dumbfounded expression, he said, "They loved it! It's going to run in this coming Sunday's edition."

"How wonderful! I knew they'd like it!" Laurel hugged Adam.

"There's more. They want me to do a whole series of stories on Alaska—one every week!"

"I'm so proud of you!" She kissed him. "You can work right from home. You won't have to move!"

"Move? Who's moving? What are you talking about?"

"I just thought you missed writing so badly that maybe we ought to move back to Chicago."

"I don't want to live there. I love it here. This is where we belong."

"When I watched you writing, you looked so happy. I figured you should write even if it meant not living here."

Adam grinned. "I'm going to write, but I'm not moving!" He scanned the letter again. "We'll be fine, just fine." He paused. "I'll have to interview a lot of the old sourdoughs around her to get more stories, but I figure I'll have time to do that and to work the farm."

"I know a lot about Alaska. With all the work I've been doing on Jessie's notes, I've learned a lot. You'll have lots of material for stories. And I'd love to do some of the research for you."

"That would be perfect." Adam threw an arm around Laurel's shoulders. "We'll be a team. You can be the researcher, and I'll be the writer!" Suddenly, he lifted Laurel and twirled her around.

Laurel laughed. "Adam, put me down. I'm getting dizzy." Once steady on her feet, she looked into her husband's eyes. *Now I can tell him,* she thought, excitement building. Keeping her hands on his muscled arms, she smiled. "I'm glad you'll be able to write, especially now."

"What do you mean, especially now?"

"Oh, Adam, everything is perfect. Our life is perfect." Laurel kissed him. "I have some news."

"What?"

"I wasn't completely honest with you about what the doctor said."

"What do you mean? Is everything all right?"

Laurel laughed. "Yes. Everything's fine." She smiled coyly. "In fact, it's perfect. We're going to have a baby."

Adam looked dumbstruck for a moment. When he found his voice, he asked, "A baby? You're sure?"

Laurel nodded.

"When?"

"December." Adam wasn't reacting the way Laurel had expected. Instead of being elated, he looked worried. "I thought you'd be happy."

Adam smiled, and his face lit up. "I am. I just can't believe it. I'm going to be a father!" He pulled Laurel into his arms, kissed her, and held her against him. "A father." Adam held Laurel away from him and placed his hand on her abdomen. "A baby's growing inside you." A question touched his face. "Why didn't you tell me? You saw the doctor a couple of weeks ago."

Laurel took a breath. "I was waiting for you to hear back from the paper. I knew you wouldn't move if you found out I was pregnant."

"I never said I wanted to move."

"I know. I just thought that maybe we should. I know how much you've missed writing."

Adam smiled. "I wouldn't have gone. Remember how hard you hung on, insisting we belonged here? Well, it took me a while to see it, but you were right." His eyes moved over farmland, wild fields, forests, and mountains, then settled on their house. "I love it here. I want to raise my children here." He hugged Laurel again. "Let's tell your mother."

"No. Not yet."

"Why?"

"What if something happens?" She glanced at her stomach. "I don't think anything will, but it hasn't been very long since Daddy died, and if something did go wrong, well, it would be so hard on her."

"All right, but it's not going to be easy to keep this secret."

"It'll just be for a little while."

Adam smiled. "All right. I'll wait, but not too long, OK?"

"OK." Laurel stepped into her husband's embrace and rested her cheek against his cotton shirt. "I'm so happy. I just wish Daddy were here. He would have been such a good grandfather."

"We'll tell him all about his grandfather."

"It might be a girl."

"Maybe." He kissed the tip of Laurel's nose. "Course I wouldn't mind. If we have a little girl, she'll look just like you, and I'll be in love all over again."

Chapter 12

JEAN PLACED THREAD AND NEEDLE IN HER SEWING BASKET AND LEANED BACK in her chair. She was weary but dreaded going to bed. The nights were long and empty. At the end of each day they loomed, and Jean would put off the inevitable. She sewed, baked, or tidied the house, anything to put off going to bed.

With a sigh she finally set the sewing aside, stoked the fire, then turned down the front room lantern. Arms wrapped around her waist, she stood at the window and stared out. It was nearly eleven o'clock, but a soft glow still touched the sky above the mountains, and dusk hung over the valley. *Maybe it would be easier to sleep if it were dark,* Jean thought. *It would only seem more bleak.*

"No reason to stay up," she said and walked to her room. Pulling back the bed covers, she sat on the soft mattress. Moving as if in slow motion, she kicked off her slippers and slid between cool sheets. Pulling the blankets up under her chin, Jean stared at the ceiling, following the progress of a small spider lithely making its way toward a distant corner. She closed her eyes and listened to the house. It was quiet except for an occasional settling creak.

The familiar aching crept over her. Why couldn't she drive it back? Pain embedded itself in her chest, and the tears came once again. She knew God was near, but she felt alone. *Please Father, help me.*

Jean ran her hand over the place where Will used to lie beside her. Most nights they had snuggled together and visited quietly, talking about the children, their hopes, and their fears. Then, clasping hands, they had prayed. For twenty-three years Jean had fallen asleep with Will's arm protectively draped over her.

Now she was only half of a whole. She had no warm body beside her, no soft snoring, no gentle touch. "I miss you," she whispered, cradling Will's pillow and breathing in his scent. Already it was fading. "I'm scared. How can I live without you?"

Anger settled in, momentarily overriding the grief. "You didn't have to die. Why did you do it? You should have thought of us." Confused and ashamed, Jean buried her face in the pillow and sobbed.

She cried until she had no tears left, then stared into a brief darkness, willing sleep to come. *Lord, I don't think I can do this. I can't bear it. I feel as if it will kill me. I want to die. At least I will be free of this agony.*

Even as the thoughts came, Jean rejected them. She had to live. Her family needed her. And the pain would ease, she'd been told. "Lord, forgive me for my selfishness. Forgive me for my weak faith. Help me to be strong."

Jean's mind wandered to more practical problems. How would she keep the farm? Luke was strong and determined, but he was only seventeen. And he couldn't live at home indefinitely. He had his own life. Before Will died, Luke had expressed a desire to move on, and he'd made it clear he didn't love farming the way his father had. Jean couldn't work the farm by herself. What should she do?

"Father, show me what to do, and give me the courage and strength to do it." Wind howled under the eves, and she felt more anxious. "Give me wisdom." She snuggled into Will's pillow again and wondered what he would have done. *He wouldn't have panicked. He'd be calm and practical and sort out the choices.* She closed her eyes. "All right, I'll wait on you, Lord."

The following morning at breakfast, Luke dragged into the kitchen and plopped down at the table.

"What's wrong?" Brian asked, scooping a forkful of eggs into his mouth.

"What do you care?" Luke asked crossly.

Jean set a plate of eggs and toast on the table in front of him. "Don't be mean. Your brother just cares about you."

"Sorry. I'm tired." Luke took a bite of toast.

Jean returned to the stove. "Eat those eggs. It's the one thing we've got plenty of. The hens have been laying up a storm. Some are giving us two a day."

"It's the long days. Alex told me their chickens are doing the same thing." Luke shrugged. "Suits me. I like eggs." Picking up his fork, he rested a hand on the edge of his plate. "Sorry for bein' so crabby. You sure don't need me grumping around here making life harder on you."

"You're entitled, but it won't make you feel better."

"Yeah, I know." He yawned and stretched. "I could use a few more hours sleep though."

"We've got work to do," Brian said. "And you told me I could help."

"Yeah. I'll be weeding. You're pretty good at that. Right?" He grinned.

"Weeding? That's what we're doing?" Brian shoved the last of his toast in his mouth.

"Yep. Can't let the weeds take over."

Susie climbed down from her chair and moved around the table to Luke. "Can I weed?"

"No. You're not big enough," Brian said, suddenly acting as if weeding were an important job.

Pouting, Susie ambled back to her chair and sat down. She picked up her fork and stabbed a piece of egg. When she tried to get it to her mouth, it fell off the fork. She tried again with the same result. Finally she picked it up with her fingers and poked it into her mouth.

"I've got to go into Palmer and see if the store has any water glass," Jean said. "I could use some company." She smiled at Susie. "Would you like to come with me?"

"Yes. But what's water glass?" Susie picked up more egg with her fingers.

Jean raised an eyebrow. "You know better. Use your fork." When Susie obliged, she continued, "I use it to keep the eggs fresh."

"How does that stuff work anyway?" Luke asked.

"I'm not sure exactly. When it sets it turns into a gel, and I guess that seals the eggs so they won't spoil."

Brian leaned his elbows on the table. "Luke, can we go fishing after we're done working?"

"Sure. If there's time."

"Make the time," Jean said, carrying her plate of eggs and toast to the table and sitting. "The more fish you catch, the better. It'll help see us through the winter." Quietly she added, "We won't have as much wild meat this year with your father gone."

"I'll do more hunting," Luke said. "We'll have enough."

Jean doubted Luke could make up the difference, but she said nothing. She sipped her coffee. "We can be thankful for all God gives us. He's put a lot of food right under our noses. Why, we have good things to eat all around us—berries, vegetables, meat, and fish. All a person has to do is go out and get it."

"True, but how do we pay off the loan?" Luke asked glumly.

Jean had wondered the same thing. God could and sometimes did work in unpredictable ways. "We don't have to know how; we just have to trust God."

Luke's expression turned dark. "I've decided to sell directly to the buyers and not use the co-op."

"But—"

"I've decided."

"You've decided?"

"I don't mean to be disrespectful, but I don't see any other way."

Jean thought through their earlier discussions about the co-op, and although she had qualms about the possible consequences, she had to admit that Luke's idea was probably their only option. "All right. We'll do it your way."

She pushed her plate away, leaving most of her breakfast uneaten. "I heard Ray Townsend's been true to his word. He's been working at building good will between the colonists and the homesteaders. He's even encouraging folks here in the valley to buy produce and dairy goods from the colonists. That ought to help some."

"It's a little late," Luke said. "If we sell, it's because we've done the work." He leaned back in his chair. "I don't care what Ray Townsend does."

"I understand how you feel, but hating him will only make things worse. You've seen what it can do. And I don't believe Ray Townsend meant for your father to die."

"It's his fault, and you know it. He sent Dad out on his own, knowing that bear was a killer. How can you talk like it just *happened?*" Luke stood abruptly, nearly knocking over his chair. "I'll never forgive him. Never." He stormed out of the room.

"Ray Townsend is a bad man." Brian said. "I hate him."

Staring at the door Luke had left ajar, Jean said, "Mr. Townsend did bad things, but he's not a bad man. He's sorry for what he did, and he's trying to make everything better." She managed a smile. "God loves him, and he doesn't want us to hate him."

Although Jean said the words, she struggled for mercy. She hadn't forgiven him. She hated Ray Townsend, maybe as much as Luke did.

Brian rested his elbows on the table. "He's mean. Do I have to forgive him?"

"If you ask God to help you love him, he'll help you."

Brian puzzled over the statement, then asked, "How come Luke doesn't have to love him?"

"God wants Luke to love him, too, but right now your brother's still hurting a lot. It's not easy for him." She bent and kissed the top of Brian's head. "Now, you better get your teeth brushed and your face washed, then get on out and help your brother. He's counting on you."

"All right," Brian said, running out of the kitchen and upstairs to his room.

Jean cleaned up the morning dishes, helped Susie dress, then headed for the store. Susie skipped ahead, stopping occasionally to examine a flower or a rock. When she picked up a butterfly and accidentally crushed it, she cried and tossed it into the air. It fell to the ground. "I killed it. I didn't mean to."

"Course you didn't," Jean said. "It was an accident."

"Will God be mad at me?"

"No. He understands." Her words echoed back at her, and she knew she couldn't put off her need to forgive for too long.

When Jean and Susie walked into the store, Celeste was standing at the counter writing in a ledger. She looked up. "Hi. It's good to see you, Mrs. Hasper." She chucked Susie under the chin. "And you too, sweetie." She turned sad eyes on Jean. "How have you been?"

"All right."

Susie discovered a display of pots and pans and was soon occupied with the lids. "We're getting along." Jean scanned the nearest shelf but didn't see any water glass. "Our hens are laying like there's no tomorrow. I was hoping you'd have some water glass."

"You're not the first one to ask for it." Celeste walked out from behind the counter and headed toward the back of the store. Jean followed. Taking a jar off the shelf, she handed it to Jean. "Here you go. How does this stuff work? I've never used it. We always eat frozen eggs during the winter."

"I'm not sure exactly *how* it works. I use one pint water glass to nine pints water, stir it around in a bucket, and put clean eggs in. The liquid turns to a gel and seals the eggs, but you can't let it freeze. Hopefully our root cellar will keep them from getting too cold. You should try it. I think they taste better, more like fresh."

"Hmm, maybe I will."

A crash reverberated from the front of the store. "Oh, no. Susie." Jean ran toward the noise. Susie sat in the midst of pots and pans, pastry tins, and a shelf she'd tipped over. "I can't leave you alone for a minute," Jean said, hands on hips. She picked up the little girl and set her on her feet.

Celeste put the shelf back in place and started picking up the cookware.

Jean helped. "She's such a curious little thing. I don't know what kind of trouble she's going to get into next. I'm so sorry. I should have kept a closer eye on her."

"No trouble. I think it's pretty normal for her age."

With the display back in order, Celeste returned to the counter. She rang up the water glass. "That'll be fifty-nine cents."

Jean dug in her change purse. "It's getting more and more expensive all the time."

"Prices are going up again. I hope that doesn't mean the depression is getting worse."

Jean handed Celeste the money. "How are things out at your place? I heard you moved back in with your father."

"Yes," Celeste sighed. "Dad feels awful about what happened. He's lost most of his bluster. Sometimes I'd almost like to have him back the way he was."

Jean couldn't imagine wanting Ray Townsend like he was, but she kept her thoughts to herself and said, "This is hard on all of us. He'll find his way."

"I hope so. It's just so hard to believe he'd do the things he did. And now he's . . . so different. Different good, but also not so good. He's sad and quiet most of the time."

Jean offered a small smile. She really didn't care about Ray Townsend or how he felt, but she did care about Celeste. She asked, "How have *you* been?"

"I'm all right. Busy. Too busy. You know how it is this time of year—everything's growing like mad, plus Mrs. Granger quit. She said she couldn't work anymore, because there's just too much to do at home. She has a passle of kids. Anyway, I'm working her hours plus mine. We need to hire someone soon."

Jean's heart picked up its pace. "You're thinking of hiring someone?"

"Yes. That's what Mr. Woodson said."

Maybe this was God's answer. *Lord, should I take an outside job? Can I do what I need to do at home and work?* "How many hours would it be?" she asked.

"Oh, twenty-five, give or take."

"How much does it pay?"

"Thirty-five cents an hour." Celeste looked hard at Jean. "Why? You interested?"

"Maybe. I've been praying for an answer to our money troubles. I think I could handle twenty-five hours a week."

"What about Susie and Brian? Who'll take care of them?"

"I think Laurel would."

"She loves those two." Celeste smiled. "Mr. Woodson's home. You could go right over."

Jean considered the opportunity. Should she jump into this? She'd prayed and here was a job. *If this is not your will, Lord, I pray you'll close the door.* "I'll talk to him," she said.

"How wonderful! I'd love to work with you!" Celeste's blue eyes sparkled.

With Susie clutching her hand, Jean walked toward home. *I got the job. Now what?*

Everything had happened so quickly. She'd gone to Mr. Woodson's home, and almost before she'd said three words, he'd hired her and asked her to start the following morning.

She had so much to do—talk to Laurel, figure out a schedule, and take care of chores she couldn't do during the week. It would mean that Luke and Brian would have to do more around the house. She'd have to talk to them. It all felt a little overwhelming. "Hmm. A working woman. Who would have thought?"

When Jean approached her driveway, she spotted their Guernsey grazing alongside the road. "How did she get out?" She scanned the fence line. It looked all right, but the pasture was empty—no horses, sheep, or goats. It was empty!

"Oh Lord, now what?" Taking Susie's hand, she approached the grazing cow. "Come along now, Penny, let's get on home," she said gently. With a glance at Jean and a flick of her tail, the bovine moved further down the road. She had no intention of returning home just yet. A pair of goats chomped on greenery along the fence line, and one of the horses pulled tufts of grass up by bunches along the Jenkins's property line.

Susie held out her hand toward the cow. "Penny. Come on, Penny," she said in her sweet voice.

Jean scanned the field, searching for Luke and Brian. They were nowhere in sight. "I wonder if those two took off to do some fishing." She hefted Susie and hurried to the house, calling for Brian and Luke. They didn't answer.

Walking past the gate, she noticed it was open. "Those boys. It was probably Brian." She pushed the gate open wide, then headed into the house.

Luke and Brian weren't anywhere inside. Setting Susie in her crib, she said, "You be a good girl," and handed her a doll. "I'll be right back. You play with your baby."

Leaving the house, she ran for the barn. Grabbing a pail, she filled it with grain and headed back to the road. "This ought to work," she said, walking cautiously toward the goats. With a bleat, they dodged out of her way and settled into another batch of tender willows. With a sigh, she changed her target and approached the cow. "All right, Penny, you love grain. Come on now." She shook the pail. Grain rattled. Penny glanced at Jean and kept munching as she meandered away.

Jean stopped. *How am I going to get them back inside the pasture? Grain just isn't tempting enough when they've got fresh clover and tender grass.* Pretending to ignore the animals, she walked nonchalantly down the road. Maybe if she got past them, she could herd them back down the driveway and into the pasture. But the animals were onto her, and each time she got close, they simply walked on.

Her frustration growing, Jean looked up and down the road and across the pasture to the Jenkins's. She needed help, but who? Tom and Adele had gone to Anchorage. Robert was in town with his family. Where were the boys? "Luke!" she yelled. No answer. "Luke!" Still no answer.

Jean thought a long while, then decided that the only answer was to climb through the fence and walk beyond the animals inside the pasture, then climb back over and herd them home. She set the bucket of grain on the ground, pulled the back of her skirt between her legs, and tucked it into the front waistband. Pushing down on the bottom fence wire with her foot and lifting the middle one, she stepped through. Her skirt caught on a barb. Trying to free it, she pricked her finger. "Ouch!" Blood oozed. Putting it to her mouth, she suppressed growing aggravation. "Lord, I need your help," she said, freeing herself. She walked a little way out into the field, passed the animals, then with trepidation climbed back through the fence, this time without injury.

Breaking off a willow branch, she walked toward the animals, swinging the spindly limb back and forth. The animals turned and walked ahead, occasionally grabbing a mouthful of greenery. As they approached the end of the driveway, Jean wondered how she would turn them.

Maybe the grain will work now, she thought and picked up the bucket. Shaking it, she said, "Come on now. Let's get on home." The cow swung her big head around, looked at Jean, and moved past the drive. A goat leapt over a clump of berry bushes and started munching. The other one followed. Swishing away mosquitoes with its tail, the horse stopped and shook its hide.

Pesky insects were devouring Jean's bare legs. She could feel itching welts rise, but she ignored them and walked up to the gelding, running her hand down his back and tempting him with grain. He buried his nose in the bucket and munched, then happily followed Jean down the drive. She walked through the gate, and the horse followed.

"That's one," she said with some satisfaction. She headed for the road only to find that the rest of the animals had continued their wandering. She walked back down the drive and stopped at the road. "What am I going to do? I can't just leave them out," she said, feeling the sting of tears.

She sank to the ground and sat leaning against a post. "Will, I need you." Resting her arms on bent knees, she allowed the tears to come. "I can't run this farm without you."

A pickup backfired, and Jean looked up to see it and the animals heading her way. Quickly wiping away the tears, she stood, hoping for help until she saw that the driver was Ray Townsend. She tensed. He was the last person she wanted to see.

He stopped and clumsily climbed out of the truck with his bum leg. "Afternoon, Mrs. Hasper. Seems you could use a hand."

"Someone left the gate open, and the animals got out," she said, watching her livestock amble past.

Ray hobbled toward her and stopped, resting his weight on one crutch. His leg was still in a cast. He studied the livestock. "Do you have grain? Usually all you have to do is let them know you've got it, and they come running."

Jean lifted the bucket. "I've tried that," she said caustically. "The only one interested was the horse."

"Hmm. Usually works." He scanned the bushes alongside the road. "Guess there's too much good stuff out here to eat." Ray tottered back to his truck. "I s'pose I could stand here and keep them from getting by while you drive them back this way." He leaned against his truck. "Wish I could be of more help."

Jean clambered through the fence, then climbed back through when she got ahead of the animals. Breaking off another willow branch, she herded them toward Mr. Townsend. The cow and sheep ambled along and automatically turned in at the drive. The goats weren't ready to settle down and tried to dart past Ray. He managed to head them off by extending one of his crutches, and they finally trotted down the driveway.

"Climb in," he said. "I'll give you a ride."

"I'll walk." Jean barely glanced at him.

Ray climbed into the truck and followed her, then helped her guide the animals into the pasture. Leaning on the gate, they watched Penny graze, seemingly content to be home.

Ray turned and looked out over the farm, his eyes wandering from the house to the barn and over the fields. "This is a lot for a woman to take care of."

"I have my son and Adam, and the neighbors," Jean said curtly.

Her sharp tone didn't put off Ray. He continued pleasantly. "You've been on my mind. I've been wondering how you're faring."

"We're fine." Jean didn't want to have a conversation with this man. "Thank you for your help. I'd better get inside."

"I wanted to tell you again how sorry I am—about everything." Ray rubbed the back of his neck. "I want to help. I'm sure you could use an extra hand."

Jean eyed Ray's bum leg. "Doesn't look like you're in any condition to help, Mr. Townsend."

"I'll only have it a couple more weeks, and it doesn't keep me from swinging an axe and doing odd jobs. I'm pretty good around the house. I know a little about plumbing and carpentry. I can repair most anything. And after this cast comes off, I can do more."

Jean needed the help, especially now that she'd taken the job at the store, but she wasn't about to let Ray Townsend soothe his conscience by working for her. "We're not your responsibility Mr. Townsend, but thank you for the offer." Barely able to look him in the eye, she added, "We don't need your help."

Ray didn't look as if he believed her. "All right then. Still, if you find yourself needing anything, let me know." He hesitated. "Will asked me to look after you."

Jean felt as if a jolt of electricity had hit her. Will had asked this man to help?

"Celeste said you'd be working at the store, so I 'spect you'll have less time to put in here at home."

"How did you know about the job? I just got it."

"I stopped by to say hello to Celeste before coming out here. I don't think she meant to gossip."

"Of course not. I was just wondering how you knew. I barely know." Jean managed a smile, and Ray returned the gesture. Uncomfortable, she started for the house. Jean didn't want to be friends with Ray Townsend, but not wishing to be rude, she stopped and looked at him. "Thank you for your help," she said in a dismissive tone and continued on.

"Anytime. I was glad to do it. Just remember, I'm here if you need me."

"We'll be fine," Jean said, not bothering to look at him as she started up the steps. She didn't want Ray Townsend to be kind. And even if it were true that Will had asked him to help, it made no difference.

Chapter 13

Pastor Sunderson closed his Bible and left the pulpit while the choir filed onto the stage. Mrs. Hudson, the director, took her place in front of the group, her broad hips swaying from side to side as she walked. She turned and smiled at the congregation. "Please turn to page 325 in your hymnal and join us in worship while we sing 'It Is Well with My Soul.'"

Jean nearly groaned out loud. She wasn't sure she could get through the song. It had been written in 1873 by Horatio Spafford after his wife and three children perished at sea. *How could he trust after losing his entire family?*

Mrs. Hudson and the choir began, and the congregation joined in. "When peace like a river attendeth my way, when sorrows like sea billows roll; whatever my lot, thou hast taught me to say, it is well, it is well with my soul. It is well, it is well, it is well with my soul."

The song tore at Jean's heart, and she couldn't stop the tears. She tried to sing, but sorrow choked off the words. *Lord, I need that kind of peace. I feel like I'm falling apart.*

The song closed, and the minister returned to the podium. "Such a beautiful song, written by a man who clearly knew his Savior." He opened his Bible. "We read in Isaiah 66:12 and 13, *'For thus saith the Lord, Behold, I will extend peace to her like a river, and the glory of the Gentiles like a flowing stream: then shall ye suck, ye shall be borne upon her sides, and be dandled upon her knees. As one whom his mother comforteth, so will I comfort you; and ye shall be comforted in Jerusalem.'*"

He looked up. "Like a mother comforts, so I will comfort you. What a picture of tenderness. We are the Father's children. He will hold us close and carry our burdens."

Jean knew God offered comfort, but she could only feel grief. His promised peace seemed out of reach. She fought to listen to the minister's words.

"God is here with you, right beside you. Reach out and take his hand. He will pull you to his side."

Jean visualized the Lord standing beside her, and she felt a touch of peace and quiet. If only she could hang on to it.

The minister finished his sermon, then closed in prayer. Jean still felt the touch of God. She was afraid to open her eyes. The world's reality waited for her. If only she could hold it off, even for just a few moments.

The congregation was dismissed. Susie wiggled, then turned and hugged her mother around the neck. Jean was forced to open her eyes, but God's presence remained, and a gentle voice whispered to her. *You are not alone. I am here, always and forever.*

The voice had seemed almost audible. Jean glanced around to see if someone had spoken, but Laurel and Adam were visiting with another couple, and Luke and Brian were already heading for the aisle. No one could have said what she heard.

The words felt like salve on the raw aching place inside. Jean knew peace would replace her loneliness—maybe not today, but one day. She kissed Susie's cheek. "I love you."

"I love you," the little girl said and tightened her hold.

With a smile, Jean eased her off her lap and stood, then sidestepped toward the aisle.

Ray Townsend's eyes caught hers. He smiled, but his eyes remained sad. Jean quickly looked away. She wasn't ready to be cordial or friendly and hurried down the aisle, hoping to avoid him.

Luke waited for her at the back of the church. He nodded at Ray Townsend. "What's he doing here? He shouldn't be allowed in the door."

"Hush. Someone will hear you," Jean whispered.

"I don't care. Everyone knows what kind of man he is."

"No. Only God knows, and it's none of our business."

"None of our business?" Luke asked incredulously. "He killed my father, your husband."

Jean gripped her son's arm and looked straight at him. She hated being forced to defend Ray Townsend, but she knew for Luke's sake she must. "He didn't kill your father. It was an accident. And whoever Ray Townsend is or isn't has nothing to do with us." She took Susie's hand and headed for the door.

Luke followed. "If I had my way, he'd be the one dead. I don't understand a God who lets a good man die while someone like Ray Townsend lives." He spit out the name *Townsend* with venom.

"God's ways are not our ways," Jean said. She'd heard those words so many times and believed them, but now they sounded empty.

She stepped onto the porch and into the July sunshine. The minister grasped her hand. "So good to see you this morning, Mrs. Hasper." He smiled at Susie. "And you, too, young lady." Susie flashed him a bright smile. He turned warm eyes on Jean. "Remember, if there's anything we can do, please let us know."

Jean nodded and forced a smile. "I will. Thank you, Pastor Sunderson."

He continued to hold her hand. "The pain of losing a life partner can feel unbearable. I remember when my father passed away—it was extremely hard on my mother. She seemed lost for a very long while. Please don't expect too much too quickly. It takes time."

"I'll try not to." Jean didn't want to talk about it. She just wanted to get away, to run home and hide from the world. She pulled her hand loose and started down the steps.

Luke took his mother's arm. "Me and Laurel and Brian are here for you. We'll help."

"I know. Of course . . ." She hesitated and managed a smirk. "I hope you don't help the way you did when all the livestock got out."

"That was Brian's fault, although I admit I should have checked."

Jean patted his arm. "I'm only teasing. Things happen."

Miram Dexter and her bosomy mother and squat father walked past them. Mrs. Dexter nodded. Miram slowed her steps and offered Jean a smile. Hitching up her glasses, she said, "Nice to see you, Mrs. Hasper."

"Good to see you, Miram. I hope everything's well at your home."

Miram shrugged and hurried to keep up with her parents.

"I worry about that girl. She seems lonely," Jean said, watching her.

Laurel joined her mother and Luke. "Who, Miram? I think she is. Mrs. Dexter is more of a jailer than a mother. Poor Miram can barely turn around without her mother being there. And I don't know what's going to happen between her and Ed Ketchum. Mrs. Dexter doesn't like him, and she's doing everything she can to keep them apart."

"Poor girl."

Nothing was said for a moment, then Laurel asked, "Mama, would you like to have supper at our place?"

Jean felt weary. She loved spending time with Adam and Laurel, but today she needed the comfort of home. "Maybe some other time. I'd really just like to go home."

"Are you feeling all right?"

"I'm fine."

"Well, how about if we come to your house? I'll do the cooking."

"I'd like that."

Adam walked up, and Laurel tucked her arm into his. "Adam, we'll be having supper at Mama's, but I'm doing the cooking."

"Sounds terrific," Adam said.

Laurel looked up at her husband, her eyes full of joy. She was absolutely beaming.

Jean studied her. "Something's up. What is it?"

"Nothing," Laurel said, her smile bright. "We just want to spend time with you." She kissed the tip of Susie's nose. "We'll go on home and change, then be over. I'll bring supper fixings." Arm in arm, she and Adam sauntered toward their truck.

Jean spotted Ray Townsend striding toward her and looked for a way of escape. She couldn't find one, so she smiled and greeted him.

"Mrs. Hasper, I wondered if you'd thought any more about my helping out. As you can see, I got the cast off and my leg's nearly good as new." He slapped it as if to prove his point. "I'm ready for any kind of work."

Luke stepped between his mother and Ray. "We don't need your help. Stay away from our place." He grabbed his mother's arm and led her away.

Although unhappy at her son's disrespectful behavior, Jean didn't know what to say. She glanced back at Ray. He stood with Celeste and Robert, his eyes grieving. Jean could feel his pain, and her mind reeled at the injustice done to him. How would it feel to be accused of being a murderer if the charge weren't true? She stopped, and Luke's hand lost its grip. "We're not going to behave this way."

Luke gaped at her. "What way?"

"I understand your anger, but you're a Hasper, and disrespect is not acceptable. And I don't need you speaking for me or making decisions about the farm, including who works for me and who doesn't." Taking another quick look at Ray, she realized he *needed* to help them. He'd taken on the burden of Will's death. Maybe it was his fault, but he hadn't decided Will should die. It was Will who'd done that. "It must be awful to think you're responsible for someone dying," she said quietly.

Jean looked at Luke. "Ray wants to make amends. He feels responsible and obligated to us. I think we ought to let him help. It might make it easier for him to put this awful situation behind him." Jean couldn't believe what she was saying.

"Why should we care how *he* feels?"

"Because Jesus would. And because your father *asked* him to look out for us." Jean headed for Ray.

Luke walked beside her. "What are you doing? We don't need him. And I can't believe Dad would ask anything of that man."

"Well, he did." Jean stopped and looked intently at Luke. "I know you're hurting. So am I. And so is Ray Townsend. We have to forgive. There's no other way." She hesitated. "Luke, you've got to let it go."

"You're saying you've forgiven him? Just like that?"

Jean didn't know the answer. She wanted to say yes. Finally she said, "No. I can't say that, but I see now that I must begin to forgive and that God will help me. However, he can't help if I'm not willing to take the first step." She looked at Ray, now seeing his torment clearly. "I have to begin by reaching out to Mr. Townsend. He's suffering too."

Luke's harsh gaze settled on the homesteader. "Him? I don't think he has a conscience. How could he be suffering?"

"I understand how you feel. I felt the same way until just this morning. But I'm beginning to see, and I'm taking him up on his offer."

"I'm not having any part of it." Luke folded his arms over his chest. "I can't forgive him."

Her voice gentle, Jean said, "That's your choice. But I have to do what God's asking of me." With that, she walked toward Ray, still uncertain just what was happening but knowing that God was leading.

Celeste said, "Hello."

Jean put on her warmest smile. "It's nice to see you outside of work. Seems that's the only time we see each other these days. Maybe you and Robert can come for supper some time." She looked at Robert. "We've missed you."

"The feeling's mutual. But you know how it is this time of year. Work, work, work." He leveled serious eyes on Jean. "How are you?"

"I'm all right. You? I've been wondering how you've been faring." It had been only six months since Robert and Laurel split, and although she'd heard Robert and Celeste were seeing each other, she'd wondered if he'd fully recovered from Laurel's rejection.

"I'm fine. And my family's well. As you know, it's still a challenge trying to find buyers for produce, but sales are picking up." He linked arms with Celeste and looked at Ray Townsend. "Sir, I was wondering if you and Celeste would come out to our place for lunch? My mother's a good cook. She said there's plenty, and she'd like the company."

"Thanks for the invite, but I don't think today would work. I've got a horse that needs shoeing and a fence that's down. Maybe another time."

"Can I go?" Celeste asked.

"Sure," Ray said. "Go and have a good time."

"Thanks." Celeste gave her father a kiss. "It was nice seeing you again, Mrs. Hasper."

Robert nodded, and with Celeste on his arm, the two walked down the road.

Ray and Jean stood alone. "It's a nice day," Ray finally said, scanning the blue sky.

"Yes, very nice. Even seems the mosquitoes have gone in search of shade." She smiled. "We'd best keep to the sunny places." Clearing her throat, she continued, "I was thinking about your offer. We could use the help. With me working and it being the middle of summer and all . . ."

"I'd be pleased to," Ray cut in. "Anything I can do I will. I'll be there first thing in the morning."

"That's not necessary. Just come by whenever it suits you. I don't want to cut into your time. I know you've got plenty of work around your place."

"Thank you," Ray said, shaking her hand.

Jean winced inwardly at his gratitude. "It's me who should thank you."

"No, ma'am. That's not right." Ray looked at the ground.

He reminded Jean of a guilt-ridden child.

"I owe you." Ray removed his hat. "Well, I'll see you tomorrow," he said and walked away.

Jean watched him go, thinking that his step looked a little lighter and realizing she wasn't angry with Ray Townsend. *Thank you, Father,* she prayed, knowing the healing had begun.

"Mama, you stay put," Laurel said, clearing away dishes and setting them in the sink.

"You've been bursting to tell me something all afternoon. What's going on?" Jean asked.

Laurel grabbed plates out of the cupboard, then cut into a rhubarb pie she'd baked. "Nothing." She slid a piece onto a plate. "I hope you like this. It's my first try all on my own."

"Looks delicious." Jean pricked the crust with her fork. "Perfect crust."

"Looks good," Brian said, leaning back on his chair and lifting the front legs off the floor.

"Brian, stop that," Jean said.

He let the chair drop and reached for pie when Laurel carried two plates to the table. Laurel moved them out of his reach. "You wait. These are for Mama and Adam." She returned to the counter for two more plates. One she set in front of Brian and the other she handed to Luke. Grabbing the last two pieces, she put one in front of Susie and kept the last one for herself.

Jean looked around the table at her family. "This has been a nice afternoon." Her eyes settled on Laurel. "Thank you for doing the cooking. What a treat."

Laurel set her fork on her plate. "I love being here. Sometimes I miss this house. Daddy used to . . ." Laurel stopped. "I'm sorry. I don't want to upset you."

"No. We should talk about him. I mean, I think about him all the time. We had a wonderful life."

The room was silent. No one knew what to say. Finally Laurel said, "I think we should lighten the mood. Adam and I have some news." She glanced at her young husband and smiled.

"News?" Jean asked.

"Yep." Laurel waited a moment, then blurted, "We're going to have a baby."

For a moment no one said anything, then Brian exclaimed, "A baby! Will it be a boy? If it is, I can take him fishing like Luke takes me fishing?"

"We won't know if it's a boy or a girl until it's born," Laurel said with a laugh. Her eyes settled on her mother. "Mama? You haven't said anything."

Jean's emotions were all mixed up. A grandchild. It was wonderful news. But Will would never get to see it. She forced a smile. "I'm so happy for you."

"I still can't believe it! A baby!" Laurel rested her hand on her abdomen. "I'm not showing yet, but soon."

Brian looked at Laurel's stomach. "Is it inside you?"

"Uh-huh."

"Where?"

"In my stomach."

"How did it get in there? I can't see it."

"It's a miracle from God," Jean said. "And you can't see it because it's very tiny right now. But it's going to grow and grow until it's time to be born. By then Laurel's stomach will be very big. You remember before Susie was born, don't you?"

"Kind of."

Jean leaned on the table. "When is it due?"

"Around Christmas."

"What a wonderful time to be born." Jean walked around the table and embraced her daughter. "I'm thrilled. I can hardly wait to be a grandmother."

A knock sounded at the door.

"I'll get it," Luke said, walking to the door and opening it.

Ray Townsend stood on the porch holding a salmon in one hand.

Luke didn't say anything at first, then asked, "What do you want?"

Jean hurried to the door. "Hello, Mr. Townsend. I thought you weren't going to be here until tomorrow?"

Hefting the salmon, he said, "Well, I caught two big ones and thought you might like one."

"I catch plenty of salmon," Luke said, his voice hard.

Jean shouldered past her son and took the fish. "Thank you for thinking of us. Would you like to come in?"

Shock moved across Luke's face, then he stormed out of the room.

"I'd better not. I brought you some wood. Where would you like it unloaded?"

Jean peered past the big man to his pickup piled with split fir. "You didn't have to do that. We've got enough for now."

"Well, I had it around and figured a person can't have too much firewood. Winter will be here before you know it."

"Well, I guess by the woodshed would be best."

"All right then." Ray stepped off the porch and headed for his truck.

"Thank you," Jean said, not sure how she felt about this man and wondering if she'd done the right thing when she'd asked for his help. Seeing him again reminded her of how Will had died and how Ray Townsend had insulted and mistreated the colonists. She closed the door and turned back to her family.

"What's that's all about?" Laurel asked.

"Oh, nothing really. Mr. Townsend offered to help with the chores, and I think it's a good idea. We could use the help." She looked at Adam. "That way, Adam can spend more time on his writing."

"I thought you blamed him."

"I did, but . . ." Jean took a breath. "The time for that is over. He blames himself and needs to help us."

Laurel poked her fork into her pie. "In a way it was his fault."

"We can't change what's happened," Jean said firmly, walking back to the table. "We can only do what's right."

"I don't hate him anymore. I think he looks sad," Brian said.

Jean put an arm around her son. "He is, Brian. He's very sad."

Chapter 14

A HORN BLASTED FROM OUTSIDE. "THEY'RE HERE!" BRIAN SHOUTED AND dashed out the door. Susie followed.

Jean didn't want to go to the community picnic, but her family was counting on it. Wishing there was some way to avoid taking part, she gathered a waiting picnic basket and blanket.

Adam stepped into the kitchen. "You ready? Looks like we've got good weather."

"To tell you the truth, Adam, I don't feel much like going."

"You don't have to."

"Yes, I do. Brian and Susie are counting on it. And they deserve a happy day. They haven't had many lately."

Adam draped an arm around her shoulders and gave her a squeeze. "You deserve one too." He took the basket and headed for the door. "The only time you get out is when you're working at the store. It's time you had a little fun."

"I don't know about fun, but I'll try."

"Didn't see Luke. Is he coming?"

"Yes, but he'll be late. He and Alex went fishing."

The festival was being held at the fairgrounds. When Adam pulled up, people were already crowding around booths, hawkers called to passers-by, and the air smelled of frankfurters, popcorn, and cotton candy. It felt like a fair.

Brian ran ahead. "I heard they're having fireworks!" he called over his shoulder. "I love fireworks!"

Her eyes alight, Susie tugged on her mother's hand and tried to hurry her. When she spotted a clown juggling balls, she ran to join the children gathered around him and watched in fascination.

Jean couldn't help but smile. "Childhood is a precious time, full of wonder and discovery."

"I never thought much about what it means to be a child," Laurel said, resting her hand on her stomach. "Not until now, that is. It's hard to believe I'm going to have a baby." She smoothed her cotton dress over her slightly rounded abdomen. "I'm already showing."

Jean eyed her stomach. "You sure are."

"How long before I feel it move?"

"Oh, it'll be a while yet. I don't think I felt any of you until I was at least four months along. The first time you feel the flutter of life is like nothing you've ever experienced. It's an incredible joy when you feel your child move. Your father . . ." She stopped abruptly, her eyes tearing. "Your father was more excited than I was when we learned you were on the way. You and Adam have so much ahead of you."

Laurel caught her mother's hand and held it. "I hope we're as good of parents as you and Daddy."

Adam picked up a ball from the ground and tossed it in the air. "I don't know anything about being a father."

"It'll come to you," Jean said. "We all begin with love and learn as we go."

"The waiting is hard," Laurel said. "It seems like an eternity until the baby gets here."

Adam tossed the ball to a nearby youngster. "For both of us."

"The time will pass more quickly than you think." A breeze caught at Jean's hair, blowing it across her eyes. She brushed it aside. "You're looking good, Laurel. How are you feeling?"

"Fine—still a little queasy in the mornings, but it's not so bad." She leaned against Adam. "Adam's so good to me. If I'm having a bad morning, he lets me stay in bed and brings me tea and toast." She watched Susie, who was still mesmerized by the clown's antics. "I'm a little nervous—about having the baby. I know how to take care of it, seeing that I was the oldest of five, but the actual birth—well, I'm not sure what to expect."

"Every mother's nervous. It's not easy, but you'll do fine. You're strong. I'll stay with you, and Dr. Donovan knows what he's doing. He'll see to you." She smiled. "When it's all over, you and Adam will have a beautiful baby."

Susie ran up to her mother. "Can I have some?" She pointed at a vendor selling cotton candy.

"After lunch, sweetie. I don't want you to ruin your appetite."

"Why don't we get a place over by the corrals?" Laurel suggested. "The rodeo's going to be there. That way we can eat and watch the contest at the same time."

"Sounds good to me," Adam said.

"Those trees will be a perfect spot." Laurel set off toward the small grove of birch.

"I'll get Brian." Adam headed for a game booth where the boy stood, gazing at a man tossing darts.

"Thanks." Jean retrieved Susie and followed Laurel.

"This is just right," Laurel said spreading out two blankets beneath the trees. "We can see all the activities from here."

Jean set the picnic basket down and sat while Susie headed for the corrals. "Susie, you stay here with us."

The blonde youngster wandered back reluctantly and sat beside her mother. Soon, having forgotten about the animals, she picked wild-flowers growing in the grass alongside the blanket.

With Adam close behind, Brian ran for the corrals. He pressed his face between the fence boards and stared inside the corral. The rodeo was about to begin. Onlookers crowded around the small arena, horses were rounded up and saddled, and steers were moved into a small enclosure.

"Brian, you get back here," Jean called. He acted as if he hadn't heard. "I don't like him over there. He's liable to get hurt."

"Adam's with him. He'll keep a close eye out," Laurel said, sitting beside her mother. She leaned back on her hands. "Whew. It's warm. I'm glad for the shade." Mosquitoes buzzed around her head and she slapped at them. "Seems the mosquitoes like it too."

A man walked by, leading two horses. Susie pointed. "Those are pretty. Can I ride one?" She ran after the man, blonde curls bouncing.

"Susie," Jean said sharply. Scrambling to her feet, she captured the little girl. "You stay with us. I don't want you getting hurt."

"Mama, she's fine," Laurel said. "She wasn't going to get under the animal's feet. She's been around livestock since the day she was born. She knows how to stay out of harm's way."

"She's too little to know better."

Laurel plucked a flower and twirled the stem between her fingers. "Mama," she began hesitantly, "lately you've been extra protective of Brian and Susie. You seem to worry a lot, maybe too much."

"So now that you're a married woman, you think you know better than I how to raise my children?" Jean snapped.

"I didn't mean it that way."

Jean stood, and with her lips pressed tightly, watched Brian and Adam.

Pushing herself to her feet, Laurel said, "I just think you're being a little over-careful. That's all."

Jean felt unreasonable anger and hurt. She swung around and glowered at Laurel. "You haven't lost a son and a husband. Maybe when you do, you'll know what it's like to be afraid of losing someone else."

Almost immediately, shame and regret fell over Jean. Her eyes filling, she said, "I'm sorry. I didn't mean that. I don't ever want you to know what I'm feeling."

Laurel pulled her mother into her arms. "I'm sorry too. I should be more understanding. Of course you're afraid. I would be too."

Jean pressed her face into Laurel's shoulder and wept. After a few moments she stepped back, wiping away tears. "I hate how I am. I just can't seem to shake my grief. If I'm not sad, I'm angry. And I know I worry too much." She glanced at Susie, who played quietly with her doll. "I keep the children in sight all the time. If they're gone at all, I worry something will happen to them. I even worry about you and Adam and the baby."

She pressed her back against the cool bark of a birch and gazed up through its limbs. A breeze touched teardrop-shaped leaves, setting them to dancing. "You think God's watching over and taking care of the people you love, then something awful happens and you realize no one is safe."

She shook her head. "I don't know why any of this happened. Your father and I always lived our lives loving God and doing our best to serve him." She blinked away fresh tears. "It was foolish to believe nothing bad could touch us." Jean's eyes wandered to her two youngest. "I guess that's why I'm scared. I know terrible things happen."

"Mama, God's still here, watching and caring."

"Yes, but he allows things . . . things that hurt."

Laurel stripped away a piece of white bark from the tree. "I wish I knew all the answers. I don't. But you've always taught me, and I believe it, that he does what is best."

Jean nodded. "I know, but that doesn't change how I feel. I don't like what God's allowed. I want my family back. I just don't understand any of it." She sniffled and wiped at her tears. Trying to smile, she added, "I don't know what's wrong with me today."

Laurel rested her forehead against her mother's. "I remember when Justin died, you told me that life is like the blink of an eye when you compare it to eternity. And eternity awaits us all. We'll see Daddy and Justin again."

Jean nodded. She wished she could feel the reality of the words, but they seemed to drift away like a leaf caught by a breeze and carried out of reach. She looked at her daughter and saw the same steadiness she'd known in Will. "You remind me of your father. He was always the strong one."

"Mom! Guess what!" Brian yelled, running up to her. "I'm gonna ride a bull!"

"What?"

"Not a bull," Adam corrected, running after the boy. "A calf."

"It's almost like riding a bull," Brian said.

"I don't understand. Why is he riding a calf?"

"He wanted to sign up, so I told him we'd ask you. They have calf riding for the kids."

"Oh, I don't know. It doesn't sound safe."

"Mom, I'm not a baby! I'm eight and a half years old. Lots of other boys are riding."

"You could get hurt."

A long pause of silence followed, then Laurel said, "It's all in fun. I don't think you have to worry. The calves aren't that big."

Jean envisioned her son lying in the dirt, injured. She couldn't bear the thought. But if what Laurel said was true, she needed to let go of

Brian a little, let him experience life. Taking a deep breath, she said, "All right. I guess it wouldn't hurt." She bent and held his face in her hands. "You hang on tight. Don't let that critter buck you off."

Brian grinned. "I'll stick to him just like glue." Without another word, he turned and raced to the registry table.

The rodeo started with calf roping and bareback riding, and then it was the boys' turn to try their hand at calf riding. Jean joined Laurel and Celeste at the fence. Susie stood beside her mother, her doll in one arm. Adam, Luke, and Robert were with Brian, giving him last-minute tips.

Two boys went ahead of Brian. The first managed to stay on until the whistle sounded and bailed off without incident. The other took a hard fall but quickly stood up and dusted dirt from his britches.

Brian climbed aboard, and Jean gripped the fence. "I shouldn't have let him do this."

Laurel gave her mother a one-armed hug. "He'll be fine."

Celeste and Robert joined them. "He's a natural," Robert said. "He'll do great."

"I don't understand why males have to do things like this," Celeste said.

A gate opened, and Brian, atop a black whiteface, shot out of the chute. He gripped a thick length of rope, and his legs hugged the animal. The calf twisted and jumped, but Brian held on.

"Go Brian!" Robert yelled. Glancing at Adam, he said, "That's a hard-bucking calf."

Her stomach churning, Jean watched as Brian's legs flew away from the animal and he slid to one side. "Hang on! Hang on, Brian!"

Clinging to the rope, Brian managed to stay with the animal another second; then the calf leapt up, landing straight-legged, head down. Brian flew over the calf's shoulders, still clinging to the rope. One more buck and the rope came loose. Brian landed with a hard thud.

The calf bucked away. Brian didn't move.

"Oh, my Lord!" Jean said.

Ray Townsend strode across the arena and kneeled beside Brian. He rested a hand on the boy's chest.

Adam, Robert, and Luke catapulted over the fence. Jean squeezed between the railings.

Brian wasn't moving.

Running to her son, Jean prayed, "Please, no, Father. Let him be all right." She pushed through the onlookers and fell to her knees beside Brian. He was breathing, but his eyes were closed. "Brian! Brian! Can you hear me?"

At first he didn't respond. Then his eyes fluttered open. Gazing at his mother, he asked, "Did I make it?"

Everyone laughed with relief. "Almost," Ray said. "It was a good ride."

Brian pushed himself up on his elbows. "What happened? How come everyone's standing around?"

"You were knocked out," Jean said, bracing his back. "Are you all right?"

Brian looked at himself. "I think so."

Ray grabbed one of Brian's arms. "Up you go."

Luke took the other, and glaring at Ray, said, "I've got him." He hefted his brother to his feet.

Brian stood completely still for a moment while he regained his bearings.

"You sure you're all right?" Jean asked.

"Yeah." He dusted off his pants. "Hey, that was a pretty good ride, huh?"

Relieved, but sick to her stomach, Jean said, "We're going home."

"Home? Why?" Brian asked. "I want to watch the rest of the rodeo."

Jean took his hand. "No. We're going home."

"Mama, he's fine," Laurel said.

"Maybe. He was unconscious. He needs to rest." She pressed her hand to her mouth. "I have to go, and Brian and Susie are coming with me." She met Laurel's eyes, and despite the disappointment she saw, she'd made up her mind. "Enough is enough."

"I'll take you," Ray volunteered. "That way the rest of the family won't have to miss the festivities. I've seen a lot of these in my day. It won't hurt me none to miss it."

"No. I'll take her," Luke cut in.

"I can walk. I don't want any of you to leave."

"Mrs. Hasper, I was just about ready to go anyway," Ray said. "It's no trouble."

Jean wasn't comfortable around Ray Townsend, but to refuse him would be rude. "All right then."

"I'll get the car and be right back. Meet you over there." He pointed at a field just beyond the paddocks.

As soon as Ray was out of earshot, Luke started in. "Why not let me take you home?"

"It's not necessary. You heard Mr. Townsend; he said he was leaving anyway."

"How can you spend a minute with him?" He glanced at Celeste. "I . . . I'm sorry, but . . ."

Celeste said nothing, but her eyes revealed her hurt.

"I'm riding home with him. Who I ride with or don't ride with is no concern of yours."

Ray Townsend pulled his car in beside a truck and trailer. He honked, then climbed out and waited. *Why am I doing this?* he wondered. *I'm just making things harder on her. Jean Hasper hates me. I don't blame her.* He glanced at Luke, who was still fuming. *And Luke hates me even more.*

Holding Susie's hand, Jean crossed the field. Brian ambled along behind. Ray nodded at her. Although he'd told himself he only cared about her because she was a widow in need, he couldn't help but notice her good looks—hair the color of ginger, soft hazel eyes, and a slender build. The fire in her eyes had dimmed, but he remembered how they could blaze.

He wished he were more like Will Hasper—even-tempered, kind, and compassionate. If he had been, Will Hasper would probably still be alive, and the light in Jean Hasper's eyes would still be there.

Ray admired Will Hasper and had decided he'd do everything he could to be more like him. Now, with Christ living in him, he had hope that such a change was possible. He'd promised himself that he'd never be mean-spirited or raise his voice to anyone again.

"Climb on in the back, kids," he said, opening the door.

Brian leaped onto the seat and bounced. "Wow, this is soft!"

Ray held the front door for Jean, and she slid onto the seat, careful to tuck her skirt in out of the way of the door. Susie climbed onto her lap. Brian was still bouncing. "Brian, stop that! Sit down and behave yourself."

Brian sat, but his eyes roamed over the lush interior. "I've never been in a car like this. Did it cost a lot of money?"

Ray settled his large frame behind the wheel. "No. Didn't cost much. I won . . ." He stopped. He'd nearly told the boy he'd won it in a poker game. That's all he needed—for Jean Hasper to know he'd been a gambler too. "Uh, a friend of mine sold it to me cheap."

"He must be a good friend," Jean said.

"Yeah, he is." Ray started the engine, already feeling guilty over lying about the car. Then he quietly said, "I won it in a poker game." He kept his eyes straight ahead.

Jean said nothing.

They bounced across the field, then pulled onto a gravel road. Ray glanced over his shoulder at Brian. "That was a good ride you had today. You hung on right up to the last. It was a tough calf to ride."

"Yeah? You think so?"

"You seem to have a real knack for it."

"I do?" Brian asked incredulously, then smiled and leaned on the back of the front seat. "I figure I'll try it again next year. I betcha I stay on 'til the whistle."

"I'll bet you do," Ray agreed.

With a sidelong glance at Ray, Jean said, "I don't know that you'll be doing any more riding."

"Ah, Mom."

She glanced at Ray. "Thank you for taking us home."

"No problem. I'm glad to. It's the least I can do." He gripped the steering wheel. "I mean . . . well . . . it should be me that's dead."

"No one should be dead, Mr. Townsend, and you don't need to keep apologizing."

Ray closed his mouth, embarrassed. He knew he should stop telling her how badly he felt but couldn't seem to help himself. Too many people still believed he didn't care about what happened. "Well, I am sorry. Just want you to know that. And I want you to know I've turned over a new leaf. I'm not the same man I was."

Jean looked at him. "That's good. The man I knew wasn't very nice."

Ray kept his eyes on the road. He hadn't expected her to throw barbs. Of course, he deserved it.

"I think you're nice," Brian said, resting his chin on the back of the front seat. "I thought you were mean before, but now you seem real nice. I like you."

Ray smiled. "Well, thank you."

"You're welcome." Brian tucked his legs under him and sat on his knees. He gazed out the window. "What's your favorite place in Alaska?"

"You talking to me?" Ray asked.

"Yep. You've lived here longest."

"Well, that's hard to answer. This is a big country; I like lots of places." He thought a moment. "I've been up to McKinley and down to Cordorva and Seward. I've even been all the way up to Barrow. Can't say I like it up there much. Too empty and cold." He scratched his dark beard. "I guess I'd have to say Fire Island."

"I remember. We saw it from the train. How come you like it so much?"

"Well, late in the summer it looks like it's on fire because of all the fireweed growing on it. Ellie and I used to take Celeste there for picnics."

"Who's Ellie?" Brian asked.

"She was my wife."

"Where is she?"

"She died," Ray said, his voice glum.

"Oh." Brian was quiet a moment. "So, you're like Mama. Are you lonely too?"

"Brian, that's enough questions."

Brian sat back against the seat.

"It's all right," Ray said. Then he asked, "Have you been to Fire Island?"

"Nope." Brian leaned forward again. "I just saw it from the train when we first got here, and I heard about it. But I'd like to go. Could you take us?"

"Brian," Jean cautioned.

"Can we?" Susie asked, looking up at her mother.

Ray cast an easy smile at Jean. "I don't mind taking you as long as your mother doesn't mind," he said, certain Jean would decline. He'd just been making polite conversation. He didn't really want to go back there and hadn't gone since Ellie's death. The memories were still raw.

"Please, can we go?"

"I don't even know where it is."

"It's on Cook Inlet. Remember, we saw it from the train," Brian said impatiently.

"Oh." She glanced at Ray Townsend. "Well, I suppose we could. But I'm sure Mr. Townsend is too busy to take us."

"You're not too busy, are you, Mr. Townsend?" Brian asked.

"Please, Mr. Townsend," Susie added.

Ray cleared his throat, searching for a way out. "Well, I have been pretty busy."

"But there's no trapping or hunting right now."

"No. Well, I suppose we could go."

"When?"

"I don't know, uh, sometime this summer."

"OK. When?" Brian pushed. "Can we go tomorrow?"

"Tomorrow? Sorry, partner, but I can't."

"Brian, Mr. Townsend is a busy man."

Ray looked at Brian in his rearview mirror. He sat with arms folded over his chest, his mouth in a pout. Ray didn't want to disappoint the boy, especially since he was a changed man and he liked the youngster. He figured Will Hasper would have made time. "I s'pose we could go, but not for a while."

"Next week?"

"Brian," Jean said.

"No. I've got things to do next week. How about the week after?"

"Great! I can't wait to tell Luke! He'll want to go! I remember when we were on the train he said he wanted to go there!" Brian returned to staring out the window.

Ray could imagine what would happen when Brian told Luke they were going to Fire Island with him. *How did I get myself into this one?* he wondered, trying to concentrate on the road.

Chapter 15

A CAR HORN BRAYED FROM OUTSIDE. "ADAM AND LAUREL ARE HERE!" BRIAN called, dashing for the door and yanking it open.

"Brian, come back here," Jean said. Brian reluctantly returned to the kitchen. "I need you to carry the extra clothes."

He picked up the box, headed for the door, and disappeared outside. Susie followed. "Camping. I like camping. We're going camping."

"Luke, could you get the box of food? I'll carry the bedding."

Luke glowered at the box of provisions sitting on the floor beside the door. "I'll carry it out, but I'm not going."

"No one said you had to go."

Picking up the box, he asked, "How can you go anywhere with that man?"

"He invited us. And Brian and Susie want to go. It will be good for them." Jean settled her eyes on Luke. "I'm not going to let hatred control me, and neither should you. We have to go on and accept that what happened wasn't anyone's fault."

"I don't know how you can say that. He could have done things differently, but he didn't. He let Dad die."

Adam appeared at the door. "You two going to take all day?" His smile faded when he saw the intensity of Luke's expression. "Sorry. I didn't mean to interrupt."

"No. It's fine," Jean said. "We're ready."

"*You're ready,*" Luke corrected.

Adam took the blankets from Jean. "You're not going?" he asked Luke.

"Nope."

"I was hoping you'd join me for some beach fishing. I brought my pole."

A glimmer of interest touched Luke's eyes. "Beach fishing? I've never done any. Heard it could be good."

"Well, get your pole then. We'll learn together."

"I don't know."

"Brian's going to be real disappointed if you don't go. He's out there talking about all the things you two are going to do." Adam rested a hand on Luke's shoulder. "Weather's good, the food will be great, and the fishing ought to be interesting at the very least."

"Nah, I don't think so." Luke walked to the truck and set the provisions in the back.

"You're really not going?" Adam asked, placing the box of bedding beside the food.

"You think I'd spend a night camping with Ray Townsend? I wouldn't go anywhere with him."

"I was counting on your company."

Luke shook his head. "If he wasn't there, I'd go, but . . ."

Adam folded his arms over his chest. "I thought you read everything I write."

"I do."

"How about the article I did on your father?"

"That fable?" Luke said with a smirk. "I'd pay attention to it if it were true. I suppose the drips back in Chicago eat that stuff up. Too bad it's drivel."

"It's not. You've seen the changes around here." Fixing his eyes on Luke's, he continued, "You can't carry a grudge forever."

Luke glared at Adam. "I'll decide what I do and when." His gaze faltered. "You don't know what it's like."

"I don't, huh?"

A flicker of realization touched Luke's face.

"I understand hate and fear. I've seen what it can do. The devil uses it to tear us down, and if we're filled with hate, we leave no room for God."

Luke looked like he was about to retaliate, then unexpectedly, his hostility slipped away. "All right. I'll go."

"Great!" Adam said, clapping him on the back.

"I better pack."

"Don't bother," Jean said with a smile. "I already did it."

"What?"

"I thought you might change your mind." She hugged Luke, then turned to watch Ray Townsend's car turn into the driveway.

"I'll go, but I'm not talking to him."

"No one said you had to, but you will be respectful. You're still my son and your father's."

"All right. I'll try."

"So, Ray's been to Fire Island?" Adam asked.

Jean leaned against the door of the truck and patted Laurel's arm resting on the open window. She smiled at her daughter. "That's what he said. I guess he and his wife and Celeste used to visit during the summers. When I first said we'd go, I figured it would just be for the day, but Mr. Townsend said it wouldn't be a real visit without a night on the beach around a campfire."

"It's a long way to go for just one day anyway," Laurel said. "Besides, summer's almost over, and it's time for a little adventure."

Ray stopped his car and climbed out. After retucking his blue flannel shirt, he ambled to Adam's truck.

Celeste walked beside him. "Hi, everyone."

"Morning," Jean said. "Nice to see you."

Celeste leaned on the pickup door. "Laurel, I'm so glad you're coming with us."

Looking a little ill at ease, Ray said, "Mornin'," and shook hands with Adam and nodded at Jean and Laurel. His eyes found Luke. "Mornin' to you."

Luke didn't answer.

Brian bounced up to the man. "Good morning, Mr. Townsend."

He looked down at the boy, then kneeled in front of him. "Howdy. You ready to see the island?"

"Yep. I got my stuff."

He tousled the boy's hair.

Susie stood at his feet and looked straight up at the big man. "Good morning, Mr. Townsend," she said with a smile. Ray bent and picked up the little girl. "Well, good morning to you too." He turned to Jean. "We better get moving. Daylight's burning." He set Susie down. "Did you bring some warm blankets and clothes? It'll be cold."

"I did."

"So did we," Laurel said.

"Good." Ray headed for his car. "Who's riding with me?"

"Me!" Brian yelled, running after the man. "You have a neat car. I like it."

"Thanks. I like it too."

"I'm riding with Adam and Laurel," Luke said.

Jean followed Ray. "I s'pose Susie and I can ride with you."

Ray opened the back door, and Brian and Susie climbed in. This time Brian knew better than to bounce, and he sat with hands tucked between his legs, his feet dancing.

"Can I sit with you?" Celeste asked.

"Sure," Brian said.

"No, Celeste. You sit up front. I'll sit in back with the children," Jean offered.

"No. I'm fine back here." Celeste slid in beside Brian. "So, you ready for an adventure?"

"Yep. I'm ready," Jean said, not at all certain she was.

"Me too," Susie said.

Ray climbed in behind the steering wheel. He pushed in the clutch, started the engine, then shifted into first and set off toward Anchorage.

Brian was out of the car almost before it stopped. He ran for the dock.

"Brian! Get back here!" Jean called, climbing out of the car. "Oh, that boy."

Adam's pickup pulled in beside Ray's car. He leaned out the open window. "He's not excited, is he?" he chuckled.

Planting hands on hips and wearing a small grin, Jean watched Brian skip back toward her. "I don't know, what would you say?"

Brian jumped with both feet and landed directly in front of his mother, then turned to look at the quay. "Which boat is it?"

"I don't know."

Ray opened the car trunk. "I've just got a dory, but it ought to carry us all." He hefted a duffel bag out of the car. "It's that one there on the right," he said, nodding at a wooden boat tied to the pier.

"It's not very big," Laurel said, worry in her voice.

"It's a big dory. We're not going far, and it's sturdy—we'll be fine." Hauling the duffel bag plus another satchel, Ray headed for the boat. "Let's get it loaded."

"Brian, give me a hand," Adam said, grabbing a box out of the back of the pickup. He handed it to the boy.

They all pitched in to assemble the supplies on the dock, and Ray methodically stowed them. He knew just where everything belonged, and surprisingly, everything fit. "All right, time to climb aboard. Who's first?"

"Me!" Brian said, jumping in and ignoring Ray's hand. The boat rocked wildly, and Brian ended up sitting on the floor.

"No more of that," Ray said sternly. "You've got to move more slowly, or you'll end up in the drink."

"I'm sorry." Brian slowly stood. "I'll be careful." He climbed over the seats to the bow. "This is my spot. OK?"

"Sure," Ray said. "All right, let's get a move on. I'd like to beat the tide change."

Laurel and Celeste sat together on one seat, Jean sat with Susie on her lap on the wooden bench in front of them, and Luke took the space beside her. Adam found a spot in back, alongside the engine.

Ray untied the boat, pushed them away from the dock, then sat on the other side of the engine. He pulled on a rope starter; the outboard sputtered, then died. He pulled again, and this time the nine-horse Johnson lit. Ray turned the rudder, and they moved into the inlet, the small engine straining under the load.

Mists sifted over the water, and sunlight splintered in the haze. Squawking seabirds investigated the small craft. "Watch this," Celeste said, grabbing a piece of bread and tearing off a piece. She threw it into the air, and a gull swooped down, caught the bread in its bill, then flew off to enjoy the tidbit. Celeste tossed more bread and more gulls flew in to grab their share.

"Can I do it?" Brian asked, standing.

"All right, but sit down. I'll bring you some." Moving carefully, she maneuvered to the front of the boat and handed Brian a chunk of bread.

"Me too," Susie said, holding out her hand.

Smiling, Celeste gave the little girl a slice.

Susie took a bite and chewed happily, then tore off a piece and tossed it into the water. She giggled when a bird immediately retrieved it.

Brian tossed the last of his and asked, "Can I have another one?"

"No," Jean said. "That's enough. The rest is for eating."

His smile became a pout, and Brian leaned on the edge of the boat, watching the water in front of them.

Jean rested against the side of the dory, taking in the view. Like a white and purple citadel, mountain ranges bordered the landscape beyond Cook Inlet. Whispers of clouds touched their peaks. The last of the morning mists evaporated with the sun, and the bay's waters rose and fell in soft, glistening waves. A breeze stirred, caressing Jean's face, and she felt the tension leave her. Until this moment she'd been unaware how anxious she'd felt.

"This is a beautiful place," she said to Ray. "Thank you for bringing us."

"You're welcome."

"Will would love . . ." Jean started, then let the sentence hang, realizing he would never see it. An uncomfortable quiet fell over the boat.

Finally Ray said, "Yeah, he would have liked it. Everyone does. Even my Ellie, who never had a fondness for the ocean, liked this trip. Every time I'm out here, I think of her."

Luke glowered at the swells. "Too bad my father never got a chance to see it."

Jean felt the prick of alarm at his words. He was cultivating his hatred. She glanced at her son, wishing there were some way to remove the hurt and anger. But the only one who could change it was him.

"What's that?" Brian asked, pointing at something bobbing in the water.

"An otter!" Adam called. "How about that. I've never actually seen one." He put his camera to his eye, aimed it at the brown furry creature, and clicked off a picture.

Laurel stood to get a better view. The charming animal floated on its back, his long whiskers flicking back and forth as he feasted on an ocean delicacy. "He's cute."

"Do you think we'll see more animals?" Brian asked.

"Maybe. Whales and sea lions are pretty common," Ray said.

"Whales?" Brian asked.

"Sure. We have all kinds up here."

"Do they eat people?"

"No," Ray chuckled.

"I'd like to see one," Adam said.

"Keep an eye out."

A fishing boat chugged past, and the dory rocked in its wake.

Jean grabbed the back of Susie's britches. The little girl was leaning out of the boat, trailing a finger through the waves washing against the hull. "The water's cold."

Jean hauled her in. "I'd feel better if you stayed right here beside me."

As they approached the island, Jean knew why they called it Fire Island. The paintbrush was so dense that the island looked ablaze. "I've never seen anything like it," she said. "It's covered with flowers."

"Pretty impressive," Adam said, taking pictures.

Ray steered the dory toward a small cove with a sandy beach. When the boat scraped bottom, he jumped out and began to haul it inland. Adam joined him. Ray then said, "This is as far as we're going with you on board. You'll have to get wet."

Luke jumped out and took Susie from his mother. Carrying her on his shoulders, he waded ashore.

Brian followed, letting out a yell when he hit the icy water. He hurried for the beach.

Jean climbed out, carefully lowering herself into the water. "Whew, that's cold," she said, thankful it was no deeper than her thighs. Once on the beach, she scanned the landscape. "It's bigger than I thought."

"It's a good-sized island—about seven miles long. There's so much to see and do—beaches and woods to explore, cliffs to climb. And there are lots of birds and sea animals."

Laurel and Celeste remained in the boat. Celeste stood and smiled at her father. "Dad, do you think it's light enough to pull in a little more?"

"Well now, I don't know. Would that be fair?" With a smirk, he hauled on the rope and managed to get the boat into calf-deep water.

After removing her shoes, Celeste gingerly stepped into the water. "It's freezing," she said, sprinting for dry land. With a laugh, she sat on a driftwood log and brushed sand off her bare feet.

Brian stared at his soaking shoes. "I should have taken my shoes off."

Luke headed for a trail leading up the bluffs. "I'm going to do some exploring."

"Don't go too far," Jean cautioned. "You don't know your way around."

"Well, if I get lost, all I have to do is follow the beach, and I'll find you eventually." He strode off.

"I wonder if we'll see any sea lions?" Brian asked, staring at the small waves washing in.

"You might. Keep an eye on the rocks. They like to sun themselves," Ray said. "Sometimes they'll stick their noses up and take a look at you."

He grinned, his gray eyes no longer frightening. Jean wondered why she'd been so afraid of him, then remembered he wasn't the same man he'd once been.

"I s'pose we ought to haul the boat up on the beach and get everything unloaded." He headed for the dory. "Adam, can you give me a hand?"

Provisions unloaded and a crackling fire going, Jean sat alone in the sand with her back resting against a chunk of driftwood. It was quiet except for the sound of birds and surf. A soft wind caught at her hair. She hadn't felt this calm since before Will's death.

After finishing the work, Ray had excused himself, disappearing up the same trail Luke had taken. Jean figured he wanted to be alone with his memories. Adam, Laurel, and Celeste had taken the children and headed down the beach to do some exploring. She'd simply wanted to rest, to soak in the quiet and the peace. Oh, how she needed peace.

Pushing her toes into the sand, she thought about napping. Closing her eyes, she rested her head against the log. Sleep tugged at her, and she finally lay down on a blanket, the sand like a soft mattress. Yet even in such a comfortable and peaceful setting, her heartache persisted. She longed for the man who'd shared so many years of her life. "I miss you," she said softly as she dozed off to sleep.

Jean startled awake. Momentarily confused, she sat up and gazed out at the ocean; then her eyes focused on a shadow falling across the sand and over her. She looked up to find Ray Townsend standing over her. It was very disconcerting. She brushed hair off her face, feeling the grit of sand under her fingertips. "What time is it? Did I sleep long?"

"It's going on five."

"That late?" Pushing herself to her feet, Jean brushed sand off her pants. "Where are the children?"

"Gathering driftwood for the fire. Soon as the sun drops behind the rocks, it'll turn cold."

Jean felt groggy and chilled. She sat on a sun-bleached log and bundled into her coat.

Ray sat on a log opposite her. "I hauled these in," he said, slapping the dead, bare tree. "Figured we'd need something to sit on."

Jean nodded, then stared at the lapping surf. It felt strange to be sitting here on a lonely beach with the man who'd once hated and despised her husband and who probably had some responsibility for his death.

He stood. "I'll get the fire relit. The kids will be back soon, and I'll bet they're wet." He gathered dry grass growing along the edge of the beach. For a big man he moved easily. Jean hadn't noticed earlier, but his curly hair had been clipped short, and his once wild beard was neatly trimmed. But more than his looks had changed. He wasn't as crusty as he'd once been. In fact, most of the time he was kind. Maybe it was his newfound faith. God had a way of changing people.

Kneeling in the sand, he cleared out a large round pit with his hands and set some of the grass in the bottom. "I'm ready for that wood," he said, glancing down the beach.

A few moments later Brian and Susie appeared from around a rock outcropping, their arms full of small pieces of driftwood. Susie kept dropping chunks as she struggled to walk through soft sand. Each time she lost one, she'd stop and pick it up only to lose more when she bent over. Instead of getting frustrated, she simply picked up the lost pieces and trudged on. *Her patience will serve her well,* Jean thought, knowing she'd face days ahead when it would be needed.

Brian strode up to Ray. "Where do you want these?" he asked in his most grown-up voice.

"Right here would be good," Ray said, touching the sand beside him with his toe. "Those look like just the right size."

Brian smiled and dropped the wood. Susie added her pieces to the pile.

Celeste, Adam, Laurel, and Luke appeared a moment later, their arms laden with wood. They laughed and kicked sand at each other. Luke's smile disappeared, and he turned quiet when he walked into camp.

"Where do you want this?" Adam asked.

"We need to be able to get at it. Why not over there?" Ray pointed to a place just outside the circle of logs.

Adam and Laurel dropped their wood in a pile, and Celeste and Luke added to it. Adam caught Laurel in his arms and pulled her close, then looked at Ray. "This was a good idea. Thanks for bringing us here."

"You're welcome. But you ought to thank Brian. It was his idea."

"Well then, thank you, Brian." Adam bowed slightly toward his young brother-in-law, then clasped Laurel's hand. "We're going for a walk. We won't be gone long."

"We'll bring more wood," Laurel added, allowing Adam to draw her away.

"I better get dinner started," Jean said.

"I'll help," Celeste offered.

By the time Adam and Laurel returned, a fire crackled and the smell of roasting meat and vegetables carried into the air. "Mmm, smells good," Adam said, dropping onto a log.

"It's just moose and vegetables," Jean said, pushing a stick through the handle of a cast iron pot and coaxing it out of hot coals. She lifted the lid with a hot pad and stirred the contents. A gust of wind carried away rising steam.

"Good thing there aren't bears around here," Adam said. "They'd smell . . ." He clamped his mouth shut. "Sorry." He poked at cinders with a stick.

Tension settled over the group.

Jean forced a smile. "Don't apologize. You're right. We can be thankful. I wouldn't want to contend with a bear for my dinner."

Adam offered her an apologetic smile.

Soon everyone chatted about what they'd seen; the children talked about scuttling crabs, seaweed, and iridescent abalone shells. Celeste told of rock climbing and birds' nests. With their arms intertwined, Adam and Laurel shared their sighting of a beluga. Luke said nothing.

"So, Ray, how long have you lived in Alaska?" Adam asked.

"Well, let me see now. Ellie and me came up from Montana in 1912. So, that's been a good twenty-five years." He grinned. "Just one week after we got here, Mt. Katmai blew up. Ellie was already leery of living way out here in the wilderness. And let me tell you, it was a wilderness then—nothing like it is now. There were no farms or towns, just a few cabins here and there. Anchorage wasn't even a town. I think a few folks had homesteaded down by Ship Creek, but that's about all."

"I can't imagine what it would be like to come to a place without even a town," Laurel said, huddling close to Adam.

"I loved it. 'Course, I've always been a man who likes his space, and the wilder the better. But poor Ellie—it was hard on her, especially with that mountain blowing up. We had ash all over everything. She was a real trooper, though, and made the best of it. After a while she fell in love with the valley too.

"We built our cabin; then she put in a garden while I hunted and trapped. That first season I got my first bighorn sheep. He was magnificent. Had a huge rack." He quieted and took a sip of coffee. "We had a good life." Looking over the darkening ocean, he added, "This was a favorite place of hers. We used to come here often as we could."

"I remember," Celeste said. "I loved our trips. We'd dig for clams and search the tidewaters for sea creatures." She grinned. "Do you remember the time your shirt caught on fire and we doused you with the water in our bucket?" She laughed, then explained, "Mom and I had been gathering and saving live crabs and minnows. We even had a starfish in that bucket. Oh, what a sight."

"I think you were more worried about the critters than you were about me."

"I was not." A satisfied smile settled on Celeste's face. "I knew the fire was out before I started gathering up our collection."

"Those were good days," Ray said, his voice catching.

Jean hadn't given much thought to Ray's grief. She felt a twinge of guilt at her self-interest. "We're real pleased you brought us here," she said.

"I love it," Laurel said. She looked at Adam. "Can we come back?"

"Sure."

Luke stood. "I'm going for a walk." He headed up the beach.

"Luke?" Jean called, but he acted as if he didn't hear and kept going. Watching his back, Jean felt her good mood sag. Momentarily angry with Ray for his part in this, she glanced at him.

His sad eyes followed Luke, and then he looked at Jean and held her gaze. She felt an unexpected connection with him and quickly looked away. What was it that she'd felt?

Chapter 16

JEAN WOKE TO THE SMELL OF COFFEE AND FRYING BACON. ROLLING ONTO HER side, she watched Ray, who stood over a small fire. He dropped slices of bacon into a cast-iron pan resting in coals, then sat with his back against a log and drank from a mug. He watched the surf and looked content.

A confused mix of emotions tumbled through Jean. She understood that hating Ray Townsend was wrong, but contempt prodded her. It was difficult to watch this man sit here happy and fulfilled. It wasn't fair.

Even as her mind followed this train of thought, she knew all that was in the past and best left there. And Ray Townsend had changed. He was different and clearly wished her and her family no malice.

Jean didn't want to think about it. She rolled over and burrowed beneath her blankets, circling an arm around Susie. The little girl pressed her back against her, a dreamy smile touching her lips. *Father, thank you for my children,* Jean thought, understanding that their presence eased the emptiness.

Jean heard someone moving about and looked to see Luke head toward the beach. He passed Mr. Townsend without acknowledgment. Ray watched the young man. When he returned to cooking, his smile was gone and grief touched his eyes. Feeling like an intruder, she closed her eyes.

"That sure smells good. What is it?" Brian asked, sitting up.

Looking at the boy, Ray turned on a smile. "It's breakfast. You hungry?"

"Uh-huh." Brian stood, with his blankets draped over his shoulders. "Can I help?" he asked, dropping the covers.

"Sure. Get me the eggs."

Brian leaped over a small log and marched to the box of food. Reaching inside, he lifted out an egg carrier. It was large and bulky and made of metal, so it was heavy. Brian managed to get it to Ray without dropping it.

"Thanks." Ray set the box on the ground beside him.

"Sure looks good," Brian said, eyeing the bacon.

"Won't be long now." Ray speared several slices, lifted them out of the pan and set them on a plate. "Do you know how to make toast?"

"Sure."

He set out sliced bread and nodded toward a stack of dishes. "There's a pan over there. Set it in the coals and use it to toast the bread." Ray watched the boy, and when the bread was laid out in the pan, he said, "Make sure to turn them. I don't like mine burned." He handed the youngster a cube of butter. "Spread a little of this on when they're done."

Brian was diligent. He checked each slice often, careful not to burn any. As each piece finished cooking, he slathered it with butter and set it on a plate.

Celeste climbed out of bed and sat beside her father. "Morning, Dad."

"Morning. You sleep all right?"

"Uh-huh. I always sleep well when we're here."

Adam sat up and yawned. Throwing back his covers, he stood. Laurel pulled the blankets closely around her and snuggled down. Adam sat on a log opposite Celeste. He studied the mists hovering over the cove. "Hope it clears up."

Laurel sat up and combed back her hair with her fingers. Looking about, she asked, "Luke's gone already?"

Ray nodded.

Susie opened her eyes, stretched, and smiled at her mother.

"Morning, sweetie," Jean said, giving the little girl a hug.

"Morning."

"So, how are you this morning?" Ray asked Susie. "Did you sleep well?"

"Yep." She climbed out from under the blankets. "But I'm hungry."

"Good. 'Cause breakfast is just about ready." Ray settled more bacon on the plate.

Luke returned and plopped down on the log beside Adam. He still looked sullen.

Jean was losing patience with him. "I'd hoped you'd be feeling better this morning."

"I'm fine." Bracing an elbow on his thigh, he rested his face in his hand.

Jean pushed back her blankets and stood, moving complaining muscles slowly. In spite of the cushion of beach sand, she felt stiff. Stretching from side to side, she said, "I feel like I slept on rocks."

"It's age, Jean, age," Ray said, his eyes teasing.

"I'm not that old," she retorted, feeling an unexpected angst. It ought to be Will cooking breakfast and poking fun. Willing cheerfulness into her voice, she brushed sand off her face and neck and said, "A good breakfast is just what we need to send us on our way."

"Do we have to leave right away?" Brian asked. "Can't we stay—at least for a little while?"

"It's a long trip," Jean said.

"Yeah, but we haven't seen hardly nothin'."

Ray lifted the last piece of bacon out of the pan and set it with the rest. Glancing at Jean he asked hesitantly, "What if I show you some of the coastline before we head home? There's some real pretty scenery, and we might catch a glimpse of another otter or maybe even something else."

"Yeah," Brian said. "Can we? Please?"

Jean wanted to go home. She'd had enough adventuring, but with a nod she said, "All right, but we can't take too long."

"How did you sleep?" Ray asked, cracking an egg into hot bacon grease.

"Surprisingly well. Sand makes for a reasonable bed, that is, until it's time to get up," she added with a wry smile. She shook out her hair. "I don't like the grit much."

"It's annoying all right," Celeste said. "It gets into everything."

"How's that toast coming?" Ray asked Brian.

"Just two more left." Brian looked at his mother. "I made the toast."

"I can see that. Looks good. Can I have a piece? I'm starved."

"No. You got to wait just like the rest of us."

"All right," Jean said, feigning disappointment.

It was Celeste who hurried the campers after breakfast. She told them about the eagles along the coastline south of Anchorage and how she'd watched them snatch fish out of the bay.

They loaded the boat and headed for the coast. Emerald green beaches greeted them. "Why is it that color?" Laurel asked. "I've never seen such a thing."

"When the temperatures warm up, algae grows," Celeste explained. "It's prettier than the dirty gray we have most of the year."

The tide was still out so they didn't go ashore but continued south. It wasn't long before Brian stood in the bow, and peering at the water, said, "I think I see something!" He pointed at a white blur just beyond the boat. Like ghosts, white shadows moved beneath the waves.

"What are they?" Laurel asked, moving cautiously toward the middle of the boat.

Celeste giggled.

Ray laughed and cut the engine. "Beluga whales—a whole pod of them. Don't be scared. They won't hurt us." A snow-white beluga breached, then dove straight down, its tail quivering as it disappeared beneath the waves.

"It's beautiful," Jean said. "I didn't know they were white. I've never seen one."

A whale came close to the boat, then another. All of a sudden the dory was surrounded by the white beasts. One bumped the boat.

"Maybe we ought to keep moving," Laurel said, her voice tight.

"We'll just sit tight. I'd hate to run over one with the motor."

Jean nodded, surprised that Ray Townsend was enchanted by the ocean mammals. He was a hunter and trapper. He killed animals for a living. *He's a puzzle,* she thought.

His camera ready, Adam leaned out and snapped a photograph, then another and another. He seemed oblivious to anything else. Finally he sat and said, "These will be great. I can send them in with the story I'm going to write about this outing."

The whales finally moved on, and Ray started the engine. "You want to get a good look at the eagles? We can go to a bay where there are always a lot of them."

"Yeah, I want to see," Brian said.

Ray turned the boat toward the cove. Once in the quiet waters, he spotted an eagle almost immediately. The impressive bird sat atop an old black spruce. A few moments later it lifted into the air and soared over the inlet. "Now watch him. He's hunting," Ray explained, his eyes following the magnificent raptor. Circling the sky and periodically beating the air with its huge wings, the bird searched the sea. Suddenly it folded its wings and dove, pulling up short just above the water. With a splash, it snatched a fish from the water; then with its prize firmly grasped in its talons, the eagle lifted back into the sky and landed in the spruce.

"Wow!" Luke said, forgetting to be surly. He stood and leaned toward shore. "Can we stop here and take a look around?"

"I don't know. It's probably not a good idea," Ray said. "The tide's got a ways to go before we can make it ashore, and we'd have to wade through the muck. These mud flats can be dangerous."

"I don't mind a little mud," Luke said. "Just move in close, and I'll walk."

Ray headed the boat inland, gently steering the bow into the sand. He looked at the mud and prodded it with an oar.

"What's that smell?" Laurel asked, covering her nose.

"Smells like sulfur," Adam said.

"The flats around here have a smell all their own," Ray said with a grin.

"I'm gonna walk in," Luke said, swinging his legs over the side of the boat.

"It's not a good idea. The sand is real fine and can close around your feet. You could get stuck."

Ignoring Ray's warning, Luke climbed out. He took a step. "Feels sturdy enough. It's fine." He headed toward shore. He had little trouble at first, his feet sinking only slightly with each step. Soon the mire sucked at his boots with each step.

He kept moving.

At one point Luke struggled to pull his foot out of the muck. Finally managing to free himself, he moved forward, sinking deeper and fighting for each step in the thick goo.

Jean had a bad feeling. "Luke, come back. Please!"

He glanced back, then went to take another step, but this time he couldn't pull free. His feet sank, and mud closed in around his ankles. Working hard, he managed to free one foot, but the other became more deeply entrenched. "It's getting bad. I'm coming back," he called. He wiggled his left leg, trying to work it loose, but mud wedged it in. He tried the other leg, but it sank up to his knee. He fought the muck, but soon he was encased up to his thighs and couldn't move.

"I'm stuck! I can't get out!" He pressed his hands down on the sand and tried to pry himself free, but the effort only caused him to sink further. He was lodged up to his hips.

"Oh, Lord," Jean said, grabbing the side of the boat and leaning out. Beads of sweat dripped down Luke's panic-stricken face. Fear knifed through Jean. "What can we do? We have to do something!"

"Luke, stop struggling," Ray yelled. "You're only making it worse. We'll help you; just hang on."

Adam stepped in front of Ray. "You can't go out there. You'll end up just like him."

Ray stared at Adam, saying nothing. Then his eyes roamed over the boat and across the mudflats to Luke. "He's out of reach of the oars."

"Maybe not," Laurel said hesitantly. "What if we set them on top of the sand, use them as a walkway, then pull him out?"

Ray thought. "It might work. We can try it." He grabbed an oar.

"Why you?" Adam asked.

"I'm the biggest and strongest."

"Yeah, and you're heavier—you'll sink."

"Maybe. But the oars are wide, and I'm the only one who can get him out. I'm going."

He lay one oar out flat on top of the sludge, tucked the other under one arm, and walked across the first. It sank slightly under his weight. When he reached the end, he laid out the other, picked up the first, and kept moving. He repeated the process several times before reaching Luke.

Lord, please let this work, Jean prayed, watching as Ray grabbed hold of Luke's arms and pulled. The oar sank, and although Luke threw his upper body back and forth, he made no progress. No matter how hard Ray pulled, Luke didn't budge. In fact, after all the struggling, he seemed even more deeply entrenched.

Luke turned his eyes toward the returning tide, and fear moved across his face.

Squatting on the oar now nearly hidden by the mire, Ray studied the boat, the sand, and the ocean. His gray eyes were pensive and anxious but determined. He stood. "OK, this is what we're going to do. When the tide comes in, we'll float the boat to you and all of us will pull you out. I can't do it alone."

"Wait for the tide? What if you can't get me out?"

"We will," Ray said. Luke shook his head back and forth vehemently. "Luke!" Ray's voice demanded attention. The young man looked at him. "Calm down. It will work. Once the water washes in around you, the sand ought to loosen, and it'll be easier to pull you free. For now, you rest, we rest, and then we'll be ready."

"We've got to be able to do something else." Luke's voice quaked.

"I wish we could, but I can't think of anything." Ray looked at the others, called out the plan, then asked, "Any better ideas?"

No one answered.

Ray knelt. "I'll stay with you."

"I'm no baby," Luke snapped.

"All right. I'll wait in the boat. You thirsty?"

"Yeah."

Ray returned to the dory. "He needs a drink," he said, grabbing a canteen of water.

Jean stared at her son, her arms hugging her waist. She felt sick. "What if it doesn't work?" Her eyes settled on Ray. "He could drown."

"There's got to be something else we can do!" Laurel said.

"I wish I knew what it was. I just don't." Ray glanced at Luke. "This should work."

"Should?" Laurel challenged.

"Yeah. Should. What do you want? I'm not a magician. I'm not God."

"He's right," Adam said calmly. "None of us is God. But we do need him and we need to pray."

"I've got to get this water to him," Ray said.

"No. Adam's right. Wait and pray with us first," Jean said.

Ray waited.

Fighting to quiet her spirit, Jean said, "All right. Let's pray."

Everyone clasped hands, bowed their heads, and closed their eyes. At first the prayers were silent; then Adam said, "Father, we know you love Luke. So do we. And we're asking you to save his life. Show us what to do." He paused. "And Lord, help him to be calm and give him peace as he waits."

Jean followed with, "Please Lord, I . . . I can't bear to lose him. Don't take him from me."

A long silence followed, then Ray said, "I know I'm the kind of man who does things in his own strength, Lord. This is one I can't do. I . . . we all need your power. Help us. Amen."

Taking the canteen, Adam painstakingly made his way across the sand. He waited with Luke, hoping to keep him calm and distracted while the tide flooded toward shore. When fingerlings of foam flowed around the boat and reached toward Luke, Adam said, "Looks like it's coming in. I better get back."

"I'm scared," Luke said, his voice trembling. "I don't want to die."

"You're not going to. This'll work. God will see to it."

"He didn't save my brother or my father. What makes you think he's going to help me?"

Adam didn't know how to answer. He cleared his throat. "I don't know why God allowed any of that, but I know he's here and he loves you. He's going to save your life."

"How do you know?"

"I can't explain it. I just do." He knelt and rested a hand on Luke's shoulder. "God won't abandon you."

"In a lot of ways he already has."

Adam squeezed his brother-in-law's shoulder, then stood and headed for the boat. "It's time," he said, climbing in and watching water flow around the dory.

Jean stared at her son. "He looks so scared."

Adam wished he could do or say something to ease Jean's anguish, but he couldn't. *Lord, please save him,* he prayed silently. He sought out Laurel. She sat with Susie on her lap, arms wrapped around the little girl. Brian huddled next to her. Their faces were stamped with fear.

Ray watched the waves break against the boat and creep across the sand. "I should have kept him from walking out there."

"Dad, you tried to tell him. He was set on going." Celeste stepped across the boat and placed a hand on her father's back. "It's not your fault."

"She's right," Jean said. "He went on his own, knowing it was dangerous."

Ray stared at the water, his eyes anguished.

The moment the surf was deep enough to float the boat, Ray and Adam used the oars to propel them forward.

Water slithered across the sand toward the young man. When the first swell reached him, he sucked in his breath, his face a mask of dread. Adam prayed hard. *Help him, Lord. Please, save him.* He glanced at a terrified Jean and laid a hand on her arm.

"I can't lose him," she said.

"Hurry!" Luke hollered as a swell washed around his waist. "The water's getting deeper."

"We're moving as fast as we can," Ray called. He looked at Adam. "We've got to get closer." He pushed the oar through the water and into the mud. "Push!"

Adam did as he was told, and they inched toward Luke. Finally the boat was beside the terrified young man. Seawater swirled around him.

Shaking with cold and fear, Luke gazed at them. "Hurry! It's getting deep!"

"We need to get leverage around him. Use the oars," Ray said. "Maybe we can loosen him." He pushed his oar into the sand and tried to dig away the earth, but each time he removed sand, more fell in to replace it. "That's not going to work," he said. "Luke, can you move your legs?"

Luke tried but couldn't budge them. "I'm still stuck."

"All right then. We'll just have to use more muscle." Ray grabbed a rope under one of the seats and made a loop in it. "Put this around you," he said, dropping the line to Luke who quickly put it over his head and slid it under his arms. "Everyone take hold." Ray braced his legs against the side of the boat and gripped the rope. Adam stood behind him, then Celeste and Laurel. "OK. When I say pull, you pull!"

"One, two, three—pull," he hollered. Everyone hauled on the rope. Mud and clay sucked at Luke's legs, but he inched upward. "Again!" Ray yelled. Everyone pulled.

"Ahh!" Luke cried. "Stop!" He was pale and panting. "My legs, they feel like they're going to come off." Another wave hit him, and he sucked in his breath. "It's not going to work! I'm going to drown!"

"You're not!" Ray bellowed. "Help us! Move those legs! Now!" He looked at his team. "Again! One, two, three—pull!" Luke's legs moved slightly. "Again!" They tugged harder.

Luke gritted his teeth and closed his eyes. Finally he groaned and yelled, "Stop! I feel like I'm going to be ripped apart."

"You want us to quit?" Ray demanded.

Luke's face was a mix of disbelief and confusion. "No."

"All right then. Move those feet and legs like I said!"

"I can't. I've got nothin' left."

"Do it!"

A wave washed across the sand, hitting Luke's chest and splashing his face. "OK. I'll try," he said, wiping salt water from his eyes.

Ray tightened his handhold, and so did Adam. "This is it. Now or never. Pull!"

This time Luke worked his legs back and forth, and suddenly, with a loud sucking noise, he came free. He was hauled into the boat and lay on the floor breathing hard.

Jean threw herself over him, crying with relief. "Thank the Lord. Thank the Lord." She looked at Ray. "You did it. Thank you."

"It wasn't me. It was all of us." Looking pale, Ray made his way to the back of the dory and sat down. Resting his arms on his thighs, he stared at the floor.

Luke looked at him but offered no thanks.

Chapter 17

JEAN ROCKED AS SHE FINISHED EMBROIDERING THE FINAL STITCHES ON A pillow slip. She held it up to examine the work. She had to admit, the magenta rosebay, lavender geraniums, and white starflowers were lovely and nearly lifelike. *Jessie will like it,* she thought, anticipating Christmas and how much fun it would be to present her gifts. *Too bad it's still so far away.*

The sound of an engine and tires crunching over rock in the driveway carried inside. Jean set her sewing on the chair and crossed to the window. Ray Townsend climbed out of his pickup. He glanced at the house, and seeing Jean in the window, he waved.

Jean wished Ray hadn't come, but she waved back. For the last several weeks he'd dropped by nearly every day. She couldn't argue about needing the help, but it didn't feel right to have Ray Townsend taking on so much responsibility.

In spite of the weekend at Fire Island and how Ray had helped Luke, having Ray around still made her uncomfortable. He'd proven to be an honorable man, and they'd established a friendship of sorts, but the idea of building a close bond with him just didn't sit right. And she did not want to be part of his recovery. She had enough to deal with.

Although Jean had told Ray Townsend she didn't need his help often, he'd continued to show up nearly every day. *His own place must be in disrepair,* she thought. *Poor Celeste must be swamped, what with working at the store and having to keep up the house.*

Jean returned to her chair and her sewing. She'd worked at the store the last three days and had set aside today to catch up on chores. Rocking as she sewed, Jean thought over her work schedule. She'd been averaging five days a week at the store. Although the money was a real help, she just couldn't manage to do everything. With the household chores, the children's needs, gardening, and canning—it all seemed like too much.

The sound of splintering wood and thudding axe carried in from outside. "Well, we'll have plenty of firewood this winter," she thought with a smile. Putting the last stitch in a starflower, she gently tied off the floss, folded the pillow slip, and laid it on her sewing basket. Returning to the window, she watched Ray. He split wood while Brian unloaded it from the truck. Susie stood watching, a basket of eggs in one hand. She swung the basket back and forth, and Jean knew it was only a matter of time before she spilled them. She hurried outside. "Susie, be careful with those eggs. You'll break them."

Immediately the little girl stopped swinging the basket. "I'm being careful."

"I know you mean to be," Jean said, taking the basket.

Susie looked hurt. "I was going to bring them to you."

"I'll hold them for now. When we go in, you can carry them."

That seemed to satisfy the little girl, and she turned her attention to searching for bugs. Finally she skipped out to the field and picked flowers.

"Howdy," Ray said, tipping his hat. "It's a beautiful morning, don't you think?"

"Yes, but a little chilly. Winter's not far off."

"True," Ray said jovially. "I saw a skim of ice on the puddles over at my place." He set the head of the axe on the chopping block and leaned on the handle. Gazing at the distant forest in its full autumn dress, his eyes warmed. "Fall's my favorite season—cold air, the smell of burning wood and brush, and golden leaves." He inhaled deeply, then looked at Brian. "But when I was a boy, March was my favorite time of year."

"How come?"

"The sugaring was done then. The temperatures would warm up, and the sap started flowing."

"What's sugaring?" Brian asked.

"In Massachusetts we'd plug sugar maples, drain the sap into buckets, and make maple syrup out of it. There's nothing like real maple syrup. I've got friends who send me some every year." He smiled. "I guess the sugaring would be one of my best memories."

"I thought you were from Montana," Jean interjected.

"I am, but up until I was six or seven we lived in Massachusetts."

"Mama, how come we never make syrup?" Brian asked.

"We don't have sugar maples."

"I wish we did. I'd like to have a tree full of syrup."

Ray Townsend chuckled. "Well, it's not that simple. It's hard work to make syrup. You got to boil down the sap, and I'll tell you, it takes a lot to make syrup. You got to cook most of the moisture out of it." He picked up the axe. "We better get back to work."

Brian returned to unloading wood, and Ray went back to splitting. Jean watched quietly. She'd hoped to dissuade Mr. Townsend from doing so much. When he picked up a chunk of pine, she said, "I wanted to talk to you about something."

Ray looked at her. "You sound awfully serious. What is it?"

"Well, as I've told you before, you don't need to come by every day. We're getting along well on our own. And I know you have your own place to see to."

"I'm keeping up at home fine." Ray glanced around the farm. "Seems to me, there's lots to be done, more than Adam and Luke can handle. I'm strong and able, and I have the time. I'll be busier once hunting season starts. Then I'll have guiding trips. Folks from the outside are always wanting to hunt down a moose or caribou or something."

Susie ran up with a handful of failing flowers. With a sweet smile she held them out to her mother. "Aren't these pretty?"

"Yes, beautiful. Thank you," Jean said, taking the gift. "I'll put them in water right away. It'll be nice to have flowers in the house. They're almost done for the year." She gazed at a distant potato field where Luke and Adam worked. "They're digging the last of the potatoes. It's hard to believe another summer's gone." She looked at Ray. "Well, I'd better get back to work. I've got bread to bake, and the root cellar needs straw for those potatoes."

"I'll take care of that when I'm finished here."

"I thought you were going to work less."

Ray grinned. "No. You just asked me to."

Jean shrugged. "All right then. Suit yourself." *I can't reason with the man,* she thought and turned to go.

"You're baking bread, huh? There's nothing like hot bread right out of the oven."

The thought that maybe she ought to invite Mr. Townsend to dinner flitted through Jean's mind, but she quickly dismissed it. It wouldn't be right to encourage him. Flowers in hand, egg basket swaying from her arm, she headed for the house. "Brian, Susie, come on. You have inside chores to do."

"Can't I stay and help Mr. Townsend?" Brian asked. "I already made my bed and picked up my room."

Jean studied the boy. She didn't want him spending too much time with Ray Townsend. He'd already formed a bond with the man. It wasn't good. She was certain that Ray Townsend would disappear when he felt his obligation had been met, and Brian would be hurt.

"Please," Brian pressed.

"OK, but I'd like you to clean the stalls when you're finished here."

"All right," Brian said, walking to the pickup and grabbing a chunk of birch.

When Jean removed her first three loaves of bread from the oven, Ray Townsend was still cutting wood. A large pile waited to be stacked. She stood at the window and watched. Resting the head of his axe on a chopping block, he leaned on the handle and wiped his forehead with the back of his shirtsleeve. *He must be thirsty,* she thought, filling a pitcher and glass with water, then carrying it outside. "Would you like a drink?"

"I could use one." He downed the cold water, then held out the glass. "A refill?"

Jean poured more water into the glass.

This time Ray sipped.

"You've been working all morning. I thank you for your help, but—"

Ray lifted a hand, palm out. "I haven't changed my mind."

"You're stubborn, Mr. Townsend."

He raised an eyebrow.

"You're not responsible for us."

He leveled serious eyes on Jean. "I wish that were true, but the more I think on it, the more certain I am that what happened was my fault. I should have made sure Will was teamed up with another man, and I should have forced him to leave me when that bear came at us." He glanced at Luke and Adam working in the distant field. "I am responsible, and I'll see to it that this family's taken care of."

Jean knew she couldn't dissuade him. She'd have to get used to having him around. "If that's how you feel, I guess I can't stop you. But you give God too little credit. He promises not to forsake us, and I believe he'll see us through this difficult time."

A smile touched Ray's lips. "And what if I'm his instrument of help?"

Jean was taken aback. She fumbled for something to say and finally mumbled, "I . . . I guess I hadn't thought of that." She glanced at Susie, who was jumping back and forth over the threshold of the back door.

His voice serious, Ray said, "I'm learning to listen to God. I'm not real good at it yet, but I know I'm supposed to help you. In the past I've pretty much done things my own way and didn't listen much to God, but I'm changing."

Jean didn't know how to respond, so she said nothing.

"If I keep on reading my Bible and doing what God says, I figure maybe one day I'll be less bullheaded and more like Will."

Jean had to smile. "I'll admit I have seen you throw your weight around a time or two." More seriously, she added, "I used to pray for you—before Will. I guess God was listening." She glanced at her hands. "I've been remiss in my prayers lately; I'll get back to it. But you need to be just who you are. You can't be someone else and still be who God wants."

"I know, but I figure I can be a better me." He looked at the ground. "I was better when I had Ellie."

The heartache and loneliness in his voice pulled at Jean, and before she could stop herself, she asked, "Would you like to have supper with us? We have plenty of food. I'm roasting a salmon, the one you brought by a few days ago. There'll be fresh string beans and, of course, bread."

Ray's eyes lit up. "I'd like that. Celeste isn't going to be home tonight, so I won't be missed."

"All right then. Well, I better get back to work." Jean started for the house, then stopped and asked, "Would you like lunch? I'm going to make some for me and the children—just sandwiches."

"Thanks. I am hungry."

With the baking finished and dinner cooking, Jean went to work on an apple pie. She hummed as she rolled out the crust. It felt good to be cooking for a man, even if it was Ray Townsend.

She pressed the crust into a pie plate, dumped in sweetened spiced apples, dotted them with butter, and laid the second crust on top, sealing the edges. After piercing the crust with a fork, she sprinkled sugar on top and placed it on the stove. Removing the salmon and setting it in the warmer, she slid the pie into the oven.

A knock sounded at the back door, and Laurel stepped in. "Hi." She gave her mother a hug and kiss. "Mmm. Smells good." She looked at the table set with five places. "Who's coming for supper?"

"Mr. Townsend."

"Ray Townsend? Is the pie for him?"

"Course not," Jean said, removing the lid from the string beans and stirring them. "I just felt like making one, and he happens to be here."

"He's always here."

Jean glanced out the window toward the barn. She sighed. "I just couldn't let him keep working and working and not feed him. I asked him not to do so much, but he insists. He's stubborn."

"Do you think he feels guilty?"

"Yes, and more." She focused on her daughter. "So, you here to pick up Adam?"

"Yes, but I brought you something." Laurel proudly held out a jar. "Rhubarb sauce. It's my first try at canning it on my own. I thought you ought to have some. Jessie gave me the rhubarb."

Jean took the jar of sweetened red and green vegetables. "It looks wonderful! Beautiful color. Thank you." She set the jar on the counter. "So, how's the work coming on Jessie's book?"

"Fine. We're nearly through all her husband's notes. We had boxes and boxes to go through. When we're finished with those, we can actually start on the book. I just wish we had more time to work. And once the baby comes . . . well, you know how it is. I won't have time for anything else."

Laurel headed for the door. "I better get Adam home. I've still got supper to cook. Looks like yours is almost done."

"Don't run off. We have plenty. Join us."

"Normally I'd say yes, but to tell you the truth, I don't want to be at the same table with Luke and Ray Townsend." She gave her mother a wry smile and left.

Jean contemplated dinner with Ray and Luke. *I shouldn't have asked him.*

With the sun's last rays slanting through the window, Jean, Brian, Susie, Luke, and Ray sat down to dinner. As expected, Luke was sullen. He didn't even try to mask his hostility.

"Shall we say grace," Jean said, folding her hands.

"Hey, can Mr. Townsend say it?" Brian asked.

Jean shrugged. "Mr. Townsend?"

"Sure," he said, then looking slightly flustered, Ray bowed his head. "Dear Lord, I thank you for this food and fine company. I ask that you guide our steps in the days to come. Amen." He looked up, his face flushed.

Food was passed around the table. Ray lifted two chunks of salmon off a platter. "Sure looks good. Thanks for inviting me."

"After all the work you do around here, it's the least I can do." Jean spooned out a serving of beans for herself and Susie. "You said Celeste was going out tonight?"

"Yeah. She and Robert are going to the movies."

"A Laurel and Hardy movie is playing," Brian said. "They're funny. I wish I could go. Can I?"

"Not tonight," Jean said.

Brian's mouth turned down in a momentary pout, then he said, "I saw Robert and Celeste holding hands."

"What Robert and Celeste do is none of our business," Jean said. "Now, eat."

Ray took a bite of buttered bread. "They're seeing a lot of each other. I've been wondering what's going to come of it." He glanced at his bread. "This is good. Celeste should get your recipe." He took another bite, then leaning his forearms on the table, he looked at Luke. "I'll be taking a trip up into the mountains soon to hunt sheep. Would you like to come along?"

Luke glared at him. "Hunting with you? No thanks. I'm not ready to become bear fodder." A pained expression flickered across Ray's face.

Jean couldn't believe Luke's cruel words. If he'd been sitting closer, she might have slapped him. "Luke!"

Pushing back his chair in such a hurry it tipped over, he stormed out of the room.

"Luke!" Jean repeated. He didn't respond. "Luke." She could hear him tramp up the stairs and slam his door.

"I'm so sorry," Jean said. "He's not usually like this."

"Don't apologize," Ray said, righting the chair. "I understand why he hates me. I suppose he's entitled to."

"No, he isn't," Brian said. "He makes me so mad. You're nice, Mr. Townsend. What's wrong with him anyway?" Pouting, Brian propped his chin in his hands.

Ray set his fork on his plate. "Don't be mad at your brother. All this is real hard on him. He's mad at me—rightfully so. I did some bad things."

"Yeah, but you said you were sorry. And I know you didn't mean for Daddy to die." Brian was crying now.

Susie looked up through blonde curls, her blue eyes wide. "I like you, Mr. Townsend. I'm glad you're here."

Ray smiled at the little girl. "Thank you. I'm glad to be here."

After that the meal turned quiet, and Ray quickly excused himself after he finished eating. "Better get on home. The cow will be hollering at me to milk her. Thanks again for the supper. It was delicious." He hurried out.

As soon as his truck lights headed down the driveway, Jean went upstairs to Luke's room. She was angry. She rapped on the door and stepped in before Luke could answer

Luke, who'd been lying on his bed, sat up.

"What do you think you're doing?" Jean started in. "How dare you act that way! You've no right to treat a guest in our house like that!"

"No right? He killed my father, and he's smooth talking my mother! I can't believe you invited him." He grabbed a baseball off his bed stand and tossed it into the air several times. Catching the ball and holding it, he continued, "And that pie—it was for him, wasn't it?"

"For him? No. It was for us."

Ignoring his mother, Luke continued, "He's traipsing in here, trying to take over our lives and our farm."

"He's doing no such thing!" Jean folded her arms over her chest. "He's simply a neighbor helping us in our time of need. And we are in need." Jean fought to quiet her temper. "I know he was cruel to us and others, but that's all in the past now. He wants to make amends. And whether you like it or not, we need his help. There's too much for you and Adam to do. Adam has his own place to tend to; he can't spend all his time here. We should be grateful for Mr. Townsend's help."

Luke's eyes flamed. "You've already started to forget Dad, haven't you? He's only been gone five months, and you're ready to move on— to someone else."

Without thinking, Jean slapped Luke. She stared at the red palm mark on his cheek.

Luke turned and looked out the window.

After a long silence, Jean said evenly, "I'm sorry you're hurting, but that doesn't give you the right to speak to me the way you just did. I love your father, and I will not forget him. No one can ever replace him, but that doesn't mean I can't have a life. Maybe someday I will want to remarry, but that's a long way off."

Even as Jean said the words, she knew she'd never let go of Will enough to allow room for another man. Fighting tears, she straightened her spine and threw back her shoulders. "My private life is my own. If I wish to be friends with Mr. Townsend, then I will be. Your hatred will not spill over into this family. And from this point on, you will respect him whenever he is in our home." Luke didn't respond. "Is that understood?"

"Yeah. Understood."

Jean wished she could do something to root out Luke's bitterness before it destroyed him and drove a permanent wedge between them.

Since coming to Alaska, Jean had lost two loved ones. As she now watched her angry son, she feared she risked losing another. It was out of her hands. *She* couldn't do anything to change his heart. It was between him and God.

"I love you," Jean said, but Luke wouldn't even look at her. Disheartened, she turned and left his room.

Chapter 18

TRUCK HEADLIGHTS CUT THROUGH EARLY MORNING DARKNESS AS ADAM AND Laurel bumped down the Hasper driveway. Adam stopped and shifted into park. "Well, they're up. The lights are burning."

"I'll go in," Laurel offered, opening the door and stepping out.

Brian was spooning in a mouthful of hot oatmeal. "I'm ready," he said, leaving the table and heading for the back door.

"I'll be there in a minute," Laurel said as he disappeared through the door. "Morning, Mom."

"Good morning," Jean said, meeting Laurel and giving her a quick hug. "It's awful early to be heading out, don't you think?"

"You know how it is. You can never count on the roads, and we want to get to Anchorage early enough to do our shopping and still have time for some exploring."

"Keep a close eye on Brian. You know how rambunctious he can be."

"I will. Don't worry."

"I can't help it. Seems these days, he's looking for trouble." Jean handed Laurel a bag. "He'll probably need a change of clothes, especially if you go to the beach."

"I hope the weather holds so we can."

"Come on! Let's go!" Brian called, sticking his head in the door.

Laurel hugged her mother again. "We'll take good care of him."

Unable to hide her worry, Jean said, "I know you will. Seems I'm such a worrywart these days, ever since your father died."

Still in her nightdress, Susie walked into the kitchen. "Hi, Laurel."

Laurel bent and kissed the little girl. "Hi, sweetheart."

"Can I go?"

"When you're bigger," Jean said, resting a hand on the little girl's blonde tangles.

"She can come if she wants," Laurel whispered. "We don't mind."

"No. She's too little." Jean shielded Susie with her hand as if Laurel might snatch her.

Unable to hide her disappointment, Laurel said, "All right. Another time. We better get going. It's a long drive. Does Brian need anything?"

"He's outgrown his school shoes." Jean shook her head. "His feet are growing faster than the rest of him. I gave him money for new shoes."

"Come on!" Brian called again, swinging the door wide.

Laurel chuckled. "Well, we're off."

Although the road was rutted and made for a bumpy ride, the trip into Anchorage was uneventful. Laurel was thankful she wasn't further along in her pregnancy because the trip would have been miserable. Still, it was a relief when they arrived and Adam parked on the main street. Stepping out, hands pressed against the small of her back, Laurel stretched from side to side.

"Your back hurting?" Adam asked.

"A little. The doctor said it's normal, but forty miles in that truck didn't help."

"Wish we could afford the train."

Brian stared at his sister's rounded abdomen. "How long until the baby gets here?"

"Three months or so. Not 'til the end of December."

Brian's eyes widened. "Three more months? How big is it going to get?"

Laurel rested her hand on her stomach. "Pretty big."

"How does it fit inside you?"

Laurel shrugged. "I don't know. It just does." She smiled and rubbed her back again.

Adam took her hand. "Do you want to rest first?"

"No, I need to walk." She tucked her arm into Adam's. "I hope we find a crib."

"Don't forget, I'm getting shoes," Brian said.

"We won't forget," Adam said, glancing down the street crowded with parked cars. "I guess we just start at one end and work our way down."

"Are we still going to the beach for a picnic?" Brian asked.

"Absolutely," Adam said.

They started down the street, stopping to gaze at apparel displayed behind large glass casements. When they came to a store with shoes, Adam asked, "You want to go in and see what they have?"

"Yep," Brian said, opening the door and walking in.

The shop was narrow and deep, with rows of shoes all along the side walls and down the center. "I've never seen so many shoes," Brian said, picking up a pair of oxfords.

Adam headed for the back of the store and stopped when he came to the children's department. Brian and Laurel followed. Brian picked up one shoe, then another and another. After he'd examined several pairs, Adam asked, "Do you see anything you like?"

Brian thought a minute, his eyes roaming over the racks. "Can I try this one?" he asked, picking up a boot-type shoe.

A young man wearing an inexpensive suit approached. He smiled, exposing a large space between his front teeth. "Would you like to try that one?"

Brian glanced at Adam, and when Adam nodded, he said, "Yep."

"Sit down and I'll measure your foot."

Brian sat on a chair with a padded seat and a straight back. The clerk removed his well-worn shoes and placed Brian's foot on a wooden ruler with a curved bracket on the back end and a straight one on the other. "Press your heel against the back," the man said and slid the front bracket to Brian's toes. "Looks like you wear an eight." He stood.

"I'll see if we have a pair in that size." The clerk disappeared through a door, then reappeared a few moments later with a box. "Let's try these," he said, opening the box and squatting in front of Brian. After sliding the shoes onto Brian's feet, he tied them and said, "Give those a try. See how they feel."

Brian stood and tromped around the store, jumping a couple of times to make sure of the fit. He stared at his feet. "I like them."

"Let me check," Laurel said and kneeled in front of him. She pushed on the toe of the shoe. "Feels like there's room to grow." She looked at the salesman. "How much?"

"One dollar and fifty cents."

Brian walked some more. "Can I get them?"

"They fit. You sure those are the ones you want?"

"Yep. Can I wear them?"

"No. They're for school."

Frowning, Brian dropped onto a chair, then pulled them off and replaced them with his old shoes. He dug into his pocket and pulled out a dollar bill and twenty cents change. "Is this enough?" He laid the money on the counter.

The clerk counted the change. "You need thirty cents more." He looked at Adam.

"I've got it." Adam retrieved several coins from his pocket, counted out thirty cents, and handed it to the salesman.

"Thank you," the young man said and rang up the purchase on a cash register. Placing the shoes in a bag, he asked, "Anything else I can do for you?" He handed the package to Adam.

"No. That'll do us fine." Adam gave the bag to Brian.

He hugged it against his chest. "Do you think Mama will like these?"

"Yes, I do," Laurel said. "They're good, sturdy shoes."

With an air of satisfaction, Brian headed for the door and stepped out into the cool air. He walked down the street while Laurel and Adam followed, hands clasped.

Brian kept walking, but Laurel stopped at a window display to look at a wicker bassinet draped with a downy blanket. "Isn't it beautiful?" she said, hugging Adam's arm. "Let's go in."

"Hey, Brian, wait," Adam called. "We're going in here."

Brian turned and walked back, following Adam and Laurel inside.

A smiling clerk with short red curls and red-painted lips approached. "Good morning. What can I do for you?" she asked. Her voice reminded Laurel of a trilling bird. The woman glanced at Laurel's stomach. "How much longer?"

"Three months."

"A Christmas baby. How wonderful!"

Laurel looked toward the back of the store. "Do you have cribs?"

"We certainly do. We pride ourselves on carrying a full line of infant products, including furniture." She turned sharply on two-inch heels, and taking short, quick steps, pranced down an aisle. Laurel, Adam, and

Brian followed. "We have the latest models." The clerk stopped at a white enamel crib and rested a hand on the side rail. "As you can see, the workmanship is good, and it is reasonably priced."

"How much is it?" Laurel asked.

She reached out and flipped a small tag. "Only $12.45," she said with an overdone smile.

Laurel looked at Adam. "Maybe we can find a used one."

"No, I've already thought about it. I sent in a story last week, and I've got another one nearly finished. We have enough money." He ran his hand over the railing and checked the workmanship. He looked at the sales clerk. "We'll take it."

With the prized crib and an assortment of sheets, blankets, and other baby items safely tucked away in the back of the truck, Adam drove toward a secluded part of the inlet. Turning down a dirt road, he said, "I was told this is a nice place."

The street ended abruptly at a bluff overlooking the inlet. He pulled into a turnout and stopped. "Well, this is it, I guess." He gazed across the broad expanse of water toward distant mountains north of the bay, and then his eyes followed a mountain range to the regal Mt. McKinley.

"What a beautiful spot," Laurel said. "What's that small mountain there? I remember seeing it when we went to Fire Island."

"Mt. Susitna. They call it 'The Sleeping Lady,' remember?"

"Why do they call it that?" Brian asked.

"Well, if you look at it just right, it looks like the profile of a woman lying on her side, asleep."

"Oh, yeah! I can see it!" Brian opened the door and jumped out.

"You stay away from the edge," Laurel called, stepping out of the truck. The wind caught at her hair and lifted it away from her face. Taking a deep breath, she looked across the bay. "I love the ocean. I wish we could visit more often."

"Me too. The last time we were here was with Ray Townsend."

"Oh, that was awful. I thought Luke was going to die."

"You did?" Brian asked, rejoining them. "But I thought you were praying."

"I was, but I was still scared," Laurel said, remembering how frightened she'd been and how quickly her faith had evaporated. "I should have trusted God more."

"That's the story I sent in, and I think the *Trib*'s going to love it." The wind whipped Adam's hair across his face, and he brushed it back. "I'm hungry." He lifted a picnic basket out of the back of the truck.

"Can we go down to the beach?" Brian asked.

"Sure. Let's find the trail." Adam looked at Laurel doubtfully. "I don't know if you want to do any climbing."

"I want to go down."

"You sure?"

Laurel nodded.

Grabbing a quilt out of the pickup bed, Adam said, "We can find a sandy place and spread out the blanket." He headed for the ridge and walked along it until he found a trail. "Here's a way down."

Brian galloped past Adam.

"Brian, you be careful," Laurel called.

"I will," he said without looking back.

Adam took Laurel's hand and steadied her as they went.

When they were nearly at the bottom, Brian called up, "Come on. This is neat!" He didn't wait, but started exploring, stopping to stare into tide pools and occasionally squatting and reaching into the cold water.

Adam led the way to a sandy area just beyond the trail. "This looks good."

After spreading out the blanket, Adam and Laurel sat and stared at the incoming tide and at Brian who moved from tide pool to tide pool, exploring the wildlife.

"Hey, you hungry?" Adam finally shouted at Brian.

He stuffed something in his pocket, wiped his hands on his pants, and ran across the wet beach toward Adam and Laurel.

Laurel leaned against Adam. "I'm glad we did this. Do you think we'll see any belugas today?"

"Maybe." Adam studied the sand and mud. "Strange how the color of the beach changes with the seasons. In the middle of the summer it was a jade green, and now it's back to slate gray."

Brian ran up. "Look what I found." He dug an iridescent shell out of his pocket.

"That's an abalone shell," Adam said.

"It's pretty." Brian studied it a moment longer, then set it on the sand beside the blanket. "Can I go wading after lunch?"

"No," Laurel said. "There's a lot of mud and sand between here and the water, and I'm not about to let what happened to Luke happen to you."

"This isn't the same place. I'll be OK."

"No. Besides, you can explore a lot of other things."

Brian pouted, but only for a moment, then sat and peeked inside the picnic basket. "I'm hungry. Can we eat?"

"Take a sandwich," Laurel said.

After lunch Brian busied himself by investigating downed trees along the shoreline and tide pools among the rocks.

"Will the tide come in this far?" Laurel asked, leaning back and resting on her elbows.

"I don't think so. We should be fine here."

She lay back, closing her eyes and enjoying the warmth of the sun. "It's awfully warm for this time of year."

"The cold could settle in any time."

"Uh-huh," Laurel mumbled, sleep tugging at her.

The next thing Laurel heard was Brian's voice. He sounded far away and frightened. She bolted upright and scanned the beach. She couldn't see him! "Brian!" she called.

"Help! I'm up here! Help me!"

Laurel stood. "Adam, Brian's in trouble!"

Adam stood beside Laurel and searched the beach and open water.

"Where are you?" Laurel yelled. "Brian!"

"I'm up here. I can't get down," Brian shouted.

Laurel and Adam stepped away from the cliff wall and looked up, their eyes moving across the face of the bluff. Brian sat on a narrow ledge, his back pressed against the cliff face. Laurel clapped a hand over her mouth. "Oh, Lord!" She grabbed Adam's arm. "What are we going to do?"

Adam ran to the beach just below Brian. Laurel followed. The two stared up. "How in the world did he get up there?" Laurel asked.

"Brian, don't move. We're going to get help," Adam called, his voice calm.

"I . . . I'm scared," Brian said, moving along the ledge.

"Don't move!" Adam yelled as rock and dirt skittered down.

The ledge broke away and Brian slid. Then he grabbed at something and it held. He dangled, facing the cliff and kicking his feet. Then the fragile handhold gave way and he slipped, at first sliding down the face of the cliff, then plummeting the last several feet. Adam tried to break his fall, and the two tumbled to the ground.

For a moment neither moved. Finally Adam sat up. "You all right?"

Brian lay still, breathing hard, then pushed up on one arm and cried out. "It hurts." He grabbed his right arm.

Laurel kneeled beside her brother. "Let me see."

"It hurts, bad."

Gently she touched his arm. "Please, can I see it?"

"No! Don't touch!"

"OK. I won't touch it. Just let me look. Can you move it?"

Brian tried to hold out his arm, then winced and groaned.

"We need to get you to a doctor," Adam said. "You'll have to be brave. Tuck your arm in close to your body." He carefully lifted Brian and carried him to the truck.

Several hours later, when they pulled into the Hasper driveway, Jean stepped onto the porch even before they stopped. When she saw Adam carry a sleeping Brian with a cast on his arm, the anxiety on her face deepened. "What happened? I've been worried sick."

"He's all right," Adam said. "Just a broken arm. It was a simple break and will heal just fine."

"What happened?" she asked, her voice laced with accusation. "I told you to watch him, Laurel."

"I know. It was my fault," Laurel said. "I fell asleep, and he climbed up a cliff."

"I wanted to get the big pine cone," Brian said groggily. "For you."

Jean caressed her son's brow. "That was sweet of you, but you shouldn't have done something so dangerous."

After Brian was tucked away in bed, Jean joined Adam and Laurel in the front room. She dropped onto the sofa. "How could you allow him to do such a thing? I shouldn't have let him go."

"I'm sorry, I . . ."

"Mrs. Hasper," Adam cut in. "Brian's a young boy, and boys get hurt. It's part of growing up. He's curious and bold. I agree, we should have been watching more closely, but no one can protect children all the time." He leaned forward, resting his arms on his thighs. "After what's happened to you the last couple of years, I understand why you're afraid. The world isn't safe, but it never has been. You can't let this fear keep you from living or allowing your children to live." He paused as if weighing his next words, then looking straight into her eyes, he added, "You need to trust God more."

Jean stared at Adam, and for a moment it looked as if she might retaliate. Then her face crumpled, and the tears came. "I know. You're right. I am afraid." She stood and walked to the window, staring out into the darkness. She took a slow, deep breath, then turned and faced Laurel and Adam. "It's not your fault. I shouldn't have blamed you. I'll try to trust more. It's just that I remember thinking God wouldn't let anything bad happen to my family."

Laurel crossed to her mother. "Mama, nothing touches us that God doesn't allow. You taught me that." She brushed her mother's hair back as she would a child's. "I don't understand how it all works, but I know we can trust him." Laurel put her arms around her mother and held her tight.

After allowing the tears and releasing some of her anguish, Jean stepped back. Sniffling, she smiled at her daughter. "I feel God's love and care every day. And I know your father and brother are with him. But it takes time for a heart to heal, longer than I thought."

"It hasn't been that long since Daddy died. Give yourself time."

Jean nodded and brushed away the last of her tears. "So, would you like some coffee and cake? I made an apple cake this afternoon while I was waiting."

Chapter 19

A KNOCK SOUNDED AT THE DOOR, AND BRIAN RAN TO GET IT. "THEY'RE here!" He flung open the door. "Hi."

Laurel stepped inside. "Hello."

Susie ran to her sister and hugged her legs. "Laurel!"

Taking Susie's hand, Laurel walked into the front room. Looking at her mother, she said, "You look beautiful! I love that dress. Is it new?"

"Yes. I needed something, so when I came across this piece of blue cotton, I decided to make a dress." She looked down at the hem. "You don't think it's too short?"

"No. It's perfect for a harvest party."

Jean sat on the sofa. "I don't really feel like a party. I was thinking of staying home. Would you mind taking the children for me?"

Laurel rested her arms on her rounded stomach. "Yes, I do mind. You need to get out and have some fun. You've been working too hard."

"Mama, you have to go," Brian said, poking a straightened coat hanger between his cast and arm.

"Brian, stop that."

"But it itches," he said, removing the hanger.

Jean knew she should go, but she didn't want to face all the couples.

"Please, Mama." Brian walked up to his mother. "I want you to watch me bob for apples. I'm good. I figured I'd get us both one."

Jean had no way out of it. "All right," Jean conceded. "I'll go." She stood and looked about the room. "Now, where did Susie get to?" After checking the kitchen, she headed for her bedroom where she found the little girl kneeling on a chair in front of the dresser mirror, lipstick in hand. Susie turned and smiled. Her lips were painted red. Jean was reminded of clowns she'd seen.

"Pretty," Susie said.

With a sigh, Jean said, "No, you're not pretty. Makeup is not for little girls." She hurried across the room, grabbed a washcloth off the top of the bureau, and dipped it in the washbasin. "You've made quite a mess," she said, wiping the little girl's mouth. A touch of pink remained, so she rubbed cold cream on Susie's skin and gently removed the last remnants of lipstick.

"I remember doing the same thing once," Laurel said, leaning against the door frame.

"As I recall, you made quite a mess," Jean said with a smile.

Laurel chuckled. "I thought you were going to skin me alive, but as always, you were patient." She ran a hand over her stomach. "I hope I'm as good with my children."

"You'll do just fine."

"I never gave it much thought before."

"Worrying about it isn't going to help." Jean sat Susie down and looked at her in the light. "Good as new." She set her on the floor. "We better get moving, or Adam'll start worrying."

"I doubt it. He's probably working so hard getting things set up that he hasn't thought about us."

"I wouldn't count on it. I'll wager he's thinking about dancing with his beautiful wife." Jean circled an arm behind Laurel and guided her toward the door.

Cars and trucks crowded the parking area outside the community building. "Looks like a lot of folks are here," Laurel said, her voice touched with excitement.

Jean opened the truck door and stepped out into cold air. "Looks like people are ready for some fun."

Brian climbed over Laurel and out of the truck and ran to the front steps. Susie followed.

The large room was crowded with people who were laughing, talking, and eating. Children played tag between tables; some scurried underneath. Everyone appeared to be having a good time. Luscious-looking desserts were laid out on two tables, sandwiched between large punch bowls at either end. One was filled with a pink beverage and the other with a red beverage. At the front of the room the band was setting up and tuning instruments.

Mr. and Mrs. Prosser stood across the room, talking with Tom and Adele Jenkins. Arm in arm, Robert Lundeen and Celeste Townsend cruised the dessert table.

"Laurel," Adam called, catching up to his wife. "I was beginning to worry."

"See, I told you," Jean said cheerfully, but inside she felt out of sorts. She didn't fit. "How are you, Adam?"

"Good. Ready for a party." Taking Laurel's hand, he said, "I have someone I want you to meet." He led her away.

Pressing her back against the wall, Jean wished she could disappear. She felt alone and out of place. *I never thought about what it would be like to be single in a world of twosomes.*

The band started playing "Red Sails in the Sunset," and couples moved onto the dance floor. Jean remained close to the wall.

"Hello, Jean," Jessie said, her eyes and voice kind. "Looks like a good turnout, wouldn't you say?"

"Yes, it sure does."

Jessie watched Laurel and Adam dance past. "Even in her condition, that daughter of yours is light on her feet. What a dear she is. And such a help." She was silent a moment. "It's difficult to be single in a world of couples," she said gently, offering an encouraging smile. "It gets easier. I won't say that one day it'll be fine, but it will get better." She rested her hand on Jean's shoulder.

"I don't mind being alone," Jean lied.

"Oh? You're doing better than I did. After my Steward passed away I was real lonely. Seemed I'd never get over it. And being at these functions only made it worse."

"To tell you the truth, I didn't want to come," Jean confessed. "And I'd be happier if I could go on home right now."

"I understand, but it's good to get out and be with friends." She turned her attention on the dancers. "God tells us we're supposed to bear one another's burdens. That way the load's not so heavy." She looked at Jean. "Please come by my place any time. I'd be happy for the company."

"I'd like that."

Adam swept Laurel past, then turned and stopped. "Evening, ladies," he said with a smile. "Good to see you."

"Hello, Adam. How have you been?" Jessie asked.

"Good. I've been doing some writing. There's so much to write about this part of the world, and people like reading about it."

"Of course. This is a remarkable place." Her eyes sparkled with pleasure. She turned to Laurel. "And how are you feeling?"

"Good, only the baby's beginning to keep me up nights with its kicking."

"Probably settling into its schedule for after it's born," Jessie chuckled.

The song "Pennies from Heaven" carried across the room. "You up to dancing a little more?" Adam asked. Laurel nodded and they moved away.

Jessie remained at Jean's side. She hummed along with the song. "I like this one. It's new, isn't it?"

"I think so."

An older man Jean didn't know well approached them. He smiled at her, then turned to Jessie. "Would you like to dance?"

"I think I just might," Jessie said gaily, taking his hand. They joined the other couples.

Jean remained glued to the wall—alone. She tried to think of an excuse to leave.

"Hey, Mom. You want to dance?" Brian asked.

Jean looked down at her son's smiling face. His blue eyes shimmered with merriment. "I'd love to," she said, allowing him to guide her onto the dance floor. Acting very adult, he took her right hand in his, rested his cast on her waist, and moved to the music. Jean did her best to follow his awkward steps.

She felt slightly better. She caught the eye of friends several times and exchanged smiles. Before long she was actually enjoying herself.

When the dance was over, Adam stepped up and asked Brian if he could dance with his mother. Brian gave his permission, and when the music started, Jean followed Adam, and Brian steered Laurel around the dance floor. Susie stood with Ray Townsend and talked happily with the big man.

Adam smiled at Jean. "Looks like lots of homesteaders and colonists are here celebrating together. Things are better."

"Yes . . ." Jean said with a twinge of resentment. "But at what price—my husband's life?"

"It was his choice."

"I know, but it doesn't help." She glanced at Ray Townsend. "If I could change it, I would."

The musicians took a break, and people gathered into small groups. Many congregated around the dessert table. Children lined up to bob for apples, and others waited at a beanbag toss.

Brian and Adam bobbed for apples while Jean and Laurel cheered them on. Carefully holding his casted arm out of the way, Brian came up with one clenched between his teeth and immediately presented the prize to his mother. After that, the family moved on to the beanbag toss where they all took a turn, trying to pitch a small bag into a clown's gaping mouth.

They also tried the cakewalk, and Adam happily won a chocolate cake donated by Mrs. Prosser. Brian tried several times to win one but never managed to land on the right spot.

When the band started playing again, Ray Townsend walked up to Jean. "Would you like to dance?" he asked, holding out his hand.

At first Jean didn't know what to do. Although they had a working relationship and had established a friendship of sorts, dancing with him was something else all together.

"That's all right. You don't have to," Ray said.

Jean realized she'd been staring at his hand. Embarrassed, she cleared her throat. "No. I'd like to."

"You sure? I don't want to embarrass you."

"Don't be silly," Jean said, taking his hand and stepping into his arms.

Ray was more self-assured on the dance floor than Jean had expected. At one point, Celeste and Robert waltzed past, and Ray winked at his daughter. His high spirits must have been infectious because soon Jean was glad to be dancing.

When the song ended and another began, it felt natural to continue. *It's nice to be in a man's arms again,* Jean thought with a touch of guilt. She glanced at her partner. She wasn't attracted to Ray Townsend, but his strength and guidance felt right.

"Are you having a good time?" he asked.

"Yes. I wasn't going to come, but I'm glad I did."

When the music ended, Ray led Jean to the punch bowl. "I'm thirsty. How about you?"

"Yes. I am too."

He filled a cup with punch and handed it to her. He swigged down one cup, then another. "Not bad."

Jean sipped hers and wondered if she ought to move on and visit with another friend. She didn't want Mr. Townsend to feel obligated to stand with her.

Frank Reed and Tom Jenkins joined them. They nodded at Jean. "How you been, Mrs. Hasper?" Frank asked.

"I'm well. You?"

"Not bad. 'Bout time to head up to the mountains. Figure I'll be taking off come next week." He looked at Ray. "You goin' up on your own, or you got a huntin' party you're takin' out?"

"Goin' alone."

"Mountain sheep?" John asked.

"Yep. I've got a good spot up in the Chugach."

Jean was out of her element and searched for a polite way to excuse herself. She looked for her children, hoping she was needed. Jessie had Susie, and the two were sitting together eating cake. Brian was with his friends. Laurel and Adam were dancing. She couldn't find an acceptable distraction.

"So, what do you think about that, Mrs. Hasper?"

"I'm sorry. Did you say something?"

Frank smiled. "I was askin' you what you think of women and hunting?"

"I've never gone."

"So you agree, hunting's for men?"

"No. I think it's for anyone who likes it."

"Women don't have the strength and endurance for hunting."

"Endurance?" Jean asked incredulously. "Sir, I brought five children into this world, and I don't think anything takes more strength than that."

Frank pushed his wad of tobacco further into his cheek. "That's different. Women are made for that kind of thing."

Jean folded her arms over her chest and met Frank's eyes. "I guess you haven't been paying attention, Mr. Reed. Lots of women, including myself, work a full day on the farm, take care of the kids, do the baking and housecleaning, make supper, then in the evening do the mending and so on. Plus, I work at the store several hours a week. I'd say that takes stamina."

"No need to get your dander up," Frank said.

"I'd do just fine on a hunt."

"You think so?" Frank grinned. "Well, Ray, didn't you say you were going up next week?"

Ray answered hesitantly. "Yeah."

"Well, why don't you let the lady prove what she's sayin'? And we'll see who's right."

Ray looked at Jean, then back at Frank. "She doesn't want to go. It's not a good idea. It's rough country."

Jean's ire grew. *Rough country!* she thought. *What's that got to do with anything?* Before she thought, she said, "It's not too rough for me. I could do it. And I will." She tipped her chin up slightly.

"Now, Mrs. Hasper, you don't know what you're getting yourself into," Ray said.

"I want to go." Already Jean wished she could take back the words. This was foolishness. She didn't want to go hunting, but how could she let these men get away with such narrow-mindedness?

"Jean, you don't have to do this. These guys are just teasing. You're a strong woman, and they know it. You don't have to prove anything." Ray glanced out over the room, then looked at Jean. "I really don't think it's good for a woman to hunt when she's not used to going."

"Now, what are you scalawags up to?" Jessie asked, sidling up to Jean and laying an arm around her waist.

"Mrs. Hasper's going hunting with Ray," Frank said. "She says a woman's just as good as a man." He gave Jean a smug smile.

"Well, I suppose if Jean said she can do it, she can. She doesn't have to prove it."

Tom Jenkins chuckled. "I think a lot of you, Mrs. Hasper, but I don't think you're cut out for hunting."

Knowing she ought to take the way out, Jean couldn't bring herself to give in. "I'll go." She looked straight at Ray. "When are you leaving?"

"I planned to head out day after tomorrow. But Mrs.—"

"Sounds fine to me. I'm sure I can get the time off work, and Laurel will watch Brian and Susie. I'll be ready."

Ray looked troubled, then shrugged. "All right. I'll pick you up Friday morning 'bout six o'clock."

"Good. I'll see you then."

For a moment nothing more was said. Then the band started playing "Ain't She Sweet."

"Would you like to dance?" Ray asked.

"Certainly," Jean said, thinking a dance was an absurd way to end the conversation, but to turn him down would seem like giving in.

They danced for a long while, neither saying a word. At one point, she found Luke glaring at them. She felt scalded by his disapproval. She looked away and wondered how she'd gotten herself trapped into a hunting trip. *How foolish of me. What will people think?*

Ray cleared his throat. "You don't have to go. Those guys were just trying to get your goat. They know women don't hunt."

"I know women who hunt," Jean said, wondering why she couldn't take the easy way out.

"I won't say a thing. We'll just let it drop."

Something in Jean wouldn't allow her to let go of it. She'd said she was going and she would. "No. I want to go. When I make a deal, I stick to it. Besides, I've always wondered what it would be like to hunt. I should have gone with Will while he was still alive."

The song ended, and Ray stopped dancing. "All right. But it's not easy. You'll have to do a lot of riding and hiking, and sometimes it's so cold, your face and hands go numb. Once we're out there, I'm not turning back."

"I understand. I'll be fine."

Ray shrugged. "All right. Make sure to bring warm clothes and comfortable boots."

Jean nodded, wondering where she was going to get a good pair of boots at the last minute.

"I'll bring the food and the rest of the gear. You have a rifle?"

"My husband's."

A question flickered across Ray's face. "It's not the one he—"

"No," Jean cut in, the memory of Will's death suddenly fresh and painful. "It's a different one."

Ray was quiet a moment, then matter-of-factly said, "Make sure it's clean and ready to go. Have plenty of ammunition. And if you haven't shot it much, you'd better practice."

"I will."

"All right. I'll see you Friday." Ray turned and walked away.

Jean stood rooted to the floor. "I'm going hunting," she said, feeling panic rise along with a touch of excitement. Maybe it won't be so bad. It might actually be fun.

She thought of her family. How would she tell them? Luke was already furious. She took a deep breath and tried to think of a casual way of telling him. "I'll just say I'm going, and that will be that," she said and walked toward Laurel and Adam who stood with Luke.

Luke challenged her before she said anything. "Why were you dancing with Ray?"

"He asked me, and I didn't want to be rude."

Luke scowled and set his jaw.

"I suppose now is as good a time as any."

"What's as good a time as any?"

Jean looked from Luke to Laurel and Adam and back to Luke. "I'm going hunting . . . with Ray Townsend."

An explosive silence enveloped the four.

"You're what?" Luke finally demanded. "No. You're joking. Right?"

"Mama, you're not really, are you?" Laurel asked.

Jean swallowed hard. "I am." She quickly went on to explain, "The men were talking about it and pretty soon . . . well, they acted as if a woman couldn't do it. And I can." She lifted her chin.

"I didn't think you hunted," Adam said.

"She doesn't." Luke glowered at his mother.

"Well, now I'm going to learn. And I don't want to talk about it any more," Jean said and walked away, wondering just what she'd gotten herself into.

Chapter 20

A TRUCK WITH HIGH SIDEBOARDS RUMBLED UP THE DRIVEWAY AND STOPPED. Luke looked out the window, then turned to his mother. "You're not really going?"

"I am," Jean said, grabbing her coat and pulling it on.

Luke said nothing but slammed a pot into the sink. "I can't believe you're going!"

Jean had decided not to fight, and she struggled to maintain her composure. "Quiet. You'll wake the children." She grabbed a bulging duffel bag off the chair. "Laurel promised to be here by ten to get Brian and Susie. You'll be on your own. I'm counting on you to take care of things."

"What are you going to tell people? They're going to talk, you know. It's not right for you to go traipsing off into the mountains with a man. It looks bad."

"People in this town know me well enough to know I wouldn't do anything improper. And if folks want to gossip, let them. I'm not backing out. I can't do that."

Luke stood in front of the doorway. "I won't let you go."

"You won't let me?" Jean asked incredulously. "Luke Hasper, just because you've taken on a lot of your father's responsibilities around here doesn't make you the head of this house. You're my son. I'm a grown woman, and I'll make my own choices. Now, I've been invited to go hunting, and I'm going."

A knock sounded at the door.

Mother and son stared at each other.

Finally Luke stepped aside. "I can't believe you're doing this," he threw at her and headed for the front room. His steps were heavy as he climbed the stairs.

Another knock. *What am I doing?* Jean asked herself. *Am I crazy to go off with him?* She walked to the table. *I am. I can't go. This whole thing is crazy.*

"Jean? You in there?" Ray asked through the door.

Intending to tell him she'd changed her mind, Jean walked to the door and opened it.

The big man gave her a stiff smile. "Good morning. You ready?"

Jean didn't answer right away. The argument with her son was still playing through her mind. Should she let him tell her what she could or could not do? She remembered the smirking faces of the men who'd challenged her, and resolve replaced reticence.

"Mrs. Hasper? Is something wrong?"

"No. Everything's fine. I'm ready to go." She hadn't spent much time camping and had never been hunting, but it couldn't be all that difficult. This would be an adventure. She managed a smile. "How are you, Mr. Townsend?"

"Good. Hankering to get to the mountains."

Jean picked up her bag.

"Is that all you've got?" Ray asked.

"Yes. And my rifle." She nodded at the gun leaning against the wall and felt a pang of grief. As many years as she and Will had been married, that rifle had been in the house. He'd purchased it just before their wedding. "Was I supposed to bring bedding and food?"

"No, I've got everything. I'm just used to women wanting to bring everything plus the kitchen sink," he kidded, taking the bag off her shoulder and hefting it onto his own. Glancing at her boots, he asked, "Those keep your feet warm?"

"Uh-huh. They're lined with fur. I borrowed them from Jessie. She guaranteed me they'd be comfortable and warm."

"They fit you all right? We'll be doing some hiking." Ray didn't wait for her to answer but headed for the truck.

Jean followed, feeling like she'd been dismissed. "I wore them all day yesterday, and they feel fine."

"Good," Ray said, chucking the bag into the back of the truck with three horses. They whickered and stomped their feet. "You ever ride?"

"Yes. Not often, but I can handle a horse when I have to."

"Good. We'll ride today and most of tomorrow, then we'll leave the horses at a friend's and hoof it the rest of the way."

"That's fine by me," Jean said, climbing into the front of the truck.

They headed out of Palmer and toward the mountains. When the road came to an end, Ray stopped the truck alongside an ancient pickup. "That rig belongs to old Sam Goodman. He parks it here and walks up to his cabin." His eyes sparkling, he added, "He doesn't come down much—couple times a year is all."

Jean didn't think she'd like living so isolated but didn't say anything. "How far is it to his place?"

"More than a day's ride this time of year. During the summer you can make it in a day, but there's not enough daylight for that now. We'll make Sam's sometime tomorrow morning." He climbed out. "From here on it's either horseback or our feet." He closed the door and moved to the back of the truck.

Jean followed, wondering how she would fare. Her stomach was doing little somersaults.

Ray slipped the latch holding a gated door, slid out a catwalk, then climbed inside. He reappeared a few moments later, leading a saddled bay mare. "She's gentle and sure-footed," he said, handing the reins to Jean and disappearing into the truck again. This time he appeared with a stocky, black gelding saddled with gear. He tethered the animal to a willow, then returned to the truck to get his white stallion.

The stallion pranced and jerked on its lead, anxious to get moving. "This is Jack. Your horse is called Jill," he said with a grin. "Celeste named them. Hopefully they won't fall and break their crowns—whatever that means."

Jean had never heard Ray actually crack a joke, and although she didn't think it was very funny, she laughed anyway. She wondered what else she might discover about Ray Townsend in the days to come.

Ray attached the lead of the packhorse to his stallion, then slid his rifle into a pouch and climbed on. Jean did the same with her gun, then put her foot in the stirrup and tried to push herself up. Her foot slipped, and she fell against the horse, gripping the saddle horn. Without looking at Ray, she tried again and managed to climb aboard. Settling herself in the saddle, she got a comfortable hold on the reins. "All set," she said with a smile, embarrassed at her clumsy mount.

They headed up a trail leading away from the road and into the forest. The trees quickly closed in. The smell of spruce and fir permeated the air, and a chill wind stung their faces. The last hardy leaves clinging to alder and birch shivered in the breeze, and the trail was carpeted with their red and yellow predecessors.

Jean kept an eye on the thickets, watching for wildlife, especially bears. Since the encounter with the grizzly at the farm and Will's death, she'd been cautious of wandering too far into their territory. Sometimes she'd find herself looking over her shoulder when going from the house to the barn.

A lynx darted out of a willow grove and across the trail. Jill spooked and nearly unseated Jean, who hauled on the reins. "Whoa!" The lynx sprinted across a meadow, and the horse pranced. Finally able to quiet her horse, Jean gazed at the wild cat.

Ray kept his eyes on the animal until it disappeared into the underbrush. "Beautiful animals," he said with admiration.

Surprised to hear wonder in this big man's voice, Jean said, "They are." Her mount sidestepped and blew air from its nostrils. Once she had the mare steady, Jean pulled off the knit gloves she'd been wearing, shoved them into a pocket, and replaced them with leather ones. "It's colder than I thought."

Ray looked at the blue sky. "It'll be a frigid night, and as we climb into the high country, it'll get colder. But you've never seen anything like it," he said, prodding his horse and moving on.

Jean watched Ray's back. Here in the wild, he seemed a different man. His voice had softened, and he was more relaxed. Clearly he was at home in these surroundings, and he had a reverence for the wilderness she hadn't expected. She felt some of her anxiety ease and began to believe that this adventure might have been a good idea.

By afternoon Jean's back ached, her hips and legs were cramping, and the insides of her legs were chafed from rubbing. She was hungry and wanted off her horse, but Ray gave no indication of stopping. Jean wasn't about to complain, so she gritted her teeth and acted as if she was having a fine time.

Finally, when the sky turned pink and the sun settled behind the mountains, Ray pulled up and looked over a clearing. "This looks like a good place to stop," he said, climbing off his horse. "I'll tether the horses here. Put your tack there by that cottonwood. Keep your saddle with you. It'll give you something to rest against." He went to work unsaddling his horse. He made no offer to help Jean.

Jean stared at Jill and the saddle with its cinches and straps. She'd never done this before. She watched Ray and copied him. The cinch knot was tight, and she struggled to loosen it, breaking a fingernail right down to the quick in her efforts. She stifled an oath and kept working. She didn't dare fall too far behind, or she'd be lost. Finally she lifted the heavy saddle off and lugged it toward the center of the clearing.

"Those can be pretty heavy," Ray said, taking her saddle and carrying it to a grassy spot. "We need firewood and kindling. Why don't you get us some?" He started digging out an area for a fire.

Her frustration growing, Jean dropped the horse's blanket beside the saddle and went to search for kindling. After the long day she'd had, he wanted her to gather firewood? And he wasn't going to help? Her body ached, and her legs felt weak and bowed. She wasn't about to give him the satisfaction of seeing her hobble, so she threw back her shoulders and forced her legs to move normally. She managed to find broken tree limbs and bark and carried them back to camp.

Ray lit dry grasses and added tiny pieces of wood. "You got that kindling?" he asked, turning and looking up at her.

She dropped the wood without a word. Her stomach growled loudly, and she rested a hand on her abdomen.

"Thank you," Ray said, poking kindling into the fledgling fire. Without looking up, he said, "I'll get you something to eat in two shakes." The fire flamed and caught. "Good thing the weather's dry. Makes fire building a lot easier." He glanced at the twilight sky. Wisps of pink clouds were fading as darkness overtook the heavens. "Looks like the weather's going to hold."

Jean moved her saddle closer to the fire and sat beside it, leaning against the hard leather.

"We need more firewood—lots more," Ray said, adding kindling. "It's going to be cold tonight." He added a limb to the flames. "See what you can find, and I'll cut some from the bigger chunks." He grabbed an axe out of his pack, set a large piece of wood on end, and with one swing, split it. While Jean scavenged for timber, he made a pile of split wood and added to the fire until he had a substantial blaze.

Jean added another armload to the stack. Weary, she wanted nothing more than to sit, bundled beneath a blanket, and sleep. "Is that enough?"

"It'll do."

"Is there anything else I need to do?" she asked, hoping he'd say no.

Ray glanced around the camp. "Whatever else you need, do for yourself. You might want to start with your bedding." He stood and grabbed bedrolls out of the gear. Tossing one to her, he said, "Roll that out. It's easier than sleeping on the hard ground." He handed her two blankets, then spread out his bedding. "Stay close to the fire, or you'll be more than cold by morning." He offered her a smile. "I'll have supper cooking in no time."

Jean nodded and wished she'd stayed home. The men had been right. This was no place for a woman. She didn't know what was worse—her aching body, her fatigue, or her empty stomach. Already cold, she leaned against the saddle and pulled both blankets around her.

Ray set a can of beans in hot coals away from the flames and he spooned coffee grounds into a pot. "The creek's just over there," he said, nodding toward the woods and standing. "I'll fill up the pot and be right back." Ray disappeared into the gloom.

Feeling alone, the night sounds pressing in, Jean hugged bent legs. When a branch snapped, she jumped and peered into the forest. She wished Ray would hurry.

A few moments later he reappeared. "Looks like that creek has some trout. How would you like fish for breakfast?"

"Sounds good."

He set the pot in the coals, then dug in his bag. He tossed two hard biscuits to Jean. "This ought to quiet your stomach. No meat tonight, but with luck, we'll have some for breakfast." He spooned beans onto two tin plates, taking a larger portion for himself. "That enough for ya?" he asked, handing her a plate.

"Fine." Jean bit into the biscuit. It was dry but tasted good. She ate a spoonful of beans. She didn't usually care much for beans, but these tasted delicious. Quiet settled around them.

The coffee was ready as Jean ate her last bite. "You want a cup?" Ray asked.

"Sounds good. I'm cold."

Shoving the last of a biscuit into his mouth, Ray picked up the pot and filled a cup. Handing it to Jean, he said, "Boy, I was hungry. You feeling better?"

"I'm fine, just a little tired."

"We covered a lot of miles. You did well."

Jean felt a flush of satisfaction at his compliment. She smiled. "Thank you. How much farther is it?"

"Couple more hours; then we'll go the rest of the way on foot. I figure we can make camp about dark."

"When will we see mountain sheep?"

"Tomorrow night we'll get a good night's rest, then head for the high country first thing the next morning. We probably won't see any until we get into the upper meadows and the rocks. They stay up in the peaks where they're safe from almost anything, except a rifle." He patted the gun resting at his side. "It's not easy to hunt them, but I rarely come home empty-handed." He chucked another piece of wood into the fire, then filled another cup with coffee.

Leaning against his saddle, he took a drink and stared at the flames. He glanced at Jean, took another drink, then said hesitantly, "It's been a long time since I went hunting with anyone except hunting parties. 'Course, then I don't do any hunting. I generally like being alone out here." He paused. "Ellie used to come with me. It's been five years since our last trip."

"It must have been hard to raise Celeste on your own."

"Oh, yeah. She's been a handful." He grinned. "She's a gem, though. Celeste and her mother were real close. They not only looked alike; they also thought alike. Both of them could be as cantankerous as a stubborn mule."

Jean wasn't one to pry, but she felt a prompting to ask more. She didn't speak for a minute, but the nudge to ask grew into a compulsion. Finally she asked, "How did Ellie die?"

"She was trying to have our son." Ray kept his face a mask and stared at the fire. "Something was wrong, and there was no doctor." His eyes glistened, and he worked his jaw. "It was my fault. I brought her here to Alaska."

"You couldn't have known you were going to need a doctor. You can never tell about those kind of things." Jean picked up a piece of dried grass and broke it in half. "Will and I set out as newlyweds, hoping for a good life. God stayed with us every step, but the world is filled with pitfalls. Things don't always work out they way we plan." She felt the familiar ache of loss.

"I've never been hunting before. Will always went out on his own. I wish I'd gone with him. Now it's too late." She pulled her legs up close to her chest and hugged her knees, wishing away the pain. "There will never be anyone like him again," she said softly.

"I know how you feel. I still miss Ellie. Sometimes when I've got something important to share, I plan on how she'll react when I tell her, then I remember she's gone." He shook his head. "I don't think I'll ever get used to living without her." He pushed a stick into the flames, then pulled it out and stared at its glowing tip. "Sometimes I can still smell her perfume." He pushed the stick back into the coals. "I should never have brought her here."

"From what you've told me and from what I've heard, she liked it."

"Oh, she did. And the more wild the country, the more she enjoyed. But I should have gotten her to civilization when it got close to her time."

Jean could hear sorrow in his voice. "You couldn't have known."

"Maybe not, but out here you've got to plan for the worst."

Hoping to change the subject, Jean said, "You've done a good job with Celeste. She's a wonderful young woman. You must be proud of her."

Ray straightened. "I am. She's a lot like her mother, though, and sometimes I worry about what's going to come of her."

"All parents worry about their children. I fret about all of mine, especially Luke. Ever since Will died . . ." her words faded. She hadn't intended to bring up the animosity between Luke and Ray.

"His troubles are my fault." Jean started to object, but he held up his hand. "I know what you're going to say—that it's not my fault. But I know the truth, and I can't blame Luke for hating me." With a sigh, he added, "Hope he finds a way to forgive me some day. Bitterness has a way of eating through a person. I know 'cause it just nearly killed me."

Before Jean realized what she was doing, she reached out and laid a hand over Ray's and squeezed. "It wasn't wrong of you to try to find a good home for your family. And no one could have predicted Ellie's death or Will's."

Chapter 21

ALTHOUGH STIFF AND SORE FROM THE PREVIOUS DAY'S RIDE, JEAN FELT optimistic about the upcoming day. Her stomach was full from the trout breakfast, and she felt more secure aboard Jill, although she still hadn't found a comfortable position for her sore legs and posterior, unlike Ray, who looked at ease atop his stallion as he led the way into the mountains.

Jean tried to distract herself from the discomfort by concentrating on the fresh air, free of mosquitoes, the raucous squirrels, and the last birds of the season. When the trees parted, she gazed at the mountains draped in white.

Despite her discomfort, the morning passed quickly. They splashed through lively streams of swirling white and quiet pools where bright stones looked up from the bottom and trout swam in place. The horses muscled their way up steep grades and shouldered through grass thickets.

When deep grasses surrounded them, Ray was more alert and kept his rifle in hand. Finally Jean asked, "Are you worried about something? Or do you hear something?"

"Why?" Ray asked over his shoulder.

"You're carrying your gun, and you seem extra cautious."

"Just making sure no bear sneaks up on us. Can't see them in this tall grass, and they seem to like it."

Fear shot through Jean, and she sat taller, gripping her saddle horn. She inadvertently pulled on the reins, and Jill threw back her head and danced off the trail and into the bushes. Whinnying in fear, she jumped forward. Jean sawed on the reins, but Ray had to grab hold of the harness to steady the horse. "Thanks," Jean said, wishing she were a better rider.

Mid-morning the trees parted, and a tiny log cabin appeared in a small clearing. A trail of smoke rose from a rock chimney, and a spruce hugged a porch that stretched across the front of the house. Ray rode past the house to a barn with a small paddock where he dismounted. Jean followed and gratefully climbed down from her horse.

Ray unsaddled his stallion, led him inside the paddock, then unhooked the bridle and slapped his rear, sending him running around the enclosure. Clearly happy to be free of his restraints, the horse tossed his head and pranced, then stopped at a crib filled with hay and buried his nose.

Jean was struggling with her saddle when Ray came up behind her and lifted it free of the animal, then carried it into the barn. "Thank you," Jean said, but Ray didn't act as if he heard. She led Jill into the paddock and let her loose. She joined Jack at the crib.

Leaning on the fence, Jean watched the horses. "They look content."

"Don't take much to make horses happy—a little hay and a load off their backs. And they've been here before. They know Sam'll treat 'em good."

"I don't see any other horses."

"Sam spoils his little packhorse. The minute the weather turns cold, he puts him in the barn." He brushed hay off his jacket. "Let's see if he's got anything to eat. I'm starved." He strode toward the cabin.

The moment Ray stepped onto the porch, the door opened. A small man with watery blue eyes and a grizzled beard stepped into the sunlight. He wore a big smile, exposing tobacco-stained teeth. "I was wondering how long it would take you to get here." He slapped Ray on the back and opened the door wider. "Come on in."

Stepping inside, Ray gave him a one-armed hug. "Good to see you, friend. It's been too long." He glanced at Jean. "I'd like you to meet a friend of mine." He nodded at Jean. "This is Jean Hasper. Jean—Sam Goodman."

Sam held out a gnarled hand. "Nice to make your acquaintance. Don't get many visitors up here." He raised an eyebrow. "I s'pect you're here to do some huntin'?"

"We are," Ray answered. "Plan on getting one of them big rams." He rested a hand on his stomach. "Before we go, I was hoping to taste some of your home cooking."

"Haven't got much, just pork gravy and biscuits." Slightly bent at the waist, Sam hobbled toward the stove. "Heard there's a good herd this year." He lifted a lid off a pot and stirred the contents. "I was just about to have me some of this, so it's plenty hot." He glanced at Ray, a twinkle in his eye. "Truth is, I've been cooking some extra the last few days—been expecting you." He grinned. "With your appetite, though, I doubt I have enough." He chuckled and carried a plate of biscuits to a scarred wooden table.

With their stomachs full and heavy packs strapped to their backs, Jean and Ray set off. As they passed the corral, Jean looked at Jill, and in spite of her soreness, she wished they were riding. Ray had made it clear the hike would be challenging.

It didn't take long for Jean to become winded. Ray was tall and took long strides. In order to keep up, she had to take two steps to every one of his. She kept her dilemma to herself, not wanting to be a burden, but soon her muscles were tight and she gulped cool air. Finally she stopped and sat on a log. "Can we rest a minute?" Ray kept moving. "Can we rest a minute?" she asked again, only louder.

Ray stopped and looked at Jean. "You all right?"

"Yes. Just tired from trying to keep up with you."

"I'm sorry. I didn't mean to run you ragged." He sat on the log. "I could use a rest."

Jean knew he was lying. He hadn't broken a sweat, and he wasn't breathing hard. This was a stroll for him. She wiped sweat from her brow.

Ray grabbed the canteen slung over his shoulder. "You thirsty?" he asked, holding it out to her.

Jean took the container and gulped down several mouthfuls. "Thank you." She handed it to him and leaned back on the log, allowing her eyes to roam across the countryside. Beyond the sparse forest, steep peaks, a patchwork of green meadows, rock outcroppings, and patches of snow stretched out above and below. She took another breath, still feeling oxygen deprived. "I don't usually get so winded."

"It's the elevation. The air is thinner up here."

"Oh. So I might not be as unfit as I was beginning to think?"

Ray only smiled.

"How much farther?"

"Not far. In fact, we should see some sheep soon." He stood. "You ready?"

"Yes." Jean pushed herself to her feet and tramped alongside Ray when the trail allowed and behind when it narrowed. The fact that he'd slowed his pace didn't go unnoticed.

Nearly an hour later, Ray stopped. Gazing at a distant ridge, he held up his hand, signaling silence. Jean's eyes followed his, searching craggy cliffs and stopping on white blotches on dark rocks. Ray put a pair of binoculars to his eyes and studied the rock ledges. Handing the binoculars to Jean, he said, "I see a couple of real nice rams in that bunch."

Jean gazed at the sheep. She counted eight. They all had horns, but two of the bigger animals had very large horns that circled the sides of their heads. "Incredible."

Jean returned the binoculars. "How close do we have to get?"

"A lot closer than we are now."

"How do we do that without them seeing us?"

"We stay low and move real slowly."

Ray skimmed off his pack and started down a small hill. Jean did her best to keep up. When they reached the meadow at the base of the rise, Ray lay on his stomach, rifle resting on bent arms. Jean did as he did.

The going was slow and difficult. Ray stopped when an animal looked their way and sniffed the air. They were downwind and went undetected. Jean's stomach jumped in anticipation, and her arms and elbows felt raw from scraping against the ground. The coldness of the earth penetrated her vest and shirt.

When they were close enough to see the animals without binoculars, Jean studied them with admiration. Their white coats looked clean against the dark rocks where they lounged. They seemed content and docile; Jean could almost imagine them grazing in the pasture at home. The two largest had huge curled horns, and when they turned their heads to gaze out over the valley, they looked regal.

It suddenly struck Jean that in a few moments she was expected to kill one of these beautiful animals. *How can I?* she asked herself while trying to think of survival and food. Her family could use this meat. *Killing is just part of life in the wilderness,* she told herself, remembering the men's teasing. She couldn't return without making a kill.

Ray rested an elbow on the ground and propped his rifle barrel in one hand, pressing the butt against his shoulder. Silent and still, he sighted in a sheep. Lowering the rifle, he whispered, "We need to get closer." He crawled forward.

Jean followed, but it was hard work to stay quiet. She panted, the cold air fogging with each breath.

When they were several yards closer, Ray stopped again and sighted in his rifle. "I'm going for that big one on the far right. He must be 150 pounds. You aim for the other large ram just below him. If we fire at the same time, they won't scatter before we've both gotten off a shot. So, after the count of three, we'll take one breath and then pull the trigger. All right?"

"OK," Jean said, wishing she were a better shot. "I could have used more practice," she whispered, then took a deep breath to quiet herself. She quaked and fought to hold her gun steady as she waited for Ray to begin the count. Gazing down the barrel at the magnificent animal, she prayed for a clean shot. It would be heartbreaking to wound the ram and cause more suffering.

"One," Ray said and paused. "Two." Another pause. "Three."

Jean took a breath, squeezed the trigger, and then pulled it through. The rifles' blast shattered the tranquil scene. Jean felt a sharp pain in her shoulder as the rifle recoiled. Her animal jumped and stumbled. "Oh, no!" She raised the gun again and aimed. Another blast and the ram fell.

Ray's lay still as well, while the rest of the herd sprinted away, disappearing over a rise.

"Good shooting!" Ray shouted and headed for his animal.

Jean stood and stared for a few moments. She'd done it! She'd shot her first bighorn sheep. Finally reclaiming her wits, she headed for it. It had fallen alongside a ledge. Jean jumped up on the rocks above it. The animal's white coat was stained red, its eyes stared. Sadness crept over Jean as she looked down at the ram. Its vigorous beauty was gone. She kneeled beside it and ran a hand over its dense coat.

Ray pulled out a knife. "I'll take care of mine, then I'll do yours."

"I'll butcher my own," Jean said. "I figure, if I killed it, I can slaughter it." She unsheathed her knife. "For years I've been telling Luke and Will that if they catch a fish, they clean it. Otherwise I tell them not to bring it home."

She slit the animal's throat, then proceeded to gut and skin it. She managed quite well for the most part, but quartering the sheep was difficult, and she allowed Ray to help.

All the while Ray kept an eye out, periodically searching the landscape. Finally Jean asked, "What are you looking for?"

"Bears. To some the sound of a rifle means fresh meat, and if one is close, it can smell the blood. I'd hate to be surprised by one."

Jean felt a chill go up her spine. She looked about, relieved to see that no bear was headed their way.

"We better get this meat to a safe place," Ray said. "It's too late to head for Sam's. We'll have to camp for the night. We can hang it from a tree. In the morning we'll bag it and haul it back down the mountain." He smiled at Jean. "I'll be happy to tell the guys about how you brought down that sheep."

"It took two shots," Jean said regretfully.

"Don't apologize. You did a good job."

It took them more than an hour to haul and hang the meat. Jean couldn't ever remember working so hard. Just before heading down with the last of the kill, she stopped to look out over the view. A broad green valley touched with patches of red and yellow bushes stretched out below, reaching to distant foothills at the feet of distant mountains. Clouds rested among the peaks, casting shadows over the basin. A darker band of clouds stacked up beyond the range. A sharp wind whipped at her hair and coat.

"Looks like a storm's moving in," Ray said. "We better get to it. I wouldn't want to be stuck up here." He hefted the last of his meat onto his shoulder and headed down.

Jean pushed hers up onto her shoulder and followed Ray, walking along the edge of the ridge. Unable to resist taking in the panorama, she let her eyes roam for just a moment. She missed a step, and her foot slipped. Believing it was only a simple blunder, she chucked her load onto the path and grabbed for a handful of grass to catch herself. It pulled loose, and she fell backward. Letting out a yell, she snatched at a bush, but it slipped from her fingers and she skidded over the edge.

Hugging rocks and granite, she bounced down the face of the bluff, her hands frantically grabbing for a handhold. There was nothing. Her chest and chin bounded off the rough wall, and her legs thudded against rocks. She didn't know what lay below. She envisioned herself being launched into open air. Fear was all she knew. *God! Help me!*

Her hand closed around a small evergreen, and her feet struck a shelf. She stopped with a jolt. She didn't move for several moments, lying flat against the cliff face. She gulped in air, fearing for her life. She peered over her shoulder, and her stomach dropped. The ledge she stood on was only a foot wide, and below lay a deep chasm. She hugged the rocks, resting her face against the jagged stones.

"Lord, help me." She searched for a way to climb up, then grabbed hold of a rock and pulled while pushing with her feet. The rock came loose and tumbled into the chasm below. Tears of fear and helplessness filled her eyes. She started to shake and felt faint. "I need to sit," she said, carefully sliding down until she was sitting. She closed her eyes.

"Jean! Jean!" Ray called from above, his voice panicked.

"I'm here!"

"Are you all right?"

"Yes. But I can't get back up. I'm stuck."

"Hang on. I'm coming."

Jean wondered how he thought he was going to help. She turned to look up but nearly tumbled off the narrow refuge. Pressing her back against the rock wall, she held completely still and waited. She could feel the sting of cuts and scrapes and the ache of battered limbs. *Please hurry, Ray. Hurry.*

A rope fell from above and slapped the rocks beside her. Bits of rock and dirt tumbled from above. Jean could hear Ray's heavy breathing as he made his way down.

Finally she heard him just above her. "I'm here, Jean. I'll get you up." His voice sounded gentle and calm. "I'm going to lower myself down to you, and then I want you to cinch this rope around you. I'll show you how."

He managed to maneuver down until he was beside her. "You all right?"

"Yes. Just scared. I'll feel a lot better once I'm back on top."

He made two loops in the rope and showed Jean how to put it around her and between her legs. She slipped one arm at a time through one loop, and then while trying to get her leg through the other, she lost her balance. Ray grabbed her, holding steady. With a tremulous smile, she pulled the rope tight around the top of her thigh. It wasn't comfortable, but it would hold her more securely while he pulled her up.

"I'm going up, and then I'll pull you up."

"Please hurry," Jean said, unable to keep her voice from quaking.

With an encouraging smile, Ray started up.

Clinging to the rope, Jean watched him climb. He made his way slowly but steadily, searching for tiny handholds and shelves to wedge his feet.

When he reached the top, he called down. "I've got the rope secured. I'll pull while you climb. Use your feet and hands like I did. Don't be afraid. The rope will hold you. You won't fall."

"Sure, don't be afraid—do it like he did." Jean glanced down and shuddered, then because she had no other alternative, she began. Her fingers sought places to grip, and her feet pushed against outcroppings and propelled her upward. More than once she lost her hold and swung away from the rocks. For a few moments she would huddle against the cliff, sucking air and rebuilding her courage, but with Ray pulling from above, she managed to make the top.

Ray grabbed her under the arms and pulled her over the rim. For a long while she lay hugging the ground. When she sat up, she had to fight off tears. Looking at Ray, she whispered, "Thank you."

He wore a broad smile. "You scared me. When I saw you disappear over the edge, I thought you were gone for sure."

Jean looked at the meat she'd tossed to safety. "Well, I managed to save the meat," she chuckled.

"You did at that," Ray grinned. "I can't wait to tell the guys." A brisk wind whipped across the bluff. "You able to make it back to camp?"

Jean pushed herself upright. She was weak and trembling. "Aside from a few bruises and scratches, I think I'm fine."

Ray looked across the valley toward the mountains where dark clouds were pushing toward them. "We better head down. I'd say those clouds are carrying snow. I wouldn't want to get stuck up here."

He turned to go, but Jean stopped him by resting a hand on his arm. "Thank you. You saved my life. You didn't have to climb down and get me."

"Yes, I did. No self-respecting man would have done otherwise. I couldn't take a chance of you putting on that harness wrong." His smile faded. "I don't know what I'd do if something happened to you." He acted as if he were about to reach out and touch her face, but instead he said, "Let's go before that storm catches us."

Chapter 22

JEAN GRIPPED THE STEERING WHEEL AS SHE BUMPED UP ADAM AND Laurel's snow-covered driveway. When she stopped, Laurel stepped out her door, fastening the last button on her coat, which stretched over her protruding stomach. Jean smiled. In less than two months her first grandchild would be born. *If only Will were here,* she thought sadly.

Laurel took the steps carefully and walked to the truck, waddling a little like a plump goose. "Good morning," she said as she opened the door and slid in while Brian shuffled Susie onto his lap.

"Careful with that arm," Jean said. "Just 'cause you got the cast off doesn't mean it's good as new."

"The doctor said it is," Brian responded.

"Hi, Laurel," Susie said, wearing a bright smile, her cheeks pink from the cold.

"Hi." Laurel gave her little sister a quick kiss and patted Brian's head. "How are you all today?"

"Good," Brian said, then without taking a breath, he asked, "Do you know if John is going to be there? 'Cause if he's not, I won't have anyone to play with."

"I saw Adele at the store yesterday, and she said the boys would be there," Laurel assured her brother. Laurel looked at her mother. "It's cold." She rubbed her gloved hands together for emphasis. "But I need to get out. A quilting at Mrs. Prosser's is just the thing."

"I'm already tired of the weather." Jean shifted into reverse and backed up the truck. "It's been too long since I've gotten together with my friends. Back in Wisconsin the ladies used to meet all the time."

Heading down the driveway, she glanced at the gray sky. "Looks like we're in for more snow. Hope it's not an all-out blizzard."

"Adam's holed up in his little corner of the house, writing. I don't think he even noticed I left. He was a little curious about quilting parties though." She grinned. "Probably hoping to find an angle for another story."

"Is that going well? Is he getting work?"

"Yes. Pretty regularly now. The readers love stories about Alaska."

"Well, this quilting is about neighbors helping neighbors. He could write about that."

"How is Mrs. Fletcher feeling?" Laurel asked, settling back in her seat and resting her hands on her belly.

"Edna's still feeling poorly, but she's ninety-eight years old. I s'pect we'll lose her before winter's passed. Hopefully this quilt will lift her spirits."

"I can hardly believe she still lives on her own."

"Her children and grandchildren do a lot for her."

"Mrs. Fletcher looks real old, like maybe a hundred and twenty," Brian said. "I've never seen anyone with so many wrinkles."

"Brian!" Jean said, taking her eyes off the road for just a moment to frown at her son.

"But she's real nice," Brian quickly added. He brooded a moment, then added, "She does have a lot of wrinkles."

"She does, Mama," Laurel said with a grin.

Jean smiled and nodded. "I suppose she does." The truck slipped sideways, and Jean gripped the steering wheel, struggling to control the slide. When the pickup straightened, she relaxed slightly. "I'm still not very good at this. I liked it better when your father drove."

"You're doing fine, Mama. It's good that you drive. Lots of women do nowadays. Adam said after the baby's born he'll teach me."

Still gripping the wheel and keeping her eyes straightforward, Jean smiled slightly. "Good. Then you can drive for me."

When they arrived at the Prossers', Brian and Susie ran ahead and knocked on the door. John Jenkins opened it, and the children disappeared inside.

Wiping her hands on an apron, Norma Prosser stepped onto the porch. "Good morning. How nice to see you. Come in before you get frostbitten." She draped an arm around Laurel's shoulders. "You're looking wonderful. How are you feeling?"

"Just fine," Laurel said, stepping into the house.

Jessie, who had been in the middle of saying something, stopped and smiled at the latest arrivals. Miram Dexter and her mother, Margarite, looked at Laurel and Jean and nodded their greeting.

Adele Jenkins stood. "Hi, neighbor. Good to see you." She smiled.

Mattie Lawson smiled and nodded.

Jean was happy to see that Mattie had been included. It was just like Norma to think of inviting the native girl. She'd been struggling to fit into a woman's world and a white world.

"How are you feeling, Laurel?" Jessie asked, approaching the newcomers.

"Good, just big. The doctor says the baby and I are doing very well." She smiled and rested a hand on her stomach.

"I miss seeing you every week, dear."

"I'm feeling fine and could come by and work on organizing some of the chapters."

"Oh, no." Jessie patted Laurel's hand. "I decided that until the baby gets here, you're to take it easy. We've got plenty of time to finish that book."

Norma took their coats and carried them into a bedroom. When she returned, she asked, "Are you ready for a hot cup of tea?"

"Sounds good," Jean and Laurel said simultaneously.

Miram stood and walked across to Laurel. Crinkling up a cheek to readjust her glasses as she often did, she said, "You must be so excited. It won't be long now. Sometimes I dream of what it will be like to be a mother." Her voice sounded shrill and nervous as always. She leaned closer and said softly, "Are you scared?"

"A little. I've never been a mother before."

Miram sniffled and dabbed at her nose with a handkerchief. "Thank goodness for Dr. Donovan. I'd hate to think of having a baby way out here without a doctor."

Norma handed Laurel and Jean each a cup of tea, then returned to her place at the table. "All right, ladies. We can chat while we work. We still have a lot of work to do on this quilt."

Laurel and Jean sat on either side of Miram, the only free places at the table, which wasn't unusual. People didn't dislike Miram, but she almost always reeked of camphor, which she used to relieve her nasal congestion. Jean smelled it immediately and turned away slightly. She noticed Laurel had done the same.

"I've always been so fond of crazy quilts," Adele said, pushing a needle through the material.

"This one's special," Norma said. "The pieces of material came from Edna's children, grandchildren, and great grandchildren's clothing. Every time she uses it, she will be wrapped up in memories."

"It's snowing again," Adele said with a sigh. "I'd hoped it would hold off."

"It's just barely coming down, and the wind's not blowing," Miram said. "We have nothing to worry about." She gave her mother a sidelong glance as if waiting for a reprimand. Margarite didn't even look up from her work.

"We've already had quite a winter," Jessie said, "one of the snowiest I can remember for this early in the year." She sat back, letting her hands rest on the quilt. "I'm grateful for all the help Adam and Ray have given me. Why, between those two, I have enough wood to keep me warm through two winters."

Margarite looked up and lifted an eyebrow when she glanced at Jean, then returned to her sewing.

Norma took a sip of tea. "Jessie, you still working on your book?"

"Not right now. I can't do much without Laurel." She smiled at the young woman. "I figured that with her time so near it wouldn't be a good idea for her to be traipsing back and forth to my place, especially with the weather being so cold."

"I'm perfectly fine. The doctor said so. And he said walking is good for me," Laurel explained. "I'd love to start on it again."

"Oh, no. I definitely don't agree with that," Margarite clucked. "You need to take care with that little one. Why, I remember when I was expecting Miram I had to go for water every day in the dead of winter, right up to the last days. I know that's why she came early. It had to be the cold and all that walking." Her eyes rested on her daughter. Miram nervously dabbed at her nose. "I've often wondered if all that walking and cold and being born so early might have something to do with her nasal troubles." She leveled a serious look on Laurel. "I caution you, young lady—no walking—and stay out of the cold." She sniffed and sat straighter in her chair. "You can never be too careful, you know."

"I'll be careful," Laurel promised.

"Well, I can't believe that a brisk walk in cold air will hurt anyone," Jean said. She smiled at her daughter. "Seems to me, the stronger you are the easier things will go for you."

Her mouth pinched, Margarite turned dark eyes on Jean. "Hmm, well I must say I've always heard that cold weather and exercise are to be avoided when one is in her condition. My mother did a good job of raising me. I never had a sick day in my life, not until we moved up here." Her eyes still on Jean, she tipped up her chin. "I'd say she knew a good deal more than you, Mrs. Hasper."

Jean could feel a retort on her tongue, but she knew better than to try to win an argument with Margarite Dexter. The woman never backed down. Working hard to maintain a calm exterior, Jean took another stitch. "Well, I suppose we all have to be careful when it comes to being outside in this weather."

It was too late. Margarite's fire had been lit. "I heard Ray Townsend's been over at your place quite a lot lately," she said with the acid of accusation.

Jean kept sewing and said evenly, "Yes, he has. Since Will died, Mr. Townsend has been very kind and helpful."

"I also heard you and him took a trip into the mountains together . . . just the two of you."

Jean knew where Margarite was heading. She pushed her needle into the material and looked at the woman. "We did. Mr. Townsend was kind enough to take me hunting."

"And you brought back a nice ram, didn't you?" Norma interceded, her voice a bit tight.

"Uh-huh. I shot it myself. The meat will be important to us this winter."

"Well," Margarite said, her voice huffy. "I would never travel alone with a man."

Jean was getting angry. She bit her lip. "We weren't exactly alone," she said.

"Oh?"

"No, it was me and Mr. Townsend and God." She couldn't keep the smirk off her face. "I'd say God is a good chaperone, wouldn't you?"

Momentary confusion touched Margarite's face, but Jean's sarcasm didn't stop her. She continued the inquisition. "So, how many days would you say Ray Townsend visits your farm in a week?"

Jean wanted to tell her it was no one's business, but she simply kept sewing. Anger fueled her adrenaline, and she was unable to keep her hands from trembling. The needle slipped, and she stabbed her index finger. "Ouch," she said, examining the wound, then putting the tip of her finger to her mouth to staunch the flow of blood. Finally she said, "I don't know just how often he comes by. I suppose a couple times a week."

"That's not what I heard." Margarite raised an eyebrow. "He's over there very nearly every day, and sometimes he stays to supper."

Jean's anger bloomed, and now she didn't care. "Yes, sometimes Mr. Townsend stays for supper," she said tersely. "He works hard, and it only seems fair to feed him."

Margarite pushed further. "So, you two are alone? Often?"

The other women had stopped sewing. Laurel's face was crimson.

"Of course, we're not alone. Luke, Brian, and Susie are always around."

A satisfied grin touched Margarite's lips. "But you were alone when you went hunting."

Jean didn't reply. She wished she hadn't come today and wondered if she could find a polite way to excuse herself.

"I've done my best to be charitable to you and your family," Margarite continued. "Especially after your husband was killed. I've bit my tongue many a time, but it's time something was said. It wouldn't be Christian of me to remain silent any longer. I'd just be allowing you to stumble." She met Jean's eyes. "It's downright indecent of you to be spending so much time alone with that man. What kind of example is it to your children?"

Jean stood. "Nothing improper is going on between me and Mr. Townsend. He's a friend, and he's good to the children. Without Will we needed the help." Jean could feel tears burning the back of her eyes, and that made her more angry. She wasn't about to let that woman make her cry.

Laurel joined her mother and placed an arm around her shoulders.

"And about the hunting trip, Mr. Townsend was simply being generous. My family needed the meat, and he offered to teach me. He's the best hunter in these parts."

"And what about your son? He could have taken you. And didn't he go hunting himself? I see no reason why you needed to go traipsing off into the mountains with a man."

Miram stood and rested her hands on the table. "Mama, hush. This is none of your affair."

Margarite's eyes opened in surprise, then hardened as they fell upon her daughter. Her tone cruel, she said, "You'll be still."

Miram's chin quivered, and she pressed her lips together. Her eyes brimmed with tears, but she said nothing more.

"That's enough," Norma Prosser said in a booming voice. She stood with her hands planted on her hips and faced Margarite Dexter. "I asked everyone here to do a good turn for Edna and to enjoy each other's company. This is not the time or place for finger-pointing. Margarite, you need to keep your opinions to yourself."

Margarite's face turned red, then purple. She shoved her needle into the quilt. "Well! I was only trying to help. It's my Christian duty to show a sister the error of her ways." She scanned the others around the table. "I can see I'm not welcome here." She tipped her chin into the air. "It doesn't really matter anyway. We're leaving this valley."

Miram gasped.

Mrs. Dexter scanned the faces at the table and settled on Miram. "We'll be leaving before the middle of the month."

"Leaving?" Miram asked, her face grief-stricken. "You never said anything. We can't go."

"Oh, yes we can. And we are." Margarite stepped away from the table. Heavy hips swaying, she walked to the coatrack and retrieved her and Miram's coats. "It's time to go." She shoved the coat into her daughter's arms, then pulled on her own, swept a scarf around her neck, and pulled on gloves. Finally she pushed a hat over her short dark curls and looked at her daughter, who still stood holding the coat. "We're going."

Miram didn't move at first. She pushed up her glasses and looked at her friends. "I'm sorry," she said meekly, then pulled on her coat and gloves and followed her mother out the door.

Still feeling the pall of the afternoon's clash, Jean stuffed wood into the stove. A knock sounded at the door. "Now, who could that be? It's dark as pitch out there, and I didn't hear a car." She opened the door.

Miram Dexter stood shivering and gripping a lamp in a gloved hand. Her fur-lined hood was pulled tightly around her pale face. With her shoulders hunched up and her voice smaller than usual, she asked, "Can I come in?"

"Of course." Jean rested a hand on the young woman's shoulder and guided her inside. "You must be frozen. Let me get you something hot to drink. Do you like tea or coffee?"

Miram sat at the kitchen table. "Tea, I guess. Thank you." She managed a small smile. "I'm so sorry to bother you, but I . . . I didn't have anywhere else to go." If it were possible, her face crumpled more, and she looked even more sorrowful.

"What's happened?" Jean asked, pouring tea into a cup and setting it in front of Miram.

Miram loosened her hood and pulled it off, remaining silent.

"The children are in bed, and I was just about to have a cup of tea. It's nice to have someone to share it with." She smiled encouragement and filled her own cup, then sat across from the young woman. Warming her hands on her cup, she waited. Miram still said nothing. Finally Jean asked, "So, what brings you to my door this time of night?"

Miram's response was tears. Her eyes filled and flooded her red cheeks. She reached for her handkerchief, pressed it to her nose, and blew. "I'm sorry," she managed to say. After blowing again, she blubbered, "I need a place to live."

"What about your parents?"

"They're leaving. You heard my mother." She straightened slightly. "But I'm not. I told her I'm staying. I can't go. This is the first place I've ever had real friends. And Ed, well, we're nearly engaged. I can't leave."

Her hands trembling, she picked up her tea and sipped. Carefully she set it down, then looked at Jean. "I was wondering . . . well, since your husband passed away . . . well, there's so much work for just one woman . . ." She let the sentence hang, then began again. "Is it at all possible that I might stay here with you? I'd be a real help. I'm a hard worker. I can sew and cook, and although I've never done much farming, I'm sure I can learn."

Miram's words tumbled out quickly. Jean took a moment to absorb the request.

"I'm sorry. I shouldn't have come," Miram said as she stood up. "It would be an imposition. I should never have come," she repeated. "I'm sorry." She headed for the door.

"Miram," Jean said gently. "Please. Sit. Let me think a moment." She offered what she hoped was a cheery smile, and the young woman returned to her chair. Jean hadn't considered sharing her home with anyone outside the family, but maybe it wasn't a bad idea. There was a lot of work to do, and having another woman's company would be nice. The house had seemed empty without Laurel.

She looked at Miram and thought over what kind of person she was. Miram could be slightly annoying, what with her constant sniffing and the smell of camphor wafting about her. Her sharp, high voice grated, but she was kind and honest. Jean had often felt sorry for her, having to live under her mother's authoritative control.

Miram stared at her hands.

"Have you talked to your mother and father about this?" Jean asked.

"No. I just told them I'm not leaving Alaska. They insist that I go with them." Her eyes brighter now and more confident, she added, "I'm a grown woman—twenty-five now. It's time I was on my own." All of a sudden her eyes were swimming in tears again. "If I leave the valley now, I may never marry. Ed is my only chance for a husband. He loves me just the way I am. I know I'm no catch. I doubt that anyone else will ever want me."

Jean's heart ached for the girl. She reached out and laid a hand over Miram's. "Of course, you can stay."

Chapter 23

OVER HER PARENTS' PROTESTS, MIRAM MOVED INTO THE HASPER HOME. Luke and Adam carted her few possessions, and she moved into Laurel's old room, sharing the space with Susie.

Susie welcomed the company, and Brian was happy to have a guest in the house. He liked Miram. Luke, on the other hand, wasn't pleased. Miram's personality grated on him, but it didn't take long before her sweetness and caring won him over.

The day of the Dexter move was a sad one for Miram and her parents. Mr. and Mrs. Dexter came by the evening before, hoping to convince their daughter to join them. As luck would have it, Ray had stayed for supper. Margarite gave both Jean and Ray a knowing look and a perfunctory greeting.

She and Miram retreated to the porch. Margarite's voice carried inside as she pleaded with, then threatened, her daughter. Miram wouldn't budge. She'd made up her mind to stay, and that was that.

Jean silently cheered for Miram. It was time for the young woman to be out from under her mother's control; it was time for her to grow up. Jean was proud of her and told her so when she came back inside.

Miram hugged her and with tear-filled eyes said, "Thank you. Thank you for your help and for believing in me."

Jean smiled and gave her another hug. As she watched the young woman leave the room and head upstairs, she had the sense that she'd inherited another daughter. Sadly, she considered what Margarite had lost. It was a shame.

"I s'pose I ought to get on home," Ray said.

"How about a cup of coffee first? I could use the company. I'll put

Brian and Susie to bed, and we can enjoy a hot drink and a visit." The words were out before she could stop them. She didn't know exactly why she wanted him to stay.

"I always like your coffee and your company."

Jean headed for the front room, and Ray followed. Brian and Susie lay on the floor, working a puzzle. Brian knew where all the pieces went, but he let Susie find most of them. Jean shook her head. Brian was such a mix of temperaments. On one hand he could be like a whirlwind, hurrying from one activity to another and giving no thought to anyone or anything, and the next moment he could be thoughtful and sweet. Jean glanced at the clock on the mantle. It was seven o'clock. Luke should have been home long ago.

"Time for bed, you two," she said.

"Ah, Mom. Can't we stay up a little longer?" Brian asked.

Ray reached down and scooped him up, swinging Brian out in front of him.

Brian giggled.

"You've got school tomorrow," Ray said. "Now, how are you going to be smarter than everyone else if you don't get your sleep?"

"I don't care if I'm smart."

"Well, one day you'll wish you were," Ray said, setting him on his feet.

"I won't either," Brian said, heading for the stairs.

"Come on, Susie," Jean said, picking up the puzzle and putting it in its box.

"Mommy, I don't feel good," Susie said, swiping her hand over her eyes.

Jean set the box in a cupboard, then felt Susie's forehead. It was warm. "You do feel like you've got a fever. Do you hurt anywhere?"

"My head hurts."

"Is that all?"

Susie nodded, her blue eyes brighter than normal.

"I'll just give you some aspirin—that ought to help." She picked up the little girl and glanced at Ray. "I'll be down in a few minutes."

Susie waved at Ray. "Good night."

Ray smiled. "Good night."

She hugged her mother around the neck. "Can Ray stay? I like it when he's here."

"No. He has to go home. But he'll come back to visit." That seemed to comfort Susie because she rested her head on her mother's shoulder. "I like Ray."

"I like him too," Jean said, realizing she did care for Ray Townsend, maybe more than she should. He was kind to the children—good to all of them, including Luke. Although Ray tried to keep his tenderness in check, he was a gentle man. Jean's mind moved over the moments when he'd exposed his tender heart—memories of his wife and daughter, sorrow over Will's death, worry over Brian's broken arm, and even tonight concern had touched his eyes when he'd heard Susie was feverish.

He is a good man, she thought, realizing her fondness for him had grown. The feelings were inappropriate. Will had been gone less than a year. How could she even begin to think of anyone else? She felt shame. *It must be because I'm lonely,* she told herself. *Or because he's been so kind. I'd feel fondness for anyone who'd been so helpful.*

She pulled the covers over Susie and kissed her forehead. She and Ray Townsend were simply friends. It would never be anything more. Nor should it be. Aside from Will's death, they had very little in common. *What an awful thing to link two people.*

After saying prayers with Brian and Susie, Jean returned to the kitchen, wishing she could find a way to send Ray home.

He stood at the sink, looking out the window. When Jean entered the kitchen, he turned to her. "Looks like the wind is picking up."

"I can feel the chill even in here," Jean said, adding wood to the fire-box. "Maybe you ought to go home before it gets worse."

"It's not bad. I'll take that cup of coffee you offered, then head out."

Jean nodded. "OK. Would you like some apple pie to go with it?"

Ray smiled. "How could I turn down your apple pie?"

The coffee was still hot from supper, so Jean poured them each a cup and cut two slices of pie. "Why don't we eat it in the front room? Sometimes it seems I spend my life in the kitchen." She walked to the sofa and sat, placing her cup on an end table and taking a bite of pie.

Ray pushed his fork through the crumbly crust and well-cooked fruit and took a bite. Chewing, he smiled. "Delicious as always."

"We could listen to the Mukluk news."

"You have any music? I don't get to listen to it much."

Feeling a little unsettled, Jean set her pie on the end table and crossed to the phonograph. Opening the cabinet, she fingered several records. "How about 'East of the Sun' or 'I Got Rhythm' or . . ."

"You pick. I don't know much about music."

Jean selected "I've Got Rhythm." It seemed safe enough. She returned to the sofa. "You like music?"

"Yeah, but I don't know any of the newfangled stuff." Ray took another bite of pie and gently tapped his fork against his plate to the rhythm of the song. He grinned. "This would give Mrs. Dexter something to gossip about, wouldn't it?"

Jean set her fork on her plate. "I guess it would," she said, realizing the atmosphere was far too romantic for two adults who were only friends. She sipped her coffee and steered the conversation to a more comfortable topic. "Actually, I'm sorry Miram's parents are leaving town. This is hard on her."

"I think it's time she got out of that house."

"Yes, but getting out of the house and being left here while her family moves hundreds of miles away are two different things. She needs her independence, but not like this."

"How's it working out having her here?"

"Good. Oh, we had our adjustments in the beginning, but she's a fine person and a lot of help. Now it feels like she belongs here."

A strong gust of wind hit the house. Jean and Ray glanced out the window. All they could see was blackness. "The wind's picking up. Probably another storm," Jean said.

"When I was out at the barn earlier, the temperature was dropping." Ray pushed himself to his feet. "I ought to get home." He headed for the kitchen, coffee cup and plate in hand. "Wouldn't want to give the gossips too much ammunition."

Jean joined Ray at the sink and ran water into both their cups. Although Ray's arm pressed against hers, she didn't feel awkward. It seemed natural to be standing side-by-side at the sink.

Ray moved away. "You know, we make jokes about the gossip, but folks have been talking. Not just Margarite." He paused. "I don't want anyone thinking badly of you. You're too fine a woman." He leaned against the counter. "Maybe I ought to stay away for a while. You're pretty much set for wood, and with Miram here you could probably manage most of the milking."

"We can manage just fine. I never expected you to take on so much of the workload. But I don't want you to stay away. You're a good friend."

Ray's cheeks flushed. "Thank you. I think of you as a good friend too. But it seems my being here is causing trouble. I can still come around and take care of anything that needs fixin' or anything else that comes up with the animals or whatever, but I'll come, then go. No more meals," he said glumly.

Jean was tempted to go along with his suggestion, but she knew it was wrong. She folded her arms over her chest and said, "You'll do no such thing. You're a friend of this family—"

"What about Luke?"

"Luke will have to work out his problems. And he will. Just be patient." Jean rested a hand on Ray's arm. "You're welcome here any-time. And you can stay to supper from time to time if you like. If some people in this town have nothing better to do than gossip, then so be it." She smiled. "Eventually rumors will die down, and our friends will stand by us."

"I hope you're right."

A wail came from upstairs. "Oh, no. That's Susie." Jean hurried up the stairs. It wasn't normal for her to wake up once she was asleep. Jean hoped her fever hadn't shot up. She opened the door.

The light was on, and Miram was leaning over the little girl. She glanced at Jean. "I think she's worse. She feels awfully hot."

Jean hurried across the room. Susie's face was bright red. Jean laid a hand on her forehead. "Oh dear, she is really hot." Jean gathered the little girl in her arms. Heat radiated through Susie's nightgown. "It's all right, sweetheart. Everything's going to be all right."

"What do you think is wrong? It's not serious, is it?" Miram asked.

"I hope not." Jean headed for the door. "She needs to see the doctor." Holding Susie closely, she hurried down the stairs. "Ray, I need to get her to the doctor." The wind howled, and a smattering of ice tickled the window.

"I'll go for him. You don't want to take her out in this." Ray shrugged into his coat. "I'll be back in two shakes," he said and left.

With Susie in her arms, Jean stood at the window and stared out into the darkness. Where was Luke? He should have been back by now. *He's probably in town with Alex,* she decided, hoping she was right.

By the time Ray returned with the doctor, the storm had intensified and snow blew in with them. Luke was still not home, but she'd have to deal with that later.

"Evening, Jean," the doctor said. He looked at Susie. Her eyes were bright and her cheeks scarlet. "So, what have we here? You not feeling so good?" Susie nodded. "Well, we'll take care of that." He smiled, fine lines creasing the edges of his mouth and eyes. Susie huddled closer to her mother. The doctor took her from Jean and sat her on the sofa. Ray stood beside the little girl, and she took his big hand in hers. Then he sat on the sofa beside her.

After taking her temperature and listening to her heart and lungs, he said, "Susie, could you open your mouth for me and let me take a look at your throat?"

Susie obediently opened her mouth. "Now, stick out your tongue." He examined her throat. After taking a good look, he gently kneaded her neck, then did a quick examination of her trunk and legs and palpated her stomach. He straightened. "Anything hurt?"

"Just my head."

He turned to Jean. "She's fine—nothing serious. I'd say she just has the bug that's going around. Keep her in bed and give her aspirin for that fever. She'll be under the weather for a few days, then she should be fine." He returned his stethoscope to his bag. "If she develops a cough, bring her in to see me." Another burst of wind rattled the house. "Sounds like a real storm out there." He buttoned up his coat.

Ray stood. "I'll take him on home, then head for home myself."

"No, please don't go," Susie whined. "I want you to stay."

"But I have to take the doctor home."

"After, come back. Please."

Ray glanced at Jean, his eyes asking her what to do.

"I'll make up a bed on the sofa," Jean said after a moment's hesitation.

"You sure?"

"Uh-huh."

"All right, then. I'll be back just as soon as I can." Ray bent and kissed Susie's cheek.

She circled her arms around his neck and hugged him. "I love you."

His cheeks flushed. "I . . . love you too," he said and straightened.

"Thank you, Dr. Donovan," Jean said.

He nodded and left with Ray.

Jean smiled at Miram, who'd been sitting quietly. "People will surely talk now."

A furrow formed on Miram's forehead. "I wouldn't worry about what others say. I'll set them straight."

"Maybe having you in the house will quiet some wagging tongues."

"I hope so."

After giving Susie an aspirin, Jean took her up to bed, tucked her in, and said prayers. When she returned to the front room, Luke stood munching a raisin cookie and staring out into the darkness. "Was that Ray's truck I saw leaving?"

"Yes."

"What was he doing here so late?" The question had a sharp edge.

"He's taking Dr. Donovan home."

"The doc? Why? What happened?"

"Susie's sick."

"She bad?"

"No. He says it's just a little bug." Jean headed for the kitchen. "Why are you so late? I was worried."

Luke followed her. "I was with Alex. We went to a dance in town. I told you."

Jean nodded and carried the nearly empty coffeepot to the sink where she dumped the last of it, then rinsed it out.

"I don't like Ray being here so late."

Jean turned and faced Luke. "*You* don't like it? If you'd been home, he wouldn't have had to fetch the doctor for me." She ran a towel over the pot. "You might as well know. He's coming back and staying the night."

"What?" Luke nearly choked. "Why?"

"Susie asked him to. She's sick and scared, and she feels safer with him here. I couldn't tell her no."

"She's a little girl. You can tell her whatever you want."

Setting the coffeepot on the back of the stove, Jean said, "I don't like your tone, young man. You have no reason to be disrespectful. Your sister's sick, and Mr. Townsend is being kind. There's nothing improper about him staying here if it will make her feel better. He'll sleep on the sofa." She folded the towel and set it on the back of a chair. "I don't know what you're worried about—you and Miram and the children are here in the house."

Luke glared and chewed his cookie. "You know how I feel about him spending time here." His voice rose. "Why did you invite him to stay the night?"

"I didn't. Susie did. Stop yelling. You'll wake the whole house."

"I don't care who I wake up. That man's not staying here."

Jean fought to control her emotions. She had to admit that Luke was partially right. There really wasn't a reason for Ray to stay. Susie was already asleep. And people *would* talk.

"He's not staying. I'm telling him to leave when he gets back," Luke said evenly.

Jean didn't know how to respond. It didn't seem right for her son to dictate to her, but she also understood that he needed to feel respected and to have some say in household decisions. After all, he was a man, this was his house too, and his father had died. "I'll check on Susie," Jean said, "and I'll tell Ray he doesn't need to stay."

"Ray? It sounds like you two are getting chummy."

"I mean, Mr. Townsend." Jean hadn't realized she'd allowed herself to drop Ray's more formal name. Placing her hands on her hips, she met Luke's eyes. "Doggone it, Luke, I'll call him Ray if I want. He's a friend."

"He's not my friend. And he never will be. He's a murderer. Have you forgotten?" Luke hesitated. "And why is he your friend? What's happening? He killed your husband."

"Luke, let's not go through this again." Jean felt tired, very tired. Without another word she headed up the stairs to check on Susie. She was asleep and felt cooler.

Jean padded out of the room and walked downstairs to her bedroom. She thought over the events before and surrounding Will's death. Ray hadn't killed Will; it had been an accident, but it did seem strange that someone who had once been her enemy was now a close friend. Was their relationship becoming too casual?

She sat on the sofa to wait. When Ray returned, she'd tell him he had to go. She hated the idea. It was unfair, but then, how often had she told her children that life wasn't fair?

By the time the knock came, Jean was asleep. She roused herself and went to the door, tidying her hair. She opened the door. "Hi. I'm glad you made it back safely." She glanced over his shoulder. "The storm bad?"

"No, not too bad."

"Good." She took a slow breath. "I think it would be better if you stayed at your house tonight. Susie's asleep. She won't know."

"Sure. That would probably be best."

Jean nodded. Neither spoke for a moment, then Ray turned and walked away. Feeling weary and sad, Jean closed the door.

Chapter 24

LIGHT SNOW, CARRIED ON SOFT BREEZES, SWIRLED AROUND THOSE GATHERED outside the Palmer train station. Temperatures hovered around twenty degrees. Oddly, Laurel didn't feel cold. Usually she tussled to acclimate to the early months of winter when the first frigid weather set in. *Good thing,* she thought. *I'm going to be out in the cold most of the day.* Against Adam's wishes, she'd insisted on joining him and their friends for a day of skiing. She didn't plan on skiing, considering her condition. It would be fun just to watch.

"This was a wonderful idea," Celeste said, her eyes sparkling. "Alex, I'm so glad you thought of it. Last winter I was so busy working that I only got to the slopes a couple of times." She looped her arm through Robert's and smiled up at him, then looked at Laurel and Adam. "I get to teach Robert."

"I've never been," Robert explained. "Hope I don't make too big a fool of myself."

"You won't be the only one learning," Luke said. "I've never been either." He glanced at Mattie.

She smiled, and her dark eyes shimmered. "I can teach you. I'm not as good as Alex, but I know enough." She looked at her brother. "Of course, Alex is really good."

A flush touched Luke's cheeks. "Maybe you both can help."

Alex grinned knowingly. "I'll show you the basics, then Mattie can take over."

"All right. Sounds good to me." Luke grinned. "You're so good at everything. I figured hanging out with you would make me a better swimmer, hunter, and fisherman, but I'll never be as good as you."

"It's the native blood," Alex said, a sparkle in his eye.

"Celeste," Mattie began hesitantly, "your friend doesn't mind that Alex and I are coming along?"

"No. Why? Because you're native?"

"Well, some people don't like being around natives."

"Mike could care less. I've known him since I was a baby, and he's never paid any mind to whether someone's native or not." Celeste patted the palms of mitted hands together. "Besides, he's only driving us to the slopes and then back to the train. It's not like we're moving in with him."

"You worry too much," Alex said. "People don't care as much as you think."

Mattie cast her brother a disdainful look but said nothing. Draping a protective arm around Laurel, Adam said, "I tried to get Laurel to stay home, but she insisted on coming." He smiled at her.

"You worry too much. The baby's not due for another two months—well, almost two months." She rested a hand on her rounded abdomen. "I feel good, and the doctor said it would be just fine for me to take a day for fun. I won't be doing as much as I do at home—just sitting on a train, then sitting and watching all of you have a good time." She pressed her lips into a mock pout. "I've never skied before."

"After the baby, I'll take you," Adam promised. "After I've written the story of what it's like to have a baby in the Alaskan wilderness."

"So, how is your writing going?" Luke asked.

"Good. The *Trib* likes the stories I'm sending in. Seems people are hungry for Alaskan adventures. With Laurel and Jessie's help, I've come up with some good tales." He hugged Laurel with one arm. "We make a great team."

"It's a good thing your writing took off, 'cause you're no farmer." Luke chuckled.

"Luke!" Laurel said.

"I'm only kidding around."

Adam smiled. "No, it's true. I'm not a good farmer. All I manage to do is get us by. Laurel's the one who saves our bacon." He gave her a little squeeze.

Mattie stomped the frozen ground with booted feet. "It's getting cold. I wish the train would get here."

"I wish we didn't have to travel so far to ski," Alex complained.

"It's not so far, and the ski bowl's always fun," Celeste said brightly. "Besides, I know you ski right here in the valley every chance you get."

"It's not the same. Not as much fun."

"I kind of like making a day of it. I've got a picnic lunch for Robert and me, and I have plenty of food for anyone else who gets hungry." Celeste hefted the basket.

"Here it comes," Mattie said, leaning forward slightly and watching the approaching train.

They all picked up their bags and sack lunches.

When the train stopped, people crowded on board. Adam and Laurel sat facing Celeste and Robert, while Mattie, Alex, and Luke took seats across the aisle.

The air felt chilled even inside the train. Adam laid a lap blanket across Laurel's legs. She wasn't cold but enjoyed his kindness.

The trip south passed quickly. The car was filled with conversations and laughter. Alex retold a hunting story, and Luke listened enraptured while Mattie stared out the window. Celeste was happily gabbing about the latest movie she and Robert had seen.

Laurel felt unusually tired. Resting her face against the cool window, she stared at the white world moving past the train. She didn't feel as if she belonged. Everyone was younger or seemed younger, including Adam, who was involved in the conversation about movies. Laurel had more important matters to think about. She would soon be a mother with responsibilities. She'd tried to imagine what it would be like. Although she'd grown up in a home filled with children, she couldn't grasp what it meant to be responsible for another person's life—a baby who relied on her for survival.

She felt a cramp grab at her abdomen. She'd been having pains for a couple of weeks. The doctor said she had nothing to worry about. She laid a hand on her stomach and watched it rise and fall as her child changed position. She smiled. The joy of motherhood superseded her fears. She imagined holding her baby and longed for the weeks to pass quickly.

Another spasm hit her, worse than the first. *It's nothing. I've most probably pulled a muscle,* she told herself. After all, she'd been working hard all week preparing the baby's room—painting, sewing, hanging draperies, and moving furniture. When Adam discovered she'd been rearranging furniture, he'd nearly lost his temper and made it clear she wasn't to do any more heavy work.

When the train arrived in Anchorage, Laurel folded the blanket over her arm. "I'll need this. Watching people ski won't keep me warm." She smiled, then felt another pain. It didn't really hurt, but she'd had more than usual and couldn't help but wonder why.

"Let's go," Adam said as he picked up a small bag of extra clothes and ushered her off the train.

Mike, a tall thin man in his fifties, greeted the group. "Welcome to civilization," he quipped, "such as it is." He helped gather up the skis and poles, strapped them to the roof of the car, and then gave instructions on how they should all fit inside the bulky Chrysler.

The ski bowl wasn't far from the depot, so the trip didn't take long. When Laurel climbed out of the car, she immediately felt the enthusiasm of the skiers. She saw the large, open hillside crisscrossed by skiers, but what most interested Laurel was a banked toboggan run that curved around the hill. Sledders crowded the broad, white hill, waiting their turn to fly down the run. Laurel was fascinated as she watched people navigate a large curve. Laughter and squeals resonated through the air, and she wished she could join the fun.

Alex and Celeste were anxious to get on the hill. They quickly strapped on their skis. "I'll just take one run," Celeste said, "then I'll come back and help you," she told Robert and headed for the towrope with Alex chasing her down. Mattie followed.

Wearing an amused smile, Robert watched her go. "It's clear what really matters to Celeste." Watching Adam strap on his skis, he did his best to duplicate the moves. It took several tries to get his skis secured. Looking clumsy and awkward, he stood and tried to move forward. He managed to travel only a few feet, then fell. Getting up wasn't easy, and he finally let Adam help him.

"Are you sure you're going to be all right?" Adam asked Laurel.

"Yes. It'll be fun to watch."

Adam seemed hesitant to leave her. "You sure?"

"I'm fine. Go on and have a good time." Laurel gave him a kiss and rested her arms on her stomach.

Adam pushed off and headed for the towrope. Luke and Robert seemed uncertain what to do.

Wearing a smile and laughing, Mattie swooshed past them and stopped. "You boys need some help?"

"We do," Robert said matter-of-factly.

Mattie patiently showed the two how to stand, move forward, and turn. She also demonstrated the right way to use the poles and the easiest way to stop. Finally, with a word of encouragement, she headed off. Celeste stopped off once or twice to check on the beginners, but the slopes called to her and she was soon off again.

After a while, Laurel's face felt frozen, and her back and legs ached. It was time to get up and find a warm place. She headed for a building that she hoped promised a place to sit and drink something hot.

Feeling clumsy, she carefully made her way through the snow. This was not a place for a very pregnant woman. Still, she couldn't deny that the cold air and the atmosphere of fun and daring had invigorated her.

Once inside, she bought a cup of hot chocolate and settled into a large cushioned chair to watch the slopes through a plateglass window. She relaxed in the warmth and comfort and soon dozed off.

It was Celeste who woke her. She was more animated than usual. Plopping down on the sofa beside Laurel's chair, she asked, "You hungry? It's well past lunch. We've all eaten. I was beginning to worry about you."

Laurel yawned and stretched. "I'm fine. How long have I been asleep?"

"Don't know, but by the looks of it, a good long while. The bus will be leaving for the train station soon. Adam told me not to wake you, but I figured you'd want something to eat before we left."

Laurel stretched again. "I can't believe I fell asleep right here with all these people around." She glanced at the families and couples using the facility.

"It's your condition," Celeste said with a smile. "You feeling all right?"

"Yes. Just sleepy." Laurel took the sandwich Celeste offered her. "I made a lunch. I don't have to eat yours."

"It seems you're a better cook than me," she said wryly. "There's nothing left of yours and there's lots of mine. So, I guess you'll have to settle for mine."

Laurel studied the roast beef sandwich. "It looks good to me," she said and took a bite.

The ride down the mountain was loud. Skiers told stories of their triumphs and their spills. Luke and Robert talked about what they'd learned. As usual, Mattie and Luke sat side by side. They talked quietly. Celeste and Robert huddled together in deep conversation, seemingly unaware of the tumult around them.

Laurel wondered if Luke and Mattie, and Robert and Celeste would end up together permanently. *I'll be surprised if they don't,* she thought as a twinge of pain reached across her back. She changed position, hoping to get more comfortable. *It can't be the baby,* she reasoned. *I'm not due for nearly eight weeks.*

"You feeling all right?" Adam asked. "You're kind of pale."

"I'm fine," Laurel lied, not wanting to worry him unnecessarily.

By the time they boarded the train, Laurel's pains were more frequent and more painful. She now knew the pains were not coming from strained muscles but hoped that once she'd settled in a more comfortable seat, she would feel better.

Laurel felt relief when the train pulled out of the station and they headed for Palmer. At least if the baby did come early, she'd be home, and the doctor would be there. She pulled the blanket up over her and settled back into her seat.

The car quieted. A day in the snow had exhausted the adventurers. Even Celeste had fallen asleep, leaning against Robert. Laurel smiled, happy for her best friend. She remembered the day she thought she might be ruining Robert's life by calling off the wedding. *I must have been awfully arrogant,* she thought. Another pain cut across the small of her back, then wrapped itself around her belly. "Ohh," she moaned.

Adam may have looked as if he was sleeping, but he wasn't. He sat up and looked at Laurel. "What's wrong? You all right?" He rested a hand on her arm.

"I've been having some pains. I didn't think much of them, but they're getting worse."

"What kind of pains? Where?"

"In my back and stomach. I've never had anything like them. They feel like a cramp."

"Do you think you need a doctor?" Adam stood and searched the car.

"What is it?" Celeste asked, suddenly wide awake.

"Adam," Laurel said, taking her husband's hand. "It's all right. Please, just sit. I don't need a doctor. We're not that far from Palmer. If I'm still having pains when we get there, we can stop and see Dr. Donovan."

Adam looked at her, uncertain whether to believe her or not. Finally he sat. "How long have you been having pains?"

"They started this morning."

"This morning?" he exploded. "Why didn't you say something? You should never have come on this trip."

"I didn't think they were anything to worry about." Laurel closed her eyes, then looked at her husband. "I still don't think they are. The baby isn't due for several weeks."

"Sometimes babies come early," Celeste said. "You can't count on them being right on time."

"Are you having the baby?" Luke asked, leaning over the seat.

"No. I'm not. I'm just having a few pains."

"At least it's not a long trip to Palmer," Celeste said, looking out the window. "The snow is really coming down. Looks like we finished just in time."

A moment later the train jolted, bumped, and slid sideways. The air was filled with the sounds of grinding, clattering, and the screams of passengers. People were thrown out of their seats. Clothing, purses, bags, and books tumbled off racks and seats. Laurel hung onto her armrests. "What's happening?"

Adam threw an arm in front of her.

Then it was over. The coach was quiet, except for soft whimpers. Laurel looked at Adam, then herself, wondering if they'd been injured. "Are you all right?"

"I'm fine. What about you?"

"I'm all right, I think." Another painful contraction spread across

Laurel's back and around her stomach. "I don't know about the baby though," she said through clenched teeth.

"Why? What's happening?"

"The pain is worse." Laurel pressed a hand on her stomach, willing away the cramp.

"We're off the track!" someone shouted.

"What?" Adam asked. People leaped to the windows to look out, but they couldn't see much in the darkness and swirling snow.

A man stepped out of the car and down the stairway. He returned a few minutes later. "We're stuck."

"How are we going to get out of here?" Celeste asked, her face white.

"Someone will come for us," Adam assured her.

Alex helped a woman who'd fallen in the aisle. A bruise and a bump had already appeared on her forehead, but she simply straightened her hat, said thank you, and sat in the nearest empty seat.

"Is anyone hurt?" Adam asked.

"I am," a woman said. Others were hurt as well, so Celeste, Robert, Mattie, and Luke moved throughout the car, checking the passengers. They found bumps and bruises, lacerations, and one suspected broken arm, but no one had any serious injuries.

Celeste dropped into the seat beside Laurel. "You all right?"

"I don't know. The pains are still coming, and they're getting stronger. I wasn't too worried, but now . . ." She gazed out the window. Snow pelted the glass. "Celeste, I can't have the baby here, not without a doctor. It's too soon." She gripped her friend's hand.

Chapter 25

A CAR DROVE UP THE HASPER DRIVEWAY, STOPPING AT THE BACK OF THE house. Susie, who was cuddled on her mother's lap looking at a picture book, said, "Someone's here."

"Let's take a look and see who it is." Jean eased the little girl off her lap.

Brian, who'd been sprawled on the floor working a puzzle, jumped up and started for the kitchen.

"Wait, Brian," Jean said. "I'll open it." She crossed to the door and looked out. "It's Mr. Townsend." The three stood on the back porch and watched him climb out of his car. He wore a troubled expression and walked with long, quick strides. "Howdy."

His voice sounded strained. Jean shivered. "Is something wrong?"

When Ray walked up to the steps, Brian catapulted himself off the porch. Ray caught him and swung him up, then set him on his feet.

"Hello, Mr. Townsend," Susie said softly.

He smiled at the little girl. "Hello there." He looked at Jean. "I need to talk to you."

"Certainly," Jean said, her stomach dropping at his serious tone. "Children, you go back inside. We'll finish reading your book in a minute." Both Brian and Susie hesitated. "Go along now." The children reluctantly ambled into the kitchen. Jean closed the door and turned to face Ray. "What is it? Something's wrong."

"There's been an accident. The train returning from Anchorage derailed."

"Oh, Lord! No!" Jean felt the strength go out of her legs. "Is anyone hurt?"

"No one seems to know how bad it is." For just a moment he touched her shoulder. "I'm going down to the station. I thought you might want to wait there."

"Yes. Of course." She glanced at the house. "I'll need someone to stay with the children. I'm sure Adele will watch them for me. Just give me a few minutes to get them bundled up and ready to go."

The children were safely settled at the Jenkins's in less than ten minutes, and Ray and Jean were on their way to the train station. "How bad was the derailment?" Jean asked, doubting Ray knew but needing to ask just in case.

"Like I said, what came over the wireless was pretty vague. It just said the train had derailed and injuries were expected. I wish I knew more." Driving fast for the conditions, he gripped the wheel while the car bounced through frozen potholes and slid over packed snow. He glanced at Jean. "I'm sure our kids are fine."

Jean didn't respond, her mind imagining the worst. She prayed for God's mercy and his miracles. *I can't lose anyone else, Father. I just can't do it.*

Cars crowded the small depot. Families had come to wait. Looking fragile, Alex and Mattie's mother stood leaning against the building. She was small with graying hair pulled back from her face. Jean approached her, not knowing how to help. "Hello, Mrs. Lawson." The woman's eyes filled with tears. Jean took her hand. "They'll be all right. God's looking out for them. I know it."

The tiny woman only nodded and tried to quiet her quivering chin.

Jean stepped inside the depot, hoping for more information. The man at the desk didn't know any more than what Ray had told her. The room was overcrowded and warm, so Jean returned to the outdoor platform, welcoming the cold air.

"There you are," Jessie said, walking up to her and pulling her into a tight hug. "I came as soon as I heard. I've been praying nonstop."

Jean stepped away. Clutching the older woman's hand, she said, "I'm scared."

Laurel felt queasy and shaky. The pains were still coming, but thankfully they hadn't worsened. Still, Laurel was frightened. What if they weren't rescued? Hours had passed, and they were still trapped. She shivered. It was cold, and the storm had intensified.

Celeste sat down beside her. "How are you feeling?"

"About the same, but kind of sick."

"A lot of people are feeling sick. I think it's the cold and the fear. Try not to worry. Someone will be here soon."

Pain hit Laurel, spreading across her back and over her abdomen. She chewed on her lip.

"You having another one?"

Laurel nodded.

"Even if this is labor, first babies take hours and hours. Everyone says so. You'll be in Palmer in plenty of time." She smiled, but even Celeste couldn't disguise her apprehension.

Adam returned with a cup of tea. "Here, I thought you might like some. The porter made it." When he talked, the air fogged.

"It's getting colder. What if they don't come soon?" Laurel asked.

"They'll be here." He handed the tea to her and tucked the blankets in tighter. "Everything's going to be fine."

"Everyone keeps saying it's going to be fine, but how does anyone know?" Laurel gazed out at the black night. Winds howled and frozen pellets spattered the window. "No one's going to come for us in this weather."

"Rescue teams do what they have to. You watch; they'll send out sled dogs or something."

"If they come, do you think they'll bring a doctor?"

"Of course."

Another pain tugged at her abdomen. It didn't hurt too badly. Maybe this wasn't real labor. Laurel closed her eyes and rested her head against the seat. *Father, please keep my baby safe. Don't let it be born out here.*

Laurel knew the baby would probably die if it came this early, no matter where it was born. It would be too tiny to survive. She grabbed Adam's hand. "Maybe we should have moved to Chicago. At least they have good hospitals there."

"Dr. Donovan is a good man. He knows what he's doing."

"I shouldn't have come today."

Adam gently smoothed back her amber hair.

Tears seeped from Laurel's eyes. "I always have to do things my way. I'm sorry."

"Hush." Adam kissed her brow. "You and the baby will be fine. Remember, the doctor said it's normal to have pains the last couple of months."

"I know, but the ones I'd been having didn't hurt. These do."

Robert peeked around from behind Adam. He offered Laurel an encouraging smile. "We'll be on our way before you know it."

Another hour passed before the barking of dogs carried over the winds. "They're here!" someone shouted.

The storm was too severe to allow anyone to leave the train, but the sleds brought a doctor and a nurse who immediately went to work suturing lacerations, binding sprains and breaks, and soothing the injured. Adam managed to get a nurse to look at Laurel.

"You think you might be in labor?" the pretty nurse asked.

"It's my first one. I'm not sure," Laurel said.

The nurse placed a stethoscope against Laurel's abdomen and listened. "The baby sounds good and strong." She rested a hand on Laurel's abdomen and waited. After Laurel had three of the cramping pains, the nurse removed her hand and smiled. "You and the baby are fine. I don't think you're in true labor. The contractions are irregular, and they're not strong." She patted Laurel's arm. "You don't have to worry. A truck is making its way here, and we'll have everyone out of the train soon."

"Thank you so much," Laurel said. "I can't believe you made it here in the storm."

The nurse grinned. "When I came up from Seattle, I didn't expect to be mushing through a blizzard to treat patients, but life is full of surprises." She moved on.

The storm had quieted by the time three army trucks with canvas-covered beds slogged through the snow. Adam and Robert helped transfer passengers from the train to the trucks. They were especially gentle with Laurel. Once in a truck, she made her way to a bench along the side of the bed and sat. The seat was hard and cold, but at least they were protected from the weather and on their way home.

Adam climbed in and sat beside Laurel. Exhausted, Laurel leaned against him. She'd be happy to get home.

"How you feeling?" he asked.

"Better. I'm not having as many cramps," she said, closing her eyes and longing for sleep. But there would be no rest. The going was slow as the truck ground its way through fresh powder. It slid and bumped, and Laurel wondered more than once if they were going to end up off the road.

Her back ached and the pains had increased again, but she said nothing to Adam, not wanting to worry him. She pulled a wool blanket up under her chin and imagined how it would feel to crawl into bed and sleep.

Hands stuffed into his pockets, Ray leaned against the outside wall of the depot while Jean paced the platform. "It's been hours," she said. "We should have heard something by now."

"We'll hear."

Stepping outside and wearing her usual calm expression, Jessie offered Jean a cup of coffee. "Here, drink this. It'll warm you up." She glanced at Ray. "Would you like some?"

"No. I've already had too much."

Jean cradled the cup between her gloved hands. She gazed down the tracks. "What's happening out there? Why won't anyone tell us?"

"They don't know anything," Ray said.

"What if no one can get to them? It's so cold."

Jessie smiled softly. "Now Jean, God knows all about the weather. He'll take care of our loved ones." She smiled, and the creases at the corners of her eyes deepened. Resting a hand on Jean's shoulder, she squeezed. "Maybe you ought to go home and get some sleep. I'll make sure to let you know when we hear something."

"I can't leave."

"Brian and Susie are probably needing you, and you can't do anything here."

A jolt of reality rolled through Jean. She'd forgotten about Brian and Susie. "Of course. You're right." She stared down the tracks, willing the train home. "I need to go." She turned her eyes on Jessie. "You promise to send someone for me as soon as you hear?"

"I promise."

"I'll take you home," Ray offered.

"Thank you," Jean said, close to tears. Ray's kindness only made it harder to maintain her self-control. She needed Will. He'd always been there to help her face a crisis. "All right. Let's go."

Leaving the protection of the depot, snow pelted her and wind ripped at her coat. She ducked inside the car and settled into the seat. Ray hurried around to the other side and climbed in. "It's getting worse again," Jean said. "Is it safe to drive?"

"Sure. I've driven in worse." He started the engine and eased onto the road.

Ray stopped at the Jenkins's and picked up Brian and Susie. Before returning to the depot, he helped get them into bed. Leaving Susie snug, he crossed the hallway to Brian's room.

Jean gave Brian a kiss.

"Mom, tonight would it be OK if Mr. Townsend said prayers with me?"

"Of course," Jean said, glancing at Ray. She walked to the doorway and waited.

Tucking the blankets up around the youngster, he stood. Brian caught his hand. "I'm scared. What if something bad happens to Luke and Laurel? And what about Adam and the baby? Could you pray with me?"

"Sure," Ray said, kneeling beside the bed. Brian kept a tight hold on his hand. "I suppose we ought to close our eyes," Ray said. Brian squeezed his shut. With a smile Ray closed his and began, "Dear Father in heaven, we know you're with our loved ones. But even knowing that, we're scared. So, Lord, we ask you to take good care of Luke, Laurel and the baby, Adam, Celeste, and all the others on that train. Bring them home safe and sound." Ray paused. "We know you're in charge of this world and everything in it and that we can trust you, but sometimes we forget. Give us peace. And I ask especially that you would help Brian and

Susie and their mama to get a good sleep. Remind them that you're watching over all of us. Amen."

Brian smiled up at Ray and threw his arms around the big man's neck. "Thank you. You pray almost as good as my dad. I wish you could be my new dad."

Ray glanced at Jean. Her face had turned red, and he offered her a small smile. He cleared his throat. "Brian, bein' your father would be a real honor, but I can't be. You already have a father. How about if we're just good friends?"

"I guess, but I still wish you were here all the time."

"I'll be here whenever you need me." Ray patted Brian's hand, then stood and walked out of the room.

"Good night," Jean said and turned out the light.

"Night." Brian sat up. "Mama, would you mind if Mr. Townsend was my new dad?"

"Well, it's not a matter of minding. I like Mr. Townsend. He's a fine man, but he's not your father."

"I know, but Daddy's not here, and I like Mr. Townsend. He's almost like my dad."

"He's a good, good friend, and you can thank God for that," Jean said with finality. "Now, good night."

When Jean walked out, Ray stood in the hallway. He glanced at her, then shaking his head, said, "I don't deserve those kids' love."

Jean hugged herself about the waist and leaned an arm against the wall. She asked softly, "Why do you say that?"

"I've done more bad than good in my life. Seems after all that, I ought to be punished rather than . . . well, rather than loved. My daughter's been so forgiving and now Brian and Susie."

"God doesn't always give us what we deserve. We're all evil. No one is perfect. But he loves us anyway." She smiled softly. "The miracle is that when he sacrificed his Son, all believers were made worthy of riches. We can stand before God sinless and pure. Even you, Ray Townsend." She grinned, then headed for the stairs. Stopping at the landing, she said, "I don't think you understand how much you've done for us. I owe you a lot."

Ray's face crumpled in anguish. "How can you say that? Your husband would be alive today if it weren't for me."

"How many times do I have to say what happened wasn't your fault before you'll believe it?" Keeping her hand on the balustrade, she took a step. "I'll pray you come to understand that and how important you are—not just to us, but to God." With that, Jean walked down the stairs.

Chapter 26

JEAN ROLLED OUT COOKIE DOUGH WHILE LAUREL HELPED SUSIE REMOVE A cookie cutout and set it on a baking sheet. "It's pretty," Susie said, patting the bell-shaped cookie.

"Look at mine," Brian said, lifting away his cookie cutter to reveal a perfectly shaped reindeer.

"That's very nice," Laurel said, leaning over the table, her round belly preventing her from reaching a Santa-shaped cutter.

Miram handed it to her.

Brian grinned. "Your stomach is sure getting big."

Running a hand over her abdomen, Laurel said, "I'm getting fat."

"It's 'cause the baby's growing. Mommy told us." Susie patted Laurel's tummy.

"We don't have long to wait now," Brian said.

"It can't be soon enough for me." Laurel sat with a groan.

"Will Santa bring a present for the baby?" Susie asked.

"I don't know. Maybe." Jean raised an eyebrow and smiled.

"I'm sure he will." Miram returned a bowl of butter to the icebox. "And maybe the baby will arrive by Christmas. What a nice surprise that would be. I'm so thankful you didn't have that child on the train."

"Me too," Laurel replied. "That was quite a scare. Just pre-labor I guess."

Jean wrapped an arm around Laurel's waist. "God was watching over you and everyone else on that trip," she smiled.

Brian popped a piece of dough into his mouth. "Christmas is tomorrow. So do you think the baby might come tonight?"

"Only God knows." Jean picked up the tray of cookies. "These are beautiful." Opening the oven, she slid the cookie sheet in.

"Mama, if I stay up and watch for Santa, will he still come?" Brian asked, cutting another Santa cookie.

"Nope. He wants children to be asleep." Jean looked at a nearly full tray of unbaked cookies. "I think these would look real pretty with a sprinkle of sugar. What do you think?"

"Yes. Sugar," Susie said, pressing a round cutter into the dough.

A knock sounded at the back door. "Now, who could that be? It's too early for Adam." Miram walked to the door and opened it. A burst of cold air swept into the room.

Celeste stood in the doorway with a big turkey in her arms. "Any solace for the cold and weary?" she asked with a smile.

Miram chuckled and pushed up her glasses. "Come in. Come in."

Celeste stepped in.

Ray stomped his boots free of snow but didn't step inside. Jean went to the door. He hefted a bulging canvas bag and whispered, "I've got something for the children." Smiling conspiratorially, he stripped back his hood.

Wiping her hands on her apron, Jean glanced over her shoulder. "I guess you can put them on the shelf." She nodded at a shelf above the washing machine.

"What's that?" Brian asked, standing in the doorway.

"Just some extra potatoes I thought you might need."

"We got plenty of potatoes."

"Well, we can always use more," Jean said, hustling the boy back inside.

Celeste held up the bird. "Dad said turkey used to be a custom in your family. We figured this Christmas would be a good time to bring back the tradition."

"Yes. I've missed it. We've tried to raise some, but I think they're too dumb to survive in this kind of weather."

Ray set the bag up out of sight of prying eyes. Susie hugged his legs, and he hefted her up. "Hi, Mr. Townsend," she said with a bright smile.

"Hello, there."

"This is a nice surprise," Jean said.

Ray rubbed his face, ruddy from the cold and wind. "Celeste and I figured we ought to come by to wish you a merry Christmas."

Jean took the turkey and carried it to the sink. "This is a wonderful gift. Thank you." She ran cold water over the bird and wondered at the change in Ray Townsend. He didn't resemble the man she'd known their first year in Alaska. Had God changed him so much? "You didn't have to do this."

"We wanted to," Celeste said, removing her neck scarf. "It was nice of Mr. Woodson to give us the day off," she told Jean.

"Yes. We've been so busy at the store I was afraid we'd have to work right up to Christmas Eve."

"Look what I did." Brian held up a finished cookie. He sniffed the air. "What's that smell?"

"Oh, dear," Jean said, hurrying to the stove. Using a heavy towel to open the door, she retrieved the burned cookies. "They were so beautiful." With the dismal tray of cookies in hand, she looked at Brian and Susie. "I'm sorry."

Susie's lower lip drooped.

"We've got more to bake," Jean said, setting the cookie sheet on the counter.

"It's OK, Mom," Brian said, holding up an unbaked Santa. "I like making cookies. We'll make lots more."

"That's a fine-looking cookie," Ray said.

Brian proudly set it on the tray.

After sprinkling cookies with sugar, Jean popped a new batch into the oven. She turned to Ray and Celeste. "Can I get you something? Some coffee or tea?"

"First I've got something to bring in," Ray said. "It's for you."

"For me?"

"I'll be right back." He hurried out the back door.

"What's he up to?" Miram asked, sniffling and dabbing her nose with a handkerchief.

"I guess we're about to find out," Jean said.

Laurel pinched off a piece of dough and put it in her mouth, then glanced at her stomach. "You wouldn't think I could eat anything," she said with a wry grin. "The baby's taking up most of the room."

Celeste grinned. "You look like you're about to burst. How are you feeling?"

"Tired and uncomfortable. I wish it would just hurry and get here. It's been quiet the last couple of days."

Celeste lifted an eyebrow. "Isn't that a sign that it's getting ready to be born?"

"Maybe it's resting up."

"As *you* should be," Jean said. "You've been on your feet all day. You sit, and I'll finish the rest of these." She went to the stove and peeked at the batch cooking.

Ray walked in, carrying a rifle. He held out the gun to Jean. "I didn't know how to wrap it. Sorry."

Jean took the rifle.

"I figured you could use it. Maybe we'll go hunting again."

Balancing the weapon in her hands, then running her hand over the stock, Jean said, "Ray, I can't accept this. It's much too expensive."

"It's yours. It has your name on it."

"My name?"

"I had it engraved on the stock. That way no one will get confused about who's the real hunter in the family." He grinned.

Jean examined the engraving, ran her fingers over it, then looked at Ray. "Well, I guess it *is* mine. Thank you."

Wearing a scowl, Luke stepped into the kitchen from the front room.

"Luke, I was wondering if you and I might play a game of checkers later," Ray said jovially.

Luke stared at the man, his eyes hard. Finally he said, "Sure. Why not? I don't have nothin' else to do, especially since I'm no good at hunting."

"Luke, he didn't mean that," Jean said, but the young man was already walking out.

Ray let out a heavy breath. "I didn't mean he couldn't hunt." Shaking his head, he added, "Seems I'm always sticking my foot in it."

"He knows you didn't mean it," Jean said. "Now, would you like some coffee and a cookie? We've got hot ones." She opened the oven door and removed the latest batch.

"Sounds good. Anything I can do to help?"

Susie handed him a cookie cutter. "We still got more to make."

"I'm not very good at it, but I'll try," Ray said.

"I'll show you." Susie cut out a cookie. "There. See. Like that."

"Ray, would you and Celeste like to stay for supper? We're just having biscuits and gravy and string beans. Nothing special, but it'll be good and hot."

"Sounds great. Celeste?"

"Sure." She looked at Laurel. "I'll help Jean and Miram, and that way Laurel can stay off her feet."

"I barely do anything these days. Even Adam's been waiting on me hand and foot," Laurel said.

"Where is he?"

"Finishing a story. He'll be by soon. He wouldn't miss Christmas Eve and fresh homemade cookies." A blast of wind hit the house. Laurel walked to the window and looked out. Trees bent in the wind, and snow shook from the limbs. "Another storm," she said with a sigh. "I'll be glad for summer."

Adam arrived just as dinner was being set out. He shook snow from his coat before hanging it up. "Looks like we've got a real williwaw blowing in."

"A williwaw?" Jean asked.

"Sorry. It's an Alaskan term that means strong wind or a storm." He bent and kissed Laurel. "I just learned about it. Sometimes when I'm writing, I get involved. I guess I'm talking in character. I figure one day I'll be a true Alaskan." He chuckled. Looking at his wife and resting a hand on her shoulder, he said, "How have you been feeling today?"

"Fine, but I'm starving. You're here just in time. We were about to eat without you."

Adam took the chair beside Laurel. "Smells good."

"Just biscuits and gravy," Jean said, setting a bowl of gravy on the table. Celeste put a platter of hot biscuits beside the gravy and sat. Miram placed a bowl of the string beans at one end of the table.

"Where's Luke?" Jean asked.

"I think he's still in his room," Laurel said.

"I'll get him." Adam started to rise.

"Why don't you say grace first, then go on up," Jean said.

"Sure."

Adam said a quick prayer of thanks and went to get Luke. A few minutes later he returned with the young man.

Still not smiling, Luke sat. In silence he served himself, and in silence he ate. Once or twice he cast a glance at Ray, but for the most part he kept his eyes on his plate.

Jean was thankful for the youngsters' exuberance. They chattered about Christmas and Santa and gifts, lifting what would have been a subdued atmosphere. This would be their first Christmas without Will, and Jean couldn't free herself from an ache that had settled in her gut. She glanced at Luke, knowing he felt it too. She forgave him his surly mood.

After dinner Ray managed to corral Luke into a game of checkers while everyone but Laurel worked in the kitchen. She was stretched out on the sofa, reading a magazine.

With the checkerboard between them, Ray contemplated his next move. He glanced at his opponent. No matter how angry or depressed Luke might be, it hadn't affected his game. He was giving Ray a real challenge. He rubbed his shaved chin. If he wasn't careful, Luke would beat him.

Luke leaned back in his chair and threw one leg over the other. "We gonna be here all night?"

"I'm studying the situation." Ray grinned, but Luke only glowered back.

"I'm done with resting," Laurel said, closing the magazine and setting her feet on the floor. "There's no reason why I can't help with the preparations." Setting the magazine on the end table, she walked to Luke and leaned over his shoulder to study the board. "I'll see if Adam wants to play the winner. I'm sure he'd be happy for a reason to get out of the kitchen." She left the two men to their game.

An oppressive silence settled over the room. Ray searched his mind for something to talk about. "So, how's trapping been?" He moved a checker forward.

"Slow." Luke didn't look up, but a smirk touched his lips as he jumped one of Ray's checkers and removed it from the board. He sat back, folded his arms over his chest, and asked, "You been having any luck?"

"Not bad. I'm holding my own." As soon as Ray saw Luke's annoyed expression, he knew he should have downplayed his success. He turned his eyes back to the board. "You're not the only one struggling. It's slow for a lot of folks."

"Except for the real mountain men, I suppose," Luke said sarcastically. He straightened and glared at Ray. Neither spoke for a long while. Finally breaking the silence, Luke said, "I want you to stay away from my mother."

"What do you mean, stay away?" Ray asked, unable to keep the challenge out of his voice. He might have mellowed, but he wasn't going to let a kid like Luke tell him what he could or couldn't do. He met the young man's eyes. He'd tried hard to like Luke, but his whiny, nasty attitude had gotten under his skin.

"You know exactly what I mean. I know what you're up to."

"I don't know what you mean. Maybe you can explain what I'm up to."

"You're courting her."

Ray jumped one of Luke's men. "You know nothing about how I feel or what I'm doing. And if any courting is going on, that's between your mother and me."

Ray couldn't deny that he'd welcome Jean's affection, but he didn't think for a moment that she would give him a chance. She'd been widowed because of him. Nothing could come of the two of them. He could never become the man Will Hasper had been.

"You are, aren't you?" Luke challenged.

The sad reality settled over Ray, and his anger evaporated. He pushed to his feet. "Your mother's a fine woman, Luke. Any man would be proud to have her, but if you want to know if I'm out to get her, the answer is no. You don't have anything to fear."

Luke stood. "So how come you're always here?"

"I'm needed. This farm requires a lot of work. And I like being here. Brian and Susie are terrific kids."

Luke's face said he didn't believe a word. "You can spend all the time you want here, and it won't change anything. You don't belong. You'll never fill my father's shoes."

Ray's anger flared. "I'm not courting your mother, nor am I trying to push my way into this family. And I never claimed I could be as fine a man as your father."

A flicker of uncertainty touched Luke's eyes. "Good, then it won't be hard for you to leave."

"Luke!" Jean stepped into the room. "That's enough!"

He fixed his eyes on his mother. "He's got you fooled, Mom. He's not who you think he is."

"And who is that?" Jean challenged.

"It's clear as the nose on your face. He's no good. He's a phony, trying to worm his way into our family."

"I don't believe that," Jean said. "And the only thing that's clear is that your bitterness is rooted. If you don't dig it out, it will destroy you."

Luke said nothing for a long moment, then walked out of the house.

"Ray, I'm sorry. He shouldn't have spoken to you that way."

"He has a right to his feelings." Ray gave a heavy sigh. "Celeste and I better get on home." He looked at his daughter standing in the doorway. She seemed close to tears. "You ready?"

She nodded and went to get her coat.

Ray followed her, pulled on his coat and gloves, then turned to Jean. "I'm the one who's sorry. I didn't mean for this to happen."

"I know."

He opened the door, and frigid air carried in tiny snowflakes. Celeste hurried for the car. "I'm real sorry," Ray said, his voice heavy.

Chapter 27

SNOW FELT LIKE TINY SHARDS OF GLASS AS THE WIND WHIPPED IT INTO RAY'S face. He pulled his hood closed and huddled low.

Celeste gripped his arm and peered into the swirling white. "Are you sure we're going the right way?"

"Yeah. This is the way," Ray said shortly.

"How do you know?"

Ray didn't answer but kept moving.

Several minutes later he rested his hand on the side rail of the small bridge just before the Haspers'. "We're almost there," he called, the wind carrying away his words.

"Thank the Lord!" Celeste yelled.

Ray and Celeste stumbled down the drive, keeping their hands on the fence line as a guide. The Hasper house appeared amidst the white squall, and father and daughter hurried toward the porch. Huddling against the door, Ray pounded on the wooden barrier.

Almost immediately the door opened and light flooded the porch. "What the . . . ?" Adam asked. "What are you two doing back here? Are you all right?"

Ray ushered in Celeste. "We're fine, I think. Just cold." He stripped off his coat and gloves. Celeste headed straight for the stove.

"I'm freezing," she said, shivering and huddling close to the heat.

Jean set down a bowl and hurried to Celeste. "What happened?" Taking Celeste's face in her hands, she examined her skin. "I don't see any frostbite." She looked at the girl's hands, then rubbed them.

Ray joined his daughter at the stove, holding out his hands to the heat.

"What happened?" Jean repeated.

"We slid off the road. Only thing to do was to come back." Ray glanced at Celeste. "The storm's really picked up. I wasn't sure we were going to make it. I'm sorry, Jean, but we'll have to stay until it passes."

"Just thank the Lord you're all right," Jean said. "We need to get you into warm, dry clothes. Laurel, could you find Celeste something to wear from my closet?"

Laurel pushed herself up.

"No, Laurel, you stay down. I'll do it," Miram offered. "I think I have some things that would fit you, Celeste."

"Thanks," Celeste said and followed Miram out of the room.

Jean sized up Ray, then shook her head. "I don't know if I can come up with something for you. Will wasn't a small man, but he certainly wasn't as big as you."

"I'm not real wet. Mostly just cold. I'll just stay here in front of the stove and be warm soon enough." He held his hands out to the heat. "Hmm. Smells like baking apples."

"I have a pie cooking. How about a cup of coffee? That ought to help heat you up. And I'll get you a blanket."

Jean hurried to her chest and removed a wool blanket. Returning to the kitchen, she draped it over Ray's shoulders.

"Thank you," he said, pulling it close.

Rubbing sleepy eyes, Brian walked into the kitchen. "What's going on? I thought I heard something. Is Santa here?"

"Sorry, Brian, it's just me. My car slid off the road, so Celeste and I had to come back."

Brian smiled. "Good, but don't stay up too late or Santa won't come."

"I won't. I promise." Ray winked.

"OK, young man. Off to bed now," Jean said.

"Where's your car?" Adam asked.

"'Bout a mile down the road—in the ditch."

"You can't do anything about it tonight," Jean said. "You're welcome to share a bed with Brian, and Celeste can have the sofa."

"I'm sorry to put you out."

"Nonsense. That's what being neighbors is all about."

"And Luke?"

"He'll understand."

Jean lay staring into the darkness. Wind shrieked around the house, driving snow against the window glass. She burrowed deeper beneath her covers, but the closeness of the blankets did little to dispel her chill and her loneliness. Will's place in the bed was still empty. He wouldn't be here for Christmas this year. He'd always been the one who cut the tree and hauled it into the house, and then he'd settle in his chair and watch the family hang the decorations. After the children were tucked into bed, he and Jean would set out gifts and enjoy a few quiet moments to reflect on the holiday. Jean had always baked Will's favorites at Christmas. This year the gesture felt empty.

She pressed her hand against her chest as if doing so would dispel the ache there. "When will the pain stop?" she asked the darkness. "Please, Lord, make it stop."

A soft knock sounded at her door. "Yes. Who is it?"

"Mama, can I come in?" Laurel asked.

Jean pushed herself up and leaned against the headboard. "Come in."

Laurel opened the door, and a splinter of light cut through the darkness. Holding a lantern high, she stepped in and walked to the bed.

"Is everything all right?"

"I think I'm in labor."

Jean's pulse picked up. "What's happening?"

"I've been having pains for a couple hours. They're getting worse and coming more often." Laurel sat on the foot of the bed. Glancing at the window, she asked, "What should we do?"

Jean smiled. "First, we thank God. We're about to have a new member added to the family." She climbed out from under her blankets and hugged Laurel. "How close are the pains?"

"About every ten minutes."

"Well then, I guess it's time to get you to the clinic. Dr. Donovan said he'd meet you there, right?"

"Mama, the storm's real bad."

Jean climbed out of bed and walked to the window. Resting her hand on the glass, she peered out. Bursts of white crystals hit the window. "Well, you certainly can't go out in that." She faced Laurel. "Someone will just have to go for the doctor."

"I heard you talking. What's going on?" Luke asked, stepping into the room.

"Laurel's in labor. We were supposed to take her to the clinic, but the storm's too bad. We'll have to bring the doctor here."

"I'll go," Luke volunteered. "Just give me a minute to get some warm clothes on." He disappeared.

Jean could hear him moving about upstairs. "How about a cup of hot tea for you?"

Laurel rested a hand on her abdomen, grabbed the bedpost with her free hand, and leaned over. She breathed slowly and evenly until the pain passed. "That was the strongest one yet. Tell Luke to hurry," she said, her voice tense.

Jean gently rubbed her daughter's back. "I will. Everything will be fine."

"They're getting worse."

"Since this is your first baby, it will probably take its time getting here. Luke will be back before then. Don't you worry." Jean smiled. "Do you think you can wake that husband of yours? We'll need to make up the bed for you." She helped Laurel up the stairs and to her room. Adam still slept.

Luke traipsed in. "I'm leaving now," he said, then turned and jogged down the hall.

"What's going on?" Adam asked groggily.

"Your wife is in labor," Jean said, unable to keep the excitement out of her voice.

Laurel sat beside her husband. "I'm going to have the baby, so Mama and I have to get the bed ready. You need to get up."

"You're having the baby now?" Adam sat up. "Here?"

Laurel chuckled. "Not *right* now, but soon."

"I thought you were going to the clinic."

"The storm's too bad. Luke's gone to get the doctor."

Adam ran his hand through his hair. "What can I do?"

Laurel doubled and hugged her stomach. "Ohhh."

"Try to relax," Jean said calmly. "It will hurt less."

"This one's bad." Laurel grimaced. "I don't know if I can do this."

Jean smiled. "I'm afraid you have no choice."

An hour passed, and Luke didn't return; another hour went by, and he still wasn't back. Laurel's pain had settled in her back, and the contractions were close together. Celeste and Miram took care of Brian and Susie and hovered around Laurel when they could. Ray was content to keep the fire stoked and coffee brewing while Adam paced and Jean sat with her daughter.

Susie and Brian asked to open their gifts, so Ray oversaw the distribution. Susie mothered a new baby doll, and Brian chugged a shiny fire truck up and down the stairway.

Adam walked to the window, the door, then back to the window. "When are they going to get here? She needs the doctor."

"They'll be here soon," Jean said, gently leading Adam out of the room. "Try to stay calm."

Swallowing hard, Adam nodded. "But they ought to be here."

"I know."

Laurel groaned, and Jean returned to her, taking her hand and smoothing the back of it. "Breathe slowly and relax; just relax."

Adam took a cloth from a bowl of water on the nightstand and wrung it out, then gently ran it over Laurel's face and neck. Laurel grabbed his wrist. "It hurts so much. I didn't know it would be like this."

He placed a hand over hers. "It'll be over soon."

"Once that little bundle gets here, you won't care a whit about the pain," Jean said. "You'll have that baby in your arms, and nothing else will matter."

Laurel dropped back on her pillows. "I wish it were here."

Jean rewet the cloth and laid it on Laurel's forehead. "Adam, could you ask Celeste to boil some water and get us some clean cloths?"

Adam hurried out the door, acting as if he were glad to have something to do.

"Mama, I'm scared. I wish the doctor would come." Laurel glanced at the window. "Where is he?"

"I'm sure he's on his way. You know how busy doctors can be."

"I don't want to have the baby here. I'm supposed to be at the hospital."

"Women have been having babies at home for centuries. You'll be fine." She patted Laurel's hand. "I'll be right back."

Jean met Adam in the hallway. "Do you know anything about delivering babies?"

"Me? No." A panicked expression hit his face. "Is she that close?"

"I think it will be soon. If the doctor doesn't hurry, we'll have to deliver this baby. I've had my own, but I've never helped with a birth." She looked at Ray, who stood at the bottom of the stairs. "You've had two children. Do you know what to do?"

Ray took a slow breath. "I helped with my son, but my wife had trouble. I don't really know much."

"Could you help me if we need it?"

Ray was slow to answer, but finally said, "Yeah. If you need me."

A cry came from the bedroom, and Jean hurried back to her daughter.

"Mama, I have to push," Laurel said. "I have to."

"All right, honey. If you have to, then do it." Jean looked at Ray, then back at Laurel. "Mr. Townsend knows about delivering babies. He said he'll help."

"The doctor's not here?"

"No." Jean forced a smile. "But you're in good hands. I've had five, and Ray helped deliver two. With God's help, we ought to do just fine."

"Ahhh." Laurel gripped the bed sheets and pushed, gritting her teeth.

Wishing he could be anywhere but where he was, Ray said, "We need to know if the baby's coming. Jean?"

Jean leaned over her daughter. "Bend your legs for me, honey, so I can check you." Keeping the sheet over her daughter's legs, Jean looked. "I can see the head. It's almost here!" She glanced at Ray. "I'll need your help."

"You have it."

"Adam, get the hot water and the washrags. And get me a pair of scissors."

Adam kissed Laurel and hurried out of the room.

"I'm scared. I've never had a baby before."

Ray leaned over her. "You're strong. You'll do it." He looked at Jean. "I need you to check and make sure the cord isn't wrapped around the baby's neck."

"I'll try." Jean did as she was told. "I don't feel anything."

Another contraction came and another and another. Laurel pushed, but the baby didn't come down. *It ought to be here,* Ray thought, sick at his stomach and remembering Ellie. Something had gone wrong then, and he knew it was happening again. *Where is that doctor? We need the doctor.* Ray wanted out. He couldn't go through this again. He stepped back.

Taking Ray aside, Jean said, "Something's wrong, isn't it?"

He nodded. "We need to check again to see if the cord's wrapped around the baby's neck."

"I already did, but I couldn't feel anything. Maybe you ought to try."

Ray wiped sweat from his forehead. "All right." He returned to the bedside. "Laurel, this is gonna hurt, but I've got to see if the cord's hung up."

Laurel nodded. "Please hurry. I'm scared. Don't let my baby die."

Ray placed his hand between the baby and the wall of the pelvis. He felt for the cord. Laurel moaned. *Yes. There it is.* "Laurel, don't push!"

"I have to." She panted. "Please! Do something! Please!"

Ray pushed the baby back slightly, got his fingers under the cord, and gently eased it back over the baby's head. He felt to make sure there wasn't another loop. He couldn't feel one. "That ought to do it."

Another contraction hit, and Laurel pushed. The baby nearly fell into Ray's hands. It was out but lay blue and still.

Ray lifted the child and gently shook it, then patted its back and bottom. It didn't cry. "No. Not again!" He grabbed a towel and started rubbing the baby all over. "Come on! Come on! Breathe!" He stared at the child, willing it to live.

First the baby whimpered, then sputtered, and then cried. "That's the way. Cry, baby, cry." Ray held up the little boy whose blue tinge was fading. The baby cried harder, and his skin began to turn pink. "He's going to be all right," Ray said, handing the little boy to Jean. "Here's your grandson."

He cut the cord, and Jean laid the baby in Laurel's arms. "Here's your son," she said, tears spilling onto her face.

Ray hurried out of the room. He stopped at the sink and scrubbed blood off his hands and arms, then pulled on his coat and headed for the barn. He needed to be alone.

He ran out into the first light of the day and stumbled toward the barn. Pushing through the doors, he ran for a stall in the back and leaned against the gate. Panting, he felt anguish and horror, as if it had just happened. It was all so near—his wife's suffering, their dead son, and then Ellie's death. Tears made paths down his face, and he gulped in cold air, wishing he were dead too.

Chapter 28

JEAN STOOD BESIDE THE BED AND GAZED AT HER SLEEPING DAUGHTER AND grandson. Little William was chubby and perfect. She tucked the quilt around the infant and planted a kiss on his cheek. He turned his face toward her. *If only Will were here. He would have been a wonderful grandfather,* she thought, blinking back tears. The little boy's mouth turned up in a dreamy smile.

Miram stood at the kitchen sink, hands immersed in soapy water. "How are they?" she asked when Jean walked in.

"Just fine—sleeping."

Miram rinsed a cup and set it on a strainer. "I've never been part of anything like that." With a look of wonder, she added, "I can't wait to be a mother."

Celeste dried the cup. "I can. I'm not so sure I want to go through all that."

Fatigue settling over her, Jean dropped into a chair. "Seems to me I heard Robert wants a big family, a whole house full. Are you two as serious as you look?"

"Very."

"Well then, you'd better have a talk about the size of your family." Jean grinned.

A frown creased Celeste's brow. "I'm sure he didn't really mean . . . *lots* of children." She picked up a plate and ran the towel over it.

Jean glanced into the front room. "Where did your father go?"

"He went outside."

"I think he's upset," Miram said. "He looked distressed."

"How long has he been gone?"

"At least half an hour." Miram washed the last dish and handed it to Celeste.

"You really think he's upset?" Jean asked, remembering how unsettled Ray had seemed earlier.

"Yes. In fact, he seemed very troubled."

Jean pushed to her feet. "I think I'll check on him. The cows need milking anyway." Pulling on a coat and gloves, she started for the barn. Morning sunlight touched a clear sky. The storm was gone, leaving behind a pristine world of white. Fresh powder squeaked under Jean's boots, and frigid air burned her lungs.

Pulling open the barn door, she stepped inside. A quiet dark world enveloped her. When her eyes adjusted to the shadowy interior, she walked toward the back stalls and spotted Ray leaning on a gate, watching a cow. "I was wondering what happened to you."

Ray turned and looked at her. His face and eyes were red. His stance reminded her of a wilted fruit tree, like the ones they'd left behind in Wisconsin. "You all right?"

"Yeah." He wiped his nose with the back of his sleeve.

Jean knew something was wrong. Should she try to help or leave him be? She took a step closer. "Are you really all right?"

Ray shook his head and shifted away from Jean.

"I'd like to help."

"You can't. No one can."

Jean tried to think of what to say.

"I can't talk about it."

Jean rested a hand on his arm. "Sometimes talking helps."

Gripping the top rail of the gate, Ray cursed under his breath, then walked to a back window. Unlatching it, he threw the wooden shutter open and gazed out.

Jean waited.

Finally ending the silence, he said, "It's not that simple. Talking won't make this better." He turned tortured eyes on Jean. "Being in there with Laurel brought it all back. It's been years, but it felt like yesterday." He wiped away fresh tears. "I watched my wife and my son die, and it was my fault."

His pain was palpable and took Jean's breath away.

"They're dead because of me."

"Life and death are in God's hands," Jean said.

"I'm the one who insisted we live in this wilderness. Ellie didn't want to come. She was afraid, but I had to have my way."

"I thought you said she loved it here."

"After a while she did." A smile touched Ray's eyes. "She became a real sourdough."

The torment returned. "When Ellie went into labor with Celeste, it took a long while, but Celeste came out pink and crying. With our son, it was different." Ray returned to staring outdoors. "By the time we knew something was wrong, it was too late. No doctor was around to help." He balled his hands into fists and hit the barn wall.

"Ray," Jean laid a hand on his shoulder.

He took a shuddering breath. "A neighbor tried to help . . . but it wasn't enough. The baby was dead—the cord was wrapped around his neck." Ray's voice had gone quiet. "Ellie had worked so hard . . . and the bleeding wouldn't stop." Ray's eyes were haunted.

"You couldn't have known." Jean gently squeezed his shoulder.

Ray worked his jaw.

"As awful as last night must have been to you, I'm thankful you were here. God knew we needed you. If it weren't for you, William would be dead." Reality hit Jean, and she pressed a fist to her mouth. "Without a doctor . . ."

"Yeah, without a doctor. That's my point. Out here you never know what'll happen." He looked straight at her. "We shouldn't be here, none of us. My wife, my son, your husband, your son—they'd still be alive."

Ray's declaration stunned Jean. If anyone belonged here, Ray did. "What happened to your wife and baby wasn't your fault, and what happened to Will wasn't your fault. And this valley neither gives nor takes lives. Life is uncertain no matter where we live." She grabbed his hands. "There are no guarantees, Ray."

Ray looked at their hands, then disengaged his. "What Luke said to me last night made sense. When it comes down to it, I'm no good. When Will showed up for that hunt, I could have made him leave or made sure he had a partner."

"I thought you'd let go of all that. You couldn't have kept Will from going, and whether he had a good man with him or not, we can't know what the outcome would have been. God allowed it, and he used it."

Ray was quiet. "I hated Will. I hated most everybody, including myself. Maybe I wanted him to die. Most of my life I've done what was right for me and only me."

"That can't be true. Look at Celeste. She's kind and thoughtful. She didn't get that way all on her own."

A smile touched Ray's lips. "Celeste has always been special, easy to love." He nudged a bale of hay with the toe of his boot. "The minister says God loves me." He plucked a piece of hay. "I believe him, but I know I'm not worthy of anyone's love, 'specially not God's."

Jean leaned against the gate. "We can't measure God's love against ours. No one *deserves* his love. We're all wicked. God chooses to love us anyway."

"In my head I know that's true, but—"

"No one deserves his love and forgiveness. It's only Jesus' sacrifice that makes us worthy of God's riches." She met Ray's eyes. "Stop doubting God, Ray. Trust him."

"I know you're right." Ray took a deep breath. "But when I think about all that's happened . . . Ellie and Will would still be alive."

Jean was beginning to lose patience, and her tone grew firmer. "You don't know that. And have you forgotten the lives you've saved? Not just William last night, but what about Adam? You pulled him out of the river, remember? And Luke, we might have lost him that day."

Ray pursed his lips.

"Laurel and Adam certainly haven't forgotten, and they have even more to thank you for now." She took his hands. "You are respected in this valley because of the man you are and what you've done for the people over the years."

Ray gazed into Jean's eyes. "I wish I could be like Will. He was always cool-headed, steady."

"Will was Will," she said, trying to keep her tone light but suddenly feeling uncomfortable. "And you are you. That's how it should be." She released his hands and stepped back.

"If I was more like Will, do you think you could love me?"

The question took Jean by surprise. What could she say? "Will was a wonderful man. I loved him. I still do. And you're a good man, Ray, just the way you are. You're not supposed to be Will. God created you to be Ray Townsend."

A wry smile touched Ray. "Even when I hated him, I wanted to be like him. He was the kind of man people looked up to. I admired his faith." Ray glanced out the window, then at Jean. "I still want to be like him."

"You're strong and steady in your own way." Jean smiled. "A little loud from time to time, but God's given you faith. All you need to do is grab hold of it."

Ray nodded thoughtfully, then asked, "And what about the rest of my question?"

Jean stared at him.

"Do you think you could ever love me?"

Jean glanced at the barn floor, then looked at Ray. "I can't answer that. I'm not ready to love anyone else yet. I might not ever be ready."

"I shouldn't have asked. I'm sorry."

"No, it's all right. I love Will. Sometimes I forget he's not here, and I expect to see him come in from the barn with the milk. Or sometimes Brian or Susie will do something funny or special, and my first thought is to tell him . . ." her voice trailed off. "He's still here." Her eyes filled with tears.

"I understand. Not a day goes by that I don't think of Ellie—even after all these years." Grief lined his face.

Jean's heart ached for Ray. She knew what he was feeling and wished she could ease his pain. In an effort to comfort him, she hugged him lightly.

Suddenly Ray was wrenched out of her arms.

"Get away from her!" Luke spat, shoving him.

"Luke!" Jean grabbed his arm. "What are you doing?"

Ignoring his mother, Luke yelled, "You stay away from my mother!"

Keeping his voice calm, Ray said, "Settle down. Nothing's going on here."

"Nothing? You call what I saw nothing?"

"What you saw was friendship. Your mother was comforting me." His voice had an edge to it.

"*You* need comfort?" Luke sneered.

"Take a step back and calm down. You're making more of this than it is." Ray attempted a smile, but it came off more as a smirk.

Luke's face reddened. "Don't make fun of me. Never make fun of me. I'm not a boy." He threw himself at Ray, shoving him against the wall.

Ray didn't retaliate.

His face only inches from his adversary, Luke yelled, "You haven't changed. Oh, you put on an act so people will think you're better, but you can't fool me. The man who hated outsiders and who murdered my father is still here!" Luke thumped Ray's chest with his index finger. He turned on his mother. "Did you want my father out of the way so you could have him?"

Jean felt as if she'd been slapped. "No! Never! How could you even think such a thing?"

"Enough, son. You've said enough." Ray's voice was hard.

"You want to lay into me?" Luke taunted. "Well, maybe you should. I'd say it was time we had this out."

"Luke, I've been patient, but I've had just about enough. I don't want to fight you. I just want to go on my way." Ray looked at Jean, who stood just out of his reach. "There's no reason for any of this. It's only hurting your mother."

"Were you thinking about her when you killed my father?" Luke grabbed a pitchfork and thrust it at Ray. "You won't be part of this family!"

Ray lifted his hands in a sign of surrender. "I can't change what's happened." He backed away. "I'm not a murderer. I've done things I'm not proud of, things I'll regret all my life, but I never meant for your father to die." He stood squarely facing Luke. "Every day I think about what happened and wish I'd done it differently. Then maybe your father would be alive. I wish he were." He dropped his arms. "I don't want to fight you. Put down the pitchfork."

Luke glared at Ray. "You're gonna fight. It's your turn to pay." He lunged at Ray, but the bigger man easily avoided his assault. The red in Luke's face deepened. "I've never hated anyone, but hate isn't a strong enough word for what I feel for you. The sooner you're out of our lives, the better." He lunged again.

Ray avoided the sharp tongs. He stared at the boy and the impenetrable rage in his face.

Luke waved the pitchfork menacingly.

"You can come at me, but I'm not moving. If you really want me dead, then do it and we'll be done with it." Ray let his arms hang loosely at his sides.

"Luke, please," Jean said. "Stop this."

Luke didn't seem to know what to do. He glared at Ray.

"We don't have to be friends, Luke, but we've got to find a way to settle our differences."

"There's no way to settle them. There's only one way to make sure you never set foot on this property again." He lunged, but Ray didn't move. The pitchfork ripped through the larger man's coat, slashing through his shirt and piercing his skin. Ray looked down at the wound, seemingly unperturbed.

Staring at the blood seeping into his adversary's shirt, Luke stepped back and dropped the pitchfork, then ran from the barn.

Chapter 29

"PRETTY," SUSIE SAID, POINTING AT AN ICE-ENCRUSTED WINDOW SPLINTERED by sunlight.

"Yes. Very pretty," Jean said, settling her daughter into bed. "You go to sleep now."

"Brian doesn't have to take a nap. Why do I?"

"He's at school. Big boys don't take naps." She pulled a quilt up under her daughter's chin and kissed her forehead.

"Please read another story."

"I've already read two. I'll read you another one tonight."

"I wish I could read. When can I go to school?"

"Two more years, then you can go. I'm not ready for you to go off to school yet. I'd be lonely without you. It's hard enough that I have to leave you when I work." Jean pressed her face against the little girl's chest.

Susie giggled and twisted her fingers into her mother's hair.

Jean sat up and smiled down at her youngest.

"Laurel could bring William to see you. Then you wouldn't be lonely."

"Yes, but she can't come every day. She has her own chores to do." Jean stood. "Now, enough of this. It's time for sleep." She walked to the door, stepped into the hallway, and pulled the door nearly closed.

She already felt lonely. With Will and Justin gone, Laurel married, Luke off hunting or trapping most of the time, and Brian in school, the house was empty. Sometimes she felt more alone than ever. *It's been nearly a year. When will the healing come?* she wondered, feeling discouraged. What would she do when all the children were grown and gone?

That's something better left to another day, she told herself and headed down the stairs. For now, she had bread to bake and washing to do.

When she reached the bottom of the stairs, she crossed to the over-stuffed sofa and plumped a throw pillow. A nap would be nice. *Just a little one,* she told herself and dragged a blue afghan off the back of the sofa. Lying down, she positioned the throw pillow under her head and pulled the afghan over her.

Sun slanted in a window, and dust particles glistened in its light. She gazed at bare rosebush limbs pressing against the glass and imagined how they would look in July clothed in greenery and red blossoms. Maybe by then her sadness would lift.

A car rumbled up the driveway. Jean sat up and looked out the window. It was Ray. Jean wasn't sure if she felt good or bad about seeing him. *The kids have missed him,* she thought. Since his argument with Luke, he'd stayed away. *At least he wasn't hurt that day,* she remembered. The wound Luke had inflicted had been superficial.

Ray climbed out of the car, closing the door firmly. Huddling in a heavy coat, he plodded through the snow, keeping his head down and hands in his pockets. He didn't look like himself.

Jean tidied her hair and headed for the back door, the thought of seeing him lifting her spirits. He knocked before she could reach it. Opening the door, she smiled. "Hello. Good to see you. I was wondering when you were going to get around to visiting. We've missed you."

"I've missed you all too," Ray said, his tone serious. "Can I come in?"

Something is wrong. Jean swung the door open and stepped aside. "Would you like some coffee?"

"Is it made?"

"No. But I can make it easy enough."

"Nah. I don't want you to go to the trouble." Ray pulled off his gloves and shoved them into his coat pockets, then pushed back his hood, revealing a tangle of dark curls. "Actually, I came by to talk to you about something." He glanced around the kitchen. "Luke around?"

"No. He's checking the traplines."

"Good."

Jean settled on a kitchen chair and folded her hands in front of her. She knew something was coming.

Ray sat across from her and leaned on the table, staring at his clasped hands.

"It's usually best just to say whatever you have to say."

He looked up at Jean and took a deep breath, then blew it out slowly. "Since the last time I was here, I've been doing a lot of thinking. After Will died I only meant to help, not to cause trouble. I . . . I felt obligated. Will had asked me to look after his family. I never thought we'd become friends, but we did . . . I think."

Jean offered an encouraging smile. "Yes. I'd say we're friends."

"Seems my best intentions have gone wrong. I didn't mean to bring trouble, but I have." He pressed his palms together. "I've been thinking . . . it would be better if I didn't come around anymore."

His words jarred Jean. "Not come around? For how long?"

"As long as it takes for Luke to get over being mad."

"He might never forgive you," Jean said, trying to absorb this new loss. "Brian and Susie will miss you."

"I'm going to miss them, but . . ." Ray shook his head. "Every time I set foot in this place, Luke raises his hackles."

Jean stared at her hands. "It doesn't seem right, his hatred controlling what we do."

"It's not, but I don't see any other way." Ray stood and pulled on his gloves. He was silent a moment, then said, "Well, see ya," and walked out.

Weeks passed, and Ray was good to his word. He didn't set foot on the Hasper farm, but he didn't dismiss his promise to look out for Will's family. Several times a week Ray sent someone by to check on them and to do chores. They almost always brought gifts of meat or fish.

Jean was grateful, but the visits from others only served to remind her how much she missed Ray. He was very different from Will. He had a quick temper, and on occasion he still bullied his way through situations, but she liked him—maybe it was his straightforward way of approaching life. And she couldn't deny he was a man of honor. He'd promised Will that he'd keep watch over his family, and he was.

With Ray's absence Jean and Luke did not argue as much and the house was more peaceful. But it also felt as if someone had been misplaced. Brian and Susie often asked about Ray and couldn't understand why their friend no longer came to visit. When Jean tried to explain, it only created friction between the two youngest and their older brother.

Occasionally they'd see Ray in town, and he always made time to chat. Susie and Brian would be animated and pleased, but when the visit ended, they were always let down, for each time they would invite their big friend to visit, and he would decline. Jean began to pray that either they wouldn't see Ray while in town or that Luke would have a change of heart. She waited for the right time to talk to Luke again.

Spring arrived, and the cold and snows were tempered by sporadic warm spells. The earliest spring flowers broke through the wet earth, hugging tree trunks and foundations of homes. Breakup was imminent, and the townspeople began to make bets on the exact day and time the ice would break free.

After finishing chores one morning, Luke sauntered into the house. "Morning. Looks like a good day," he said cheerfully.

This is as good a time as any, Jean thought. "Luke, I was wondering if we could talk about Ray Townsend."

"What about?" he asked, his voice guarded. "Things have been better since he's been staying out of our way." He took a chunk of cheese from the icebox.

Jean bit back a retort and poured hot water into the sink.

Luke sliced the cheese and slapped it between bread. "I guess he finally got the message."

Picking up the knife Luke had used and setting it in the sink, Jean asked, "And what message would that be?"

"That he doesn't belong here and that I'm the man of this house."

Jean turned and leaned her back against the counter, then folded her arms over her chest. "No. That's not it. The message you gave is that you're not a man yet and you're unforgiving."

Hurt flickered across Luke's face, then insolence settled in.

"Ray didn't want to cause more trouble between us. That's why he hasn't been around."

Luke smirked. "I'd say he's scared."

Jean's anger and frustration boiled up. "I'm ashamed of you, Luke, and if your father could hear you, he would be too."

Luke's smirk disappeared.

"Ray Townsend isn't afraid of you. He cares about us. He figured he had to stay away to keep the peace." She briskly folded a towel and slapped it down on the counter. "You're the one causing the problems."

Luke scowled. "I didn't make the trouble. He did. He should have stayed away from the beginning. He wasn't welcome here, and he knew it."

Jean pressed her hands down on the counter and waited for a wave of rage to pass. Taking a deep breath, she turned and crossed to her nearly grown son. Resting her hands on his shoulders, she said softly, "I miss the young man I used to know—the one who loved life and looked for the best in people, the one who was quick to forgive." She could feel the sting of tears. "Luke, hate is eating you up. The fine man I know is disappearing right before my eyes."

Luke stared at his mother, then shrugged away. "I'm not naïve like I used to be. A man like Ray Townsend doesn't deserve forgiveness. I'm responsible for this family. I'm just trying to protect you. I'm sorry you can't see that."

Jean smoothed the towel, hoping to quiet her growing anger, "Luke, it's an honorable thing to feel responsible and protective, but my life and this farm are not your responsibility. They're mine." Luke started to say something, but Jean held up her hand. "I will finish," she said sternly. "Your behavior will not be tolerated any longer. You are old enough to know better. And you need to know that God will hold you accountable for your behavior. He doesn't look kindly on hatred and bitterness. I won't have you interfering any longer. Do you understand?" When Luke didn't answer, she repeated, "Do you understand?"

"Yeah, I understand," he growled, shoving two sandwiches and two apples into a bag.

"Alex and I are going to the river." With that he left, slamming the door behind him.

Jean stared at the door. She'd prayed and prayed, but still he clung to bitterness. What would happen to him? *Lord, you have to do something.*

"Hey, what's with you?" Alex asked, leaning against the bridge.

"Nothin.'" Luke stared at the river, hands stuffed into his coat pockets.

"Right. You've been bad-tempered all morning. Even though it looks like we might win that bet, I think the breakup's starting today."

Luke clenched his teeth. "It's Ray Townsend. He's trying to weasel his way into my family, and my mother can't see it. She thinks he cares."

"Maybe he does."

Luke looked at his friend. "You really think he could? He murdered my father."

"It was an accident, Luke. Your father's the one who insisted on going. And he decided to stay with Ray. Ray didn't make him." Alex glanced away, then continued. "He should never have taken an old rifle like that. He knew better."

"I never thought *you'd* turn against me. I thought you understood."

"I do, but you've got to let go of the past. Let go of your hate. Your father's death wasn't Ray's fault."

With a look of astonishment, Luke said, "I can't believe it. He got to you too. I thought you were smarter." He shook his head. "Seems I'm the only one who can see the truth."

"Maybe you're the one who's wrong," a soft voice said from behind Luke.

He whirled around to face Mattie. "What do you mean?"

"It doesn't make sense that everyone else is wrong and you're right."

"You don't know Ray Townsend the way I do." Luke glowered. "I don't want to talk about it anymore." He returned to staring at the river.

"Anything happen yet?" Mattie asked.

"Nope," Alex said. "Just a lot of groaning and popping."

Luke cut in. "Why do you think I'm the one who's wrong?"

"I thought you didn't want to talk about it," Mattie teased, her dark eyes smiling.

Clenching and unclenching his jaw, Luke's eyes followed the curves of frozen ice. They looked like ribbon candy.

"It's just that everyone else thinks he's fine, including me." She stepped in front of Luke and met his eyes. "People change."

"Not him."

A loud pop fractured the air.

"I just wish you would think about it, Luke. He's different."

"And, of course, I'm the one who's wrong."

Neither Mattie nor Alex said anything. They watched the ice.

"You two can think what you like." Luke strode down the bank and leaped across the soft ice along the river's edge and onto more solid ice.

"What are you doing?" Mattie asked, her voice shrill. "Get off the ice! It could go at any time, and the water's deep here."

Ignoring her warning, Luke said matter-of-factly, "It's a little soft, but I'd say it's got a way to go before it breaks loose." He walked out farther.

Alex followed his friend, stepping carefully and feeling his way.

"Hey, you boys get off the ice!" a man called. "You loony?"

Suddenly Alex's foot broke through. He jerked it up and shook off water. "We better get out of here." He turned and headed back.

The ice shifted. Alex stopped and stood completely still.

"Get out!" Mattie yelled.

Luke gingerly headed toward shore. "It's ready to go."

Alex took another step. His foot broke through again. He stepped back and stood completely still, studying the ice. It creaked and groaned. A crack appeared with a splintering sound. "It's gonna go!"

A fissure widened, and the ice writhed and slanted upwards, tossing Alex into the frigid water. He disappeared, then his hooded head bobbed to the surface and he gasped, grabbing for a handhold. The ice was slick, and he couldn't get a grip to climb out.

The frozen river was moving beneath Luke. He lay on his stomach and crawled toward his friend. "Hang on, Alex, hang on!" He searched for something to hold out. Spotting a limb, he shouted, "Mattie! Throw that to me!"

She quickly climbed down the bank, grabbed the small branch, and chucked it toward Luke. It landed several feet away, but he cautiously moved across shifting ice, grabbed it, and headed back for his friend.

Alex beat the water with his arms. "I can't get out! I can't make it!"

"Yes, you can! Grab this!" Luke called, sliding the limb toward Alex.

He grabbed for the branch, but his fingers wouldn't close around it. Ice and water swirled around him. He disappeared.

"Alex! Alex!" The native boy reappeared. "Grab hold!" Luke shrieked. "Do it! Now! Forget the cold. Look at me! You can do it!"

Alex's eyes locked with Luke's.

Luke knew he was saying good-bye. "No!" he shrieked. "Live!"

The young native man's arms slapped the water, and he tried to swim toward his friend. A chunk of ice rammed him and he disappeared again.

"Alex! Alex!" Luke searched the water. "Come on! Alex!" His friend was gone. Luke pressed his face to the ice and sobbed.

"Luke, get out of there," a man called.

Luke looked up to see Tom Jenkins standing at the river's edge.

"Get out, or you'll be next."

Luke tried to refocus, but all he could see was his friend—dying. It was his fault. He ought to be the one dead.

"Luke! Come on! Get out of there!"

Still on his stomach, he crawled across the moving ice. Tom threw a rope and pulled Luke toward shore and onto the bank. Shivering, Luke pulled his knees to his chest and sat staring at the place where he'd last seen his friend.

Mattie sat beside him crying.

Luke draped an arm around her shoulders and stared at the river. "I'm sorry. I'm so sorry."

"I can't believe he's gone," Mattie said between sobs. "How could this happen?"

"I shouldn't have gone out on the ice," Luke said, remembering the day he'd met Alex, his first Alaskan friend.

Tom Jenkins clapped a hand on Luke's shoulder. "I'll take you on home, son. This isn't anyone's fault. Things just happen."

Luke wished he could believe that. Tom lifted him, but his legs felt as if they didn't belong to his body as he stumbled up the bank. He climbed into Tom's truck and watched as Mattie joined the others searching the river for Alex's body.

As Tom drove away, Luke stared at the distant mountains and wished he'd never come to Alaska.

Chapter 30

TAKING LONG STRIDES AND LETTING HER ARMS SWING FREELY AT HER SIDES, Jean headed for town. The June sunshine felt good. She took in fields dotted with yellow buttercups, purple cress, and white starflowers. She couldn't remember feeling this happy in a very long time. A flock of tiny birds skittered away as she approached the fence they rested on. A truck flew by, bouncing over the rough roadway, but Jean didn't slow her steps as she entered town.

Celeste stopped sweeping the mercantile porch and said, "Morning, Mrs. Hasper. How are you?"

"Good. Wonderful, in fact. You?"

"I'm well," She leaned on the broom. "How's Luke?"

"Still not himself. It'll take him a long while to get over Alex's death, if he ever does."

"Time will take care of it."

"I'm sure you're right," Jean said with a smile, wishing she were confident of that. "Alex's death has added to Luke's cavern of unhappiness."

Jean stepped into the post office. "Good morning, Mrs. Wilkerson."

"Hello, there," the plump woman responded. "You look chipper this morning."

"I feel chipper. It's a beautiful day."

The door opened, and Ray Townsend walked in. "Hi, Ray," she said, feeling slightly flustered. He looked good. His wide shoulders seemed broader than she remembered, and he wore his coat open and his shirt tucked in. His curls were cropped short, and his beard was neatly trimmed. He looked almost refined. If she were meeting him for the first time, she'd never guess he was a mountain man. She wondered if

Celeste had something to do with the change or if another woman had entered his life.

"Howdy," Ray said. "What are you up to on such a beautiful day?"

"Oh, just mailing a letter to an old friend." She set the letter on the counter. "You?"

"I'm going to do some fishing. They're running heavy right now." He leaned on the counter.

"Where you going?"

"To Cook Inlet. I've got a spot I go to a couple times a year."

"I wish you luck." Jean glanced out the window. "You have perfect weather."

"Have you fished in the inlet?"

"No."

"Then I'd say it's time you did. I'll show you some real fishing."

"Oh, I don't know. Laurel's waiting for me. She's watching Susie."

"I'd sure enjoy the company," Ray pressed.

"It sounds fun, but . . . well . . . I thought we were supposed to keep our distance."

Mrs. Wilkerson dropped the envelope in her mailbag. "I'd go," she said. "Not that it's any of my business, but . . ." She smiled and her cheeks rounded. With a shrug, she waddled toward the back of the building.

"It's just fishing. I won't be at the house."

Jean wanted to go but knew it would only stir up trouble. "I don't know. Luke's still upset over Alex dying and—"

"It's been too long since we've had a good chat. Fishing is the perfect way to catch up."

Jean wanted to go. *Luke can't run my life*, she decided. "All right. Sounds like fun. If Luke raises a stink, well, too bad." She chuckled, then looked down at her clothes. "I'll have to change and get some fishing gear. I don't think Laurel will mind watching Susie. And Brian won't be home until this afternoon." She headed for the door. "When will we be back?"

"Early evening. I've made a good-sized lunch. I've got plenty for both of us."

With her gear tucked in the back of Ray's pickup, Jean sat beside the big man feeling ready for an adventure. They bounced over the rough road and slid through muddy ruts as they headed south. She wondered about what she was doing but decided it was time she did something just for herself.

Groves of birch hurried past the window, and Jean remembered the times she and Will had picnicked under the birch at home. Would he care that she was with Ray? *No. He'd want me to have a good time,* she decided.

Jean rested her arm on the open window. Early summer rains had filled the ponds, and water lilies, pond grasses, and heavy bog orchids crowded the pools. Aspen and cottonwood bordered swampy lowlands, and distant mountains stood like broad-shouldered sentinels.

The road followed the inlet's finger called Knik Arm, and Jean breathed in the pungent odor of the mud flats. "I ought to get down here and do some clamming. Jessie's assured me that digging for razor clams is a real adventure."

"It can be," Ray said, keeping his eyes on the road. "They're fast, and as soon as they know you're after them, they fly, straight down. You've got to be fast to catch 'em."

Ray turned off the main road and headed toward the beach. He stopped at a long wharf leading to a cannery. A cannery tender had moored in the bay. Ray's dory was tied to the dock.

He stopped the truck and climbed out, then hurried around to open the door for Jean. "You'll need that coat," he said, nodding at the jacket she'd left on the seat.

"Oh. Of course," Jean said, picking it up and draping it over her arm.

Ray closed the door, then grabbed the picnic basket and rain gear out of the back. He handed them to Jean then retrieved the fishing gear. He held out his pole straight in front of him and gazed down the length of it. "Yep. It's a good day for fishing," he said and headed for the wharf.

Jean followed, no longer enjoying the ocean smells. The air was heavy with the odor of rotting fish. Seabirds swooped over the bay, then spreading their wings, landed on the gray mud where they picked at carcasses littering the cove. Dirty seawater washed around the moorings while a fishing boat unloaded its catch.

"Looks like the fishing's good," Ray said. "Smells like it too." He chuckled. "I'd hate to work in a cannery—spending every day in this stink, gutting fish."

"Sounds awful," Jean said, stepping onto the dock.

Ray stopped at his battered wooden dory. He stepped in, throwing his arms out as the boat floated away from the wharf. After stowing the gear, he hauled on the rope and pulled himself alongside the dock. Taking the rain gear from Jean, he said, "Never can tell what the weather's going to do." He took the picnic basket and set it under the middle seat. Straightening, he looked at her. "You ready?" He held out his hand.

Jean took his hand but wondered if she should have stayed in Palmer. She stepped in and the dory wobbled. Climbing around the fishing poles, she sat on a wooden bench and laid her hands in her lap. *How did I go from taking a morning walk to being here?* she wondered as she gazed at the open water.

Ray released the small boat and pushed away from the dock. He started his engine, and it thrummed softly as they headed into the inlet. Keeping a hand on the motor's handle, Ray sat with a straight back and gazed out over the water. With the cannery disappearing into the shore-line haze, he said, "I know a good spot west of here, just beyond the Susitna River. Figured we'd start there."

Her hands pressed between her knees, Jean studied the landscape. "That's Mt. Susitna, right?" She pointed at a low-lying mountain north of the inlet.

"Yep, and the big mountain beyond is McKinley." Ray kept his eyes on the water in front of them.

Jean scanned the coastline with its mix of spruce, birch, and alder forests, swamps, and open meadows. Beyond, to the north and east, were mountain ranges. "Seems there are mountains just about every-where you look." She rested an arm on the edge of the boat.

"That's true," Ray said, never taking his eyes off the waves.

Jean settled back. Among the trees along the shore, birds flitted through boughs, busily building nests and squabbling over space.

Finally Ray cut the engine and tossed out an anchor. "This is it."

"How do you know?"

He smiled incredulously. "I've been coming here for years." He pointed at the mouth of a river. "That's the Susitna."

Jean nodded, picked up her pole, and threaded the line.

By the time she was ready for her hook, Ray had his line in the water. "You need a hand?" he asked.

Holding up her pole and line, she said, "It's been a while."

Ray took the gear and quickly had it ready to go. He took a herring out of a bait bucket and secured it to a large hook. "All set." He handed the pole to Jean. "Now, let's see what you haul in."

Jean cast out her line and settled down to wait. Neither spoke as a companionable silence settled over the boat. Soon, with the warmth of the sun and the gentle rocking of the boat, Jean felt sleepy and wished for a comfortable place to nap. Instead she studied the shoreline, gazed at a curious sea lion, and watched hungry seabirds. It was a peaceful setting, and Jean was glad she'd joined Ray.

"So, you come here a lot?" Jean asked, breaking the silence.

"Oh, I'd say half a dozen times during the summer. Usually get enough salmon to last the year. 'Course, I fish the rivers too." He grinned. "I can count on Celeste to cook what I catch. She takes good care of me."

"You can be thankful you have a woman to look after you," Jean said, then wished she could take back the words. An uncomfortable quiet fell over them.

Finally Ray said, "I used to come here with Ellie. She was a good fisherman." He eased his pole up. "Those were good days."

Jean nodded, hoping to leave memories alone for a day. She concentrated on her fishing.

Morning drifted into afternoon. The salmon were plentiful; Ray landed four, and Jean caught two. By the time they stopped to eat, clouds skittered across the sky, and a sharp wind cut across the waves, sending spray into the air. "Looks like we're in for some weather," Jean said as she bit into a venison sandwich.

Ray shoved a peanut butter cookie into his mouth. "We need to head back." He took a swig of water, then held out the container of cookies. "Try one. I made them."

"You?" Jean took one. "I never figured you for a cook," she said, taking a small bite. "Delicious." She took another bite.

"Don't sound so surprised. When Ellie died, I took over the cooking. I'm pretty good at it, although nowadays Celeste does most of it."

Jean finished the cookie. For reasons she couldn't explain, knowing Ray cooked made her like him more.

"So, I suppose Luke's working from daylight to dark these days," Ray said.

"Even at this time of year we don't seem to have enough daylight. In fact, I ought to feel guilty for being here. I shouldn't be goofing off."

"You're working," Ray said with a grin. "You now have more fish to hang in your smokehouse."

"It doesn't feel like work." Wind caught Jean's hair and whipped it across her face. She pushed it back. "Most of the planting is done, thanks to Adam and the fellows you sent over."

Ray took another drink of water and climbed to the back of the boat. "And how's Luke?"

"Fine, I guess, but if you're asking how he feels about you . . . well, nothing's changed."

"I'm sorry to hear that."

A wave slammed against the boat, splashing over the sides. The clouds had turned dark.

"Weather's changing fast," Jean said, unable to disguise her anxiety.

"We better get a move on." Ray started the engine and pointed the bow toward Anchorage.

They'd barely started back when the rain started and the wind picked up. Waves rolled close together and dipped into deep troughs. The small dory rocked wildly and dropped to the bottom of watery valleys. Jean gripped the wooden bench, certain they would capsize at any moment.

Ray reached under his seat, pulled out a raincoat, and tossed it to her. "Put it on." He didn't bother with one for himself but gripped the rudder handle. "I know a place where we can hold up until the storm passes," he called over the wailing wind. He steered toward the mouth of the Susitna.

As they entered the river, the waves became more erratic and choppy, and the dory bounced violently. Jean prayed. *Brian and Susie need me. They've lost so much already, Father. Please, not now.*

Finally they cleared the chop and entered the calmer waters of the river. "Where are we going?" Jean asked.

"About a mile inland there are a couple of small cabins. The seal hunters use them during the season."

Meadows of tall grasses spread out away from the river. As they moved inland, alder thickets replaced the fields. Ray steered toward a clearing. Maneuvering the boat into the shallows, he jumped out and pulled the dory to shore.

"How did you know about this place?" Jean asked, pulling her hood around her face to shut out the wind.

"I've been here a lot of years, remember?" He chuckled. "In the winter you can get here by dogsled." He offered his hand to Jean and steadied her as she climbed out. "The cabins ought to keep us warm for the night," he said, grabbing a pack.

"The night? You mean we're going to be here all night?"

"This storm isn't going to let up anytime soon."

"My family will worry."

Ray headed up a trail leading away from the river and stopped in front of two tiny cabins standing side by side. A canoe lay alongside one, and each had a single window in front and a smokestack protruding from its roof. Wood was stacked alongside one cabin.

"Not much," Ray said, "but it'll do." He peeked inside one, then walked in. Jean followed. It seemed even smaller from the inside, measuring approximately ten feet by eight feet. A small wood stove stood in one corner, and a wooden bench sat beneath the only window.

Ray walked back outside, then returned a few moments later with an armload of wood. "We can be thankful for whoever was here before us. The person left a supply of firewood." He set the split birch and alder on the floor beside the stove and took a newspaper from a stack along the wall. He crumpled it and shoved it in the stove, then added kindling. Retrieving matches out of his pack, he lit the paper, and soon a small blaze crackled. He added larger pieces of wood and closed the cast iron door. "That'll do it."

After sharing what was left of their lunch, Ray and Jean sat on the floor and settled into a comfortable silence. Burning wood crackled and popped, and the cabin turned warm.

A burst of wind swept over the cabin. "What would we have done if these cabins hadn't been here?" Jean asked, glancing at the window.

"We'd be sleeping under the trees, trying to keep from shivering our teeth loose." Ray grinned. "Or we would have sheltered under the boat. I've done that before."

"You've done just about everything."

"And more," Ray said.

"Do you think we'll be able to leave in the morning? My family will be frantic."

"Probably." Ray leaned his back against the wall. "Don't worry about your family. Celeste will know where we are, and she'll tell them."

Jean hugged her knees. "Do you think it's this bad in the valley?"

"Maybe. We get some strong storms rolling through."

"The crops won't stand up to this kind of beating."

"It's early in the season. Could you replant?"

Jean looked at Ray. "I haven't been completely honest with you about the farm. We don't have enough money for replanting. Even with a good crop, I don't know if I can hang on to it. Luke's talking about joining the navy as soon as he's eighteen. That's only six months from now."

"You think he'll leave in the middle of winter? I thought he was all excited about running the farm."

"He was, but ever since Alex died, he hasn't been the same. He blames Alaska and wants to leave." She shrugged. "Even if it means I lose the farm, I think it's good for him to get away." A sharp pop reverberated from the stove. "I've been thinking about moving."

"Where to?"

"I don't know. I want to be close to Laurel and Adam and William. I was thinking maybe Anchorage. Maybe I could find a job. I've also thought about Wisconsin—work is more plentiful there, but the people I care about are here."

"I thought you were working at the store."

"I am, but it's not enough. And as long as I live on the farm, I have an obligation to work it. That's part of the contract Will and I signed."

Ray pushed to his feet and walked to the window. He watched the storm. "I've never been a real farmer, but I liked the work I did for you. It's good, honest labor." He turned and looked at Jean. "I know I'm not Will. I've prayed and wished I were. I've even tried to make myself like him, but I'm not." Jean started to say something, but Ray raised his hand. "Let me finish.

"God's been working on me, helping me become a better Ray Townsend. My temper's not so bad as it was; I'm steadier, not so quick to fly off the handle." He offered a sideways grin. "I doubt I'll ever be a quiet man, but I'm working on it."

He pressed his palms together, then swiped a hand through his dark curls. "I can't replace Will, and I don't expect you to love me, but I could be a real help to you and the children." He didn't look at Jean. "I was thinking . . . maybe I could move in to your place and work it full time." His eyes met Jean's. "With Luke leaving, there won't be a problem between him and me."

Jean stopped breathing. Was Ray asking her to marry him, or was he just saying he'd live at the farm to help out? "Oh, I don't know. Luke would be awfully upset."

"Jean, you can't live your life according to what your son wants."

"I know, but he is my flesh and blood. I have to think about his feelings." She added wood to the fire. What should she do? She didn't want a marriage of convenience, but Ray might be the only way she could stay in Alaska. Could she love him? She liked him and respected him. Was that enough? Obviously he didn't love her, or he would have said so. *It's the children he loves,* Jean decided. *And Ellie. 'Course, I still love Will. That will never change.*

Ray waited.

Jean knew she needed to say something. Finally she said, "I'll think about it. That's all I can do for now. I promise to think about it."

Chapter 31

WAKEFULNESS PULLED AT JEAN, BUT SHE WANTED TO LINGER. SHE AND WILL stood together beside the barn. He was tall and handsome; she could feel her heart pounding. Will took something from his pocket; it was a ring. She'd known it would be. They'd been so young, so in love.

The smell of coffee cut into Jean's dream. *No. Let me stay a little longer.*

A door closed, and daylight pressed against her eyes. She rolled to her side and remembered she was sleeping on the floor. *Oh yes, the storm.* Jean opened her eyes and found Ray sitting on the bench looking at her.

"Morning," he said.

She pushed herself up on one elbow. "Is that coffee I smell?"

"Yep." He sipped from a cup. "Found it in the other cabin. I also found some powdered milk and dishes. I heated the milk." He nodded toward the stove. "It's still warm."

Sitting all the way up, Jean combed her hair with her fingers. "I hate warm milk," she said, wrinkling her nose. "But coffee sounds good."

"You should drink some of the milk. It'll fill you up. A marauder took our fish."

"What? Oh, no."

"I should have been more careful."

Jean pulled her blanket around her. "What do you think it was?"

"Any number of critters—fox, wolf . . . a bear."

Unable to keep herself from looking, Jean glanced at the window. The idea of a bear prowling around while they slept was unsettling. Her stomach rumbled. "I guess I'll try the milk, but I won't like it."

Ray grinned. "You never know. 'Course, I could catch us another fish."

"Are we staying?"

"No, going. The storm's moved on. It's a little breezy, but we ought to do all right." He held out half an apple. "I found this in my coat pocket. I ate part of it."

"Thanks." Jean took the apple and bit into it. "We can't take time to fish. My family will be worried." She headed for the stove, and tucking the apple between her arm and her side, she poured warm milk into a cup. Sitting on the bench beside Ray, she took a sip and made a face.

"Try taking a bite of apple with it."

Jean took a bite, then a drink. Swallowing, she said, "Better, but still not good. I'd rather enjoy the apple," she said, taking a big swig of milk followed by a shudder. Looking at the bottom of her cup, she said, "I'll add coffee to the rest of this."

Ray laughed. "You do beat all."

Warmed by his laughter, Jean walked to the stove and filled the cup with coffee. She stared out the window. "The wind is still gusting. You sure it's all right to head back?"

"Yeah. There'll be some chop, but the boat's sturdy. We ought to be fine.

"Laurel and Luke must be worried sick."

"I'm sure Celeste is with them. She'll set 'em straight. Like I said, I'm sure she's figured out where we are." His voice gentle, Ray caught hold of Jean's hand. "Try not to worry."

The contact was unexpected, and Jean flinched. Ray let go immediately. "Sorry, I didn't mean to—"

"No, it's fine. I just didn't expect it, that's all." Jean hated the wounded expression in Ray's eyes. She didn't want to hurt him. "I'm not offended, and it's not that I find it—"

"No. It's nothing. Don't worry about it," he said brusquely and crossed the room. Picking up two blankets at once, he said, "We better get going." He stuffed the blankets into the duffel bag.

Jean finished her coffee and the apple, then gathered up her things, puzzling over her reaction to Ray's touch. Nothing was wrong with it. Why had she reacted so negatively?

Ray headed out the door with the duffel bag. "Let's get a move on," he said, his gentle mood gone.

The trip across the inlet was silent and strained. The seas were rough, and Jean prayed they wouldn't have to turn back. She couldn't face another night alone with Ray.

Keeping her eyes trained on the distant shoreline, she was thankful the rough waters kept Ray distracted. That way they didn't have to talk. What could she say to his proposal? She didn't even know just exactly what he was proposing.

They'd been enemies, then friends, and now . . . what were they now? If he wanted to marry her, would they become lovers? Husbands and wives generally were. Was he suggesting they marry and simply live a life of convenience? Or did he just mean to move onto the farm and be a help to her family? She imagined the embarrassment when she'd have to ask him to explain.

If he were suggesting marriage, how did she feel about it? The idea wasn't unpleasant. Was it possible for her to love someone other than Will? In so many ways he was still with her, and she'd never stop loving him. Wasn't that unfair to Ray? Brian and Susie would be ecstatic. They loved Ray. Luke, however, was another matter. She could barely bring herself to think what his reaction would be. What if he was angry enough to walk away for good?

Jean breathed a sigh of relief when the boat glided up to the pier. Ray climbed out, tied the dory, and offered Jean a hand. His grip was strong and sure. *Just like him,* she thought, her mind touching on the image of him as a marriage partner. She could never marry for convenience. Standing on the dock, she said, "It's good to be back."

"We've still got a long drive ahead of us." He started unloading their gear.

They headed for Palmer, and weariness settled over Jean. She longed for the quiet of her room and time to sort out her thoughts. She glanced at Ray. His big hands gripped the steering wheel; his eyes stared straight ahead. Maybe now was a good time to ask him what he'd meant when he'd talked about helping her and the kids.

"I'll bet Luke's hotter than an angry yellow jacket," Ray said, flashing Jean a smile. "I don't suppose we could hope he's not there."

"No. I'm sure he's home . . . and waiting." The thought of facing her fuming son made Jean's stomach turn.

Ray reached across the seat and patted Jean's hand. "Don't worry. I'll handle everything. Luke knows things can happen. He's been here long enough to understand."

"He knows, all right. He just doesn't want any adventures that include you."

"Not all adventures are bad." Ray chuckled.

Jean was glad things were back to normal between her and Ray. Maybe she wouldn't have to decide anything for a while.

Quiet settled over the cab, and Jean was content to watch the scenery move past the window. As they approached home, her stomach growled loudly. Pressing a hand against her abdomen, she said, "I'm starved. I'm sure you are too. Would you like to stay for supper?"

"I don't know if this is a good time. It would be like putting a burr under Luke's saddle, if you know what I mean."

"He's going to be mad no matter what."

"You have a point," Ray said, pulling into the driveway.

Brian and Susie tore out the back door, and Jean took a strengthening breath, knowing she was about to face Luke's ire. Putting on a smile, she waved at her two youngest.

The truck had barely stopped when Brian yanked open the door and threw his arms around his mother. Jean inched off the seat and climbed out with Brian still clinging to her.

"Where were you?" he asked. "I was scared you weren't coming back."

"Of course I was coming back. I'm sorry you were worried. A storm blew in and we had to stay in a cabin up on the Susitna River."

"Mommy," Susie said, throwing herself at her mother.

Releasing Brian, Jean hefted her daughter into her arms and hugged her. "Oh, how good to see you. I missed you."

The little girl looked at her mother, her blue eyes bright. "Are you all right? You look all right."

"Yes. I'm fine. Mr. Townsend took good care of me." She rested a hand on her stomach. "But I am hungry."

Celeste and Laurel strode up to Jean and Ray. "It's about time," Celeste said with a grin, giving her father a quick hug. "I was beginning to worry."

"You know better," Ray said.

With William in her arms, Laurel embraced her mother. "I'm so glad you're all right. You scared us."

"I'm sorry." Jean kissed William. The little boy smiled and flailed his arms. Jean circled an arm around Laurel's waist. "We went fishing, then a storm chased us inland for the night." They headed toward the house.

Adam met them halfway. "Glad to see you back safe and sound. Did you get any fish?"

"We did, but some scavenger stole them in the night," Jean said.

"Let me give you a hand with your stuff," Adam said and headed for Ray.

Wearing a scowl, Luke stood on the porch, hands in his pockets. "You had us worried, you know."

Jean hugged him. "I'm sorry. I didn't mean to. The storm came up all of a sudden."

"It wouldn't have been a problem if you hadn't been out there in the first place."

"It was a beautiful day, and I needed some time off." She tried to smile. "Some things just can't be helped."

"Yes, they can be." Luke strode toward the truck.

"Luke. Don't." Jean followed him. "We all know how you feel." She grabbed his arm. "I told you to stop. You have no right to interfere."

Yanking his arm free, Luke whirled on her.

Jean forced herself to stand her ground, throwing back her shoulders.

"I have every right. This is my farm, and he isn't welcome here." Without another word, he headed for Ray and hurtled himself at the man. Pressing his fists against the big man's chest, he yelled, "What do you think you're doing taking my mother out on the inlet like that? You could have killed her. 'Course, you're pretty good at that kind of thing."

Adam tried to step between the two men. "That's enough, Luke."

"No. It's not . . . enough."

"It's all right, Adam. I'll handle this," Ray said evenly, facing the young man. "I never intended to put your mother in harm's way. We just went fishing. You know how changeable the weather can be. I didn't know a storm would come up. You can't predict those kinds of things."

Luke glared and didn't respond. Ray continued, "I've been out on that stretch of the bay more times than I can count. I know my way around." He glanced at Celeste. "Isn't that right?"

"We've gone fishing there ever since I was a kid. You didn't have to worry, Luke. I told you that."

"That's what you said, but how can I believe you? You're his daughter. You're loyal to him." His rage growing, Luke turned back to Ray. "I told you to stay away, and I meant it."

"You did, and I have. And yesterday when I set out, I never planned to take your mother along. We just bumped into each other at the post office. It was a beautiful day, and on the spur of the moment, I asked her to join me. I'm not sorry I did. I enjoyed her company; I've missed her." He glanced at the children. "And I've missed Brian and Susie."

Brian sidled up next to Ray and rested an arm around the man's waist. "Yeah, and we miss him. You don't have to be so mean, Luke."

"Yeah, Luke," Susie said, sticking out her lower lip and joining Brian. She looked up at Ray and smiled. "We like you. You're our friend."

If it were possible, the red in Luke's face deepened. "You're kids. What do you know? Have you forgotten he's the one who murdered our father? And now he's trying to take away our mother and our house."

"That's not true," Brian said. He looked up at Ray. "Is it?"

"No. It's not," Ray said, a sharp edge to his voice.

Jean touched Luke's arm. "Please, Luke . . . enough's enough."

Ray's eyes were angry now. "I've had enough, Luke. I've tried to get along with you, but you won't listen, and I don't like your accusations." His voice was calm but threatening. "I didn't murder your father. It was an accident. And I don't plan to take over your home." His eyes rested on Jean for just a moment.

"You're after our mother. I can see it. Don't deny it."

Ray didn't respond right away. His eyes moved from his daughter to Adam and Laurel, then stayed with Jean. Finally he said quietly, "I guess you do have one thing right. I am crazy about your mother. But please believe me when I say it didn't start that way. Before your father died, he asked me to watch out for you all. In the beginning you needed help. And I just wanted to lend a hand . . . do what your father asked. Then gradually it became something else. I couldn't help it . . . I fell in love."

He turned his eyes back to Luke. "Your mother's a special woman. It would be hard for anyone to know her and not love her." He looked at Jean. "I didn't want to make things harder on you or your family. I'm real sorry." He turned and climbed into his truck. "I'll see you at home, Celeste?"

"Yes," she said softly. "Soon."

Ray drove away.

Stunned, Jean watched the truck. He loved her. Now what should she do?

When the pickup was out of sight, she turned to Luke. Anger boiling up, she stared at him a long moment before speaking. "Cruelty isn't something this family believes in. I never thought I'd say this, but if your father could see you right now, he'd be ashamed of you." She balled her hands into fists. "I thought you'd finally understand . . . especially after what happened with Alex."

A pang of sorrow seared Luke's eyes, and Jean immediately wished she'd kept the words to herself. Suddenly drained, she walked to the porch and sat on the steps, resting her arms on her legs.

Adam stepped closer to Luke. "It's time you faced the truth. Your father's death wasn't Ray's fault any more than Alex's death was yours. You're doing nothing but hurting yourself and your mother." Shaking his head, he added, "I expected better from you."

Chapter 32

JEAN STOOD AND BRUSHED DIRT FROM HER HANDS. ALTHOUGH IT WAS nearing eight o'clock, the sun still hung above the mountains. The kids would be hungry. Shading her eyes, she watched Brian shovel dirt into the back of his dump truck. Susie sat on the edge of the vegetable patch, braiding wildflowers into a necklace. Jean smiled, remembering how Laurel used to do the same thing when she was little.

Noticing her mother's interest, Susie jumped to her feet and ran to her. "Look what I made," she said, displaying the colorful band.

Jean bent to examine it. "How beautiful! It's the best one yet."

"Yeah, but this flower's broke," Susie said, touching a daisy with a twisted stem.

"Oh, that's all right. Now it's more interesting."

"You think so?" Susie smiled. "I made it for you." She handed the necklace to her mother.

Jean draped it around her neck. "Thank you," she said and gave Susie a hug.

A truck approached, kicking up dust. It bounced over the bridge, then moved on. A frown touched Susie's mouth. "Is Ray ever going to come and see us?"

"I'm sure he will. He's been busy." Jean scanned the field and studied Luke, who drove the tractor up and down rows. Sadness settled over her. If Ray showed up, there'd be a war.

"I'm hungry," Susie said.

"Me too," Jean said. "I was working and forgot about supper. I've got a roast cooking. All I need to do is add vegetables."

"And bread?"

"Of course." Jean picked up her hoe and followed Susie to the house. "Brian, could you run and tell your brother supper will be ready soon?"

"OK." Brian parked his truck, then skipped toward the tractor.

"Be careful," Jean called after him, remembering Will's accident on the tractor. It had seemed devastating then. She smiled, suddenly aware the memory didn't bring the usual gut-wrenching pain. Now she felt a sense of loss and savored the sweet memory of her husband's courage and determination. *Maybe I'm getting better,* she thought.

"Mommy, what are you thinking about?" Susie asked, standing on the porch steps.

"Your daddy."

"Do you still miss him a lot?"

"Yes. But sometimes I just remember what a fine man he was."

"I don't remember him too good."

Jean scooped up the little girl and nuzzled her. "Oh, he loved you. He liked to say you were his sunshine."

"I remember that." Susie leaned away from her mother. "Will I have a different daddy some day?"

"I don't know. Maybe . . . someday."

Brian trudged in just as Jean set the roast on the table. "Luke said he has to finish. He'll come in when he's done." Leaving dirty footprints, he walked to the table and pulled out a chair. "Looks good," he said, picking at the meat.

"Oh, no you don't," Jean said, swatting his hand gently. "You go and wash up, then you can eat." Brian walked to the sink and stuck his hands under running water. A knock sounded at the door.

Susie ran to answer it. "Hi, Ray," she said, holding up her arms so he could lift her.

"Hi," he said, scooping up the little girl and walking in.

Jean immediately knew Ray had a reason for his visit. Otherwise, he wouldn't have chanced an encounter with Luke. "You're just in time for supper."

He looked at the table. "I figured you'd be finished by now. I'll come back later."

"We have plenty. Luke's out working, so you can take his plate."

Ray skimmed off his hat. "All right, if you're sure you have enough." He looked about the kitchen. "Where's Miram?"

"In town visiting a friend."

"Ed," Brian said with a knowing smile. "I think Miram loves him. What do you think, Mama?"

"I think you should ask her," Jean said firmly. "Now, let's sit down and eat. I'm hungry." She sat and so did everyone else. For the moment the room was quiet. Jean looked at Ray and asked, "Would you mind saying grace?"

Ray bowed his head. "Dear Lord, thank you for this family. They're good people. I ask that you bless them. And Father, thank you for the food and for Jean's hard work in preparing it. Bless her for being such a good mother and a good . . . friend. Amen."

Jean's eyes met Ray's, which seemed oddly intense. He'd said he loved her. Was that what she saw now or had the words been unintended and simply slipped out in the heat of the moment? *No matter,* she thought. *It feels right having him at our table.* "Thank you, Ray," she said and handed him the platter of meat.

"How are things going for you?" he asked.

"Good," Brian said. "I've been doin' a lot of fishing. I caught a real big trout this morning, and yesterday I reeled in a salmon. It's big."

"Really?" Ray asked, taking a slice of bread. "I'd like to go with you some day."

"That'd be fun." Worry furrowed Brian's brow. "Luke wouldn't want you to come with us." He thought a moment, then smiled. "Maybe just you and me could go."

"Sounds like fun," Ray said, cutting his meat. He took a bite and chewed. "This is good."

"Thank you." Jean buttered a slice of bread. "How did your fur sales turn out?"

"Not bad. Good enough to see me through the year."

Susie dipped her bread in thick, brown gravy and slopped it into her mouth. "Mama, what if Luke comes in? Won't he get mad?"

"Probably."

Silence fell over the table. Brian laid his hands one on top of the other and rested his chin on them. He looked at his mother, then Ray, and asked, "Do you love my mother?"

"Brian! You don't ask such things!" Jean said.

"You told me I should ask Miram if she loves Ed."

"Well, that's different. Ed's not here."

"Oh." Brian poked his fork into a small potato. "Well, never mind then."

Ray's face had turned red. He finished off the last of his bread and sipped his coffee. "Actually, I was hoping I could talk to your mother about that," he finally said, looking directly at Jean. "Could we talk?"

Jean knew her cheeks were flaming. "Now?"

"Well, just as soon as you're done eating if that's all right."

Jean looked at her plate, uncertain she could manage another bite. She nibbled on a slice of bread, then pushed her plate aside and said softly, "I'm finished."

Ray stood, his eyes on her.

Jean was afraid. What would she say if Ray wanted an answer? "Brian, can you and Susie clear away the dishes?"

"All right," Brian said in a whiny voice. "But Susie's not much help. She makes a mess."

Jean stood and moved around the table to her daughter. "Susie, I need you to put the dishes on the drain board. OK? Brian will do the rest."

Susie nodded. "I'm a big girl. I can do it."

Jean kissed her forehead. "Good." She looked at Ray. "So, you ready?"

"Yep."

Feeling as if her legs were made of wood, Jean walked to the back door. Ray quickly reached around her and opened it. Taking a deep breath, she stepped out. Her eyes immediately went to the mountains where the sun rested on the peaks, transforming the sky and strands of clouds into a golden pallet. "It's beautiful."

"It sure is." Ray rested a hand on Jean's waist. "Maybe we could walk down to the creek?"

"All right." Jean's voice wavered, and she hoped Ray hadn't noticed. His hand burned against her back.

They followed the trail to Justin's apple tree and stopped. "It's really grown," Jean said. When we first moved here, it wasn't much more than a twig. She smelled a white blossom. "Maybe we'll have apples this year." She turned and looked back at the house. "Back in Wisconsin we had a big orchard. This tree was a seedling cut from one of Will's father's original trees. Justin and Brian used to swing from branches every chance they got." Jean could feel the tears. "I miss Justin," she said, glancing at Ray and walking toward the creek bank.

"He was a fine boy. He was the serious one, wasn't he?"

"Yes. You noticed? You didn't even know him."

"I knew more than you thought. I wasn't hard all the way through. He was smart. I wish I'd known him." Ray's voice faltered.

"Ray, what is it?"

He blinked hard. "Just thinking about my own boy. I wish I'd known him too." He looked at Jean. "You and Will did a fine job of raising your children. You can be proud of them, all of them—even Luke."

Jean smiled softly. "It was more God than us."

"That Luke can be a hothead, but I understand that," Ray said with a grin. "He's mad at me, but a big part of his anger is because he loves you and he feels protective." Ray picked up a rock and tossed it into the creek. "He's a fine young man."

"I'm worried about him. He's still so angry. And since Alex died, he's withdrawn."

"He'll be fine. I can't envision God leaving him to muck around for too long."

"I hope you're right."

"I know what it's like to feel the way he does and it's no fun. Hopefully he won't fight God as long as I did." He took Jean's hand. "I see a nice spot down here."

Ray moved ahead of Jean, walking sideways down the bank and holding her hand. When they reached the bottom, he kept hold of her hand. His grip was strong.

He sat on a log and gently pulled Jean down beside him, then circled an arm around her shoulders. It felt natural to nestle close, so Jean did.

For a while they silently watched the stream sweep past, tickling grasses along the bank and dancing over rocks. Then Ray cleared his throat and said solemnly, "I meant what I said."

Jean gave him a questioning look.

"I do love you. I tried not to. I knew it would be complicated if I did, but I couldn't help myself. You're so beautiful and so decent." He gently brushed her auburn hair back off her shoulder.

Jean trembled. She had never been this close to any man except Will. She felt something like love for this uncommon man. But could she trust her feelings? "I've been doing a lot of thinking." She hesitated. What if she was wrong? "I've been thinking, and . . . I believe I love you. I guess I do." She chewed her lip and searched his face—his serious, gray eyes probed hers. "I do love you," she said. "I love you."

Ray cupped her face in his big hands and kissed her forehead. "I never thought I'd hear you say those words. I prayed . . . but I had a hard time believing." He smiled. "I'm not like Will. I still have a hot temper, and my faith is puny, but I have a powerful love for you."

"What about Ellie?"

Ray took Jean's hands and held them against his chest. "I love her. I always will. But that doesn't mean I can't love someone else." He pressed her hands to his lips. "I believe God gave us hearts big enough to love lots of people." He pulled her against him and held her for a few moments. Setting her away from him, he asked, "And Will? It hasn't been very long."

"I know. I've been lonely." She glanced away, then back at Ray. "I was afraid that my loneliness would keep me from thinking clearly." She turned his palms up and ran a fingertip across his callused hand. "You have good, strong hands." She rested the back of his fingers against her cheek. "You aren't Will—and you shouldn't be. You're Ray Townsend." She hesitated. "I love Will, but my heart has room for you too." She smiled.

"I want you to be my wife."

Jean took a deep breath. She knew this had been coming, and the idea of it took her breath away. She glanced up the bank. "What about Luke?"

"You can't wait to live your life until he's ready to live his."

"I know. But he hates you. How will you abide that?"

"I'd rather tussle with Luke than live without you."

"Does Celeste know?"

"Yes." Ray smiled. "She was sure you'd say yes."

"I have to admit, it's all I've thought about since the storm."

"You haven't answered. Will you?"

"Yes. I'll marry you."

Ray pulled Jean into his arms and held her as if he were afraid to let go. Finally he set her away from him. "I don't have a ring yet, but I'll get you one."

"Rings don't matter." Jean felt as if she could melt into this man, and as she thought of Will, she was certain he was smiling and grateful that she and the children wouldn't be alone anymore. Then Luke's angry face intruded into her thoughts. He hated Ray. Would he hate her too?

Chapter 33

Norma Prosser looked at the ladies sitting around the quilt. "Would anyone like some apple cider?"

"I'd love some," Jessie said, pushing a needle through the quilt and directly into her finger. "Ouch!" She glanced at the wound, then pulled a handkerchief out of her blouse pocket and wrapped it around her finger to stop the bleeding. "I was never very good at this. I'm much better with a paintbrush."

"We appreciate your efforts," Norma said.

"I'd love some cider," Miram Dexter said in her high-pitched voice. "However did you manage to keep from drinking all of it? Ours never lasted past early spring."

"I guard it with my life," Norma said, holding up a wooden spoon like a weapon. She chuckled. "My family loves cider, so if I don't keep a close eye on it, it's gone long before spring."

"I just can't seem to discipline myself," Jean said. "The children and I drink it right up."

Jessie looked at Jean. "So, when is the wedding?"

"We decided August 14 would be a good day. The weather should be good; we'll have a few weeks to plan."

"Where are you going for your honeymoon?" Norma asked.

"Into the mountains—the same place we went hunting."

"That's so romantic," Miram said.

"I hope you'll let me take care of the flowers," Jessie said. "August is a perfect time. Lots of different varieties will be in bloom. The narcissus will be out, and daisies, of course, and the asters. Oh, and geraniums are beautiful, plus lots of fireweed . . ."

Jean laughed. "Of course, you can take care of the flowers. You know them all."

"It's just that I love wildflowers."

"I trust you completely," Jean said. "Whatever you choose will be perfect. And wildflowers are just right. Ray and I both want a simple wedding . . . since we've been married before and all."

Miram abruptly left the table and walked to the counter.

"Oh, I forgot your cider," Norma said, quickly getting the jug out of the icebox and filling Miram and Jessie's glasses. She set the juice on the counter and looked at Miram who stood sipping. "Is everything all right, dear?"

"Yes, fine." She returned to her chair, careful to keep her eyes on the quilt. The room turned quiet. Miram tried to sew but finally let the fabric go and looked at her friends, sad eyes finally settling on Jean. "I don't mean to take anything from you. I'm very happy you and Ray found each other, but . . . well, I just wish *I* was the one getting married. I'm beginning to think Ed is never going to ask. And my mother isn't making it any easier."

"Yes, I heard she was in town," Norma said with a gentle smile.

"You know she's welcome to stay with us," Jean said.

"No. She wouldn't hear of it." Miram resumed her sewing. "She's just as happy to stay in town."

Norma rested a hand on Miram's shoulder. "You don't need to worry about Ed. I've seen the way he looks at you. He'll come around."

"I hope you're right." Miram's eyes filled with tears. "And I don't know what to do about my mother. She doesn't like Ed. She's always saying something about the way he dresses, his work, or his . . . well, his everything. I wish she'd never come."

"You don't really mean that," Laurel said. "She's your mother."

"You know what she's like. And, well, she's not like your mother." Miram dabbed at her eyes with a handkerchief. "I wish she were."

"Your mother loves you," Jean said gently.

"I know." Miram blew her nose. "But I wish she were a little kinder—not just to me, but to everybody. She's been going on about everyone in town, and especially about you and Ray."

Jean felt a stab of anxiety. Margarite Dexter and Luke weren't the only ones unhappy about the wedding. Others were also nettled. "I know our getting married doesn't sit well with everyone; even my own son says he won't be there." Jean felt the sting of tears and quickly blinked them back. She pushed her needle down through the material and up again, then stared at the square of gingham in front of her. "I pray we're doing the right thing," she whispered, then looked at her friends and smiled. "I have to admit, I'm nearly as surprised as everyone else. I never imagined Ray and I would get married."

"I think it's wonderful," Miram said.

Laurel patted her mother's hand. "It's a shame Luke can't see what a good man Ray is. For a long while I tried to believe he was a fine person beneath all his bluster, and now I know. Poor Celeste used to try to tell me about the man she knew. Now she says her father's whistling again."

"Oh, I've noticed a big change in him," Jessie said. "He's the old Ray I used to know."

"Where is Celeste?" Norma asked. "I was hoping she could join us."

"She had to work. Guess she takes all the hours she can. Business is down."

"So many colonists are leaving." Norma shook her head. "I thought we'd made it."

"We haven't lost the battle yet," Jean said. "A lot of us are still here."

"Yes, but for how long? It looks like the country is heading back into hard times."

"We'll make it, don't you worry." Jean returned to working on her portion of the quilt, her mind more on Luke than the economy. She couldn't imagine the wedding without him.

Jean woke early to bright sunlight. She climbed from beneath her blankets and walked to the window, shivering slightly in the morning coolness. Gazing at the pastures dotted with clover and wildflowers, she thought about the day. In a few hours, she would become Mrs. Ray Townsend. It didn't seem possible. Fifteen months ago she'd considered Ray Townsend a life-long enemy.

The back door banged shut, and Luke trudged toward the barn, a milk pail in each hand. Taking long strides, he kept his eyes on the ground. He didn't swing the buckets but held his arms stiff, his shoulders rigid.

He's angry. He won't be there, she thought with a sinking heart. *Lord, what will it take? Am I going to lose him? I couldn't bear it.*

She walked to the bureau, picked up a brush, and ran it through her auburn hair. Gazing at her reflection, she studied her face. She wasn't the beautiful young woman Will had married, but she had to admit, she was still attractive. Her hazel eyes were spirited, and her skin looked soft and smooth. She smiled. "You're not bad looking for a grandma." She turned from side to side and studied her still trim figure. "Forty isn't that old," she said, turning away from the mirror and heading for the kitchen.

Brian and Susie were already sitting at the table. They each had a glass of milk and a piece of bread.

"You're up awfully early," Jean said.

"We couldn't sleep." Brian took a bite of bread. "We're too excited."

"Are you hungry enough for some eggs?"

"Yep. I could eat a bunch."

"Me too," Susie added, dipping her bread into her milk and taking a bite. "Could I have toast?" she asked, her mouth full.

"Certainly," Jean said, setting a cast-iron skillet on the stove. She cut several slices of bread, buttered them, and set two in the pan. She melted bacon grease in another skillet and broke eggs into it. She glanced at the clock. *Seven o'clock. Only six more hours.* Jean's stomach did a little tumble. It would be strange not to be Mrs. Hasper.

She turned the eggs, took out the first pieces of toast, laid in two more, then filled a cup with coffee. "Luke made coffee?" she asked, looking at Brian.

"Yep. Before he went out. Said he couldn't wait. He needed some good strong coffee right away."

Jean looked at the dark brew and took a sip. "It's strong, all right."

Brian shoved the last of his bread into his mouth. "Are you scared?"

"No, but a little nervous. Are you?"

"Nah. I know all about weddings. I was in Laurel and Adam's, remember?"

"I remember," Jean said with a smile. Sadness touched her. It had been such a joyous day. They'd had no clue Will would be gone a few weeks later. She brushed aside the memory and looked at the youngsters. "Did you know that you are two of the most important people in my life?" She smiled.

"Yep. I know. Especially because today I'm going to carry your rings."

"I get to carry flowers," Susie said petulantly, "and I'm going to wear a real pretty dress." She smiled, her cheeks dimpling. "It's pink and has ruffles."

Brian stood. "I'm wearing a suit, and I have new shoes." He ran to get the shoes he'd left in a box on the back porch. "Ray helped me pick them out. He said they look just like his."

"How come I didn't get new shoes?" Susie asked, sticking out her lower lip.

"The shoes you have are beautiful," Jean said, sliding an egg out of the pan and onto a plate. Carrying it to the table and setting it in front of her daughter, she added, "You'll both look perfect."

"I'm going to like having Ray for my dad," Brian said.

The back door slammed, and Luke walked in with the milk. He looked like a thundercloud. "He's not your dad. You already have a dad." He slammed the pails on the counter, spilling milk.

"I know that, but he's kind of like a dad."

"He's not."

"Luke, let it be. If Brian wants to think of Ray as his father, that's just fine."

Luke glared.

"I can have two dads," Brian said.

"Yeah," Susie added. "We can have two dads."

Luke headed for the door.

"Please, Luke, can't we talk?" Jean asked.

"There's nothing to talk about." He yanked open the door and walked out.

"How come he's so mad?" Brian asked.

Jean shook her head. She had no adequate answer for a nine-year-old boy.

Brian walked to the door and stared after Luke. "I like Ray. I'm glad you're going to marry him."

Jean kneeled in front of the youngster and pulled him into her arms. "I'm glad too. Maybe Luke will be one day."

A knock sounded at the back door. "Who could that be so early?" Jean walked to the door and opened it. Mrs. Dexter stood with gloved hands clasped over her bulging stomach. She straightened her pillbox hat and smiled, then pursed her red lips. "Why, hello, Mrs. Dexter," Jean said, apprehension rolling through her. "I didn't expect anyone so early."

"I know, but I figured I ought to get over here first thing."

"Please, come in."

Holding her purse close to her chest, Mrs. Dexter squeezed her bulk past Jean.

"Would you like a cup of coffee or tea?"

"Coffee, please."

Jean knew Margarite Dexter hadn't come calling simply for pleasure. She grabbed a cup from the cupboard and filled it. "Do you like anything in it?

"Milk and sugar."

Jean set the cup on the table along with a spoon and sugar. Then she retrieved milk from the icebox.

Brian and Susie stared at the woman. Margarite nodded at them.

"Brian, why don't you take Susie upstairs and help her get dressed," Jean said, knowing that whatever Mrs. Dexter had to say the children didn't need to hear it.

Brian took Susie's hand and led her out of the room.

Mrs. Dexter poured milk into her coffee, then added three heaping spoons of sugar and stirred. She looked around the bright room. "This is very nice, especially compared to that Townsend house—if you can call it that. I wish Miram was still here with you."

"She felt it would be better if she stayed with Celeste since they're both single women and Ray will be moving in here."

Margarite gave a little sniff. "That man has animal heads mounted on the walls and skins on the floor and thrown over the sofas. It's down-right heathen."

"He's a hunter and a trapper," Jean said, feeling her anger rise.

"I suppose a person can't expect much from the folks up here." She scanned Jean's kitchen. "At least it hasn't affected you too badly." Margarite took a drink of coffee, then set her cup on the table in front of her. "This place has some semblance of civilization. I just can't bear the thought of Miram living in that hovel. And if she marries that Ed fellow . . . well, I hate to think."

"He's a nice young man."

"He's slovenly and uncivilized. Miram is far too well-bred for a man like him." She took another sip. "I haven't been able to get her to listen to reason."

"I know Ed cares for her."

"Well, if that's so, why hasn't he asked her to marry him? Not that I'd like him to."

"Ed's kind of quiet, a little shy. I'm sure he'll get around to it."

Margarite rested her arms on the table. "If only Miram would leave with us. She'd be much better off. Do you think you could talk to her?" She added another spoon of sugar and stirred, the spoon clinking against the sides of the cup. "She thinks a lot of you. I thought maybe you could help her see she doesn't belong here."

"Miram's a grown woman, and if she's made up her mind to stay, I'm not going to try and change it. She's done wonderfully here. She has friends and a good life. She's happy."

Margarite's eyes narrowed. "I expected you to say something like that. How do you know she's happy? I understand her better than anyone, and I can see she's not."

Jean figured Miram certainly wasn't happy with her mother around. "Well, I'm sure you know your daughter well, but Miram told me she never felt like she fit in anywhere before. She told me that here she feels like she belongs."

Margarite compressed her lips, and her cheeks turned bright pink. "I didn't come to talk about Miram. I wanted to discuss something else."

Jean waited, preparing for the worst.

Margarite clasped her gloved hands on the table in front of her. "Your poor husband, God rest his soul, must be turning over in his grave at what's going on."

"What are you talking about?"

"The wedding, of course. Do you think for one moment he'd want you to marry Ray Townsend, his enemy, the man who killed him? And it hasn't been very long since his death."

"First of all, Ray didn't kill my husband, and he wasn't Will's enemy. Will chose to stay and protect Ray." Jean looked at Margarite's gloved hands, then at the woman herself. "As to getting married too soon—well, Will's been gone more than a year. He wouldn't want me to be alone, and Ray Townsend is a good man. Will would approve."

Mrs. Dexter raised an eyebrow. "And why would you think that? Ray Townsend is nothing like your husband, who was a godly and well-mannered man. Everyone in this community respected him. Ray Townsend, on the other hand—"

"Ray Townsend is also godly and respected," Jean cut in, considering ordering the woman out of her home.

"What about that boy of yours? I hear he's not even going to the wedding. It's not right turning against your own flesh and blood that way."

The words cut into Jean. She'd struggled with herself about going ahead without Luke's acceptance.

"It must be so hard on that boy, what with his father barely in the ground—"

Jean stood, pressing her hands on the table. "It's been more than a year, and he's not in the ground. He's in heaven."

"Well, yes, of course, you know what I mean."

"Yes. I'm afraid I do."

"Please understand, I just want to help," Margarite said in a sweet voice. Still clutching her purse, she stood. "Will was your husband for so many years. If you get married so soon, it looks bad—almost as if you've shoved him aside for another man."

"I would never shove Will aside. I love him, I always will, but—"

"If that's so, then why are you marrying so willy-nilly? People are talking. You could ruin your reputation."

Jean could feel herself losing control. "My reputation?" she asked incredulously. "Nothing inappropriate has happened between me and Ray Townsend."

"Of course not. But then, well, you did have that overnight stay with him during the storm."

"I assure you that nothing happened."

"And the issue of the way your husband died. It looks very bad—almost as if you two planned it."

Jean couldn't take any more. Shaking, she pointed at the door. "I want you out of my house! Out!"

Disbelief flittered across Mrs. Dexter's face. "Why, I never . . . I'm just—"

"Go. Before I say or do something I'm sorry for."

Margarite headed for the door. "It will never work. Never. You two are going against God."

Jean pressed her hand against Mrs. Dexter's back and propelled her toward the porch. Shoving her out, she closed the door and leaned against it. Tears came. "I hate that woman! I hate her!"

"Mommy, what's wrong?" Brian asked, tentatively approaching her.

Jean wiped at the tears. "Nothing. Everything's fine."

"But you're crying. Did Mrs. Dexter say something mean?"

Jean walked to the table and picked up the cups. "She was just trying to help."

"She's right, you know," Luke said, stepping in from the front door. "People are talking. And Ray won't make you happy. He'll never replace Dad."

"I'm not trying to replace your Father. I could never replace him."

Luke took the cups from Jean and set them in the sink. "I know I've been awful lately, and I'm sorry." He turned and faced his mother. "I want you to be happy, but I don't think marrying Ray Townsend is the way to do it. He isn't who he says he is. If I really believed he had changed, I'd say OK to all this, but . . . well I just can't swallow it."

"You're wrong, Luke. He isn't what you think. Please give him a chance."

"I can't . . . just can't. Please don't marry him."

"The wedding is today. How can I change my mind now?"

Luke didn't answer; he just walked out of the house. As she watched the door close behind her son, Margarite's words reverberated through Jean's mind. *That poor boy. It will never work.*

Was she doing the right thing? And what about Luke? Would she lose him?

Chapter 34

THE MORNING PASSED, AND JEAN DID HER BEST TO PUT MARGARITE AND Luke's words out of her mind. Marrying Ray was the right thing to do. It would be good for Brian and Susie, and she needed a partner. Maybe it was too soon. Maybe her reasons to marry weren't the right ones. And what about Luke? He was her son. He mattered.

Each day since he'd first heard of the wedding, Luke had grown more distant. He'd packed his things and was ready to move in with Adam and Laurel, refusing to live in the same house as Ray Townsend. *What if he never accepts the marriage?* she wondered.

Jean hung her wedding dress in the kitchen while she waited for the iron to heat. It was a soft, yellow chiffon with a scooped neckline. Fitted at the waist, it flared just above her ankles. It was a lovely dress. She knew it would draw Ray's admiration. Only now, she didn't care so much about that, and she didn't feel the anticipation she'd expected. Jean wasn't even certain she ought to get married.

She headed upstairs to finish her last-minute packing. Warm clothes were a must for camping. When Ray had suggested they return to the mountains where they'd hunted, she'd thought it romantic. Now she only felt confused and anxious.

Maybe Margarite had been right, and she was blinded to the truth. But how could she call off the wedding on such short notice? She imagined Ray's reaction and felt sick at the thought. And if she didn't marry him, what would she do? She couldn't manage the farm on her own. She'd have to move. *But security isn't a good enough reason to get married,* she thought.

Jean stuffed an extra pair of pants and a shirt into her duffel bag. "Maybe I ought to take a pillow."

"Look, Mommy," Susie said, prancing into the room wearing her new dress. She twirled, arms straight out from her body. The skirt of her pinafore swirled away from her. Wearing a bright smile, she stopped twirling.

"You look absolutely beautiful," Jean said, folding the little girl in her arms. "You'll make a perfect flower girl." She straightened. "That dress needs ironing though."

"OK." Susie danced away.

An ache settled in Jean's chest. Susie loved Ray. She and Brian were thrilled to have a father. How could she hurt them by calling off the wedding? They'd already lost so much.

What matters is, do I love him? I do. Don't I? She'd thought it was clear in her mind. Now she wasn't sure. She closed her eyes. *Lord, clear my mind. Show me what to do.*

Susie carried her dress to her mother. Jean took it downstairs and laid it out on the ironing board. Carefully running the iron over the cotton material, she pressed out the wrinkles. Next she turned to her dress. The chiffon rustled as she worked.

Brian walked into the room. "Mom, I can't get this buttoned." He held up his arm.

Jean did up his cuffs. "Do you need help with your tie?"

"Nope. Ray taught me."

She smoothed the shoulders of his shirt. "You look very handsome."

"I'll look even better with the jacket. I'll get it." He ran out of the room and galloped up the stairs.

Luke walked in and was about to pass by without saying anything. "You get all those stalls done?" Jean asked before he disappeared.

"Yeah." He stopped, half in the kitchen and half in the front room. He rocked from one foot to the other. "They needed cleaning pretty bad. Figure I'll do some weeding this afternoon."

"So, you won't be at the wedding?"

He shoved his hands in his pockets and stared at the floor.

Jean searched for the right words. "Luke, this is an important day for me. It doesn't seem right, your not being there."

Keeping his eyes on the floor, Luke said, "The way I see it, it doesn't seem right for me *to* be there." He headed for the stairs.

Brian ran into the room and nearly bumped into him. Looking up at his brother, he asked, "What do you think? I look pretty good, huh?"

Luke managed a small smile. "You sure do."

"You still not going?" Brian asked, his voice cheerless.

"No. I've got work to do," Luke said brusquely and moved past him and up the stairs.

Brian's shoulders drooped. "I wish he would go. Can't you make him?"

"No. It's something he has to decide on his own."

"It won't be the same without Luke."

"I know."

By the time Adam and Laurel arrived, Jean and the children were ready. Laurel walked in with Adam right behind her, baby William in his arms.

"Mama, you look absolutely beautiful!" Laurel said, hugging her mother. "That yellow is perfect on you. I knew it would be."

"You look nice, Mrs. Hasper," Adam said, shuffling the baby into his other arm. "I swear, pretty soon this boy will be too heavy to carry. I'll be glad when he can walk."

"Don't hurry him too much," Jean said.

"So, how do I look?" Brian asked.

"Real sharp," Adam said.

Susie twirled. "How about me?"

"You are beautiful." Laurel bent and kissed her little sister, then straightened and looked at her mother. "Is Luke coming?"

"No."

"Do you want me to talk to him?" Adam offered.

"No."

"I wish he would come with us," Brian said.

Jean was tempted to go upstairs and try to convince Luke, but this was a decision he had to make on his own.

"Well, I think it's time someone talked some sense into that boy," Adam said and hurried out of the room and up the stairs. Several minutes later he reappeared.

"Well, what did he say?" Laurel asked.

Adam shrugged. "I don't know if he'll be there. Maybe."

Laurel forced a smile. "Well, we better go then. You ready?" she asked her mother.

"As ready as I'll ever be." Jean glanced at the camping equipment she'd set by the back door. "Ray and I will come by for the gear after the wedding." She walked into the front room and glanced at the stairway, feeling the pull to go up.

Hugging her mother with one arm, Laurel said softly, "Maybe he'll be there. He knows how important this is to you."

With a sigh, Jean said, "I don't think so. He says he'll be moved out before we get back."

When they pulled up at the church, Jean was surprised to see several cars already there. Jessie emerged through the front doors and waited on the porch, a bouquet in her hands. "You look lovely." She hugged Jean and handed the flowers to her. "For you."

"They're beautiful," Jean said, taking the bouquet made predominantly of bright pink fireweed, with sprinklings of yellow daisies, white anemones, and blue forget-me-nots. "Thank you."

Jean wanted to talk to Ray. *Maybe just seeing him will settle my doubts.* She glanced about. "Is Ray here?"

"Yes, but you can't let him see you. It's bad luck." Jessie grinned, her eyes crinkling at the corners.

"I was just hoping I could talk to him."

"Oh, no you don't," Celeste said, walking up to Jean and giving her a hug. She steered her into a small room off the church foyer. "You wait here. Someone will come and get you when it's time." She stopped at the door and looked at Jean. "In a few minutes you'll be my stepmother." She walked back to Jean and gave her a kiss and a hug. "I'm happy you're marrying my father," she said and left.

Gripping her bouquet, Jean sank into a chair. "Oh, dear. What am I going to do? How can I disappoint so many people? But what if what Luke said is true. What if Ray isn't what he seems?" She walked to the door. "Of course he is," she said and peeked out. *If I could just talk to Ray.*

Jessie hurried by with more flowers. She stopped when she saw Jean. "Is everything all right? You look a little pale."

"I'm fine. Just nerves," Jean replied, wondering if she ought to tell Jessie about her uncertainty. Jessie had experienced a lot in her life, and she always gave sensible advice, but Jean couldn't bring herself to voice her doubts and instead repeated, "I'm just nervous."

"That's to be expected. I still remember how scared I was on my wedding day. Oh my, that was so many years ago. It doesn't seem possible." She pushed back a loose strand of gray hair. "Well, I haven't finished setting out all the flowers yet." She hurried away.

The door opened, and Norma Prosser stepped in. She wore a sensible, floral cotton dress. "Just thought I'd check in on you. So, you ready?"

"No."

Norma looked startled for a moment; then her usual levelheaded expression returned. "No?"

Jean let out a shaky breath. "I'm confused. I need to talk."

"Certainly." Norma pulled another chair around in front of Jean and sat.

"I'm not sure what to do."

"About what?"

"Me and Ray. We haven't known each other very long, and Will only died last summer. Luke's angry and absolutely against the marriage. And he thinks Ray is a fake." Her eyes filled with tears. "Luke isn't planning on being here. He's packing. I'm afraid I'm going to lose him."

Norma pulled out a handkerchief tucked into her dress sleeve and dabbed at Jean's eyes. "And I thought I was going to be the one needing this."

Jean almost chuckled. "I never expected to be crying before the wedding." She took the hankie and daubed at her tears. "If I marry Ray, I don't know what my life will look like. What will happen between me and Luke? What if I really do lose him?"

"Oh, now, I don't believe that for a minute. That boy loves you. He would never just walk away—not for good. Give him time."

"That's just it. He's had more than a year to get over his anger and his hurt, but it's getting worse."

Norma thought for a moment, then asked, "Do you love Ray?"

"Yes. Well, I think I do. It's not the same as when Will and I got married, but I don't suppose it should be. I'm more mature now."

Norma smiled kindly. "I can't say for sure how someone ought to feel, but I would think that youth brings a lot of intensity with it. Usually we get steadier as we get older, more levelheaded. And the feelings wouldn't be the same—this isn't you and Will, it's you and Ray. You're two different people." She folded her arms over her bosom. "But your love should be strong. It has to be."

Jean nodded. "I do love him."

"Then what are you troubling yourself about? You need to live your life, and Luke must live his." She gave Jean a tight hug. "I really think you have a case of pre-wedding jitters."

"I suppose."

The door opened, and Jessie looked in, her eyes lighting on Norma. "Ah, there you are. We need some help. Could you give us a hand?"

"Sure." Norma stood. "Now Jean, all you need to be thinking about is what a wonderful life you and Ray are going to have. You hear?" She smiled, then followed Jessie out of the room.

Jean remained in the chair and waited, and although her exterior demeanor was calm, her mind tumbled with questions. She could hear guests arriving. Brian and Susie came to visit more than once, and Celeste checked in on her twice.

Just before the wedding was to begin, Laurel came to wait with her mother. She was nervous and paced. Every few minutes she'd stop and look out into the foyer. "People are still arriving. Looks like the whole community is here." She turned and looked at her mother. "It's almost time. You ready?"

"I suppose," Jean said, but she wasn't. Her mind was still unsettled, and she didn't know what she was going to do. "Have you seen Luke?"

"No, but he might still come." Laurel faced her mother. "Don't let him ruin this day." She smiled. "You are so beautiful. I'm very proud of you. Thank you for asking me to be your matron of honor."

"Well, I wouldn't have asked anyone else." A rush of memories assailed Jean—strolls with a handsome beau, a life with a devoted husband, a houseful of busy children, a new farm. . . . Jean could feel tears burning the back of her eyes. "When your father and I started out, I never considered that one day I might marry someone else. We planned on spending our years together, raising children, farming, and growing old together. It feels strange to be minutes away from being someone else's wife."

"I know Daddy's happy for you. He wouldn't want you to spend your life alone."

Jean nodded.

Celeste looked in, her blue eyes alight. "It's time. You ready?"

Gripping her flowers, Jean stood and walked into the foyer.

She'd chosen to walk the aisle unaccompanied, her children preceding her. Organ music filled the sanctuary and drifted into the foyer. Susie smiled up at her mother, and with some guidance from Celeste, finally headed down the aisle. Brian followed. Before Laurel stepped into the church, she whispered, "You ready?"

Why is everyone asking me if I'm ready? Maybe I'm not. Jean offered Laurel a smile and watched as her oldest walked into the sanctuary. She stepped into the doorway and finally saw Ray. He stood in front, tall and broad-shouldered, his eyes riveted on her. Jean felt a flash of panic rather than the security she'd hoped for. The love in his eyes only made her feel more uncertain. Did she love him enough?

Keeping her bouquet clasped in front of her, she fought to keep her hands from shaking as she started down the aisle. Her friends and neighbors offered smiles and nods of encouragement. She managed to keep moving and smiled back, but inside she felt turmoil. She searched for Luke. He wasn't here. Would this be the day he stepped out of her life? Should she call off the wedding until she worked out the differences with her son?

She moved past Celeste, who smiled warmly. As she approached the front, Ray moved toward her and took her hand. Jean was afraid to look at him, afraid of the trust and love she would see in his eyes. *I do love him. I do,* she told herself, staring at the minister.

"Dearly beloved," the reverend began.

Jean's inner turmoil drowned out his words. *I must decide. Now. I can't marry Ray if it's not right.* She managed a glance over her shoulder.

Even if it means stopping the ceremony in front of all these people. She dared a glance at Ray. How could she even consider hurting him that way?

She was trapped. No matter what she did now, it would be wrong. *If only Will were here. He'd know what to do.* Jean was shocked at the thought. This was wrong. It was wrong. She needed to stop it.

She heard a door open and close softly. Turning to look, she saw Luke standing in the back. Their eyes locked, then he smiled and nodded.

"And do you, Jean Hasper, take this man to be your beloved husband?" the minister asked.

Jean looked up at Ray, searching his eyes. She knew what to do. "Yes. Yes, I do."